# Allison

**ALSO BY STEVE GANNON**

*STEPPING STONES*

*GLOW*

*A SONG FOR THE ASKING*

*KANE*

*L.A. SNIPER*

*INFIDEL*

*KANE: BLOOD MOON*

# ALLISON

# Steve Gannon

A
*KANE*
NOVEL

# Allison

"Summertime" lyrics by DuBose Heyward and Ira Gershwin; Songwriter
George Gershwin

Library of Congress Cataloging-in-Publication Data
Gannon, Steve.
Allison / Steve Gannon.
p.   cm.
ISBN  978-0-9849881-3-6


Printed in the United States of America
10  9 8 7 6 5 4 3 2 1

For Susan
my Solfagnano muse

And as always, for Dex

*Life is what happens to you*
*While you're busy making other plans*
~ John Lennon

# Allison

# 1

Friday, July seventh, on the third anniversary of my rape, I awoke feeling unsettled and depressed. Rolling over in bed, I opened my eyes and stared at the ceiling, plagued by a vague sense of disaster that always accompanied my unwilling observance of that day three years past.

Until the summer I turned seventeen and my brother Tom died and I was attacked and everything changed, I always believed I was more than the things that had *happened* to me, or that I had done, or that I hoped to do. Deep down, I believed I was more than that. I believed an essential part of me, a core part of me, was immune to the forces of life. I believed that the part of me that was truly *me* would remain forever unchanged, no matter what. Looking back, I realize now how naïve I was.

Years ago, in the telling of one of her stories, my mother tried to impart to me something about life. Her tale involved a group of people who were offered a magical gift: They were given the opportunity to rid themselves of their most painful, heartrending memory. Gladly accepting the offer, everyone piled his or her greatest sorrow in the center of the room. Newly unburdened, each person was then told to select a sorrow from the pile. In the end, without exception, everyone there once more embraced his or her own heartbreak.

At odd moments since, I've thought about my mother's story. I'm not certain I would want to forget what happened that summer. Once rid of the memory, however, I don't know whether I would have the courage to pick it up again. One thing is certain: I was forever altered by losing my brother Tommy and by my sexual assault and by the other things that happened that year. I was changed, essentially and indelibly. Until then I had been living a dream—a careless, carefree dream in which I thought that nothing and no one could touch me. Afterward, it was as if a veil had been lifted. I had crossed a threshold from which there was no turning back. No matter how much it hurt, I had joined the human race.

Outside my dorm window, the first fingers of dawn were beginning to light the sky over UCLA. Resolving to think of something else, I eased up on one elbow and squinted at the clock on my nightstand: 5:25 AM. Reaching over, I flipped on a lamp and swung my legs from beneath the covers. Time to get up.

Though reluctant to admit it, I knew that rising early was a trait I had picked up from my police detective father, along with my powder-keg flashes of temper, disregard for authority, and a near obsessive resolve to succeed at whatever I attempted. Despite hating to leave a warm bed, I also conceded that if nothing else, rising early gave me time to write before getting caught up in the distractions of the day.

After slipping my feet into a worn pair of slippers, I stumbled to the adjoining bathroom, used the toilet, splashed cold water on my face, and brushed my teeth. During my freshman and sophomore years at UCLA, I had always had a roommate. Most of the girls with whom I'd lived in the defunct Delta Zeta sorority house—a sorority row structure that had eventually been converted to a private boarding facility when the Delta Zetas moved off campus—were gone for the summer. My most recent roommate, a petite, bright, messy young Asian named Janice, had left as well. In her absence, my customarily crowded living quarters seemed almost spacious, especially the bathroom.

My reasons for deciding to remain at school for the summer, rather than returning to my parents' beach house in Malibu, had been threefold: First, I would be transferring to the USC School of Journalism in the fall, and taking one last upper-division literature class was necessary to complete my transfer credits. Second, staying at school for summer quarter provided me a final opportunity to enjoy the atmosphere of exploration and freedom that I had enjoyed at UCLA over the past two years. And third, and possibly most important, it gave me an excuse not to move home.

Gathering my hair in a ponytail and securing it with an elastic band, I inspected myself in the mirror. In the image peering back I saw startling hints of my mother, Catheryn—a strong chin, high cheekbones, and large, inquisitive green eyes—qualities that in

2

Mom appeared refined and beautiful, but that in myself, at least to my eye, seemed subtly coarsened by my father's Irish lineage. True, my long reddish hair—a genetic gift from my father that as a child I'd despised—had ultimately mellowed to a deeper auburn similar to my mother's. Around the same time, a rash of freckles across the bridge of my nose and cheeks had faded as well, but my body, spare and lanky over the course of several explosive teenaged growth spurts, had continued to grow, and at nearly five-foot-eleven in my bare feet, I stood inches taller than my mother and almost every other woman I knew.

Ruefully, I turned from the mirror and marched back to my bedroom, trying to recall where I had left my running shoes. In the wake of Janice's departure, I had spread out in the cramped room—my clothes, books, and other personal items expanding into the vacuum of my roommate's absence. My eyes traveled the small space, taking in my rumpled bed, an oak dresser I had brought from home, a pair of Churchill swim fins, and a bodysurfing wetsuit heaped by the door. Beside the room's single window, a small TV and a DVD player sat on a bookcase I had also brought from the beach house, along with a maple table that doubled as a desk. Atop my makeshift workstation was a Mac laptop, HP printer, and a full-sized ergonomic keyboard—a refurbished computer setup that my father had given me several years back. Nearby lay stacks of writing projects in various states of completion. Guiltily, I remembered that I still hadn't finished an article I was writing for the *Daily Bruin*, the UCLA school paper. The deadline was Tuesday. Promising myself to work on the piece as soon as I returned from my run, I continued my search, at last spotting my Nikes beneath Janice's bed.

Kneeling, I retrieved my running shoes, kicked off my slippers, and shrugged out of the oversized tee shirt I had worn to bed. The room was chilly and I dressed quickly, pulling on underwear and shorts, a nylon windbreaker with yellow UCLA letters blazed across the back, and my shoes. Next I checked my jacket pockets. My fingers closed on the comforting cylinder of pepper spray I always carried when I ran. The campus was relatively safe, but in early morning when almost no one was around, it didn't hurt to take precautions.

Moving quietly so as not to wake any of the other girls living in the house—or worse, Mrs. Random, our resident housemother—I grabbed my cell phone, locked my room, and descended the staircase to the main floor. After easing out the front door, I made my way down a flight of tiled steps to Hilgard Avenue. There I paused on the sidewalk, breathing in the crisp morning air. Across the deserted street, in the cactus section of the Mildred E. Mathias Botanical Garden, the shadowy arms of forty-foot-high euphorbia, stands of aloes, and acres of spine-covered succulents rose in thorny thickets into the dawn skyline. I stood a moment enjoying the view, then started off at a brisk clip. After crossing Hilgard, I cut left onto a walkway bordering the garden. Another turn brought me past the botany and plant physiology buildings and onto UCLA's main campus. Upon reaching the Health Sciences Center, I turned right.

I routinely varied the routes of my morning jogs, not only for safety, but also because I liked visiting different parts of the university's lush campus. After passing the inverted fountain near Franz Hall, where water spilled down a huge central hole, I proceeded north to Dixon Plaza, skirting its sprawling sycamores and stately fig trees. Briefly I contemplated circling the Murphy Sculpture Garden as well, then decided against it. I had taken that route yesterday. Besides, going that way would lengthen my run, and I had things to do before my 10 AM literature class.

Increasing my pace, I turned west past a procession of older, ornately bricked buildings and descended to the athletic fields flanking Sunset Boulevard. After passing Pauley Pavilion, I continued west to the student recreation center and the encircling dorms that comprised UCLA's western border. Until then I had seen almost no one. Fighting an encroaching sense of unease, I remained alert as I headed back past the tennis courts and made another circuit around the athletic fields. As always, my eyes and ears took in everything around me. Since my assault, caution had become second nature: parking in well-lit spaces, approaching my car with my keys out, wearing sensible shoes in case I had to flee, and carrying pepper spray when alone. I hated living in fear of another attack. On the other hand, I was determined it would never happen again.

Three quarters of an hour after starting out, following a final sprint along a dirt path paralleling Sunset, I returned to my dorm. Dripping sweat, I punched the entry code into the keypad outside and opened the front door. By then Mrs. Random, a prim woman in her early forties, was working at her desk in the housemother's office, just off the entry. She glanced up from her paperwork as I stepped inside.

"Morning, Mrs. Random," I said, trying to sound cheery.

"Good morning, Allison. How was your run?"

"Great."

Peering over half-moon glasses, the older woman studied me thoughtfully. "For the life of me, Ali, I don't understand all this exercise you do," she said. "I realize you have more energy than any other three girls here put together, but you already have a perfect figure for a young woman your age, and—"

"I just like doing it," I interrupted. Although I knew she meant well, we had tilled this ground before, and I knew no good would come of it. Actually, I liked Mrs. Random a lot, for despite her strict demeanor, the housemother cared about all the girls living under her charge, including me, and had proved it many times.

"Hmmph."

"Why don't you join me sometime?" I offered with a grin. "Who knows? You might enjoy it."

Mrs. Random frowned, clearly peeved at having her advice go unheeded. "I don't think so, dear," she replied, pursing her lips like a disapproving librarian. "Don't wake the other girls on your way up."

"I won't," I promised. "I'm going to fix some tea," I added. "Maybe some breakfast, too. Want me to make you anything?"

"I don't think so, Ali," she answered, finally gracing me with a smile. "I've already had my coffee. But thanks."

After returning to my room, I stripped off my running clothes, showered, and pulled on a thick pair of socks and a terrycloth robe. Still drying my hair with a towel, I descended to the first-floor kitchen. Meals, normally provided to house residents during the school year for an all-inclusive boarding fee, had been suspended until fall, but students staying over the summer still had refrigerator and hotplate privileges. I put a kettle of water on to boil and rummaged hopefully through my assigned section of the refrigerator, coming up with a partial package of bagels and an apple that somehow the other girls hadn't pilfered. Although each student was responsible for her own food, in actuality the refrigerator was considered fair game by most, especially late at night, and I was pleasantly surprised to find anything left at all. Resolving to eat a more substantial lunch at the student union after my literature class, I toasted two of the remaining bagels and brewed a cup of peppermint tea, sweetening it with a teaspoon of honey.

Food in hand, I returned to my room and plopped down at my desk. There, after booting up my laptop, I worked steadily for the next hour roughing out a first draft of the *Daily Bruin* piece. Deciding I would have plenty of time for a rewrite and polish over the weekend, I next turned to a project with which I had been struggling for the past two years: my novel. A world apart from the school newspaper articles and a handful of short stories I'd had published, my novel had undergone interminable rounds of revisions, each new draft seeming to engender a host of previously undiscovered problems. Glumly, I suspected that the revision process could go on forever.

So what if it does? I thought, my mood plummeting as I highlighted and then deleted a paragraph that yesterday I had struggled hours to write. No one's ever going to read this anyway.

So why am I writing it? I wondered.

As usual, no answer came.

At 9:45 AM I glanced at the clock, surprised to see so much time had slipped by. After saving my work, I closed the computer. If I hurried, I would just have time to make it to class. Rummaging through my dresser, I selected a clean white blouse, fresh underwear and bra, and a faded pair of jeans. As I slipped out of my robe and began pulling on my clothes, my cell phone rang. I hesitated, then crossed to the bed. Retrieving my cell phone from my jacket pocket, I answered on the sixth ring. "Hello?"

"Hi. I'd like to order a super large deluxe pizza," a girl's voice announced on the other end. "Sausage, pepperoni, mushrooms, and extra cheese. And throw in a six-pack of beer, too."

"McKenzie!"

"Home from Dartmouth at last."

I finished wiggling into my jeans, phone wedged between my shoulder and chin. McKenzie Wallace and I had grown up together, been best friends for most of our childhood, and gone off to college at the same time—she on scholarship to Dartmouth, I to UCLA. Though we hadn't seen much of each other since, our friendship was one we could pick up exactly where we'd left off, no matter how much time had passed. "When did you get back?" I asked, buttoning my blouse and jamming my feet into my tennis shoes.

"I've been home awhile now. Sorry I didn't call earlier. My parents dragged me down to Newport Beach for our annual family vacation. Ugh. We just got back."

"How was it?"

"Newport? Actually, great," answered McKenzie. "Matter of fact, I met a drop-dead gorgeous lifeguard there over Fourth of July weekend. His name is Jeff, and he works at the Wedge," she added, referring to a popular bodysurfing spot at the tip of the Balboa Peninsula, forty miles south of Los Angeles. "I'm heading down there this morning to meet him. Why don't you join me? Maybe he can find a friend for you."

"I'd love to, but—"

"C'mon, Ali. It's a beautiful day, and I hear that big surf is hitting the coast."

"Mac, I have a class at ten."

"It's summer. You're getting your usual straight A's, right?"

"Yeah, but—"

"But nothing. Missing one class won't kill you. Besides, I need another body in the front seat so I can use the carpool lane."

"I knew there had to be a reason you called," I noted dryly.

"I'm serious, Ali, and I'm not taking no for an answer. Look out your window."

"Why?"

"Just do it."

Puzzled, I walked to the window and gazed down at the street. Angled into a no-parking zone out front was a powder-blue VW convertible. McKenzie was sitting behind the steering wheel, grinning up at me from the car her father had bought her as a high school graduation present. She waved. "I don't have all morning," she said, speaking into her cell phone. "Get down here."

"I'm tempted, Mac. But I can't."

"Yes, you can. We're going."

"Mac . . ."

C'mon, Ali. We haven't seen each other since Christmas, and we have a lot of catching up to do. Am I going to have to come up there and drag you out?"

I hesitated a moment more, then smiled in resignation. I knew from experience that when McKenzie made up her mind, there was little use arguing. "You win," I sighed. "I suppose I can get today's lecture notes from someone in class. Gimme a sec to change."

After swapping my school clothes for a one-piece Speedo swimsuit, a pair of sweats, and sandals, I grabbed my surfing fins and a beach towel and headed for the door. When I arrived outside, McKenzie smiled at me warmly. "Great to see you, Ali," she said, reaching across to open her passenger door.

"You, too," I shot back, feeling like a kid playing hooky as I climbed in. McKenzie was wearing an abbreviated pair of shorts and a sleeveless blouse over a red bikini top. As usual, she looked stunning, but something about her had changed. McKenzie had always been a head-turner, but over the past year she had transformed in some way I couldn't quite define. Though she still parted her dark, shoulder-length hair in the

8

center, neatly framing her amber eyes, patrician nose, and generous mouth, there was something different about her. A moment later I had it. Always a bit on the shy side, McKenzie now seemed to exude an aura of confidence that I wished I felt in myself. "How's school going?" I asked, stifling a tinge of envy.

With a perfunctory glance over her shoulder, McKenzie slipped the VW into gear and executed an illegal U-turn that sent us south on Hilgard toward Westwood. "My design and architecture courses are going fairly well," she answered with a shrug, selecting an oldies station on the radio and turning up the volume. "Unfortunately, I can't say the same for my science classes. Plus my love life is almost nonexistent. Wayne and I broke up last month."

"I'll notify the media."

"Nonetheless, I *do* have prospects," McKenzie added cheerfully, ignoring my sarcasm. "Lifeguard Jeff, for instance. How about you? Anyone special?"

"Nope."

"Who are you going out with?"

"Whom."

"Excuse me?"

"You're excused."

McKenzie groaned. "Ali . . ."

"*Whom* are you going out with," I corrected, attempting to dodge her question. "Even better, 'Whom are you seeing?' would eliminate that nasty dangling preposition."

"Thank you, Ms. Perfect English. I've missed your enflamed sense of grammar. Okay, *whom* are you seeing?"

"Nobody."

"Nobody?"

"I'm not dating much, Mac. Actually, I'm not dating at all. I don't have time."

"Don't have time? Ali, sometimes I think you're afraid of men."

I felt myself flush. "That's not it," I said, realizing that my friend had struck closer to the truth than she knew. With the exception of my parents and a rape-counseling therapist, I had never told anyone about my attack, not even McKenzie.

"What, then? You don't like fraternity guys?"

"No."

"Why not?"

I scowled, trying to hide my embarrassment. Thankful that McKenzie had her eyes on the road and not on me, I replied, "Well, for one thing, most of them display an intellectual maturity somewhere in the range of broccoli—not to mention being about as subtle as a pair of brass knuckles. Or as romantic as a love scene from *Alien*," I added, warming to the subject. "By the way, I'm an English major, so don't try to use those similes at home."

"As usual, you're letting your brain do too much of your thinking, Ali—especially when it comes to men," McKenzie said as we turned right on Wilshire and took the 405 Freeway on-ramp south. By then rush hour traffic had thinned a bit, but even at 10 AM, commuters still crowded the highway. After negotiating the Santa Monica Freeway Interchange and proceeding south, McKenzie edged into the 405 carpool lane and picked up speed. "I simply think a little romance in your life might be a welcome improvement," she added.

"As I said, I don't have time for that right now."

"So make time. And don't tell me you're not interested. Remember that short story you wrote about a blind girl falling in love for the first time? It was so romantic, I cried at the end. What was the title?"

"I don't recall."

"Sure you do. Your main character went through all these changes, only to finally discover what she truly wanted in life was to have someone who really *knew* her—what food she liked, her taste in music, what side of the bed she slept on, how to make her laugh. In the end, she realized that sharing herself with someone was the one thing that could make her feel complete."

"She was a character in a story, Mac. A *short* story. Perfect for people like you with short attention spans."

"But you said that when you write, you put parts of yourself into your work."

"It was just a story," I insisted.

"Well, I think it's a big contradiction for someone to be able to write so movingly about something they don't feel themselves. It doesn't make sense."

"Life doesn't make sense. And contradictions make characters interesting."

"In fiction, maybe. In real life, contradictions lead to trouble." Then, noting my darkening mood, McKenzie finally relented. "So you're off to USC this fall?"

"Right," I replied, grateful for the change of subject. "UCLA doesn't have an undergraduate journalism curriculum, and USC does. I can transfer most of my lower division credits and still graduate in four years. Tuition's considerably more at SC, but my folks have worked it out."

"Your dad's borrowing on the beach house?"

"He planned to, but Grandma Dorothy offered to help—at which point my mom unilaterally accepted. Dadzilla wanted to handle everything himself, of course, but even he knows better than to tangle with Mom and Grandma at the same time. He didn't take kindly to being overruled, however."

"I can picture it now," laughed McKenzie. Then, keeping her voice light, "When you start at SC, will you be seeing much of Trav?" she asked, referring to my older brother Travis, who was attending USC on a music scholarship.

I shrugged. "More than I see of him now, I suppose. For the past two summers the Kane family prodigy has been touring on his Van Cliburn recitals, leaving for parts unknown the minute school lets out. Right now genius boy is in Washington, D.C., preparing for a concert with the National Symphony Orchestra."

McKenzie nodded. "On my way to your dorm this morning, I stopped by the beach house. Speaking of which, the rebuilt version looks terrific. Not as much character as your old house before the fire, but it's great," she added.

I remained silent at McKenzie's mention of the fire, for the second time that morning finding my thoughts venturing into territory I didn't want to revisit.

"Anyhow, while I was there, your mom told me about Trav's concert," McKenzie went on. "You're going?"

"Uh-huh. Mom and I are catching an early flight to D.C. next weekend. Which reminds me. Now that you've broken up with your college flame, do you want me to tell Trav you're available?"

"Don't you dare!" McKenzie squealed.

I grinned. McKenzie had been sweet on Travis in high school, and I knew she still wasn't over her crush. "Whatever you say, Mac."

"Your mom invited me to a barbecue at the beach house tonight," McKenzie continued, trying to cover her outburst. "Will you be there?"

"Yep. My dad's cooking. There's no way I'm going to miss one of his meals."

McKenzie smiled. "Me, neither."

As we drove south under a cloudless Southern California sky, the high-rise condos and office buildings of Westwood gradually surrendered to a succession of retail businesses, warehouses, and car dealerships lining the freeway from West Los Angeles to Orange County. Continuing our rambling conversation, McKenzie and I brought each other up-to-date on our lives. Forty minutes later, still engaged in our nonstop exchange, we exited the freeway on Brookhurst and turned left on the 101 coastal route. A few miles farther on, as we swung right on Balboa Boulevard, a newsbreak came on the radio.

McKenzie turned up the sound. "Have you been following this?" she asked, her eyes wide with excitement.

I leaned forward to hear.

". . . disappearance of Jordan French, teenaged star of the popular TV series, *Brandy*," the announcer's voice was saying. "Miss French was reported missing from her Pacific Palisades home over a week ago. Authorities still have no clue regarding her whereabouts. Although no ransom demand has been received, investigators are not ruling out an abduction. A spokesperson for Paramount Studios, where Jordan was shooting a feature film, announced today that work on the project will continue in the hopes of her speedy return. In other news—"

McKenzie twisted off the radio. "Weird, huh? A newspaper I saw in the supermarket says she was recently spotted in Europe with an Italian movie star. Another said she's in rehab at Betty Ford."

"I wouldn't call those rags you read at the checkout stand newspapers."

"Good point. Anyway, the *tabloids* are probably exaggerating, but something's going on," McKenzie maintained stubbornly. "You ever watch Jordan's show?"

"*Brandy*? Occasionally," I confessed. Jordan's fictional TV series centered on the life of Ambassador Harold Wilkenson, a widowed American living in England with his adolescent daughter Brandy, played by Jordan. Every week as regular as clockwork, Ambassador Wilkenson ran afoul of some convoluted, ill-conceived but well-meaning attempt by Brandy to assist him in various affairs of state—not to mention her occasional schemes to find him a wife. Despite its pedestrian premise, the show worked surprisingly well thanks to imaginative writing, and it was one of the few TV shows that I followed. "I watch it when I have time," I added with an embarrassed shrug.

McKenzie grinned. "Yeah, sure. So what do you think happened to Jordan?"

Again, I lifted my shoulders.

Noting something in my manner, McKenzie looked over questioningly. "You know something, don't you?"

"No."

"I'll bet your dad's got something to do with the case. C'mon, spill it."

My father, LAPD Detective Daniel Kane, had for the past several years served as the West Los Angeles Division's supervising homicide detective, and his jurisdictional boundaries included the Pacific Palisades area where Jordan had vanished. "It's not a murder investigation, so my dad's not on it," I said.

"But I'll bet he knows who's running the case, and I'll also bet he has an inside track on what's going on," McKenzie insisted. "C'mon, Ali. I can keep a secret."

"Well . . . my dad *does* know the MAC detective in charge," I admitted.

"MAC?"

"Major assault crimes. A detective named Carl Peyron is investigating Jordan's case. Dad's known Carl for years."

"And?"

"And I heard Dad talking on the phone to Detective Peyron about the investigation. There *are* a couple of things that haven't been released to the press."

McKenzie frowned. "Jeez, this is like pulling teeth. Are you going to tell me or not?"

"Not. There's not much to tell, but Dadzilla would send me on a one-way trip to the moon if it ever got back to him that I blabbed about the case."

"He won't hear it from me."

"Sorry. Like I said, if my—"

"I get the picture. Your dad will go postal if he finds out you talked. Don't worry; it'll be our secret. Now give."

I hesitated a moment more. Then, with a sigh, I said, "Despite what's being reported in the news, the Frenches *did* receive a ransom letter. The envelope contained a locket belonging to Jordan and a demand for money."

"Are her parents going to pay?"

"They were willing to," I answered. "Unfortunately, the kidnappers haven't been in contact since."

"Why not?"

I shook my head. "Nobody knows for sure. But my dad has a theory."

"And that is?"

"He thinks Jordan French is dead."

# 2

Mike Cortese swung his telephoto lens across the beach, searching for the best angle to frame the gigantic waves. He had already shot fifteen minutes of the colossal slabs of water slamming off the Newport jetty, but he still hadn't captured the images he wanted. He mentally weighed shooting a short video clip with lifeguard tower W in the foreground, the guard station flying a red storm-surf flag and a black-ball pennant that signified no flotation devices allowed. Adjusting the focus, Mike assessed the shot, then rejected it. Shooting past the tower foreshortened the waves, negating the chaotic violence of the storm surf he wanted to show.

From experience, Mike knew he needed another object in frame with which to gauge the size of the La Niña-generated waves. Normally a sequence like this included someone in the water—a bodysurfer, for instance—to provide a visual reference. The trouble was, the waves were simply too big for anyone to ride, especially in the Wedge "bowl," where reflected energy from the rock jetty rejoined the main swell to throw it up even higher. Only a handful of local bodysurfers who called themselves the "Wedge Crew" had dared to enter the ocean, and even they, the best of the best, were treading water far outside the break line and taking off only on intermittent ten- to twelve-footers between sets.

With a sigh of exasperation, Mike lowered his camera. Around him the beach teemed with girls in bikinis, boys in baggy shorts, and families with picnic baskets. Most of those there that morning stopped whatever they were doing to stare in awe whenever a particularly large wave thundered ashore, drumming the sand like a monstrous footfall. In an effort to communicate the power of the swells, Mike recorded several minutes of crowd reaction, then returned his attention to the ocean. At last he found the shot he wanted. To the left of the guard tower, three young girls were playing along the shoreline—wading up to their knees during calmer intervals, then retreating with excited squeals of laughter as the next upsurge approached.

Mike moved closer to a berm running the length of the beach. After a quick refocus, he framed the nearest of the girls in his lens, shooting her scrambling from the water as an oncoming wave threatened in the background. It was perfect, the teenager's slim body giving Mike the size reference he had lacked earlier. Getting ambient sound with the camera's shotgun microphone as well, he widened the shot to include the wave just as it crashed offshore.

"What're you doing, mister?"

Mike continued shooting as the girl and her friends once more entered the water, this time wading up to their thighs. Then, lowering his camera, he turned, finding a young boy standing behind him.

"You look like a sharp kid," Mike answered. Kneeling, he rested the camera on his knee. "You tell me."

"You're shooting the big waves for TV. Channel 2 News, right?"

"How'd you know?"

"The eyeball," the boy replied solemnly, pointing at the CBS logo on Mike's camera.

Mike pretended to be surprised. "Hmmm. I forgot about that."

"All the TV stations have camera logos."

"You're right," Mike laughed, ruffling the boy's hair. "I knew you were a sharp kid."

"Dex, don't bother that man while he's working," a tanned woman in shorts and a halter top called from a nearby blanket.

"It's okay, ma'am," Mike called back, raising his voice to be heard above the surf. "He's not bothering me."

The woman, an attractive brunette in her early thirties, smiled at Mike with obvious interest. "Not *yet*, maybe," she shot back.

Mike smiled in return, then kept working. He had to get the beach footage to the newsroom by 3 PM, and time was getting short. But as he started to turn back toward the ocean, a pair of young women caught his eye. They had apparently just arrived and were laying beach towels on the sand near the lifeguard tower. One, a raven-haired beauty who wiggled out of a skimpy pair of shorts and a sleeveless blouse to reveal a tiny red bikini, had great legs and knockout figure. But it was the taller of the two who drew Mike's attention.

Momentarily forgetting the waves, Mike watched as she stripped off a pair of gray sweats. Beneath the sweats she was wearing a black Speedo swimsuit cut high at the hips and low in the back, accenting a captivating figure that was both athletic and feminine. Shaking free her tousled mane of reddish-auburn hair, the girl looked up. Her pale-green eyes turned quizzical as they noticed Mike watching, her unabashed look displaying a startling directness that held his gaze.

At that instant the boy began tugging on Mike's arm. "Hey, mister. Look!"

Reluctantly, Mike glanced toward the ocean, noting that the teenaged girls who earlier had been playing in the shallows had ignored a warning from the lifeguard and ventured into deeper water. Caught in the outflow, they were now having difficulty making it back to the safety of the beach. Abruptly, a strong backwash buffeted the trio, sweeping two of them over a sandy drop-off. Realizing the danger, Mike kicked off his sandals, asked Dex to hold his camera, and started for the water. He hesitated when he saw a lifeguard bolting from the guard tower, orange rescue tube in tow.

A second backwash surged seaward, carrying away the third girl. With a chill, Mike realized that the situation had turned deadly. Noting another guard running from a tower a hundred yards distant, Mike retrieved his camera and resumed shooting, knowing he would probably need saving himself were he to enter the water. He was a good swimmer, but not *that* good.

Trailing his rescue tube from a nylon shoulder strap, the first guard dived in and swam toward the closest girl. He reached her just as a six-foot crest of boiling foam rolled over them. Mike kept his lens trained on the spot where they disappeared. When they resurfaced seconds later, he got a shot of the guard wrapping the flexible orange tube around the girl's body, securing the device with a brass clip. By now the other guard had arrived. Mike shot him entering the water, then raked his camera across the ocean, searching for the other girls. A head popped up forty yards out. No sign of the third girl.

The second lifeguard had entered the water in an outflowing riptide, which was rapidly shuttling him seaward. Mike kept shooting, hoping the guard would reach the teenager before she was carried into the breaking waves farther out. From down the beach came the distant wail of a siren. Mike turned. A lifeguard jeep was speeding toward them, its lights flashing as it raced along the hard sand at the water's edge. It wouldn't arrive for minutes.

With a sense of dread, Mike kept shooting. By now every eye on the beach was following the unfolding drama. The second guard in the water had covered half the distance to the flailing girl farther out. It appeared he would reach her before the current carried her out to the break line, but getting her to safety would be another story. The first guard, victim in tow, had given up taking a direct route to shore and was swimming parallel to the beach, attempting to move laterally out of the strong riptide. The second guard would have to do the same.

Suddenly Mike spotted the third girl, far from shore. He adjusted his telephoto lens, bringing her into focus. She had been dragged through the break line and was lying facedown in the water. Mike pulled back to reveal the two guards already in the surf. Busy with a rescue apiece, there was no way they would reach the final girl in time.

All at once Mike saw the taller of the two young women he had noticed earlier running toward the shoreline. The girl paused in knee-deep water to pull on a pair of swim fins, then took a breath and dived in.

Jesus, Mike thought as he kept shooting. She's going out there!

\*     \*     \*

Heart in my throat, I pulled toward the oncoming waves, arms slashing the choppy surface. Having grown up on the beach, I was strong swimmer and an excellent bodysurfer. I was terrified nonetheless, never having been out in waves this big. Upon arriving at the Wedge and seeing the size of the waves, I had resolved that under no circumstances would I be surfing that day. That was before I spotted the girls in trouble. The lifeguards who'd already responded had their hands full, and the rescue jeep wouldn't arrive in time. Someone had to help.

The outflowing riptide carried me swiftly to a smaller inside break. An eight-foot wall of foam boiled toward me. Caught in the rip, I knew there was no turning back. After taking a hurried gulp of air, I scratched for the bottom an instant before the hissing surge reached me. Moments later I emerged on the far side and continued swimming. The worst was yet to come. I still had to get past the outside break.

Normally I would have waited for a lull between sets before trying to make it out. Because of the situation, I didn't have that luxury. Momentarily raising my head, I checked the waves. My stomach sank as I saw an eighteen-foot-high swell approaching. I had to reach deeper water.

Increasing my strokes, I kicked for all I was worth, arms and legs driving me toward the onrushing wave. Being caught inside the break of a wall that large meant disaster. In a shallow-bottomed area like the Wedge, getting slammed down from a height of eighteen feet could break a shoulder, a neck, or knock a swimmer unconscious—all of which could prove fatal.

The riptide continued to ferry me seaward. For a moment I thought I might surmount the looming wave before it curled. Relentlessly, the gigantic swell moved toward me with the fury of a freight train, an angry plume of spray trailing from its crest, the wave soaring ever higher as the ocean bottom threw it skyward, rising . . . rising . . .

It's too close, I thought, trying not to panic. Dive.

Taking one last breath, I submerged again, pulling for the bottom. The mass of the wave moved over me, trying to pull me back. I kicked with every bit of strength I possessed, thanking God I had taken the time to put on my fins. My fingers scrabbled against sand. I could go no deeper.

Forward, then.

Blood pounding in my ears, I struggled against the terrible sucking force of the wave, its power weakened by my depth but still strong enough to drag me into its churning maw. My lungs burned. My legs ached. My thighs were beginning to cramp.

I couldn't stay down much longer. Making one last effort, I kicked another few yards, chest skimming the bottom, hands pulling to either side, fins raising billows of sand behind me. And still the wave pulled at me, unwilling to release its grip.

If I get out of this, I thought, I'll never go out in big surf again.

An eternity passed.

And then it was over. Aware I had only seconds before the next swell arrived, I shot to the surface. I choked down several gasps of air, the crash of the passing wave roaring in my ears. I peered seaward. The next wave looked even larger. There would be no rest if I were to make it over. And I had to make it over. Another dive like the last was out of the question. I didn't have the strength.

I started out once more. Though tempted to check the approaching wave, I kept my head down and swam for all I was worth, knowing even a few feet could make the difference between safely topping the swell and being swept backward over the falls. Moments later the toe of the wave began to lift me.

Keep swimming, I told myself grimly. Keep swimming.

Panic roiled in my chest as I clawed up the rising face. For a sickening instant my momentum slackened as I reached the crest. I was certain I would be pulled over backward. Then, with an overwhelming flood of relief, I felt myself descending the backside, the power of the wave sliding harmlessly beneath me.

Another minute of hard swimming brought me to a position of relative safety, at least for the moment. Treading water, I searched for the third girl. Another swell passed, raising me high in the air. Using my temporary elevation, I scanned the waters around me. Nothing.

Did I miss her?

Though fearing the girl might have already slipped beneath the surface, I continued searching. Shivering and exhausted, I was beginning to think I had lost her when I spotted a small shape in the water thirty yards toward shore.

The girl was lying facedown when I reached her. Apparently the rip current had carried her through the breaking waves, but not without cost. I threw an arm over her shoulders and rolled her onto her back. She was unconscious. Her lips were blue, her skin pale as death.

Now what?

Try to get her breathing.

With an arm across the girl's chest, I used my free hand to tip back the girl's chin and force open her jaw. Legs scissoring to keep our heads above water, I blew awkwardly into the girl's mouth. I felt her chest inflate slightly. And again.

Other than the involuntary lift and fall of the girl's ribs in response to my breath, there was no effect.

This isn't doing any good.

All at once I sensed danger behind me. I turned. Another giant wave was approaching, this one easily the largest of the day. In swimming toward shore to reach the girl, I had forfeited precious yards I'd fought earlier to gain. And while attempting to revive the girl, I had drifted even closer to the beach.

With a renewed surge of panic, I realized that I was inside the break line again.

I tightened my grip on the girl. Pulling with my free arm and kicking with both legs, I started swimming toward the approaching wave.

I'll never make it, I thought. Not dragging the girl. Drop her.

The wave rocketed skyward, dwarfing me with its size.

She's probably dead, a voice inside me insisted. Let her go.

Despite a paralyzing surge of fear, I held on and kept swimming, my breath now coming in ragged gasps.

Drop her, my voice insisted.

No, I thought grimly. We're making it together or not at all.

And then we were climbing the impossibly lofty face. The wave began to curl as we neared the top. For an instant I was certain we were going to be sucked backward over the falls and buried beneath tons of water.

Don't give up. Keep going . . .

Spurred by a nauseous rush of adrenaline, I rallied my last bit of strength. Kicking furiously, I teetered on the wave's summit, marveling in a detached portion of my mind at how high the swell had raised us. I could see more waves marching in past the tip of the Newport breakwater, a flash of yellow emerging from the mouth of the rock jetty . . .

Keep going. Don't stop!

Another kick . . . and another . . .

And we were past.

Though trembling with exhaustion, I kept swimming, determined not to be caught inside the break line again. Despite being impeded by the girl's body, I eventually put a comfortable distance between us and the beach. It was then that I heard the roar of an engine farther out.

I saw the yellow lifeguard vessel as the next wave lifted us, concluding that the approaching boat must have been the flash of color I had spotted at the mouth of the breakwater. As the boat neared, I saw that it was one of several Newport Beach rescue craft I'd noticed on previous visits to the Wedge. At the time I had never imagined I would ever be so grateful to see one.

Its seven-hundred-horsepower engine revved up full, the lifeguard vessel slammed through the waves. Twenty yards from us it abruptly veered left, catapulting a rescue swimmer from its stern. The guard's high-speed entry and a series of strong overhand strokes quickly put him at my side.

"She's not breathing," I gasped as the guard began securing a rescue tube around the unconscious girl.

The guard finished clipping his flotation tube beneath the girl's shoulders. Then, treading water, he turned to me. "You okay?"

"I'm fine," I answered, my teeth chattering.

The guard shook his head, giving me a look that said he couldn't believe I was out there.

By now the yellow boat had turned and was backing toward us, the operator keeping a wary eye on the waves. An incoming swell forced him to retreat to deeper water. After recircling, he waited for another break in the waves, then backed toward us once more. When he reached us, the guard in the water slithered onto a submerged swim-step at the stern, hauling the girl's body with him.

Another wave approached. As I attempted to pull myself onto the swim-step, a blast of prop wash from the boat thrust me back. "Move away!" the guard on the stern yelled, fighting to maintain his grip on the girl.

Though puzzled, I released my hold on the boat and let the prop wash sweep me a dozen feet away. An instant later the swell rolled beneath the boat, first raising the bow, then the stern. As the keel seesawed over the crest of the wave, the rudder came completely out of the water, then sliced down like a guillotine. Shaken, I abruptly realized why the guard had warned me to stay clear.

"Now!" the guard shouted. "Get on!"

Wasting no time, I kicked toward the boat, squirmed onto the swim-step, and tumbled over the transom. Once I was aboard, the boat operator levered the throttles open wide. The guttural sound of the engine roaring in my ears, I braced myself as we picked up speed and crashed through the oncoming waves.

For the first time since entering the water, I began to relax. The wind felt raw and cutting on my skin; the bone-rattling shock of the waves beneath the keel occasionally blurred my vision; the pitch and roll of the boat was starting to make me feel sick. Nevertheless, I had never been happier to be anywhere in my life.

A throng of medics, police, and Newport Beach lifeguards were waiting for us on the Orange County Sheriff Harbor Patrol dock when we arrived. Passing an eighty-seven-foot Coast Guard cutter and a several smaller harbor-division craft, our rescue boat nosed into its designated berth. Deeper in the harbor, safe from the waves battering the beach outside the jetty, a thicket of sailboats and yachts swayed in dockside slips, their naked masts a forest of spars and booms and rigging. At the top of a metal ramp leading up to a parking lot, a fire-department ambulance idled at the curb.

I stepped over the gunwale of the rescue boat, fins in one hand and a woolen blanket clutched around my shoulders with the other. As I made my way up the dock, I noticed that in addition to the medics and lifeguard personnel, apparently a gaggle of onlookers had driven over from the Wedge. Standing near McKenzie, I saw a nearly hysterical woman whom I assumed was probably the mother of the drowning victim. I also saw the young cameraman who had been staring at me earlier.

A paramedic team quickly offloaded the girl. Working on her all the way back, the rescue boat lifeguards had performed cardiac resuscitation, administered positive-pressure oxygen, and treated her for hypothermia and shock. Though they had managed to restore the girl's heartbeat and breathing, she still hadn't regained consciousness. Praying the girl would recover, I watched as she was bundled onto a stretcher and carried to the waiting ambulance.

A moment later McKenzie pushed through the crowd. "Jeez, Ali, I was so worried about you," she cried, throwing her arms around me. "You scared me half to death. Are you all right?"

"Just cold and tired," I answered, noting that the young cameraman, having finished shooting the medics loading the girl into the ambulance, had now shifted his attention to me. Irritated, I turned away. "Did you drive over here, Mac?"

"Yes."

"Good. Let's go."

"Miss? May I have your name, please?"

I turned back. The request had come from the cameraman, who had closed the distance between us. Powerfully built, the man appeared to be in his mid-twenties. He had thick black hair and dark, surprisingly kind eyes, along with a slightly taunting smile that seemed misplaced on an otherwise open, handsome face. "Can I have your name?" he repeated, training his camera on me.

"No."

"Why not?"

"It's already taken."

"C'mon, miss," the man chuckled, continuing to shoot. "Our viewers will want to know who the hero was out there today."

"The lifeguards were the heroes," I said, again starting for the parking lot. Seeming reluctant to leave, McKenzie trailed behind.

Not giving up, the cameraman followed and kept shooting. "Don't be so modest, miss," he continued. "If it hadn't been for you, that girl wouldn't have had a chance. Aside from the guards, no one else on the beach made a move to help. Not even the men."

I turned. "Not even the men?" I said. "Is that what this is about? You think that because someone is a girl, she can't—"

"No, of course not," the man backpedaled. Though he lowered his camera, I noticed that he had kept his finger on the trigger and was continuing to shoot. "I'm simply saying that no one else on the beach, *man or woman*, had the guts to go out there," he continued. "Only you."

Though mollified, I suddenly felt naked under the cameraman's gaze, my gooseflesh skin bare and exposed. I clutched the woolen blanket even more tightly around my shoulders. "Well, going out in big surf isn't for everyone," I said, a little embarrassed at my on-camera outburst. "It isn't for sane people, for instance," I added with a shrug.

Again the cameraman's eyes lit with a mix of amusement and admiration. "No argument there," he laughed. As he was about to say something more, one of the lifeguards from the rescue boat placed a hand on my shoulder. "Excuse me, miss. Would you come with me to the Sheriff's office, please?" he asked politely, pointing to a gray building overlooking the dock. "There are some people who need to talk with you."

Twenty minutes later, after relating my version of events to several Sheriff's officers and a Newport Beach marine safety supervisor, I rejoined McKenzie in the parking lot. By now most of the crowd had dispersed, with the notable exception of the dark-haired young cameraman.

"What's *he* still doing here?" I groaned as I saw him walking toward us, this time without his camera.

"His name's Mike Cortese and he's with Channel 2 News," McKenzie replied, as if that explained everything. "He just wants to talk with you. I don't understand why you're being so nasty to him. He's only doing his job. Besides, he's cute."

"If you like him, you talk to him," I said. "Where's your car?"

"Miss Kane?" the man called. I gave McKenzie what I hoped was a withering stare, realizing where he must have learned my name.

"I apologize if I seemed pushy before," the cameraman continued pleasantly, joining us. "And I didn't mean to imply that a woman might be any less capable than a man. In fact, I think you showed exactly the opposite." Then, extending his hand, "I'm Mike Cortese."

I shook his hand but said nothing.

"And you are Allison Kane," Mike went on, filling the silence. "I admire what you did out there. That took guts."

"It was probably more a lack of good sense than anything else," I said.

"Right," Mike agreed, his eyes saying otherwise. "Listen, your friend McKenzie says you're studying to be journalist. Have you ever thought of interning at one of the local news stations?"

Once more I squinted my displeasure at McKenzie. Clearly convinced that she had my best interests at heart, McKenzie smiled back, her brow as untroubled as a newborn's.

"Channel 2 usually has a couple of interns on staff at all times," Mike continued. "There might be a position open. I could check for you if you want."

"I don't know," I replied suspiciously. "Right now my schedule's pretty full."

Mike shrugged. "I'll look into it anyway. If it works out, fine. If not, nothing's lost."

"Don't go to any trouble on my account."

"No trouble at all." With that, Mike turned and started across the parking lot toward a late-model Toyota pickup with a sticker on the rear bumper advising: "Earth first. We'll mine the planets later."

"Damn you, Mac," I said once Mike was out of earshot.

McKenzie grinned. "Hey, somebody has to take an interest in your love life. As it obviously isn't going to be you, it has to be me."

"What are you talking about?"

"The guy *liked* you, Ali. Although considering the way you acted, I can't imagine why."

I frowned. "He was just trying to flesh out his story," I said. "'Coed Snatches Victim from Monster Waves!' and so forth. That bit about a news intern job was a load of bull."

"Maybe, maybe not. I wouldn't be surprised if he checks on it for you."

"You wouldn't, huh?"

"No, I wouldn't."

"Want to put some money on it? Say, twenty bucks?"

"Nope," McKenzie answered quickly.

It was my turn to smile. "I didn't think so."

# 3

Later that evening I sat on the redwood deck outside our family's beachfront house, gazing at the wave-tossed Santa Monica Bay. By then the sun had dropped behind Point Dumé to the west, lighting the horizon with a palette of reds and golds. A mild offshore breeze had picked up with the setting of the sun, keeping the Malibu evening warm and pleasant.

My dad was leaning over a smoking barbeque, inspecting the grill. "All right, lemme see here," he said, stroking his chin as if lost in thought. Taking his time, he straightened, cracked his knuckles, rolled his shoulders, and stretched his muscular six-foot-three, 220-pound frame. "Now I remember," he said. Using tongs, he moved a stack of foil-wrapped corn to the edge of the grill, then began transferring a pile of New York steaks onto the barbeque. "You kids like your meat nice and tough—black on the outside and extra-well done on the inside, right?"

"No way!" objected Nate, my youngest brother, calling from across the deck. "We like 'em tender and juicy, medium pink, and big!"

Having recently turned fourteen, Nate had rocketed up over the past year, his strong, compact body maturing with the onset of adolescence. His mischievous face still sported a rash of freckles, and his mop of curly red hair—as intractable as a snarl of baling wire—had, if anything, grown more undisciplined with age. Impetuous, competitive, quick to both fury and forgiveness, his loyalties unswerving and his emotions as transparent as glass, Nate, of all the Kane children, most resembled my father. And for better or worse, he seemed to be traveling that road more and more as time went on.

"Dadzilla's just teasing, larva," I said. "Have you ever known him to burn a steak?"

"No. And be careful who you're calling 'larva', sis," Nate warned. Obviously showing off for McKenzie, who was sitting on a swing nearby, he flexed a surprisingly well-defined set of biceps. "Keep talking like that and I might have to call out the big guns here."

"Ohhh, I'm *so* scared," I replied good-naturedly. "Tell you what, shrimp. I'm going to ignore that foolish threat, as I realize your adolescent brain is currently suffering the effects of your adolescent male 'butthead gene.' It's a genetic failing that cripples all members of your gender right around puberty."

"Is that what people believe on the planet you're from?"

"Yes, oh freckled-one. And you're living proof," I teased, as usual enjoying our verbal jousting—a sparring that had been part of our relationship since childhood, though now that we were older neither of us really meant.

"Is that right?" Nate retorted. "Have you discussed your 'butthead gene' theory with Dadzilla? He's a male too, you know."

"Dadzilla is where you got that particular gene in the first place," I pointed out.

"Knock it off, troops," said Dad, placing the last of the steaks on the grill. "And while you're at it, watch who you're calling Dadzilla," he added, trying not to smile. "That kinda talk might give somebody the wrong idea. Namely, me."

"Aw, Dad, you know we mean that only in the best possible way," I said. "When it comes to dads, you are without a doubt the finest, most understanding, loving, compassionate—"

"Enough, petunia. Why don't you scurry upstairs and give your mother a hand with dessert?"

"Because I would rather stay down here and bask in the glow of your culinary genius, that's why. Besides, I don't feel like scurrying."

"What *is* dessert?" asked McKenzie. "Something fattening, I hope."

"You won't be disappointed," said Dad. "My talented wife is making her famous mud pie."

"Yum," said Nate. "C'mon, Callie, let's go upstairs and see how things are going. Maybe we can get a little preview," he added to our family's four-year-old yellow Labrador retriever. Callie, who had been napping near the sea wall, cocked her ears, sprang up, and bounded after her young master.

"Have your mom check on my bean casserole, too," Dad hollered after Nate. "And take the Caesar salad out of the fridge."

"Yes, sir," Nate yelled back. "Consider it done."

With Nate and Callie gone, conversation on the deck again settled into a comfortable lull, McKenzie rocking in the swing and contemplating the diminished but still-gigantic waves offshore, my dad concentrating on his cooking. I watched as my father removed foil from a half-dozen ears of corn, placed them on the upper barbecue rack for their final heating, and flipped the sizzling steaks. And as I watched, I was struck as usual by the deftness of his thick-knuckled hands, hands that to me had always seemed more suited to bone-crushing labor than the delicate art of cooking. Nonetheless, despite my father's rough appearance, I knew he was an excellent chef. It was a talent that resulted not only from his love of cooking—a passion that in my opinion derived from his controlling nature, a failing he could fully indulge in the kitchen—but also because he had a natural flair for food preparation and an adventurous spirit in his choice of menus. Mom's meals sustained us, but my dad's occasional Friday-night feasts—spicy stir-fry, Southwestern cuisine, Thai and Chinese dishes, sushi, wild-game dinners, Italian food, and a summer barbecue like the one he was preparing tonight—were a welcome diversion eagerly anticipated by our entire family.

Shifting my gaze, I studied my father's face, finding it a contradiction of harsh lines and contrasting tenderness. In the evening light, an angry white scar traversing his right cheek reminded me of the glistening track of a tear. He had received that particular injury in the line of duty several years back. During that same incident he had also suffered a gunshot wound that left him with a slight limp, a disability most noticeable when he was tired. In addition, I knew that my father carried other scars from his years on the police force—some visible, some not.

Sensing that he was being observed, my dad turned, his slate-blue eyes searching mine. "What's up, sport?" he asked. "You seem kinda quiet tonight. Anything wrong?"

I shot a glance at McKenzie, noting that she appeared occupied with her own thoughts. After a slight hesitation, I shrugged. "I don't know, Dad. Do you ever feel like you don't know where you're going with your life?"

"All the time. Don't worry, you'll get used to it. It's part of being an adult."

"I'm serious, Dad. You have your work, Mom will get tenure soon with the Philharmonic, and Travis's career as a pianist is all laid out for him. Even Nate is showing promise on the baseball field. At the rate he's going, the kid will probably turn pro by the time he's twenty. I feel like I'm just spinning my wheels."

"Does this have something to do with what happened today at the beach?" Dad asked.

When I had arrived home that afternoon, my mother already knew of the Newport Beach incident, having seen it on the local news. Angrily, she'd pointed out that I had no right taking such chances, adding that I had Friday classes at UCLA and shouldn't have been at the beach in the first place.

"It might have something to do with today," I replied, taken off guard by my father's question. "I don't know. Maybe."

Dad, who had also seen the rescue footage on television, nodded pensively. "It's natural to feel let down after something like that, kid. Happens in police work all the time. It'll pass."

"It's more than feeling let down."

Using a knife, Dad made a small incision in one of the steaks. Noting its interior had attained a deep-red color just shy of purple, he began removing the meat from the smoking grill. "It was your mother getting on your case, huh?" he said, placing the steaks on a large platter and covering them with foil to let the meat's internal heat complete the cooking. "Listen, on this particular issue your mother and I don't see eye-to-eye. I agree with her that you shouldn't have been playing hooky, and that going out in that surf was dangerous, and so forth. But what you did today was really something, Ali. Someone had to help that kid, and you stepped up to the plate. I'm proud of you. Just don't do it again," he added with a grin.

I brightened slightly. "Okay, Dad. But maybe Mom's right about college. If I'm not taking my studies seriously, why keep going to school?"

"What are you talking about? You're getting straight A's, for chrissake."

"But what good is it doing me? I can't make a career out of getting A's in English literature classes."

"Journalism's a career. I thought that's what you wanted."

I raised my shoulders, then let them fall. "I'm not sure what I want. Mom's dead-set on my pursuing a career in creative writing, but—"

"Back up a sec," Dad interrupted. "Let's get things in perspective here. First of all, you have more on the ball than any other young woman your age I've ever met. When I was young, girls got married, had kids, and raised a family. Now, I know things have changed a bit since the Dark Ages, and I think it's great that you want to do something with your life before settling down. But as far as quitting school, don't be in such an all-fired hurry to grow up. You'll be an adult soon enough, and the years will pile up before you know it. Believe me, the only good thing about getting old is eating cheaper at Denny's."

I smiled, but before I could reply, Nate leaned over the railing of our second-story balcony overhanging the deck. "Ali, McKenzie, get up here fast," he called. "You too, Dad. Ali's on TV again!"

Once more using his knife, Dad tested the corn. "These still need a couple of minutes," he said, judging that the ears had yet to reach the proper level of chewiness, always a point of family contention. "You and McKenzie go ahead. And tell everyone that dinner will be hitting the table shortly."

Though our conversation remained unresolved, I decided to let it pass. "Okay, Dad. I'll tell them."

Leaving my father on the deck, McKenzie and I made our way upstairs, joining my mother and Nate in the living room. By then the Newport Beach TV news segment was almost over. The television screen now showed a wet and shivering me standing on the Harbor Patrol dock clutching a blanket around my shoulders.

"The lifeguards were the heroes," my image said, turning away from the camera. At that point the scene shifted to the news desk. I was shocked to see the handsome face of Peter Samson, the CBS network news anchor. Inexplicably, what had started out as a local news segment had somehow turned into network news.

"Although the mystery rescuer refused to give her name, CBS has learned that she is Allison Kane, a student at UCLA," the anchor said. "According to hospital officials, the young victim Ms. Kane assisted is in stable condition and is expected to make a full recovery. Heavy surf is predicted to continue battering California beaches through tomorrow." Then, turning to another camera angle, "In other West Coast news today, LAPD officials have reported little progress in locating fourteen-year-old actress Jordan French, reported missing from her Pacific Palisades home last weekend. Here with more from Los Angeles is CBS news correspondent Brent Preston."

The scene flashed to a residential street. My mother shook her head. "That poor little girl," she said. Then, raising the remote control, she turned off the set.

"Gosh, Ali, now you're on *national* TV," said McKenzie. "Congratulations."

"Thanks," I replied self-consciously, still stinging from my mother's earlier censure.

"Yeah! Awesome, sis!" added Nate.

"Can I have your autograph?" begged McKenzie. "Please?"

"Oh, hush, Mac," I said, covertly watching my mother from the corner of my eye. Like many of my recent confrontations with Mom, our latest argument over the beach rescue had been protracted and bitter, charged with an underlying tension that more and more seemed to color our exchanges with misunderstanding and hurt. Worse, I knew this latest conflict wasn't over yet.

As I secretly regarded my mom, I felt a familiar stab of inadequacy. Still stunningly beautiful at just over forty, Catheryn Kane, accomplished musician and the associate principal cellist for the Los Angeles Philharmonic, embodied all the virtues I felt

I lacked in myself: elegance, talent, grace, and most of all, a sense of purpose. "What do *you* think about my making the national news, Mom?" I asked hesitantly.

Mom looked over. "You know what I think," she said, her eyes flashing with irritation. "This latest newscast doesn't change anything." As she was about to add something more, the phone rang. McKenzie, the closest, picked it up. "Kane residence." A pause, then, "Yes, she's right here." Setting the receiver on the table, she turned to me. "It's for you," she said with an enigmatic smile.

"Dinnertime," my dad's voice boomed up from the deck outside. "Get your butts down here, kids! You too, Kate."

"Oh, that reminds me," said Nate, glancing guiltily at Mom. "Dad wanted you to check on his bean casserole. And he said to take the salad out of the fridge."

"Already done," said Mom. She rose from the couch. "Everything's on the kitchen counter. Let's all take something down to the picnic table as we go. And Allison, don't be long. We'll wait for you to eat."

"Yes, ma'am."

After everyone left, I crossed to the table and lifted the receiver. "Hello?"

"Allison? Mike Cortese."

"Who?"

"Mike Cortese. From the beach. The pushy guy with the camera, remember?"

"How . . . how did you get my number?"

"Your friend McKenzie. Have you seen yourself on TV?"

"Unfortunately."

"I hope you don't mind. I know you didn't want any publicity, but what happened today was news."

"Well, I suppose you were just doing your job," I conceded. "I *was* kind of shocked seeing myself on the *CBS Evening News*, though."

"I'll bet. It was just supposed to be a local-color segment, but Newspath picked it up and farmed it out to all the CBS affiliates.

Eventually network decided to use it to plug a hole in the six o'clock national lineup."

"Newspath?"

"They supply video clips to network affiliates. Sort of like a wire service."

"Oh."

"Anyway, the reason I'm calling is that I looked into an intern position for you at Channel 2. Nothing's available here at KCBS, but I contacted a friend at network. He says they might have a slot for you over there. Nothing's guaranteed, but you have an appointment at CBS first thing Monday morning. It's on Fairfax Avenue. Go to the main desk and ask for Brent Preston."

"Brent Preston, the news correspondent?"

"That's him. I know Brent from when he started at Channel 2."

As I'd told McKenzie, I had originally considered Mike's talk of a news intern job simply that: just talk. Now, presented with the possibility of actually working at a news station, and a *network* news station at that, I found myself at a loss for words. "Monday morning. I'll . . . I'll be there," I finally managed.

"I'll let Brent know," said Mike. "And good luck." With that, he rattled off Brent's phone number at the station and said good-bye, disconnecting before I had recovered enough from my surprise to say thanks.

Everyone was assembled outside at the picnic table when I finally arrived downstairs. "C'mon, Ali," urged Nate. "Get a move on. We're starving."

I slid in beside McKenzie, who had taken a seat across from Nate. From his position at the head of the table, my dad began serving salad. "Hope you like anchovies, McKenzie," he said, passing a bowl down the line. "In my book, Caesar salad isn't Caesar salad without 'em, so I use plenty."

"I've had your Caesar," said McKenzie, "and I love it. Anchovies and all."

"Let's say grace before everyone digs in, Dan," Mom suggested.

Dad ducked his head quickly. "Right."

My mother led a short prayer in which she asked God's blessing for everyone we loved—family and friends both present and absent—and especially Travis, who would be performing his own work in concert the following weekend.

"Amen," said Dad, lifting a tumbler of Coke, his customary beverage since he had stopped drinking. "And here's to the hero of the hour," he added, glancing at me.

McKenzie, who had turned twenty-one earlier that spring, lifted a glass of white wine. "To Allison."

As the rest of the table joined in, I felt a blush rising to my cheeks. Though my mother remained silent, I saw her also raise her wine glass. Nate, after clunking his mug of milk against mine and taking a drink, reached for Mom's wine. "Can I have a sip, Mom?"

"Great idea, sport," said Dad. "One more suggestion like that and you'll be doing pushups till your arms fall off."

"Never happen," said Nate, again flexing his biceps. "Not with these arms."

"Who was that on the phone, Ali?" asked Mom, smiling at Nate's posturing.

I speared a steak from the meat platter, then reached for the corn. "Somebody from school," I lied.

"Oh?"

"He, uh, wanted to borrow my notes," I explained, digging myself in deeper. McKenzie glanced at me curiously but said nothing.

"I hope he didn't want your notes from today," my mother observed dryly.

"Jeez, give the girl a break, Kate," said Dad, serving the last of the salad. "She skipped a couple of classes, saved some kid's life, and wound up on national TV. What's so wrong with that?"

"Nothing, except for the small matter that her rashness could have resulted in her death," Mom countered irritably. "This isn't the first time she's pulled a daredevil stunt like that. What's she trying to prove?"

"Kate, that kid in the water needed help."

"And Allison should have let the lifeguards handle things. That's their job."

"It's a tough call to make without being there," Dad pointed out. Then, sensing the afternoon's argument threatening to resurface, he changed the subject. "Speaking of jobs, I have the weekend off. I should be able to start on your closet organizer tomorrow."

"Really?" asked Mom.

"Absolutely," said Dad, ladling a steaming portion of three-bean casserole onto his plate, then tearing off a hunk of freshly heated French bread. "Maybe I can even get going on those living room bookshelves you've been bugging me about. You want to help, champ?" he asked, passing the breadbasket to Nate.

"Sure," Nate replied enthusiastically. "I have a baseball game tomorrow morning, though."

"Yeah, yeah, I know. I'm one of the coaches, remember? We'll get working on things here after that."

"The house is sure coming along, Mr. Kane," interjected McKenzie, gazing up at our new home. Mom's mother, Dorothy Erickson, had grown up in an ancient structure built on the site during the mid-thirties, and she had subsequently bequeathed it to my mom and dad as a wedding present. The original home, a sadly sagging construct of termite-ridden beams and quick-fix repairs that time had eventually lent an air of permanence, had burned to the sand several years back. Though our family had escaped for the most part unscathed, it had been a heartbreaking loss for all of us. Following the fire, Dad had spent a year getting the requisite permits to rebuild. After securing a bank loan to augment the fire-insurance money, he had taken substantial blocks of accumulated LAPD sick leave and vacation time to supervise the framing—later setting up a workshop in the new garage and spending every free weekend working on various finish details. Although months earlier my family had moved back to the beach from our temporary quarters in a nearby rental condo, there was still much to do.

"It really *is* coming along, isn't it?" Dad agreed proudly. "I miss the old place, though."

"I never thought I would admit it, but I do, too," said Mom, absently brushing back a lock of hair from her forehead. "Still, it's nice having a modern kitchen, not to mention a bigger music room and windows that actually open and close. And the upstairs balcony is heavenly," she added, referring to the deck above us that Dad had cantilevered off the second story.

"No argument there," said Dad. "You should use it more often, sugar. Catch a few rays. You've been looking a bit peaked lately."

I stole a glance at my mother, thinking her color did seem a little pale. A small, purplish bruise marked the skin of her forearm—a blemish that would have ordinarily gone undetected had she displayed her normal tan.

"With the Philharmonic's rehearsal schedule and helping Trav prepare for his concert, I haven't had much time to be lounging around in the sun," Mom replied. "But it's sweet of you to notice, Dan."

"Just watching out for you, honeybunch."

"How *is* Trav's concert preparation coming along?" asked McKenzie.

"Fine," Mom answered. "Trav's been in D.C. for the past two days working with the NSO music director to fine-tune his concerto, as well as rehearsing it with the orchestra. Next weekend's performances should go perfectly."

"He's really nervous about debuting his own work, though," I noted. "I talked with him last night on the phone. He says a lot is riding on this first concert."

Mom nodded somberly. "Performing his own composition will be a tremendous step up for Trav, especially if it's well received."

"How come Trav gets to play with the NOS, anyway?" asked Nate.

"NSO," I corrected. "National Symphony Orchestra. And it's because our older brother Travis is such an ineffable genius."

Nate looked confused. "Ineffable?"

"Unspeakable," explained Mom, squinting at me with irritation. "Your sister is being sarcastic. It's an ineffably unattractive trait in a young lady, I might add." Then, turning back to Nate, "To answer your question, the NSO's music director heard Trav play one of his compositions at the Kennedy Center last year. Your brother was on a recital tour that was part of his winning the silver medal at the Van Cliburn International. You remember."

Nate nodded. "And the conductor liked Trav so much he wanted him to play with his orchestra?"

"Something like that. The music director happens to be old friends with one of Trav's professors at USC."

"Mr. Petrinski?"

"That's right. Anyway, the NSO regularly supports young musicians, and Mr. Petrinski sent his friend a recording of Trav's work."

"And the rest, as they say, is history," I finished.

Once more Mom frowned at my tone. Sensing the strain, everyone at the table fell silent, and for the next few minutes the only sound heard was the clink of silverware and the incessant jangle of the upstairs telephone—the latter a distraction that Mom insisted we let the answering machine handle.

The steaks proved juicy and delicious, the Caesar salad a delightful contrast to the smoky flavor of the barbecued corn, the bread fresh and aromatic. But as usual at any Kane family barbecue, Dad's sweet-and-sour bean casserole was everyone's favorite—the savory dish demanding a second helping, and then possibly a third. Nate finished his without touching any of the other food on his plate and clamored for more.

"There *are* other things to eat," Dad noted dryly, dishing out another portion.

"I'll get to 'em soon as the beans are gone," said Nate.

My father, far more understanding with Nate than he had ever been with any of his other children, especially me, smiled patiently.

As twilight descended, table conversation ricocheted from topics ranging from my transfer to USC in September to Mom's upcoming concert season, continuing unabated until everyone finished eating. After we had cleared the table and carried the dishes up to the kitchen, we again reassembled outside for dessert. Though I could have sworn I had no room left for anything, not even a morsel, I changed my mind when Mom's mud pie made its appearance.

"Mmmm, that looks scrumptious, Mrs. Kane," said McKenzie, admiring my mother's creation of vanilla ice cream in a crumbled Oreo-cookie shell, with layers of fudge sauce and whipped cream topping the delicious-looking concoction.

"And it *tastes* even better," said Nate as Mom began cutting thick slabs and serving them on paper plates.

Once desserts had made their way around the table, everyone again fell silent, concentrating on eating. Predictably, Nate had seconds. By the time everyone finished, a full moon had risen over the lights of Santa Monica, illuminating the deck with a soft yellow glow. Pleasantly full, Dad rocked back and laced his hands across his stomach. "Okay, rookies, listen up," he said, his voice unconsciously assuming the autocratic snap of a drill sergeant. "I've been doing some thinking lately—"

"Somebody alert Mensa," I whispered to Nate.

"—and I have an announcement to make," Dad finished, ignoring my gibe.

Like all the Kane children, I had learned from experience to distrust my father's postmeal announcements, the majority of which involved summaries of each of our shortcomings and failures regarding schoolwork, chores, and family duties— invariably followed by a compulsory plan by which we could redeem ourselves.

"Oh, joy," I groused. "We have company, Dad, and we certainly don't want McKenzie getting the right idea about you. Don't forget your rule about no negativity at the dinner table."

"I'm not being negative."

I smiled. "There. See?"

"Hey, the ol' dad might have something positive to say," my father objected, feigning insult. "Don't you kids trust me?"

"No!" Nate and I laughed as one, emboldened by Dad's unusually sunny mood.

"Tough," said Dad. "You're going to hear this anyway. What I was about to propose before that rousing vote of confidence was this: With rebuilding the house and all, it's been quite a while since we've had one of our annual Fourth of July bashes—"

"Here's a news flash," I broke in again. "The Fourth is over."

"I know that, petunia," he said patiently. "Contrary to popular belief, I *can* read a calendar. I'm talking about another date that's coming up in a month or so. August eleventh, to be exact. Your birthday. Now, your mom and I talked it over, and we both agree that in the tragic absence of our customary Fourth of July gathering while we've been rebuilding, we should do something memorable to kick off your upcoming twentieth birthday."

"All right!" exclaimed Nate. "A beach party for Ali! With hundreds of people like on the Fourth?"

Dad grinned. "What's the point of having a beach party if you don't invite everybody?"

Nate's face lit up. "Can we have a bonfire?"

"It's possible."

"Fireworks?" asked Nate.

"No fireworks. It's not the Fourth. Besides, I have something else planned."

"Food?" I suggested. "You're doing something special with the food?"

"No more guessing."

"You're not really thinking of inviting every single person we know like on the Fourth, are you?" I persisted, secretly pleased but trying not to show it.

Dad gazed at the moon without answering.

I turned to my mother. "Mom? What's Dad planning?"

"It's a surprise, honey. Your father swore me to secrecy."

"C'mon, Dad," I begged. "What are you going to do?"

"You'll see," Dad answered mysteriously. "Just keep that weekend open."

*     *     *

41

In the mountains north of Malibu, the same summer moon shining down on the Kanes' deck also bathed the surface of a large reservoir. As moonlight pierced the water's inky depths, the slanting rays quickly diminished, barely illuminating a small object submerged a dozen yards offshore. Strands of hair swayed like eel grass in the slight subsurface current, billowing around a face whose eyes stared sightlessly into the dark.

Buoyed by gases of decomposition, the ghostly white shape lifted gently from the bottom, partially shedding an enclosing shroud of black plastic. Loops of rope binding the wrists and ankles prevented the body from rising more than a foot. Bit by bit, the body rotated. Cut by coils of encircling cord, a patch of water-softened skin bunched like wet newspaper, sloughing from the underlying tissue. Loosened, a cord fell free.

And gradually, as another restraining tether came undone, the body began a slow ascent to the surface.

# 4

As I wheeled into the CBS Television City visitors' parking lot early Monday morning, I still wasn't certain what I was doing there. Getting an internship at a national news bureau would be great, but I was already enrolled in class at UCLA, and I was fairly certain I couldn't do both—even if I got the job, which wasn't likely for someone with little or no experience. Making an effort to shelve my concerns for the moment and just see how things went, I proceeded down a broad driveway, stopping at a parking kiosk near the far end. There, with a disapproving glance at the beach-rusted Bronco I had borrowed from Travis, a uniformed guard handed me a parking stub and waved me past. Straight ahead, the looming hulk of CBS Television City rose above a sea of cars, its eyeball-festooned black-and-white walls and squat lines reminding me of a giant cardboard box. After minutes of searching, I found a slot at the west end of the lot, parked, and twisted off the ignition. Refusing to die, the Bronco bucked repeatedly before finally shuddering to a stop.

Struggling to suppress my apprehension, I stepped out, smoothed my skirt and wool blazer, and started for the huge, windowless building. As I approached, I noticed a number of people queued along the western perimeter, apparently waiting to see one of the daytime game shows that I knew were shot inside. After asking directions from a production assistant polling those in line, I threaded through the crowd, arriving at an artists' entrance a hundred yards east. Still inexplicably nervous, I entered.

Inside, I found myself in a small but pleasant lobby decorated in plastic and chrome. A coffee table and couch, several chairs, and a ceiling-mounted TV took up most of the space to the left; to the right, a waist-high stainless-steel counter curved toward a door opposite the entrance. From behind the counter, a portly African-American man politely asked, "May I help you, miss?"

I nodded, feeling out of place and again wondering why I had come. "I'm Allison Kane, here to see Brent Preston."

The guard slid a register across the counter and lifted a phone. "Sign in, please. I'll see whether Mr. Preston is in the newsroom."

After I had printed and signed my name in the entry record, I glanced at the TV across the room. Not surprisingly, it was tuned to Channel 2, CBS's Los Angeles affiliate.

"Mr. Preston will be down shortly," the guard informed me. Then, after checking my name in the register, he filled out a guest pass and slid it across the counter. "You'll need this."

"Thanks."

I pinned the pass to my blazer and sat in a chair across from the TV. Twenty minutes later, after viewing all I could stand of a mind-numbing morning talk show, I rose and made my way back to the desk. As I was about to ask the guard for an update, Brent Preston, a tall, sandy-haired man in his late twenties, stepped into the room. Noticing me, he smiled, his slate-gray eyes lingering on me for several seconds before he spoke. "Sorry it took so long," he apologized. "I was in a meeting."

Nervously, I smiled back, deciding that Mr. Preston looked even more striking in person than he did on TV. "I'm, uh, I'm Allison Kane, Mr. Preston," I stammered, reaching out to shake his hand. "I've seen lots of your newscasts, starting back when you were doing the local news for KCBS."

"Ah, the good old days at Channel 2," said the newsman. "Well, thanks, Allison. And please call me Brent. The bureau chief is tied up right now, but she'll be able to see you shortly. C'mon. I'll give you a tour while you're waiting."

I followed Brent through the door. A procession of promotional photos lined the walls of a wide hallway on the other side. Some pictures were of CBS news anchors, but most of the photos depicted stars of network game shows, daytime soaps, and sitcoms. "Looks like the soap-opera hall of fame," I observed, noting a conspicuously empty slot as we passed.

"More like the hall of shame," joked Brent, noticing my glance at the empty spot. "If your ratings are down, your picture's gone the next day. And we call them 'daytime dramas' around here," he cautioned with mock severity.

"I'll remember that," I laughed, beginning to relax.

Farther down the corridor the ambiance abruptly changed, the forest-green carpet replaced by industrial-grade linoleum, the acoustic ceiling tiles giving way to a maze of pipes, cables, and ductwork. A misplaced pair of promotional photos from another era—Red Skelton as "Freddie the Freeloader," and Jack Benny posing with a chimp—were the final attempts at decoration. From there, a labyrinth of passageways branched deeper into the building, their industrial mien reminding me of the interior of a factory, or possibly a ship.

Several turns took us to *The Price is Right* backstage area, an aircraft-hanger-sized chamber jammed with couches, beds, kitchen appliances, cars, boats, Jet Skis, sports equipment, and an endless array of televisions, stereos, washing machines, refrigerators, and other household items. I whistled under my breath.

"And this is only *one* of the studios here," Brent informed me. "Impressive, huh?"

"I'll say. Is the newsroom like this?"

"I wish," Brent answered. "We in the news give network a certain stature and prestige, but if the truth be known, we're fairly low on the corporate pecking order. Actually, make that the bottom of the pecking order. The reality shows, daytime dramas, and game shows are the real money-makers around here, so they get the space. I enjoyed better working conditions at Channel 2."

"But I thought—"

"Never mind what you thought. Just don't be too disappointed when we get to the newsroom. It won't be what you expected."

A quarter hour later, after escorting me through several other studios, an extensive woodworking shop used for set construction, and the CBS employee cafeteria, Brent checked his watch. "Lauren should be done by now," he said. "I suppose we should head over to the newsroom."

"Lauren?"

45

"The bureau chief. Lauren Van Owen."

My throat tightened.

"Is something wrong?" Brent asked, looking at me curiously.

"No," I lied.

"People are often surprised to learn that the bureau chief is a woman," Brent went on, misinterpreting my reaction. "When Sid Gilmore, our old chief, retired six months back, the suits in New York tapped Lauren for his spot. You may remember her. She was a reporter for Channel 2 before an accident ended her on-camera work.

"I recall the incident," I said, thinking that what had started as a promising morning had just taken a drastic turn for the worse.

\*     \*     \*

It had been more years than Kane cared to admit since he had ridden patrol for the LAPD Van Nuys Division, but the streets were beginning to come back. After turning left off Ventura Boulevard onto Alonzo, he drove into the chaparral-covered mountains that marked the southwest borders of the San Fernando Valley. New homes with bricked patios and wrought-iron fences flanked the street all the way up, but with the exception of these recent additions, the rugged hillsides of the Santa Monica Mountains still looked the same: steep, dusty, and overgrown with sage and scrub oak.

Fifteen minutes later Kane arrived at a cul-de-sac, high above the housing developments and shopping malls of the valley below. Crossing overhead, high-voltage power lines arced up the mountainside, the thick spans of electrical cables glinting in the midday sun. At the pavement's end, two black-and-white patrol cars were stationed near a dirt fire road. An eight-foot-high chain-link fence topped with barbed wire prevented access on either side. A young patrol officer, notebook in hand, guarded the open gate. Other officers stood nearby, questioning a group of neighbors.

Kane pulled up to the gate. "Detective Daniel Kane, West L.A. homicide," he said, flipping out his ID.

The young officer checked Kane's credentials, made an entry in his notebook, and waved him past. As Kane drove in, he noticed a heavy chain and a number of interlinked padlocks dangling from the gate.

The dirt fire road swung right, then steepened as it continued up the slope. Kane's late-model Ford, one of several "city cars" assigned to the West L.A. homicide unit, began to strain, its wheels slipping on loose gravel. After several hair-raising curves, Kane surmounted a steep rise. There, the road forked. To the right it proceeded higher into the mountains. To the left, several hundred yards down a steep incline, lay the blue surface of Encino reservoir, enclosed within a second chain-link fence. Unlike the outer perimeter fence ringing several square miles of mountain hillside, the inner fence ran a mere twenty yards from the water's edge. Within this secondary barrier Kane spotted three more patrol cars, two unmarked vehicles, and a gray van with a Department of Water and Power logo on the side.

Pumping the brakes, Kane eased his Ford down toward the reservoir. Finally reaching more level ground, he entered an open gate in the inner fence, arriving at a flat section of shoreline. There, beyond the parked cars and a loose knot of men, he saw the nude body of a young girl sprawled at the water's edge.

Kane turned off the engine and stepped from his vehicle. One of the men in the group saw him and started over. As the man neared, Kane recognized the round face and bulldog bearing of Carl Peyron. The ranking detective for the West L.A. Major Assault Crimes unit, Peyron had drawn the Jordan French abduction case weeks before. Kane knew that for lack of evidence, Peyron had made little progress to date on the investigation. Kane also knew that situation was about to change.

"Morning, Kane," Peyron wheezed when he arrived. "Make that afternoon," he corrected, squinting at the sun.

"How's it going, Carl?" Kane replied, noting beads of perspiration glistening on Peyron's forehead, a faint trace of Maalox ringing his lips. "A bit far from home, aren't you?"

Peyron, a stocky Hispanic in his late thirties, mopped his brow with a crumpled handkerchief. "Yeah. Now I recall why I transferred out of the valley."

Kane smiled. "Me, too." Then, his smile fading, "Is it her?"

Peyron nodded somberly. "It's her. The body's been in the water for some time, but you can still tell it's Jordan French." Peyron glanced toward the men assembled a dozen yards from the body. "The Van Nuys guys who first responded recognized her and contacted us, because they knew we were handling the abduction. Needless to say, they're more than happy to let West L.A. take over, especially now that it's turned into a homicide. Unless the parents want to involve the Feds, it's all yours."

Kane knew that although LAPD detectives had jurisdiction over the investigation of Jordan's abduction and murder, the FBI could be brought in by request to assist in the kidnap portion of the case. It was an option that neither Jordan's parents nor LAPD authorities had pursued to date, and that's the way Kane wanted it to stay, having had problems in the past with what he considered unnecessary FBI interference.

Kane turned toward the shoreline. "Who found her?"

"DWP workers who were surveying for some water-quality improvement project. Seems they're upgrading all open reservoirs in the system."

"Make sure those guys stick around. I want to talk to them." Kane thought a moment. "Where was she found? On the bank?"

"Floating a few yards offshore. One of the survey guys dragged her in."

"Anybody else touch her?"

"According to the first officers to arrive, no."

"The DWP crew had to unlock that gate at the street to get in," reasoned Kane. "Did they report any signs of tampering?"

"Nope. They said everything looked normal."

"How about the other gate?" asked Kane, indicating the one in the inner fence near the water.

"That was open. The DWP guys say it hasn't been locked all summer."

"I noticed a string of padlocks on the outside gate. Who has locks on that gate?"

"That's the first thing I asked when I got here," said Peyron. "DWP, Southern California Edison, the Fire Department, and LAPD all have locks on the chain. Nobody else."

"The dirt road I drove in on appeared to keep on going up the ridge," Kane said, glancing toward the top of the hill behind them. "Where's it wind up?"

"It connects with an unimproved section of Mulholland," answered Peyron. "One of the uniforms hiked up there. He says there's another gate at the top. Nothing looked disturbed. The chain and locks there are all intact, and no cuts in the fence."

"We'll want to recheck that, along with everyone who has keys." Kane swept his eyes over the miles of brush-covered hillside encircling the reservoir, noting a number of animal trails cutting through the undergrowth. "For that matter, it's possible our man entered from one of the nearby neighborhoods. It would have been a long hike carrying a body, but it's possible. We'll have to canvass the neighbors, too."

"Right. Inquire about any strange cars in the area, check for cuts in the fencing, that kind of thing," Peyron agreed. "I called the Van Nuys watch commander and asked him to send more guys out here for some door-knocking. I also took the liberty of contacting SID," he added, referring to the LAPD Scientific Investigation Division crime-scene unit. "I notified the coroner's office, too. They're on their way."

"Good. Anything else?"

Peyron hesitated, then referred to his notebook. "One thing. Maybe it's not important, but I asked the DWP workers about currents in the reservoir."

"To get an idea of where the body was dumped?"

"Yeah. It appears the corpse was weighted down before it broke loose. According to the DWP guys, there's a subsurface current draining toward a collector at the north end of the dam. But once the body rose to the surface, the wind could have blown it in any direction."

Kane gazed out over the reservoir. "A lot of shoreline to search."

"You've got that right."

Just then one of the patrol officers yelled to them from his cruiser. "Detectives, I got a call here from one of our guys out on the street. A news crew just arrived. They want to know whether there's any statement yet."

"Not yet," Kane yelled back. "And for God's sake, don't let them in."

"Yes, sir."

"Damn, how do those dirtbags find out so fast?" Kane muttered. Cursing under his breath, he started toward the reservoir. After a few steps, he turned. "Hey, Carl?"

"What?"

"I'll want to get together with you later and go over everything you have on the abduction. Tomorrow morning work for you?"

Peyron nodded, staring past Kane toward the water. "Sure. And if there's anything else I can do to help . . ."

"I'll let you know. By the way, good work today. If you ever want to move over to homicide, we could use a guy like you."

Again, Peyron glanced uneasily toward the water. "I'll pass."

Kane had investigated a wide range of murders over the course of his career, but those involving children were always the hardest, and he understood Peyron's reluctance. Steeling himself for what was to come, Kane made his way to the water's edge, passing a knot of somber officers. With a nod of approval, he noted that they had apparently stayed well back from the body. In all likelihood the reservoir was merely a dump site and not the place where the child's death had occurred, but you never knew what evidence might turn up.

Kane approached the corpse slowly, careful not to miss details that might later prove important. Looking like something a backhoe might have turned up, the bloated body of a female child lay in the sunlight a few feet from the waterline. Areas of scum-coated skin had sloughed from long immersion; a tangle of hair was matted around her neck and face. She rested on one side, an arm raised awkwardly above her head—presumably as result of the survey worker's hauling her ashore. Her position reminded Kane of a schoolchild raising a hand in class. Frayed nylon cord still trailed from her wrist.

A breeze drifted up from the water, carrying the odor of putrefaction. Breathing shallowly to lessen the smell, Kane moved closer. From the state of decomposition and abdominal distention caused by gases of decay, he estimated that the corpse had been immersed for at least a week, although the ambient water temperature could affect that time period considerably. Typically a body floated facedown after surfacing, and a section of the child's upper back that had been open to the air was cracked and darkened from exposure. Kane noticed tiny blow-fly larvae on areas of skin that had been above water, concluding from the maggots' size that the corpse had been floating for no more than twenty-four to thirty-six hours.

Deciding to check with DWP about water temperatures at different depths, Kane leaned over the body, still not touching it. Mottled purplish discolorations called postmortem lividity, a condition caused by blood settling under the effect of gravity, marked the grayish-white flesh of the child's right side. Because lividity "fixes" and becomes unchangeable within the first eight hours of death, the port-wine stains on the child's right thigh, hip, and shoulder indicated that after her death she had lain on her right side for an extended period of time. At some point after that she had been transported, weighted, and dumped into the reservoir, but the lividity still bore testament to the hours immediately following her death.

Staring at the corpse, Kane felt a surge of anger, wondering how anyone could have done that to a child. Fighting to pinch off his emotions, he forced himself to focus on the details of the investigation, a technique he had long ago adopted to shield himself from the horrors of his profession. But as he resumed his inspection of the body, he made a silent vow, both to himself and to the dead girl at his feet.

Continuing his examination, Kane noticed a faint lattice of marks on the visible portion of the girl's lower back and buttocks.

As he made a mental note to have the coroner investigate those injuries, Kane also noticed that several areas of sodden skin on the body's ankles had degloved from the underlying tissue. Suspecting ligature wounds, he inspected the wrists, finding similar trauma. The body rose when it bloated, sawing loose from whatever was holding it down, he thought grimly, glancing at the tag of rope still remaining on one wrist. He made another mental note to save the knots and get divers to locate whatever was used to anchor her down.

Carefully, Kane shifted to the other side of the corpse. Small aquatic animals had nibbled away much of the eyelids, lips, and portions of both eyes, but Kane could still recognize the face of Jordan French. Following her disappearance, her picture had been featured in every newspaper and plastered on every Amber Alert notice in town. Nevertheless, he decided to try for prints at autopsy to get a positive ID, and to have a sexual-assault team present, too.

Leaning down, Kane noted a small gold ring on the index finger of the girl's right hand. Because of postmortem bloating, the band had cut deeply into her tissue, its heart-shaped body and filigreed "F" inscription nearly hidden within the swollen flesh.

A moment later Kane saw the SID crime-scene van inching down the steep hillside. Standing, he shoved his hands into his pockets. Though his exam of the body had just begun, he was already certain of two things. First, the killer had stored the body for some time before disposing of it. Second, rather than simply burying the corpse, the killer had gone to great lengths to submerge it in water, most probably to ensure that no external physical evidence—hair, fibers, latent fingerprints, tissue under the fingernails, and so forth—remained to tie him to his victim.

Kane knew he would spend the next hours with the SID crime unit and the coroner's investigator directing a detailed examination of the corpse and coordinating a ground search of the reservoir area. Everything would be done by the book. That notwithstanding, he expected to find nothing useful. And unless he were lucky, he knew that the autopsy would most likely prove useless too—which left canvassing the surrounding neighborhoods as the most promising avenue of investigation. Given the concern for eliminating evidence that the killer had shown in disposing of his victim, Kane suspected that approach would also prove futile.

As the SID van reached the bottom of the incline, Kane returned his gaze to the dead girl, a child whom someone had abducted, murdered, and dumped like a sack of garbage. Sickened by the sight, Kane's thoughts turned inward, traveling back to the death of his oldest son in a rock-climbing accident several years past. Tommy's death had been a paralyzing, crushing, heartbreaking loss that Kane had eventually learned to accept, but one that he had never been able to reconcile. Again, he wondered how anyone could treat a child with such malice.

Though the odds were against him, Kane reaffirmed the vow he had made earlier, this time speaking aloud. "Whoever did this to you, kid," he promised softly, "I'm going to find him."

\*     \*     \*

CBS bureau chief Lauren Van Owen looked up at me from her desk. "I'm happy to finally meet you, Allison."

Not trusting myself to speak, I glanced around the bureau chief's office, struggling to control a rising tide of animosity. Flanking Lauren's desk, a rack of TV monitors, each tuned to a different station, covered an entire wall. A large bulletin board took up another. Beside the door, a narrow couch blocked part of a window that looked out into the newsroom.

"I wasn't sure you'd come," the attractive blond seated behind the desk continued.

"When I made the appointment, I didn't know I would be seeing you," I said, finally finding my voice.

Lauren raised an eyebrow. "But once you found out, you bulled ahead anyway."

"Something like that."

"You're like your father in that respect." Lauren motioned with a hand toward the couch. "Please sit down."

At the mention of my father, I felt a renewed rush of hostility. "I didn't come here to discuss my father."

"No. You came here to confront the hussy who almost came between your parents—and possibly give her a piece of your mind."

I squared my shoulders. "As a matter of fact, you're right."

"Fair enough," said Lauren, holding my eyes with hers. "I don't blame you. I'm sure that like most young people, you see things only in black and white, with no confusing shades of gray. So if that's what you want, fine. But first let me say that I'm not defending myself for what happened. Back then I was a hungry reporter, and your father was . . . getting into a lot of trouble at work. They were tough times for both of us, and what took place between us was a mistake. A big mistake. God knows we paid for it."

I hesitated, disarmed by Lauren's candor. The words I'd planned to spit at the woman who had carried on a brief but deeply hurtful affair with my father suddenly seemed inappropriate. "I . . . I'm sorry for what you went through afterward," I said instead, looking more closely at Lauren's face. Though I tried, I was able to detect little of the brutal slashing she had suffered at the hands of the same man who had attacked my father.

"The scars are still there, but you have to look hard to see them," said Lauren, noticing my gaze. "A little makeup and years of reconstructive surgery can work wonders. I recovered most of my vision too, though I still have to wear sunglasses in bright light."

"So that's why you, uh, switched to—"

"—working behind the camera," Lauren finished. "In a way, things turned out for the best. I'm happy in what I'm doing now, and I have more time for my daughter, Candice. She's a few years younger than you." The bureau chief hesitated, then folded her hands on the desk. "Allison, although we've just met, you and I have a lot of history between us. Bad history. I'm sorry for that."

I remained silent.

"Your cameraman friend at Channel 2 told Brent that you're a writer, and that you're taking journalism courses in college," Lauren continued, chipping at the ice.

"That's right. At least I will be," I admitted. "I've been majoring in English at UCLA, but this fall I'm transferring to USC and switching to journalism. And I just met Mike last Friday. He's not really a friend."

"Well, he spoke highly of you. By the way, congratulations on your rescue effort at the beach. That was a dynamite segment. Our ratings shot through the roof after we ran it."

"How nice for you."

"So why journalism?" Lauren asked, ignoring my sarcasm.

"Well, I've been working on the UCLA school paper, and I like it," I replied, thawing slightly. "Plus journalism might be a career at which I could actually make a living."

"As opposed to tackling something more risky? Creative writing, for instance?"

I shrugged. "I suppose so."

"I don't want to pop your bubble, Allison, but there are no guarantees in the news business either," Lauren cautioned. "What's more, when it comes to getting ahead, many of those working in the media consider a journalism degree almost worthless. They'll tell you there's a big difference between academia and the real world, and the only way to learn this job is to do it."

"And what do *you* think?"

Lauren smiled. "I think it depends on the person. Schooling can't replace ability or on-the-job experience, but if nothing else, getting a journalism degree shows desire."

I thought for a moment, finally deciding that despite my animosity toward Ms. Van Owen, working at CBS for the rest of the summer might be something I could use, and maybe even like. If I were going to be a journalist, even a print journalist, getting some on-the-job experience *would* be helpful. "So tell me about the intern position," I said, beginning to get excited.

"It's thirty to forty hours a week with no pay. Mostly gofer work, but sometimes there's a chance to get involved with the news."

"No pay?"

"Money's tight. No pay is standard for interns. Is that a problem?"

"You could say that," I said, trying to hide my disappointment. "I would have to drop out of summer session at UCLA, and no pay would mean moving back to my parents' house in Malibu."

"Friction at home?"

"There would be."

Just then Brent Preston stuck his head into Lauren's office. "Sorry to interrupt. I just got a call from one of my LAPD contacts. A body matching Jordan French's description was just found in a reservoir out near Encino."

"Take a camera crew and see what you can get," said Lauren.

"I'm on it."

After Brent left, I shook my head in surprise. I had never met Jordan French, but having seen her on TV over the years had left me feeling as if the young actress were someone I knew. "Dad was right," I said absently.

"Your father thought Jordan French was dead? Why?"

"Well, when there was no follow-up on the ransom—" I stopped short.

"So there *was* a ransom demand," said Lauren, pouncing like a cat on a crippled sparrow. "I knew the police were holding something back."

I flushed, angry with myself for my slip. "I shouldn't have said anything."

"Don't worry about it. Now that the body's turned up, there's no longer any reason for investigators to withhold that particular piece of information. I'm sure they'll be announcing it shortly. Incidentally, I didn't know your father was working on the case."

"He's not. At least he wasn't."

Lauren studied me for a long moment. "How are your computer skills?"

"I've been online since I was twelve, and I can type like the wind."

Again, Lauren paused thoughtfully. "It took guts for you to walk into my office today, knowing who I was," she said at last. "That kind of nerve is unusual for a girl your age. You remind me of myself when I was first starting out. I'll tell you what, Allison. I'm going to take a chance and give you a shot at working here. *With pay.* I'll find some way to bury the expense in the budget. We'll call you an assignment-desk assistant or an associate producer. Whatever. The position will be open for a year, but you can quit in September when it's time to return to school. As I said, you'll be a gofer for the most part, but there may also be opportunities for you to get involved in the news. What do you say?"

"I say yes!" I answered impulsively, my hostility toward Lauren temporarily forgotten.

"There *is* one condition," Lauren cautioned. "You indicated that your working here might cause friction at home. I won't get caught in the middle on this. You have to tell your parents."

"Of course. My mom won't like my dropping out of summer session, but she'll get over it. And I can handle my father."

"I'm glad someone can," Lauren noted skeptically. "When can you start?"

"I'll need the rest of today to withdraw from my literature class and tie up loose ends at school," I answered. "I have an article to finish for the school paper, too. And I'm leaving on a trip this weekend and won't be back till Monday, so I'll have to miss a day then," I added, remembering my trip to D.C. for Trav's NSO performance. "But other than that, I can start first thing tomorrow. Is that okay?"

"Tomorrow morning works fine. Be here at eight," said Lauren, reaching across her desk to shake my hand. "Welcome aboard."

# 5

Feet propped on my desk, phone in one hand, TV remote control in the other, I sat in my room later that evening talking with McKenzie. Rocking back in my chair, I lifted the remote and flipped through the channels, stopping on the *CBS Evening News*.

"So how did your mom react to your dropping out of summer session at UCLA?" McKenzie asked.

"I can hardly hear you, Mac," I said, dodging her question. "Are you in your car?"

"Yeah. Hold on. I'll roll up the window."

"Is that better?" McKenzie's voice came back a moment later. Then, without awaiting my reply, "C'mon, tell me what your mom said."

"I haven't told her yet."

"You haven't? Well, you'll have to tell her soon. I'd love to be a fly on the wall for that one. Listen, I have a date, and I just pulled into my driveway. Keep me filled in, okay?"

"You'll be the first to know," I promised.

As I hung up, I noticed a photo of Jordan French flashing up on the TV screen. Then the scene abruptly shifted to a dead-end residential street. Microphone in hand, Brent Preston stood gesturing toward a brush-covered hillside behind him. Curious, I turned up the sound.

" . . . recovered from Encino Reservoir, where earlier today a Department of Water and Power survey team discovered the body of the missing fourteen-year-old."

The picture switched to an overhead shot of a large body of water, its gray-blue surface shimmering in the foothills above the San Fernando Valley. A number of police vehicles, large block numerals visible on their roofs, were parked by the reservoir dam. Nearby, several men stood beside a white sheet at the water's edge.

"Although Jordan French was reported abducted from her home more than eleven days ago, police still have no leads," Brent continued as the shot returned to him. "In other developments, CBS News has learned from sources close to the investigation that a ransom note was delivered to the Frenches' home shortly after Jordan's abduction. When contacted, LAPD officials had no comment regarding the ransom demand, or why its existence had previously not been disclosed. This is Brent Preston, CBS News, Los Angeles."

"Damn," I said aloud, realizing with a surge of regret that my slip with Lauren was at least one of Brent's so-called "sources" close to the investigation.

"Allison! You have a visitor," one of the girls residing in the dorm hollered up the stairs.

"Be down in a minute," I called back.

Unsettled by Brent's mention of the ransom note, I flipped off the TV. Though regretting my slip with Lauren, I also realized that I had felt a deliciously guilty thrill when I'd heard Brent's on-air revelation—*my revelation*—knowing millions had been listening. With an uneasy shrug, I decided I would have to be more careful in the future. Anyway, there was nothing I could do about it now. I just hoped my father didn't find out. After donning a loose-fitting rugby shirt, I grabbed my purse and headed for the door, turning off lights on my way out.

At the bottom of the staircase I stopped midstride, my mouth dropping open in surprise. Upon hearing I had a visitor, I'd concluded that it must have been a girlfriend from lit class who had called earlier that week about possibly joining me for dinner. Instead, there in the entry wearing a pair of crisply pressed slacks, an open-collared shirt, and a leather aviator jacket, stood Mike Cortese. Obviously enjoying my reaction, the cameraman grinned, his rugged features creasing with amusement. "Hi, Ali," he said. "I wasn't sure I would recognize you in clothes."

A rush of heat flooded my face. "Just happened to be in the area and thought you'd drop by?" I asked, hating myself for my blush and wishing I had chosen something more flattering to wear than a pair of faded jeans and a rugby shirt.

"Something like that."

"How'd you know . . . ?" Then, shaking my head, I answered my own question. "McKenzie."

Mike nodded. "She gave me your address. I hope you don't mind. Listen, I realize we got off on the wrong foot last weekend at the beach, and I'm sorry," he said. "And I *did* just happen to be in the neighborhood, so when I heard about your getting hired at CBS, I thought I'd look you up and offer my congratulations."

"Thanks," I said, warming slightly. "I appreciate your help."

"No thanks are necessary. I simply made a call. You nailed down the job yourself. Brent says he thinks you'll do great."

"He said that?"

"Yep. As a matter of fact, I'm meeting him tonight in Westwood for a drink. The restaurant is just down the street. Why don't you join us? He can tell you himself."

"I don't—"

"Have you eaten? If you haven't, we could grab a bite, too. What do you say?"

"I don't think so."

"Why not?"

"For one thing, I don't know you that well. For another, I'm not dressed to go out."

"Are you kidding? You look great. As for not knowing me, there's only one cure for that. C'mon, the place I'm meeting Brent is casual, serves fresh pasta, and we can walk there in no time. That is, unless you don't like Italian," Mike added with a mock frown. "In which case we can forget the whole thing."

"No, I love Italian," I conceded, finding Mike much nicer than I remembered. And he *had* helped me get the job at CBS. Plus Brent would be there too, so going to a restaurant with Mike wasn't really a date. "And I am hungry," I added. "Actually, I'm starving."

"Good. I like a girl with a healthy appetite."

Following a short stroll down Hilgard Avenue, Mike and I pushed through the doors of The Gardens, a brick-and-tile throwback to earlier days of Westwood. As Mike spoke to a young woman at the hostess station, I let my eyes roam the restaurant, pleased by the changes that had been effected since I'd last visited. Years ago the ancient building had housed an upscale hamburger palace; now, despite encroaching high-rise office towers and multiplex theaters, the interior of the renovated one-story structure seemed delightfully rustic. Directly ahead lay a spacious room with a domed skylight and a thirty-foot tree rising from the center, its sprawling limbs shading tables set with high-backed wicker chairs. On either side, bricked archways accessed smaller dining rooms that I remembered had originally been patio gardens, while to the left lay an airy, four-sided bar with intimate tables ensconced in alcoves ringing the room's perimeter.

"You said this place was casual," I whispered when Mike finished talking with the hostess, again wishing I had worn something more appropriate.

"It *is* casual," Mike replied. "Besides, even in hip waders and a trench coat you'd be the best-looking girl here. C'mon, let's sit in the bar area. They can serve us dinner there right away."

Pleased by Mike's breezy compliment, I followed him into the bar. The hostess, a pretty young woman with a dazzling smile, seated us in a window alcove that looked out on the streets of Westwood through a wisteria-covered trellis. "Your waitress will be here shortly, Mike," the hostess said, placing menus on our table. "Want anything to drink while you're waiting?"

"Thanks, Brooke. I'll have a beer. Make it a Red Hook," said Mike, glancing at me. "What would you like, Ali?"

"A Coke."

"A Coke and a Red Hook, on the way," said Brooke, shooting Mike another smile as she departed.

"Are you a regular here?" I asked, having noted that the hostess wasn't wearing a name tag.

"I used to be," Mike answered, opening his menu. "A lot of guys from the station hang out here."

I opened my menu, finding that in addition to a selection of reasonably priced pasta dishes, The Gardens boasted a tempting variety of other entrées. "Speaking of work, you said you first got to know Brent when he was at Channel 2?"

Mike nodded. "He got his start at KCBS as a local reporter. He's moved up in the world since then, not that he needs the money. His dad's the president of Preston Development Company."

"Preston Development? The company that builds those Orange County housing tracts?"

"That's the one. PDC's one of the biggest construction outfits in the Southland, and they're not just building condos and single-family homes any more. Despite our occasional real-estate downturns, now they're putting up shopping malls, light-industrial parks, and office buildings. With no exaggeration, it's fair to say that Brent's family is filthy rich—private jet, mansion in South Pasadena, vacation homes in Sun Valley, Hawaii, and New Mexico. The guy's always had the best of whatever money can buy, though you would never know that from the way he pushes himself."

"What do you mean?"

Mike paused before answering. "Don't get me wrong," he said after a moment. "I admire the way Brent has ascended the ranks at CBS. With the exception of using his dad's connections to get his first job at Channel 2, to my knowledge he's never depended on his family's money or influence to get ahead. He wants to be a network anchor by the time he's thirty-five, and he's determined to do it on his own. I guess there's nothing wrong with that, except it's as if he's trying to prove something. You'll see what I mean. The guy's driven."

"So what would *you* do if you had his money?"

"I sure as hell wouldn't be chasing the news."

"Why not?"

Noticing a cocktail waitress approaching with our drinks, Mike closed his menu. "For someone like you just starting out in the news game, I'm not the one to be talking to," he answered. "That glint of idealism in your eyes will fade soon enough. So what are you having?"

Though puzzled by Mike's reply, I let it go. "Pasta. I heard from a reliable source that it's great."

I chose a penne dish served with a broccoli-crème sauce; Mike selected a fusilli with rock shrimp, scallops, and arugula. As a side dish he also ordered one of the house specialties—pizza with pesto, prawns, and red onions. The pizza was overkill, but I surprised myself by devouring my penne and still finding room for two slices of pizza as well.

Thirty minutes later I placed my napkin on the table, watching as Mike finished the last of the pizza. Our conversation had continued comfortably throughout the meal, sputtering along between bites. Now, pleasantly full, I decided to revisit a topic we had broached earlier. "So what's wrong with the news business?"

Mike downed a final bite of pizza crust. "Just that," he said. "It's a *business*, along with all the things that go with being a business." Then, glancing across the bar, "There's Brent. Hey, Brent! Over here!"

Hearing his name, Brent Preston looked over from the far side of the room, breaking into a grin as he spotted us. By now a number of theaters in the area had let out, and the bar was rapidly filling with moviegoers stopping by for a nightcap. Arm around a slim brunette accompanying him, Brent fought his way through the throng, arriving at our table after making several stops to speak with friends and admirers. "Hi, Allison," he said, taking my hand. "Mike told me he was going to ask you to join us. I'm glad you came. Good to see you too, Cortese."

"Back at you," said Mike, rising from the table. "Hello, Liz," he added to the woman with Brent. Then, turning to me, "Liz Waterson, Allison Kane."

I recognized the smartly dressed woman accompanying Brent as one of the CBS news producers I had met earlier that day. "Hi, Liz."

Liz frowned at Brent, who was still holding my hand, then turned to me. "Good evening, Allison," she replied with a cold smile. "I hear congratulations are in order."

"They sure are," Brent jumped in. "Van Owen is bringing Allison onboard as a full-time associate producer. With pay, if you can believe that. You must have really wowed her, Allison. I'll grab some chairs and you can tell us all about it."

Liz raised a sculpted eyebrow. "Yes, why don't you?" she suggested. "I, for one, would be interested in knowing how you swung it. I've never heard of anyone as green as you who's just starting out as an intern—oh, excuse me, as an *associate producer*—being paid from day one."

"Ali's not that green," Mike pointed out. "She's studying journalism. What's more, she already has some TV recognition going. We're still getting calls at Channel 2 about her beach rescue."

"Same thing at network," Brent chimed in, returning with two chairs from an adjacent table. "The overnight ratings were in the stratosphere after we ran her spot," he went on, seating Liz beside Mike and taking a place next to me. "We even got calls from management in New York."

"But the position for which mermaid-girl was hired doesn't have anything to do with being recognized on TV," Liz noted dismissively, as if I weren't present. "I just think that something is—"

"You guys want a drink?" Mike cut in. "I'm heading to the bar for another beer."

"I'll have a double Chevas on the rocks," said Brent.

"Vodka gimlet for me," Liz replied with another chilly smile, clearly irked at having been interrupted.

"Allison?"

"A refill on my Coke, please."

As Mike started across the room, I turned to Brent, puzzled by the animosity I felt radiating from Liz. "Mike was in the process of telling me what's wrong with the news business when you arrived," I said, attempting to steer the conversation away from myself. "Any thoughts on that?"

"A few," Brent replied. "For one thing, you have to understand that Mike is a frustrated filmmaker who resents shooting ten-second news clips. As a result, when it comes to accepting the way things are in the media, he has a chip on his shoulder the size of Rhode Island. It's a shame, too, because he's really good. UCLA Film School and all that. Maybe one of these days he'll make it in the movie biz. Did he tell you he has a documentary that's going to be shown at the Telluride Film Festival in September?"

"No."

"Well, he does. It's a huge honor simply having your work screened at a major event like that."

I decided there was more to Mike Cortese than I had thought. "You mentioned his not accepting the way things are in the media. What things?"

Brent grinned. "He didn't get that far in his analysis of the woes besetting the industry, eh? Well, it's the old journalism-versus-entertainment chestnut that people have been kicking around for years. You know—the golden age of journalism died when big corporations took over and network bean-counters began evaluating everything based on the financial bottom line. According to Mike, present-day news coverage is typified by inanity, hype, and crime. News anchors have become million-dollar celebrities reading scripts off a TelePrompTer, and in an endless scramble for ratings—once more according to Mike—news stations are broadcasting lowest-common-denominator programming, with substance replaced by weather, sports, and happy-talk between correspondents and anchors."

"That's not really fair, is it?"

Brent shrugged, absently worrying a thumbnail with his teeth. "Oh, a bit of it is. Maybe more than a bit. But the news has to make money like everything else; otherwise it couldn't exist. So we give viewers what they want. And when all's said and done, what's so wrong with that?" Noticing Liz watching him bite his nail, Brent removed his hand from his mouth and continued. "If we can inform the public and entertain them at the same time, why not?"

"Because mainstream news likes to think it's different from the paparazzi on motorbikes snapping pictures," answered Mike, returning from the bar. "But it isn't. Insights like that, by the way, mark the difference between a professional cameraman such as myself and someone with a real job," he added wryly, setting a double handful of glasses on the table. "Chevas rocks, vodka gimlet, Red Hook, and a Coke. Grab 'em while they're frosty."

"How much do I owe?" asked Brent.

"I've got this one," said Mike, resuming his place. "Sorry about breaking in on your sterling defense of the news, by the way. Speaking of which, do you have any words of wisdom for Allison?"

"Yeah. Don't fight with management," said Brent tersely.

Brent's response brought an instant nod of agreement from Liz. Then, frowning, Liz turned to Mike. "Paparazzi? I suppose you'd like to turn back the clock to the days of Edward R. Murrow and Eric Sevareid and the like."

Mike lifted his beer. "Unfortunately, Liz, that's not possible," he said evenly, taking a healthy sip. "Thanks to TV, pictures have replaced words, and in case you haven't noticed, crazed gunmen and murders du jour provide better visuals than in-depth coverage of world events. Not to belabor the point, but FBI figures show that national crime has been decreasing for years, while news stations continue to escalate their coverage of blood and guts—on average giving it twice the air time they did a decade ago. Meanwhile, among other things, international-news reporting has declined by half."

"Sad, but true," said Brent. "If it bleeds, it leads. But to be fair, all broadcast journalism isn't murder and mayhem at eleven. There's good work being done even now, and some reporters still have scruples."

Mike chuckled. "This coming from a guy who would sell his own mother for a story."

"Guilty as charged," said Brent. "In my defense, I'm no different from anyone else in the business."

"No. Just better at it than most," said Mike. "Incidentally, I caught the Jordan French spot you did today at the reservoir. Impressive."

"Thanks."

"Where'd you get the exclusive on the ransom note? None of the other stations mentioned that."

With a renewed rush of guilt, I wondered how much Lauren had told Brent.

"Van Owen received an anonymous tip," answered Brent. "I checked my sources to get confirmation. Eventually it panned out."

"So who's handling the investigation now that it's turned into a homicide?" asked Liz, reaching across the table to take Brent's hand. "Anybody we know?"

"Some hard-ass detective named Kane," Brent replied. "He wouldn't even comment on the case. Said the next of kin had to be notified first. I got most of my material from one of the Van Nuys patrol cops and a friend at the coroner's office."

"Kane," mused Liz. "Now, why does that name sound familiar?"

"No relation of yours, is he, Allison?" joked Brent.

"He's my father."

All heads at the table turned toward me. After several seconds Brent found his voice. "You're kidding."

"No."

"*Now* I recall," Liz said brightly. "Kane was on that Candlelight Killer Task Force two years ago." Then, her eyes widening, "Oh, my God. Detective Daniel Kane. It was all over the news when Lauren was attacked, remember? Kane was the cop Van Owen was, uh . . ." Liz let her voice trail off meaningfully.

"Kane and Lauren?" said Brent incredulously.

"Sure," Liz went on. "Don't you see? It explains everything. What does your mother have to say about your working for Lauren, Allison?"

"I haven't told her yet."

"You haven't?" Liz smiled, clearly enjoying herself now. "Well, sooner or later you'll have to. I would like to be a fly on the wall during *that* conversation."

It was the second time that evening I had heard those same words. Unable to hide my embarrassment, I lowered my head and rose from the table. "Excuse me. I have to go to the bathroom," I said.

After crossing the bar, I stood in the lobby taking deep breaths, angry with myself for having allowed Liz to get under my skin. I considered walking home, but decided that would only make matters worse. If I were going to work at CBS, I had to set things straight with Liz, and the sooner the better. Whatever had gone on between my father and Lauren had nothing to do with me. And if Liz or anybody else thought it did, they were mistaken.

My mouth set in a grim line of determination, I reentered the bar. As I approached our table, I noticed that Mike was now engaged in a heated conversation with Brent's date. "Jesus, Liz," I heard Mike say. "Sometimes you can be a royal pain."

Liz shot Mike a contemptuous glare, her eyes flashing like daggers. "Screw you, Cortese. *I* wasn't the one who got some cop to cheat on his frigid, ice-princess wife in order to get inside information. And now, of all things, Lauren has apparently hired his *daughter* to—" Liz hesitated midsentence, suddenly noticing me.

I stopped beside the table. Instead of sitting, I remained standing, hands balled at my sides. I stared at Liz, feeling the newswoman's words settling like spit on my face. "Let's get something straight, Ms. Waterson," I said quietly, holding the older woman's gaze with mine. "First, my father and Ms. Van Owen haven't seen each other for years. Second, my being hired at CBS had nothing to do with what happened between them in the past. And third, if you ever talk about my mother that way again, I'll make you wish you hadn't."

As Mike walked me back to my dorm, I was still simmering over my confrontation with Liz. Paradoxically, I was also furious with myself for losing my temper.

"Want to talk about it?" Mike ventured.

"No."

"C'mon, Allison. What are you thinking right now?"

"I'm thinking I shouldn't have blown my top like that," I answered.

"Liz was out of line. Way out of line."

"Yeah, but I made things worse," I said, my mood plummeting. "On the other hand, I suppose the danger of bottling up hostility is that one runs the risk of forgetting it."

"Good point," Mike chuckled.

"Anyway, thanks for sticking up for me."

"My pleasure. You know, for a moment I thought you were really going to deck her."

"I still might," I said.

"Let me know if you do. I'd like to be there for that."

"No problem. Jeez, what did I ever do to her?"

"Liz can be a real bitch about anything that threatens her at work, but I think what took place tonight had more to do with the way she saw Brent looking at you," Mike observed. "They've been an item for years, and she's definitely not the sharing type."

I didn't know what to say to that. Our discussion drifted into silence, with the remainder of our walk up sorority row passing quickly. When we reached the steps of my dorm, I was surprised to find myself wishing the evening weren't ending. "Not counting my argument with Liz, I had fun tonight," I said, wondering whether Mike would accompany me to the front door. Oh, God, I thought. What if he tries to kiss me?

"I had fun, too," said Mike, following me up the stairs.

When we reached the top landing, I turned, dreading the inevitable first-date moment at the door. I lowered my gaze, suddenly finding it hard to breathe.

Mike moved closer. "Ali?"

I looked up.

Mike's eyes found mine. "Be careful at CBS. Unless I miss my guess, your dad's being the lead investigator on the Jordan French case will cause complications. You've already made one enemy at the station. In time, you may find that some of your other new associates over there aren't what they seem, either."

"What do you mean?"

"I'm just saying be careful."

"I will."

"Good. I'll see you later." With a smile, Mike turned and headed down the stairs.

Relieved, disappointed, and irrationally irritated that Mike hadn't even attempted to kiss me—not even a quick peck—I stood on the dorm landing, watching as he disappeared into the night.

# 6

At eleven-thirty the following morning, after attending the autopsy of Jordan French at the Los Angeles County Coroner's Office, Kane returned to the West Los Angeles Division station on Butler Avenue. Upon entering the windowless, two-story building across from the county courthouse, he made his way directly to the office of Lt. Nelson Long, the division's commanding officer.

Stopping outside Lt. Long's door, Kane struggled to shake the depression he had felt since witnessing the body of the fourteen-year-old girl being laid open on a cold metal table— what once had been a living, breathing child reduced under the coroner's knife to a collection of snips and slices, a library of tissues and fluids to be minutely examined, weighed, and preserved. Though Kane had attended many such procedures, for him this had been one of the hardest.

Attempting to put the autopsy behind him, Kane rapped on the door. "Come," announced a gravelly voice from the other side, sounding like a diesel engine turning over.

As Kane entered, Lt. Long looked up from his desk. Although Long's broad, African-American features remained impassive, his eyes betrayed the perceptive intelligence that had enabled him to climb LAPD ranks on ability alone. A large man, nearly as big as Kane, Long was one of the few members of the brass to whom Kane afforded both his respect and trust.

"Good morning, Dan."

"Morning, Lieutenant," Kane replied, noticing that Carl Peyron was also present.

"Grab a seat," said Long brusquely.

Kane dropped into a wooden chair beside Peyron.

"I asked Carl here to recap MAC's progress on the abduction," Long continued. "But before we get into that, there's something I want to make absolutely clear to both of you. There are to be no further leaks on the French case. Not from *this* department, anyway."

"You're referring to the media finding out about the ransom note?" asked Kane.

"Correct. Captain Lincoln was all over my ass about it this morning. He said heads are gonna roll if it happens again."

"It wasn't me," said Kane.

"Me, neither," added Peyron. "It was probably one of those tube steaks over at the DA's office."

"I'm not accusing anyone," said Long. "Just make sure there are no repeats. If the leak is in our ranks, find it and plug it. With a high-profile investigation like this, things will be hard enough without tripping over reporters every time we turn around."

"You're preaching to the choir here, Lieutenant," said Kane.

"Fine, Dan. Let's move on. You first. What have you got so far?"

Kane took a second to collect his thoughts. "Well, to begin with, the kid wasn't killed at the reservoir. Lividity marks show that she lay on her right side for a number of hours after death, so she must have been transported afterward. And whoever put her in the water knew what he was doing. He could have just buried her."

Long leaned forward. "You're saying someone dumped Jordan in the reservoir to eliminate evidence, not just to get rid of the body?"

"Absolutely," said Kane. "And he succeeded, too. An exam of the corpse produced nothing in the way of hair, fibers, latent prints, tissue under her nails, and the like."

"What about the dump site?"

"Nothing. No footprints, tire tracks, cuts in the fence, or other physical evidence, with the exception of a length of nylon cord tied around one wrist—probably from whatever was used to weigh her down. Divers are doing a grid search later today, but it's a big reservoir with a lot of shoreline."

"How long was she under?"

"Based on the average water temperature at a depth near the shoreline, the coroner estimates her submersion time was from eight to ten days," answered Kane. "Fly eggs and larvae on her back and shoulders indicate she wasn't floating for more than a day or so. Adding that to the submersion estimate gives a time of death right around the day she was reported missing."

Donning a pair of reading glasses, Long lifted a thick, three-ring binder with block letters on the spine reading "French." Known in departmental jargon as a murder book, it was an LAPD compilation of all records pertinent to the case. At present it included only Kane's death report and his preliminary entries in the crime report. Other items relating to the investigation would soon be added, including Peyron's initial investigative work, detailed measurements of the abduction scene and dump site, pictures, autopsy findings, field-interview summaries, notes and regularly updated follow-ups, search warrants and their returns detailing material taken as evidence, surveillance reports, arrest warrants, and any other relevant documents.

Long opened the book without comment. Finding what he wanted, he continued. "Your crime report states that the access road had locked gates at both ends. Neither gate looked disturbed. You think the guy carried in the body?"

"It would have been a long haul over rough terrain," Kane said doubtfully. "But maybe. Besides the gates, there are a number of other possible points of entry. Washed-out culverts under the outer chain-link fence, for instance. A preliminary canvass of neighborhoods around the area got us zip, although a lot of residents weren't home. I contacted the Van Nuys watch commander and requested that he send out another squad tonight. It's possible somebody may remember a strange vehicle being parked in the area. We also need to run down anyone with a key to the gates. I'm putting Deluca and Banowski on that," he added, referring to two fellow detectives on the homicide unit.

"Good idea. Speaking of which, who *does* have keys to the fire road?"

"DWP, Southern California Edison, and the Fire Department. And LAPD, of course. I hate to even *think* a cop was involved, but I'm having Van Nuys detectives make discreet inquiries in the ranks to see whether anybody out there lost his keys, or had them borrowed or stolen."

"What about the autopsy?"

Kane shifted in his seat, resting his forearms on his knees. "A couple of things turned up. Like I said, Jordan was dead when she went into the reservoir. No water in her lungs or stomach. The coroner is listing her cause of death as a subdural hematoma resulting from a fractured skull. He thinks the bleeding into her brain developed over a period of hours. There was no tearing of the scalp, so the skull trauma was caused by something blunt. She also had welts on her back and buttocks, probably inflicted before death by something flat and flexible."

"Like a belt?"

"Maybe. The coroner also found a focal area of erosion on the anterior wall of her vagina. Except for a residual annular ring, the hymen was absent as well."

"Had she been raped?"

Kane shrugged. "That's up for grabs. I had the sexual-assault unit take vaginal, rectal, and oral swabs. The reports came back negative: no sperm or seminal fluid. But sperm often begins deteriorating within an hour, and sometimes elevated acid phosphatase in the vagina doesn't last more than a few days—so the negative results aren't definitive. Although rape or sexual abuse could be a factor, there were no signs of disfigurement, strangulation, or tearing of the genitalia typical in a crime of sexual rage. Which leaves abuse. I'm withholding judgment on that until we get the results of the microscopic tissue exam. Incidentally, the gastric contents showed that Jordan's last meal, pasta with some sort of red seafood sauce, had undergone a digestion period of three to four hours."

Long nodded. "That may help nail down the time of death. What about the lab tests?"

"Toxicology, vaginal sections, and microscopic slides of the welts are under way," said Kane, still continuing from memory. "We're also checking for the presence of any sexually transmitted diseases. I'll be talking with her family doctor about that, among other things," he added.

All three men knew that statistics showed childhood sexual abuse was usually done by parents or a close family member, and that when a parent or parents killed a child, they usually staged an abduction and reported their offspring missing. At that point it was a possibility no one wanted to mention, but it hung in the air like a rotten stench.

"I don't have it all figured yet," Kane continued, reading the question in Long's eyes. "What I do know is that we have evidence of vaginal penetration, although in a fourteen-year-old a missing hymen could have other explanations besides rape or sexual abuse. On the other hand, the strap marks on her back and buttocks indicate she had been nude when beaten, suggesting a sexual angle to the crime. The cause of death taking hours to develop could mean the killing was unplanned. The body being placed in water implies a killer who wanted to eliminate forensic evidence that could tie him to his victim, even if the corpse were found."

"Meaning he knew her?"

"Maybe. At least it makes you wonder. As for the dump site, the inaccessibility of the reservoir tells me the guy's a local. He knows his way around. Even if he drove in, he still had to cross difficult terrain carrying a body, so he's probably a strong male." Kane paused thoughtfully.

"What?"

"I don't know, Lieutenant. There are a couple of things that don't add up. The ransom angle, for instance. People who kidnap children usually do it for one of three reasons: profit, sexual gratification, or because they're lonely and want a child. Suspects belonging to the second and third categories *never* send ransom demands. If this is a sexual crime, as it appears to be, why the ransom demand?" Kane turned to Peyron. "Is there any chance this could have been a burglary-gone-wrong?"

"Unlikely," said Peyron. "Nothing was taken."

"On that note, this might be a good time for you to summarize your investigation into Jordan's abduction, Carl," suggested Long.

"Sure, Lieutenant." Peyron pulled a notebook from his pocket, opened it, and found his place. After referring briefly to the notebook, he cleared his throat and began. "On Saturday

75

morning, July first, my partner and I responded to a call from Mrs. Elizabeth French, who telephoned nine-one-one to report that her daughter was missing and had apparently been abducted from her bedroom sometime during the previous night. When we talked with the Frenches at their home in Mandeville Canyon, Mrs. French stated that Jordan hadn't felt well on Friday and had stayed in bed most of the day. Both parents looked in on her before retiring at around ten-thirty. The next morning she was gone."

"And no one heard anything?" asked Kane.

"No. The parents' bedroom is on the second floor; Jordan's is on the ground level in the back. No one else was in the house. Apparently the guy jimmied her window. We found footprints in a flower bed outside."

"How about the neighbors? Any of them report seeing or hearing anything?"

"No, but the Frenches' estate is huge," noted Peyron. "The nearest house is halfway down the block and obscured by a ten-foot hedge. Nobody recalled any strange cars being parked in the area, either," he added, anticipating Kane's next question. "But anyone with five bucks for a movie-star map could've found his way up there."

"Signs of a struggle?"

"Not much. The sheets were messed up; a lamp was knocked over."

"Any dirt on the windowsill or in the room?"

"Nope."

"Hmmph. Where did the guy exit?"

"The parents say all the downstairs doors were locked when they got up, so we're assuming he left the same way he got in."

"So the guy slips back out the window without making a sound, carrying the kid?"

"Seems that way."

"What about forensics?"

"Not much there," Peyron replied regretfully. "No unmatched prints, no blood, no loose hairs on the bed sheets. We took casts of the footprints in the garden. They were made by size-eleven boots or shoes with a Vibram sole, but so far we haven't been able to match the pattern to a particular brand."

"Back up a second, Carl," said Kane. "Are you saying there were *no* hairs in the bed, or just none that didn't belong to Jordan?"

"There were no hairs at all. I thought that was peculiar."

"Like the sheets had been washed?"

"Yeah."

Kane leaned forward. "Tell me about the parents."

Peyron hesitated, aware of the direction Kane was headed. "I don't know, Dan," he said. "Initially I considered them, of course, but they both appeared genuinely upset about their daughter's being missing. Mrs. French, especially. They're both upstanding citizens. She's on the L.A. County Museum board and belongs to numerous charities; Jordan's stepfather is the senior vice-president of some high-tech software company in Orange County. Plus, they've been cooperating fully with the investigation. I just don't see them doing it."

"Stepfather, huh?"

"Jordan's biological father died in a car accident when she was two," Peyron explained. "Mrs. French remarried four years later. Her new husband, Crawford French, legally adopted Jordan at that time."

"Any other suspects?"

"One. A gardener named Javier Peña who works for a Santa Monica landscape company. He was at the Frenches' estate two days before Jordan disappeared. When I ran a check on anyone who had been employed recently by the family, his name popped up on the Megan's Law database," Peyron explained, referring to a criminal register that enabled law-enforcement officials to keep track of paroled sex offenders, as well as notifying local residents of their presence. "Years back Peña was convicted of molesting his six-year-old nephew in East L.A. Peña's been out of jail since January. Because he lives in Inglewood, none of his customers in Mandeville Canyon knew his history."

"I take it he didn't pan out as a suspect."

"No," said Peyron. "He claims he was staying with his mother on the night Jordan was abducted—something Mrs. Peña confirms. They could both be lying or he could have slipped out without his mother's knowing it, but Peña strikes me as the kind who can barely tie his own shoes, much less pull off a high-risk abduction. All things considered, the chances of his being our man are about as likely as me winning a yodeling contest."

Kane smiled. "I still want to talk to him."

"What do you have on the ransom demand, Carl?" asked Long.

Again, Peyron referred to his notebook. "It arrived in the mail on Monday, July third, along with a gold locket belonging to Jordan. The postmark on the letter was from Santa Monica, dated the Saturday Jordan disappeared. The Frenches' address had been snipped from someplace and glued to the envelope; words on the note were cut from a magazine or some other glossy publication and pasted to a single sheet of typing paper. The message read, '$750,000 for your daughter. Details to follow. Notify the police and she dies.'"

"And there was no follow-up message?"

Peyron shook his head. "Nope. Nothing in the mail. We monitored calls to the Frenches' phone twenty-four hours a day, too. Nothing came in."

"Which could indicate that the ransom demand was simply meant to throw off investigators," said Kane.

"It's possible. Or maybe when Jordan died, the kidnapper got cold feet."

Again, Kane spoke up. "What's the status of the forensic exam on the note?"

"No latent prints," answered Peyron, flipping forward in his notebook. "No residual writing imprints were found on the envelope or the typing paper. As I said, the cutout words in the text had been scissored from one or more glossy-style publications. The glue used was an ordinary mucilage paste. Mrs. French opened the envelope with a letter opener, so we were able to test the envelope flap as well as the stamp for saliva. No saliva on the flap, so whoever sent the letter didn't lick it. The stamp was the self-stick kind, so no saliva there either. The lab did a transillumination analysis to check for a possible print on the back of the stamp, without removing the stamp from the envelope. No luck there, either. They did see what looked like a smeared partial print, which may mean that the sender touched the sticky side. If so, we might be able to get a Touch DNA analysis," he added hopefully, referring to a DNA testing method that required only the presence of a few cells to complete.

"Is the DNA testing being done?" asked Kane.

"Not yet. At the time we thought it would be better to wait until—"

"Maybe we should get that going," Kane interrupted, addressing Long. "If we do come up with a suspect, it would be helpful to have testing done, or at least underway."

"Agreed," said Long. "You have anything else, Carl?"

"That's about it," Peyron answered regretfully.

Long thought a moment, then shifted his gaze to Kane. "So how do you want to proceed?"

Kane unconsciously began cracking his knuckles. "As I said, we need to recanvass the reservoir neighborhood. We should take another run at the dump site, too—extend the ground search to see whether we can locate where the guy got in. And have divers continue hunting for whatever was used to weigh down the body. I also want another shot at the Frenches' house. This time we should go in behind a warrant."

"I'm sure the parents wouldn't object to another search," noted Peyron. "They've been cooperative. Why a warrant?"

"Because if we find anything implicating them, I don't want it kicked out of court on a technicality," answered Kane, punctuating his reply with a crack of cartilage. "Furthermore, I'd like to put a surveillance team on the Frenches' residence. If it *was* a nutcase who snatched the kid, sometimes those psychos like to come back and gloat. Besides, I want to keep an eye on the Frenches."

"I'll set it up with Metro," said Long. "They'll take the PM and morning watch; we'll need somebody from our unit out there during the day. Anything else?"

Kane rubbed his chin. "It's a long shot, but we could check for strangers showing up at the funeral. Jordan's being a TV star complicates things, but you never know. We might ask the Frenches to leave a personal item of Jordan's at the grave, too. A stuffed doll, something like that. Maybe the guy will try for a souvenir."

"So we'll need surveillance on the grave."

"I know it's a lot. Give it a week and see what turns up."

"I'll see whether I can get it approved," said Long doubtfully. "Anything else?"

Kane thought a moment, then shrugged. "That about covers it."

"How about you, Carl?" asked Long. "Anything to add?"

Peyron shook his head. "Nope."

Placing his fingertips together, Long sat back and sighed. "Fine. In that case, why are you two still here?"

"Right, sir," said Peyron. Rising from his seat, he glanced at Kane. "Like I told you yesterday, Dan, I'll be glad to help any way I can. Just lemme know."

"I will," said Kane as he rose and started with Peyron toward the door.

"Hold on a sec, Kane," said Long. "I want a word with you before you leave."

Puzzled, Kane turned back.

After Peyron had left, Long closed the three-ringed binder he had been studying earlier. "The media is going to be all over this," he said, removing his glasses and pinching the bridge of his nose. "You know that."

"The thought had occurred to me, Lieutenant," said Kane. "Don't worry, I can handle the press."

"It may get worse than you expect," Long noted somberly. "There was talk over at headquarters of having senior detectives from Robbery-Homicide assume the case. The brass eventually decided to let you run with it. Believe me, they weren't doing you any favors."

"Somehow that doesn't come as a surprise," said Kane, recalling a high-profile murder investigation that Robbery-

Homicide had taken over from the West L.A. Division years back. Over the course of a nationally publicized trial, the case had blown up in their faces. Kane also knew that despite closing an unprecedented number of homicide investigations during his career, his unconventional methods and abrasive manner had garnered him more than a few enemies at headquarters.

"Watch your back on this one, Dan," Long warned. "I don't need to tell you that this is the kind of case that ends careers. And usually not well."

## 7

My first days at the news station passed quickly, during which I saw little of Lauren, which was just fine with me. I spent my initial hours on Tuesday filling out employment forms, receiving a parking pass and an ID badge, and getting a more comprehensive tour of the newsroom from a friendly producer named Wendy. When I first visited on Monday, I had received only a cursory glimpse of the frenetic newsroom beyond Lauren's office. Later, as I examined the windowless, forty-by-fifty-foot space crammed with desks, filing cabinets, and computer monitors, I realized that Brent had been right. It wasn't what I'd expected.

Four staff-reporter cubicles flanked a hallway leading into the newsroom—one of which was Brent's. Another passage at the other end of the room led past a string of electronics-filled editing bays, a tiny dubbing booth, and a tape-archive storage vault—finally accessing the camera-crews' area and a metal door that exited into an alley behind the building. Circling two sides of the newsroom, several private offices including Lauren's looked out through open venetian blinds. On a wall beside Lauren's office, an illuminated CBS eyeball stood out in bold relief; above it, a second sign that could be lit from within read CBS NEWS LOS ANGELES. With the exception of the signs, the hectic chamber reminded me more of a video arcade than what I had pictured a newsroom to be. On occasion I had visited my father's squad room, and even that had seemed cheerier.

After introducing me to several other producers and staff members, Wendy had escorted me to my new workspace, a small desk in a corner surrounded by a low bookcase and two copy machines. A telephone, keyboard, and a computer monitor occupied most of the desktop; a cork bulletin board hung on a nearby wall. Behind the desk was an eight-foot-high metal rack jammed with dusty, three-quarter-inch videotapes of ancient *Twilight Zone* episodes. Noticing my glance at the titles, Wendy shrugged and explained, "They were there when I got here six years ago. They'll probably be there when I'm gone."

As forewarned, I soon learned that my responsibilities mostly consisted of gofer chores—everything from running errands and making coffee to taking messages and answering phones. A quick learner and a habitual self-starter, I rapidly picked up the rhythms of the newsroom, keeping busy by seeking out supplementary tasks when not otherwise occupied. Later in the week I typed several pages of news copy for Liz Waterson, my editing suggestions impressing even the coldly distant newswoman. I also conducted a phone survey for one of the field producers and performed some computer research for another, generally satisfying everyone with my thoroughness and accuracy.

Although I had honed my telephone interviewing skills by observing my father, my computer proficiency was an expertise I had developed on my own. In addition to the internet facilities I had used at home and at school for years, the online hookup at CBS offered a further arsenal of powerful data-retrieval services including Reuters, Dow Jones, and Lexis-Nexis. At a keystroke, these and other worldwide databanks now at my disposal could provide quick, categorized access to a staggering archive of publications, news wires, and major metropolitan newspapers. Like a kid with a new toy, I spent as much time as possible during my early days at the station exploring my expanded resources.

On Friday evening, more excited than ever about my new job, I returned to the beach house to pack for my trip to D.C. with my mother. I still hadn't told Mom that I had dropped my lit class and accepted an internship at CBS, but I assured myself that the opportunity would present itself on our trip and everything would be fine. The next morning, however, as I sat beside my mother on the giant Lockheed jetliner that would fly us to Washington, I began to have my doubts. Getting her to see my side of things was going to be hard enough, but having dropped my summer course without consulting anyone was probably going to make things impossible.

"Listen up, Mom. We're about to receive our preflight admonitions," I said as the mammoth engines began spooling up for takeoff, increasingly nervous about how she would react.

Getting no response, I nudged my mother. She looked tired, but we had been up late the previous night packing and getting ready for the trip. "These instructions could be important, like making sure our seats are in their upright and most uncomfortable position for blastoff," I continued. "And not disabling the smoke detector in the lavatory. Did you know that's a federal offense? If you're caught, you're invited out on the wing to view the in-flight movie, *Gone With the Wind*."

Mom glanced up briefly from the novel she was reading. Then, without replying, she again concentrated on her book as our plane taxied onto the tarmac.

"Really, Mom," I insisted as an instruction video began playing on a screen partway up the aisle. "The seat belt demonstration is coming up. It might be a lifesaver, especially for anyone who hasn't ridden in a car for the past thirty years."

"Ali, I'm trying to read."

"But what if we have to make a water landing? Or worse, there's an in-flight pool party? You won't know how to use your seat cushion as a flotation device."

"I don't think we cross any appreciable bodies of water on the way to Washington, honey."

"Good point. Oh, look. They're showing how to use the oxygen masks if they drop from the ceiling. You place one firmly over your nose and mouth and breathe normally. Yeah, right. After you stop screaming."

Mom sighed. "Let me know when they get to the part about those traveling with young children, or someone acting like one. I swear, Ali. This isn't like you. Why are you so uneasy about this trip?"

"I'm not."

"Then what is it? You didn't say a word to me on the drive to the airport, and now that we're on the plane you're chattering like a nervous hen. What's up?"

"Nothing."

Closing her book, my mother gave up and stared out the window. Moments later the rumble of the airliner's engines rose to an ear-splitting whine. With a lurch, the gigantic aircraft lumbered down the runway, its mounting acceleration pushing us back into our seats like an invisible hand. Outside, shadows flitted past as the plane rotated, its nose lifting skyward. Following LAX predawn noise-abatement procedures, the half-empty jetliner climbed swiftly, throttled back, and continued west over the Pacific to gain altitude.

When the aircraft finally banked and began circling back toward the coastline, my mother turned again to look at me. "Allison, with work and all, I know I haven't been myself these past weeks. I'm sorry if I've been, I don't know . . . what's the word I want?"

"Critical? Domineering? Tyrannical?"

"Impatient," she said with a tired smile. "I've been so exhausted when I get home, I haven't had much patience with anyone."

"Especially with your favorite daughter."

"I admit it, honey. But there's a reason. In many ways you're the most gifted of my children, so I expect—"

"Me, gifted? Yeah, sure. Trav's the one who got the nod in the genius department."

Mom frowned at my tone. "You have no cause to be jealous of your brother. You should be proud of him."

"Is that right? What did he do, volunteer for a frontal lobotomy?"

"That's not funny, Ali."

"Sorry, Mom. But face it. When it comes to talent, I'm wading in the shallow end of the family gene pool."

"You couldn't be more wrong. You have the ability to become a wonderful writer. How many young people your age have had their work published? I wish you would let me read some of your recent efforts. Are you still working on your novel?"

"No," I lied.

"Well, you should start again. For someone with your—"

"I don't want to talk about it."

"Of course not. You never want to discuss *anything* with me. Don't you trust me to understand?"

"That's not it."

"Then what is it?" she demanded. "Please don't be like this, Ali. This wall of secrecy you've built around yourself is hurting you as much as everyone else."

"I don't know what you mean."

"Sure, you do," Mom persisted, picking up the threads of what had become a deep-seated argument between us. "You've been shutting out everyone, including me, for a long time now. Do you know you never even say you love me anymore? It seems like ever since the night you were . . ." Her voice trailed off.

Raped, I thought angrily, silently finishing her sentence. Unwillingly, my mind travelled back to the attack I had suffered four years ago, the loathsome memories returning with abrupt and numbing virulence. My mother had been attending a concert at the Music Center that evening. My older brothers, Tom and Travis, had been out on a double date, and my dad had unexpectedly been summoned back to the West L.A. police station—leaving Nate and me at home alone for several hours. During that time two men had broken into our house, looking for money. In the course of the robbery I had been brutally beaten and sexually assaulted. After swearing Nate to secrecy, I had concealed my rape—not only from the authorities, but from my parents as well—fearing disgrace, becoming an object of pity, and most of all, the shame of admitting my own cowardice.

More than a year later, I had told my father the truth about what had happened that night. It was a revelation that had disturbed my parents deeply, particularly my mother, who couldn't understand why I had chosen to suffer my shame and degradation alone. In time my father and I had reestablished a bond of trust, but not so my mother and I. With a surge of regret, I realized that the estrangement between us now was still rooted in that terrible night, and there seemed nothing I could do to change things.

"I'm simply saying that as a creative writer, you have to be willing to open yourself and share with others," my mom finally continued, backing from the precipice that our exchange had led us. "Just as you're *supposed* to do with those you love."

"Let's drop this," I suggested, struggling to submerge the old memories. "And anyway, I'm going to be a journalist, not a novelist, remember?"

"You can still do that and also pursue a career in creative writing. I'm right about this, Ali."

"You're *always* right, Mom."

"Ali . . ."

"Look, I'm not you," I said bitterly.

"What's that supposed to mean?"

"It means that everyone can't juggle two careers as perfectly as you—matchless mother and consummate artist at the same time."

"That's not fair," Mom shot back, realizing from my corrosive tone that the old walls had slammed down once more. "You know that my family has always come before my career."

"Right. And I'm the queen of the Nile."

Though stung, my mother hesitated, unable to deny that her position with the Philharmonic *had* cut into our family life, no matter how much she had tried to make it otherwise. At last she continued. "Ali, along with your father, I love you and Nate and Travis more than anything in the world. I know there have been times when my job has imposed on our time together, but—"

"Mom, your nose is bleeding."

"What?"

"Your nose is bleeding."

Mom touched her upper lip. Withdrawing her hand, she stared at a bright red smear on her fingers. "That's odd. I don't recall doing anything . . ."

"Probably the altitude," I said, rummaging through my purse for a Kleenex. "Or maybe the dry air. Darn, I don't have anything. Keep pressure on it and tip your head back. I'll get an attendant." Reaching up, I pushed the call button.

Moments later a flight attendant who had been dispensing breakfast from a metal cart made his way down the aisle. "Yes?" he said, leaning in to reset the call button. Then, looking more closely at me, "Oh, I recognize you. You were on TV. You're the girl who rescued that kid at Newport Beach, aren't you?"

I nodded self-consciously. "My mother needs a tissue."

Suddenly noticing Mom's bloody nose, the attendant's eyes widened. "Are you all right, ma'am?"

"I'm fine, Mom answered, still pressing her upper lip. "I just need something to stop it."

The attendant reached into his serving apron, withdrew a packet of tissues, and handed them to Mom. "Here. I always carry them for emergencies."

"Thanks," Mom said gratefully.

"You're welcome. Let me know if you need anything else. And you, miss," the attendant continued, again addressing me. "That was such a brave thing you did at the beach. Your mother must be very proud."

I smiled. "You can't imagine."

For the next ten minutes Mom held a wad of tissues pressed firmly to her nose. When the bleeding finally stopped, she used a moist towelette to clean her face, then turned her attention to the lukewarm coffee that had been served during the interim.

We both sat in silence, the roar of the engines and the white-noise rush of air outside more conducive to introspection than conversation. As I sipped my coffee, I mulled over our earlier exchange, regretting that our discussion had, as usual, degenerated into argument. Despite wanting to progress to more pleasant topics—Trav's concert or the Smithsonian tour we had planned for Sunday—I knew there were things that still needed to be said.

"Mom?"

My mother turned. "Yes, Ali?"

I carefully set my coffee on the tray. "We didn't finish our conversation. About your career, I didn't mean to—"

"No, let me go first," my mother interrupted, placing a hand on my arm. "Ali, I know you feel that I've been away from home more than I should be, especially over the past few years, and I admit there are times when my career has taken precedence over my family. For that, I apologize. It's often difficult balancing time between family and work. It's something you'll undoubtedly discover for yourself when you're a successful writer with children of your own."

"I don't think I'll be heading down the old marriage highway, Mom."

"Oh? No family of your own?"

"No. And I didn't mean to be critical about your music. Actually, I don't blame you one bit. I'd give anything to have a career like yours, and I intend to. And I won't let changing diapers, cooking dinners, and cleaning up after a pack of screaming brats get in the way."

"I changed lots of diapers and cooked plenty of dinners over the years, and I still kept up with my music," Mom said. "I even did a little cleaning. And believe it or not, you four weren't screaming brats *all* the time," she added with a smile. Then, more seriously, "Ali, my career is important to me, but you children and Dan are my life's real blessings. You know that, don't you?"

"I know," I said, certain I detected another element of advice lurking in my mother's words. "Unfortunately, things aren't that simple for me."

"They can be," my mother reproved gently. "Life can be *exactly* that simple. And someday you'll realize it."

Later that afternoon, after landing at National Airport and checking into a Georgetown hotel, Mom and I showered, changed clothes, and caught a cab to the Kennedy Center. As Mom paid the fare, I stood on the entrance plaza, gazing up at the imposing structure before me. "Jeez, this place is *huge*," I whispered when my mother finally joined me.

"It certainly is," said Mom, looking resplendent in an aquamarine evening gown, matching jacket, and a small emerald pendant that accented her eyes. She glanced at her watch. "Let's go in. If we want to meet Trav and have time for a bite to eat before the performance, we'll have to hurry."

I had planned to dress casually, but at my mother's insistence I had instead chosen a black silk dress, heels, and a single strand of pearls. Glad now that I'd taken my mother's advice, I followed her through an entrance leading into the Hall of States, one of three ground-floor public chambers accessing the Center's Eisenhower Theater, Opera House, and Concert Hall—the latter the performance venue in which Travis would be playing. Once inside the building, I stood gaping at the collection of flags hanging from the ceiling sixty feet above. "Incredible," I murmured.

"There are flags up there from all fifty states," said Mom, who had been to the Kennedy Center on numerous occasions.

"I know." I craned my neck to take in the multicolored canopy. "Plus the five territories and the District of Columbia, hung according to the order in which each joined the Union."

"Right. And the Hall of Nations displays—"

"—flags from all the nations with which we have diplomatic relations," I finished. "C'mon, Mom. Let's go check out the Grand Foyer."

Amazed by my unexpected knowledge and seeming a bit disappointed not to be the one giving the tour, Mom followed me down the enormous, marble-lined hall. Upon reaching the west end, we passed through a monstrous doorway into a room that dwarfed even the one behind us. There we paused once more. To our right, marching the length of the colossal chamber, soaring windows offered views of an expansive terrace graced with fountains and elevated planters of weeping willows. To the left, flanked by mirrored panels ascending to the ceiling, carpeted steps fanned up to the doors of the Opera House, while straight ahead, on a thick pedestal, sat a spectacular bronze bust of President Kennedy, the centerpiece of the awe-inspiring room.

"Aren't the chandeliers magnificent?" Mom asked, referring to a procession of gigantic crystal light fixtures traveling the vast space from end to end.

I nodded. "They were a gift from Sweden. Each weighs over a ton. And *that*," I added, pointing to the seven-foot-high sculpture of JFK, "tips the scales at over three thousand pounds. The artist was Robert Berks. He sure captured Kennedy, didn't he?"

"That he did. You're quite the encyclopedia about this place. How do you happen to know so much?"

"I did a little internet research before we left."

"And you remember it all?"

"Sure. For instance, did you know they used 3,700 tons of Carrara marble during construction? The stone was a donation from Italy—"

Mom raised her hand. "Enough! I keep forgetting that you inherited your dad's memory. And you say you're not like him," she laughed. "C'mon. Let's go find your brother."

After passing the Opera House and turning left into the Hall of Nations, we rode an elevator up to the South Roof Gallery. Upon exiting, we found ourselves in a charming space with inviting restaurants at either end. On one side was the Roof Terrace Restaurant, which catered to those in the mood for formal dining; on the other lay the Encore Cafe, a more relaxed setting where theatergoers could have a casual meal before a performance.

"Where are we meeting Trav?" I asked.

"When I telephoned from the hotel, he said he would see us at the Encore Cafe," Mom answered, starting across the room.

Glancing out floor-to-ceiling windows at the city below, I trailed my mother down the hall. Reaching the far end, I stopped to admire a vista to the east, picking out several landmarks, including the Washington Monument and the dome of the Jefferson Memorial. To the right, a low-flying plane on final approach to National Airport traced the sluggish course of the Potomac.

"C'mon, Ali. You can take in the sights later," Mom called impatiently from the restaurant door.

Hurrying to catch up, I joined my mother as she entered the cafe, a cheery space punctuated with potted ficus trees, mirror-clad columns, and cafeteria-style seating. Scanning the room, I spotted Travis sitting on the far side, nervously sliding a coffee mug from hand to hand across the table. Tall, with our father's reddish hair but the more refined features of Mom, Travis seemed to have grown even more handsome over the past years. Working summer construction jobs had hardened his body, and his slightly angular face had matured with the coming of manhood. As if sensing our presence, Travis glanced up, his eyes drifting toward the doorway.

I waved. A moment later Travis saw us. With a look of relief, he stood. "Mom, Ali!" he called.

Hearing his voice, Mom turned. "Hi, Trav!" she called back. Together we began threading our way through the busy room. "Sorry we're late," Mom said when we arrived, giving Travis a hug. "We got stuck in traffic."

"It's okay, Mom," said Travis, who was wearing a sport coat, slacks, and a white shirt open at the collar. "I'm just glad you made it. Hi, Ali."

"Good to see you, genius boy."

Travis smiled. "You too. I caught your beach rescue on TV. They even ran it again this morning. I'm proud of you, sis."

"Thanks," I said, feeling a flush rise to my cheeks.

"I tried to call, but the line was always busy."

"After that newscast, I think everybody in the world tried to call us," Mom noted dryly.

"I'm not surprised," said Travis, missing Mom's tone. "I want to hear all about it."

"Actually, there's not that much to tell," I said, glancing at Mom.

"So make something up. You're the writer."

"Sure, Trav. After the concert," I promised, trying to get off the subject. "Do we still have time to eat? I'm starving."

"Big shocker," said Travis. "You're *always* hungry. God knows how you stay so skinny."

"Same way you do, bro. Nervous energy. Speaking of nervous, are you ready for your big concert?"

Travis's smile evaporated. "As ready as I'll ever be, I suppose."

"Your performance tonight will be flawless," Mom said firmly. "Now, let's get something to eat."

"I'm not hungry," said Travis. "You and Ali go ahead. I'll hold down the table."

"Butterflies, huh?" I teased. I glanced toward the restaurant's grill and sandwich counter, squinting at a menu displayed on a large white board. "Sure you don't want something? A big greasy bowl of chili and a couple of beers might help settle your stomach."

"Allison, hush," my mother admonished.

"I'll pass, sis," laughed Travis. "But thanks for the thought."

In addition to the chili I had suggested, the grill offered a surprisingly eclectic choice of fare. I decided on crab cakes, which came with a side of fries and a small salad; Mom opted for chicken piccata and a bowl of black-bean soup. Both of us grabbed soft drinks from a metal ice tub. After paying for our meals at the register, we rejoined Travis in the main room.

Mom took a seat next to Travis. "Has Alex arrived yet?" she asked, referring to her friend and colleague, Alexander Petrinski. Mr. Petrinski was the professor at USC who, convinced early-on that Travis had the makings of a prodigy, had guided Trav's musical instruction from the time he had turned six.

"He got here last night," answered Travis. "He said he would meet you in the Concert Hall."

"Good. Have rehearsals gone well?"

"Very well . . . although at first I had my doubts," Travis answered. "The music director wanted to begin by reviewing the concerto's dramatic architecture. There were things I thought I'd already ironed out, but he had some good ideas and it turned out to be time well spent. He found several opportunities I'd missed, and we ended up making a number of changes. All for the better."

"I'm not surprised. A debut concert like this is often a collaboration between composer and conductor," Mom pointed out.

Travis nodded. "Anyway, once we had agreed on the changes, rehearsals went smoothly. It's great having a chance to play with an orchestra once again," he added.

Pensively picking at my crab cakes, I listened to Travis and Mom's discussion without paying much attention. As usual whenever they discussed music, I felt as if I were on the outside looking in, with no hope of understanding, much less of being included. Nonetheless, I realized that Travis's last remark referred to his performing with the Los Angeles Philharmonic after winning a high-level piano competition at the age of seventeen—an experience he later confessed to finding both exhilarating and terrifying. Since then his only opportunity to play with a full orchestra had been during the finals of the Van Cliburn International Piano Competition. Despite Travis's lack of experience with larger assemblies, I also knew that my brother, unlike most young musicians who by necessity practice in isolation, had enjoyed the benefit of playing with Mom and her Wednesday night chamber group over the course of his entire music career. During that time he had developed habits of eye contact and of *listening* to other musicians, traits that facilitated reading the subtle signals of communication among performers— a nod, a bow lift, a hesitation, the dip of a scroll—wordless exchanges that knit together all musical assemblies, including an orchestra.

As Mom and Travis's conversation drifted into more arcane and inaccessible areas of music, I finished my crab and the remainder of my fries. Several times I started to speak but stopped, envious of the admiration I saw in Mom's eyes for my brother.

"What's wrong, Ali?" asked Travis, at last noticing my silence.

"Nothing. Just thinking."

"Well, don't overdo it. You might short something out."

"Clever, Trav."

"Sorry. Couldn't resist," Travis said with a smile. Then, checking his watch, he sighed. "Well, it's time for me to head down to the dressing room and get ready. Wish me luck."

"Good luck, honey," Mom said. "Not that you'll need it."

"Yeah, good luck, Trav," I echoed. As Travis rose from the table, I stood and quickly kissed his cheek. "Knock 'em dead, bro," I added softly.

Thirty minutes later, after a stroll around the river terrace, Mom and I again made our way through the Grand Foyer to the Kennedy Center Concert Hall, the largest of the Center's six performance venues. As we started down one of the hall's central aisles, I let my eyes roam the gigantic chamber, charmed by the wood-clad walls, dusty-red seats, and the handsome gold checkerboard inlays facing all three encircling balconies. Overhead, hung from an array of embossed hexagonal patterns on the ceiling, a cluster of chandeliers lit the room in a warm, inviting glow.

By now theatergoers had partially filled the auditorium, with more pouring in as concert hour approached. When Mom and I arrived at our seats in the fifth-row center of the orchestra section, we found Alexander Petrinski already there waiting. As we took our places beside him, Petrinski glanced up from his concert program, his leonine head of hair and youthful bearing belying his advancing years. "Catheryn, Allison, you're both looking as radiant as ever," he said, his face lighting with pleasure.

"Hi, Mr. Petrinski," I replied, noting that for the evening Travis's music teacher had worn a dark suit and tie. "You're looking pretty sharp yourself," I added, again thankful I had taken my mother's advice and dressed for the occasion.

"Thank you, Ali. And congratulations on surviving your recent visit to the beach. Helping that young girl showed tremendous courage. I saw it last weekend on TV."

"Thanks."

"Alex, it means the world to Travis that you're here tonight," said Mom. "Thank you for coming."

Petrinski's eyes shined with pleasure. "Oh, I wouldn't have missed this for anything. Did you get a chance to talk with Trav when you arrived?"

Mom nodded. "He tried to hide it, but he's terribly worried about tonight. Not only regarding his performance, but about the reception his concerto will receive."

"I know," Petrinski said thoughtfully. "Over the course of his Van Cliburn recitals this summer, Travis has performed a few of his own shorter compositions. All were relatively brief and sandwiched in between other works. This will be different."

"Yes. It will."

"Nevertheless, despite his apprehension, I'm convinced that Travis has the maturity to play brilliantly," Petrinski went on. "As for his concerto, I believe it will prove a lasting contribution to the symphonic repertoire. The music world will discover something wonderful tonight. As will Travis."

A late-arriving group of musicians filed onstage and quickly joined those already present in a discordant round of tuning. As I flipped through my program, I pondered Petrinski's words, wondering what he had meant about Travis discovering something. Moments later the lights dimmed, summoning latecomers to their seats. Shortly afterward the concertmaster rose at the head of the first violin section, motioning for the principal oboist to play an A. As the entire ensemble readied itself in a final cacophony of tuning, I felt a twisting in my stomach, a dampness gathering under my arms. Around me I could sense a ripple of anticipation coursing through the hall, as palpable as an electric current.

The orchestra members stood as the music director, a robust, broad-shouldered man with deep-set eyes and thinning brown hair, entered from stage right. Travis, now wearing a black tuxedo, walked at his side. Smiling at a welcoming round of applause from the audience, the music director greeted the concertmaster and the other principals, then signaled the orchestra musicians back to their chairs. Smiling woodenly, Travis also shook hands with the concertmaster. Then, eyes averted, he took his place at a Steinway concert grand piano to the left of stage center.

As the room quieted, the music director mounted the podium and paused, giving the audience time to settle. Slight rustlings and a spate of coughs echoed through the hall. Moments later the conductor raised his hands. A hush fell over the assembly. I felt the room crackling with tension.

The conductor brought the orchestra to attention, then turned to Travis. With a nod, Travis placed his fingers on the keyboard.

And then they began.

I held my breath, praying that Travis wouldn't stumble. His concerto, a work that I knew he had expanded and then orchestrated with Petrinski's help from a one-movement fantasy for piano and cello written years earlier, opened with a pulverizing tonic cord voiced by the entire assembly. Travis answered with a flawless flight of upward flourishes, his solo instrument, though unable to match the force of the combined ensemble, compensating with an eloquence and passion that hinted at the battle between piano and orchestra that was to follow.

Again the orchestra spoke, its thunderous roar filling the hall. Once more Travis countered with a stormy, knife-edged passage that I recognized as a theme I had heard drifting from the music room in our house many times in the past, often accompanied by Mom's cello. But never like this, never played against the full backdrop of a symphony orchestra. Spellbound, I listened as first the strings and then the horns and woodwinds gradually encroached on the keyboard. Slowly, other musicians picked up the threads of the idea Travis had broached and embroidered it into a more complex tapestry, then proceeded to a chillingly poignant second theme that stood in resonant contrast to the first.

As the opening passages of Travis's concerto washed over me, I felt the tendrils of anticipation I had sensed earlier in the room being replaced by something new, something magical. Fears Travis might falter forgotten, I turned to glance at my mother. She sat motionless, her eyes riveted on the stage, watching as the conductor addressed different sections of the musical body—his hands expressive, his baton raking the assembly like a rapier.

The preliminary exposition complete, Travis broke in anew with growing confidence, subtly slowing the tempo as he elaborated on the militaristic main theme he had first introduced. He sat erect at the keyboard, his manner devoid of dramatic arm movements, his fingers deceptively quiet yet fluid on the keys, his left hand alternating the cascading melody with the right. Reluctantly, the orchestra surrendered and joined him as a subordinate, arising once more like an enraged beast when he attempted to shift to the lyric second theme, the main orchestral body angrily insisting on the first.

At times a fierce rivalry between piano and orchestra, at times a seamless collaboration, Travis's concerto unfolded with inexorable, sweeping beauty. And as the minutes slipped by, I gradually began to comprehend that unlike many of the classical piano concertos with which I was familiar, my brother's composition was not simply a vehicle to demonstrate his own prowess at the keyboard. To the contrary, often Travis allowed the larger assembly to take the lead, forging a bond between keyboard and orchestra that gave his work a soaring, cathedral-like grandeur. And as I listened, I felt myself filling with an almost unbearable pride in Travis's accomplishment. Respect and admiration for his work were there as well. And to my shame, so was the aching, consuming envy I had felt for my older brother all my life.

Forty minutes later, following a heartrendingly tender second movement, the orchestra joined Travis in a majestic closing theme, building with shattering, pounding momentum toward the climax. Shocked, I realized the piece was nearly over.

His pace driving and relentless, Travis engaged the percussion section in a short staccato duel, then again took the musical initiative with a torrent of right-hand triplets, his ardent outpouring plummeting to a profoundly satisfying recapitulation that welded together with perfect simplicity the concerto's initial statements and its sublime closing ideas. And then at last, as the music rose a final time, the entire assembly joined Travis in a blazing crescendo of exaltation and triumph and joy.

Seconds passed as the final strains died away. The audience sat stunned, as if life itself had been suspended. Then, in a surge moving from those in the front rows to those in the back, the entire audience rose in recognition, filling the chamber with a deafening round of applause. Mom, Petrinski, and I rose as well, clapping furiously.

Onstage, Travis stood and took the conductor's outstretched hand, then joined him in a bow. Next, with a grin, Travis turned to the orchestra and applauded them in turn. As the smiling conductor waved the entire assembly to its feet, I noticed that Mom was no longer joining in the ovation. Puzzled, I turned, noting a clammy sheen of perspiration on my mother's face.

Without warning, my mother slumped forward. I caught her, barely preventing her from toppling over the row in front. Arm around her shoulders, I lowered her awkwardly into her seat. "Mom, what's wrong?"

"Dizzy . . ."

"Put your head down. Take deep breaths."

"I feel so silly," Mom said, dropping her forehead to her knees. "I think I stood up too fast . . ."

"Keep your head down."

"I'll be okay in a minute. I'm so embarrassed . . ."

By now several people, including Petrinski, had turned toward us in concern. I indicated that I didn't need help, then gently began rubbing my mother's back, shocked at how icy her skin felt. "It's okay, Mom," I said softly. "Just take it easy. You'll be okay."

Later that evening at the hotel, I couldn't sleep, still troubled by thoughts of my mother's collapse at the concert.

"Mom?"

A rustling came from the adjacent bed.

"Mom?"

A groan. "What, Ali?"

"Are you awake?"

"I am now."

"Sorry."

"Me, too." Mom checked the clock on the bedside stand. "It's after midnight. What's so important that you have to talk to me about it now?"

I hesitated. "I, uh, I was wondering what Mr. Petrinski meant when he said Trav would discover something tonight."

"I'm not sure," Mom yawned. "But a conductor once told me that very same thing, just before I went onstage to play the biggest concert of my life."

"The Dvorák?" I guessed, referring to a cello concerto that Mom had performed with the Los Angeles Philharmonic years earlier.

"Uh-huh."

"So what did *he* mean?"

"I think he meant that after the concert I would know more about myself as a musician."

"And did you?"

"Yes, honey, I did."

"What about Trav? Think he had some sort of big epiphany tonight?"

"Of that I have no doubt," Mom replied warmly. "Trav has a wonderful life in music ahead of him—not only as a performer, but also as a composer. And after tonight, I'm sure he knows it. And so does everyone else."

"Hmmm. I guess we'll have to start calling him 'maestro' and let him use the bathroom first in the morning and so forth."

"If you're insinuating that Trav will get a swelled head over this, you're wrong. You know him better than that. Honey, is this why you woke me? To discuss your brother?"

"No."

"What, then?"

A long pause.

"What is it, Ali?"

"I'm worried about you, Mom," I finally blurted. "As soon as we get home, I want you to go in for a checkup."

"Because I got dizzy at the concert? I told you, I stood up too quickly."

"It's more than that. What about your nosebleed on the plane? I thought it would never stop. And you've been so exhausted lately. It's not like you."

"I've been working a lot."

"I know. I still think you should go. Please, Mom?"

"Sweetheart, I have a full rehearsals with the Philharmonic starting on Thursday."

"So go in Tuesday, as soon as we get back."

"Ali, enough," Mom said sharply, her voice slipping into its no-nonsense mode. "My yearly physical is scheduled for September. I'll have a complete exam then. Okay?"

"No."

"I beg your pardon?"

"I want you to go in now. Please?"

"Ali, I don't have time."

"Yes, you do. Look, I don't want to worry Dad unnecessarily about this," I went on, taking a new tack. "But I will if I have to."

"I don't believe my ears. You're threatening to tell your father on me?"

"As a matter of fact, I am," I said stubbornly. "And if he even *thinks* there's a chance something's wrong with you, he'll *make* you go. And you know it."

Mom didn't reply for almost a minute. "If it means that much to you, I suppose I could try to bump up the date of my annual physical," she said at last.

"Promise you'll call first thing tomorrow morning. Do it before our flight."

"Ali . . ."

"Promise."

"All right, I promise," Mom sighed. "I swear, sometimes you're worse than your father. I'd hate to get in your way if you ever really wanted something."

"Thanks, Mom."

"You're welcome. Now can we get some sleep?"

"Sure. Night, Mom."

"Good night, Ali. Sweet dreams."

Although Mom fell asleep again quickly, I lay awake long afterward, listening to the soft sounds of her breathing. And when I eventually did drift off, I dreamed of running, and of giant waves, and of Travis's sure hands on the piano, and of blood on my mother's face.

## 8

The remainder of our weekend in Washington passed quickly. Mom, Travis, and I spent quiet Sunday morning visiting the Smithsonian, followed by Travis's second and equally successful performance at the Kennedy Center later that evening. During that time Mom seemed back to her old self. But by the following morning I once more sensed an uncharacteristic lethargy in her. Travis, who joined us for our return flight to California, commented on it as well. Impatiently, Mom dismissed our concern. At my continued insistence, however, she kept her promise and called to move up the date of her yearly physical, unexpectedly snagging a canceled appointment for Tuesday afternoon.

After returning to Los Angeles, feeling inexplicably let down after the trip, I spent Tuesday morning at CBS running for coffee and doing internet research for one of the producers. In a spare moment in between, I experienced an almost overwhelming desire to talk with my mother, wanting to touch base with her before her medical appointment. I dialed home. The answering machine picked up. I disconnected without leaving a message. Mom didn't answer her cell phone, either. Finally I called my father at the station, thinking he might know where she was. I was transferred upstairs from the front desk, where someone in the squad room finally picked up.

"Homicide."

"Hi, Paul," I said, recognizing the voice of Paul Deluca, a detective who worked with my father. "My dad around?"

"Hi, Ali. Hey, I caught your beach rescue on TV last weekend. Way to go, kid."

"Thanks," I said. "Although I sure didn't expect to be seeing myself on TV when I headed to the Wedge that morning."

"Don't worry, you came off just fine—even if you couldn't recall your own name," Deluca chuckled. "Hold on a sec. I'll see if I can run down your old man."

I heard Deluca's muffled voice yelling into squad room. "Anybody seen Kane?"

"He's over at the courthouse picking up the search warrant," someone shouted back. I recognized the deep, raspy voice of Detective John Banowski, another member of the homicide unit. Like Deluca, Banowski had visited the beach house many times over the years, and like Deluca, I considered him a family friend.

Deluca came back on. "Your dad's gone. You wanna leave a message?"

I looked up, noticing Brent Preston making his way across the newsroom. "I don't think so, Paul. Will he be back soon?"

"Maybe. If not, I'm meeting him for lunch, after which we're driving out to the Palisades. We'll probably be gone the rest of the afternoon. I can have him call if you want."

"That's all right. Tell him I said hi."

After hanging up, I checked the time, surprised to see it was already past noon. I was also surprised to find myself disappointed that the day was flying by so quickly. Despite less than optimal working conditions, I liked the high-energy atmosphere of the newsroom, the challenge of learning new things, and the excitement of being part of an organization that spoke to millions daily. Best of all, for the first time since the previous evening, I had occasionally been able to stop worrying about my mother.

"Hello, Allison."

I turned, finding Brent Preston smiling down at me. "Hi, Brent," I replied.

"Want to grab some lunch?"

"Thanks, but I have a ton of work to do."

"You have to eat," Brent insisted. "Union rules."

"Really?"

"No, but it sounded good, didn't it?" Brent grinned, taking my hand. "C'mon, we should celebrate your second week on the job. We'll go next door to Farmers Market. I promise to have you back in thirty minutes. Forty-five at the most."

"Well . . ."

Brent pulled me to my feet. "It's settled. We're going."

Conscious of a number of eyes in the newsroom marking our departure, I followed Brent through the camera crews' area, exiting into the alley behind the building. After crossing a line of hopeful contestants waiting outside *The Price is Right* studio, we walked a half block south to Farmers Market, a huge, open-air market on Fairfax Avenue that has long been a Los Angeles landmark. In addition to an almost endless selection of fresh breads, meats, fish, and produce, the outdoor market offered a variety of luncheon fare to those wandering its colorful passages and shaded stalls. I decided on shish-kebab, ordering skewers of chicken and beef, a side of fries, coleslaw, and a Coke. Brent ordered a fruit salad and a tall iced tea. Food in hand, we made our way to a table beneath a bright-yellow lawn umbrella.

Brent straddled a folding metal chair, sitting across from me. "You eat like this every day?" he asked, glancing at my mammoth lunch.

I grinned. "High metabolism."

"Lucky you. So how's the job going so far?"

"Great." I took a bite of chicken, doused my fries with ketchup, and downed a swig of Coke. "I really like working in the newsroom," I added, wiping my fingers on a napkin. "At first I had my doubts, but it's really exciting. Way more than I expected. Of course, I spend most of my time running errands and answering phones, but I get to do a little research and computer work, too. I even did some editing for your friend Liz."

Brent picked at his salad. "She mentioned that. She says you have a knack for writing. You may win her over yet."

"Doubtful. But somehow I have a hunch that won't keep her from dumping all her typing on me."

"Probably not," Brent agreed. "She's a tough nut. If I were you, I'd tread lightly around her."

"Don't worry. I think Liz and I have an understanding. Any other advice?"

Brent smiled. "You mean besides not fighting with management?"

"Besides that," I said, recalling our conversation in Westwood. "And not just how to fit in around the newsroom, either. I want to know how to get ahead."

"Do I detect a touch of ambition?"

"More like a whole truckload."

"In that case, you had better accept one thing right now," Brent advised. "There aren't any shortcuts in the news game. You have to pay your dues."

"I plan to," I said. "I also know that there are undoubtedly a number of ways for me to get what I want, some quicker than others."

"And what is it you want?"

"For starters, *your* job would be nice." After saying that I laughed, afraid I might have gone too far. "Seriously, Brent. You're on the fast track at CBS," I added quickly. "What's your secret?"

Brent shrugged. "No secret. I'm on my way up because I want it more than anyone else, and I'm willing to do whatever it takes to get it."

"Such as?"

"Such as hard work and clean living."

"C'mon, there must be something useful you can tell me."

"All right," Brent said reluctantly. "Don't repeat this, but as far as I'm concerned, the so-called 'news team' approach is a crock. There's no *team* approach to being a reporter. If you want to get ahead, you look out for number one. Period. You make your own contacts and protect your own sources. You develop, pitch, and fight for your own stories—digging out the facts and verifying them yourself. Last, you follow up leads, ask the right questions, and put *yourself* right in the middle of anything you're covering."

"With that attitude, I don't imagine you've garnered many selfless-reporter-of-the-year awards," I observed.

"Guys who win that prize usually aren't around long enough to collect it."

"Note taken. Anything else?"

Brent nodded. "One other thing, and it's probably the most important: Never forget that journalism is a business, pure and simple."

"So we're selling the news?"

"Absolutely."

"And in business, you give customers what they want," I mused, recalling Brent's disagreement with Mike on the subject. "So if it's entertainment they want, entertainment they get?"

"What if it is?" Brent replied defensively. "Journalists are supposed to inform the public, but that doesn't mean we always have to be ramming facts and figures down people's throats. The trick is to understand what captures viewers' imaginations and then deliver it. Believe me, ratings are all that the bastards in New York care about."

"Bastards? You mean management?"

Brent nodded. "None other. When our timeshare numbers are up, the suits are happy. When the numbers are down, you can start looking for another job. I didn't make the rules; I just play by them. And if you want to succeed, you'll do the same."

Though part of me was reluctant to accept Brent's cynical opinion of the news, another part suspected that his words held at least a kernel of truth. Realizing I had a lot to learn, I resolved to reserve judgment until later. "So that's what it takes to be a good reporter?" I asked, tossing a few fries to a particularly bold sparrow who had been pecking the ground nearby for scraps. "Investigating interesting stories and keeping an eye on the ratings?"

"There's more to it than that," Brent said patiently. "Interviewing technique is crucial—asking the right questions and knowing how to get a subject to open up, for instance. Clear, succinct writing and being able to ad-lib on camera are also essential. Plus you have to be able to work against a deadline. Some of that you can learn; some you either have or you don't. There are other things too, but a bit of advice a senior correspondent once gave me pretty much sums everything up in what he called the three basic rules of journalism."

"Three? I thought there were five: who, what, where, when, and why."

"Nope, only three. Get the story, get the story, and get the story."

I fell silent. "I have a tip for you," I said after a moment's thought, deciding to take a chance. "A good one. But along the lines of looking out for number one, I want something in return."

"You *are* a fast learner, aren't you? Okay, what do you want?"

"If what I have to say pans out, I want to go with you on location."

"And where would that be?"

"Do we have a deal?"

After a slight pause, Brent nodded. "If your information is good, I'll clear it with Lauren. Where are we going?"

I hesitated, realizing what I was about to say would increase the chances that my father would discover I was the source of the ransom-note leak. But with any luck he wouldn't, and the reward seemed worth the risk. Finally I spoke. "We're going to Jordan French's house."

Brent leaned forward. His eyes hardened, locking on me like a hunter studying a game trail. "Why?"

I smiled, enjoying Brent's reaction. By then my plate was empty. "Are you going to eat that?" I asked, eyeing his nearly untouched fruit salad.

Impatiently, Brent pushed his lunch across the table. "Damn it, Allison. What do you know about Jordan French?"

Using my fingers, I selected a plump strawberry from Brent's salad. "I phoned my father at work earlier today," I answered. "My dad wasn't there. The detective I spoke with said my father was driving to Pacific Palisades this afternoon and probably wouldn't be back for the rest of the day."

"So?"

"So when I called, my dad was at the courthouse. Picking up a search warrant."

"I still don't . . ." Brent stopped midsentence, abruptly following my line of reasoning. "What time did you call?"

"Just before we came here. If we get moving, we can probably be at the Frenches' house when the police show up."

# 9

Catheryn shifted impatiently in her chair. She had spent most of the past two hours with Dr. Porter and various assistants updating her medical history, giving blood and urine samples, and being thoroughly tapped, poked, and prodded. Begrudgingly, she admitted that an annual physical was a necessity. Nevertheless, it took time from her busy schedule, time she couldn't afford. Fall rehearsals were beginning on Thursday, and she hadn't even finished unpacking from her trip. Instead, here she was cooling her heels in a Santa Monica medical building.

Across his desk, Dr. Porter paged through the results of several in-house lab tests he had ordered. Then, closing Catheryn's medical file, he cleared his throat.

"Well? How long do I have?" joked Catheryn. "Give it to me straight."

Dr. Porter smiled. "Actually, nothing too much turned up. Your lab numbers are all in the normal range, with one exception. Your blood work shows a decreased hemoglobin and platelet count."

"So I need to start taking iron?"

"No. I don't think that's it."

"What, then?"

"I'm not sure," said Dr. Porter. "Your peripheral white-blood-cell count is within normal limits, but I'm concerned about your nosebleeds and the blood you mentioned seeing on your toothbrush. I'm also concerned about the bruises on your arms and thighs. You don't know how you got them?"

Catheryn shrugged. "Probably banged myself doing yard work."

"And your lack of energy?"

"I've been busy. I need to get more sleep."

"Possibly." Dr. Porter wrote a name and telephone number on a slip of paper. "I want you to see Dr. Kratovil for further tests. She's a hematologist here in the building. With any luck, she may be able to work you in this afternoon."

"More tests?  But—"

"I don't want to alarm you," said Dr. Porter, cutting her off. "Your platelet and hemoglobin anomaly could well mean nothing, but coupled with your other symptoms, your test results might indicate a more serious problem."

"I . . . I suppose I could find time to come back next week."

"Not next week, Catheryn.  If not today, tomorrow.  No later."

# 10

On the drive to the Frenches' estate, Kane repeatedly checked his rearview mirror, making sure the Scientific Investigation Division van was still following. Shortly after leaving Sunset Boulevard, satisfied that the SID unit was keeping him in sight, Kane cut the wheel and headed up a steep, narrow road that branched off Mandeville Canyon to the right. Sitting beside him in the front seat, Detective Paul Deluca checked a map that lay open in his lap, then resumed telling a joke he had started minutes earlier, swearing he'd heard it at church.

"'Lemme get this straight,' Adam says to God," Deluca continued, picking up the thread of his joke—as usual enjoying his own humor more than the material warranted. "'You can create a companion for me who will be loving and supportive, who'll cook and clean and wash my clothes, and who will always do whatever I say—but it'll cost me an arm?'" Deluca chortled, struggling to keep a straight face as he headed into the punch line. "So Adam thinks for a moment, scratches his head, and says, 'What can I get for a rib?'"

"Not bad," Kane chuckled. "Undoubtedly one of your wife's favorites."

"Uh . . . actually, no."

Kane smiled. "Imagine that."

Ahead, as they proceeded up a ridge guarding Sepulveda Pass, the travertine walls of the J. Paul Getty Museum came slowly into view. In the distance, framing the museum, the high-rises of downtown Los Angeles squatted like building blocks on the horizon. Bordering one side of the road as it ascended the western ridge of the valley, live oak, sycamore, and jacaranda overhung the pavement. On the other side, visible through occasional breaks in thick hedges guarding palatial estates, the hillside fell away to reveal smoggy vistas of Westwood and Century City.

"That should be it up ahead," said Deluca, referring again to his map. "The one with the fancy gate."

"I see it." Kane slowed, wheeling into a driveway fronting an opulently landscaped mansion. Through a ten-foot-high metal gate he could make out portions of the stately, slate-roofed structure. Stands of eucalyptus, strips of bark peeling like old wallpaper from their trunks, obscured the rest of the two-story, colonial-style building. Past the wrought-iron barrier and twin tennis courts adjoining the house, an ivy-covered fence and hedges of boxwood and oleander ran the perimeter of the grounds.

After waiting for the SID van to pull up behind, Kane lowered his window and punched a button on a gate intercom mounted beside a numerical keypad. Seconds later a woman's voice answered. "Yes?"

Kane flashed his shield at a TV camera positioned above the gate speaker. "Detective Kane, LAPD. I called earlier."

"Yes, Detective Kane. Come in."

After a slight pause, the gate swung inward. Kane drove down a long, cobbled driveway, parking in front of the house's six-car garage. Through an open garage door he noted several vehicles parked inside: a bright-red sports car, a silver Lexus, and a dark-blue Land Rover. As the SID van pulled to a stop behind him, Kane glanced up a flight of flagstone steps leading to the house. A heavily built man in his mid-forties and a pretty, slightly younger woman with jet-black hair stood waiting on a landing by the front door.

"How do you want to play this?" asked Deluca.

"I'll take the parents," said Kane, stepping from the car. "You run the SID team. And don't forget the house plans."

"Got 'em right here." Reaching into the backseat, Deluca retrieved a set of floor plans he had procured from the building department earlier that morning. Deluca also grabbed a copy of Peyron's crime report describing the abduction scene. Plans and report in hand, he hurried after Kane, who had already started toward the house.

"Detective Kane?" said the man on the landing, thrusting a hand toward Kane as he reached the top step. "I'm Crawford French. This is my wife, Beth."

Kane shook Mr. French's hand, noting that his grip seemed overly firm, even for a man of his size. With receding brown hair showing tasteful touches of gray, razor-thin lips over a cleft chin, and a dark, challenging gaze, Jordan's stepfather struck Kane as a typical type-A personality: intense, impatient, and controlling.

"What's being done to find the man who murdered our daughter?" Mr. French asked curtly, his voice tinged with a slight Texas drawl.

"I'm truly sorry for your loss, Mr. French," said Kane, ignoring the question. "Yours, too, Mrs. French," he added, turning to the tanned woman standing nearby. In addition to a heavy application of lip gloss and eye shadow, Jordan's mother had on a thin silk blouse and a pair of tight-fitting designer jeans. A head shorter than her husband, Elizabeth French appeared even younger than Kane had initially guessed, probably being no more than thirty-five. She was also far more attractive than he had first thought, too—although something about her wide-set eyes and full, high breasts looked just a little too perfect.

"Thank you, Detective," Mrs. French replied, nervously raising a hand to her throat, a large diamond on her fourth finger sparkling in the sunlight.

Kane nodded toward Deluca as he joined them on the landing. "This is Detective Deluca. While he's examining Jordan's room, there are a few things about Jordan's abduction that I want to go over with you."

Mr. French gazed briefly at Deluca, then returned his attention to Kane. "We'll do anything that might help find whoever took our daughter, but I don't understand the need for another search. The first officer who was here, Detective, uh—"

"Peyron."

"Right. Detective Peyron already went through everything. Where is he, by the way?"

"He's still involved with the case, but now that it's become a homicide investigation, I've taken over," Kane replied, reaching into his coat and withdrawing a thick, folded document. "This is an authorization for us to remove various articles from your house, mostly from Jordan's room," he added, handing the sheaf of papers to Mr. French.

"A search warrant?"

"Just a formality," Kane explained, keeping his tone matter-of-fact. "We'll be taking things with us when we leave. Your daughter's sheets and mattress, for instance. We need to list them on a warrant so they can be returned." Not the true motivation for the warrant, but plausible.

"Her mattress?" asked Mrs. French.

"Whoever killed Jordan might have done it in her room," said Kane. "If it happened in her bed, he might have left evidence. Fibers, fluids, those kinds of things."

Mr. French stiffened, his eyes turning as flat as porcelain. "You think she may have been raped?"

"It's possible," Kane replied. "We'll know more when the lab tests come back." Not exactly true either, but close enough. Though the initial results of Jordan's autopsy had been inconclusive regarding sexual assault, Kane wanted to rule out the possibility of chronic sexual abuse by a family member. Testing Jordan's sheets, bedding, and underwear for blood, semen, and seminal fluid could prove revealing, as could an examination of her diary, computer files, and other personal items. Kane had argued to have the search warrant authorize seizure of certain of the parents' personal property as well: clothes, cars, items that could have served as a murder weapon, and evidence indicative of an interest in child pornography. Neither the district attorney nor the judge issuing the warrant had concurred, contending that no justification existed for extending the search to that extent.

By now several officers had piled out of the SID wagon and were making their way to the front door. "We'll try to be as unobtrusive as possible," Kane continued sympathetically. "While these men are working on your daughter's room, why don't we go inside and talk? As I said, there are some aspects of Jordan's abduction that I would like to go over with you."

Clearly irritated, Mr. French shook his head impatiently. "We already told the other officers everything we know."

"I realize that, but we need to go over it again," insisted Kane. "I want to know every detail, no matter how insignificant. There may be some bit of background information or a fact you forgot that could help find the killer."

"We'll be glad to help," said Mrs. French. "We can talk in the living room." Then, turning to Deluca, "I'll show you to Jordan's room first."

"No need, ma'am," said Deluca, holding up the building plans. "Third room down the hallway past the kitchen, next to the den and game room."

Mrs. French stared. "That's correct, Detective. Well . . . I suppose we should go in."

Leaving Deluca to confer with the SID team, Kane followed Mrs. French into the house. Mr. French trailed a few steps behind. After crossing a hardwood foyer with a broad staircase curving to the second floor, they entered a cavernous living room decorated with tapestries, crystal glassware, and expensive-looking paintings. Mr. and Mrs. French sat together on an overstuffed couch near a marble fireplace; Kane took a seat in a matching armchair nearby. Between them, a glass coffee table displayed an abstract metal sculpture and a fan of designer magazines including *Elle Décor*, *Coastal Living*, and *Architectural Digest*.

Mr. French leaned forward. "I still want to know what's being done to find the man who killed our daughter. So far no one's told us anything."

"As soon as we make any progress, you'll be the first to know," Kane replied patiently. "At present I'm just trying to put together the pieces, and your cooperation would be helpful."

Mrs. French shot her husband a look as cutting as an arctic morning. "As I said, Crawford, we'll do anything we can to assist," she reiterated firmly.

"Thank you, Mrs. French," said Kane.

"Call me Beth. Please."

"All right, Beth. Let's begin with the twenty-four hours prior to Jordan's disappearance."

"That was all in the statement we gave Detective Peyron," Mr. French objected again. "Don't you people talk to one another?"

Kane frowned. "I read his report. Now I want to hear it from you."

Mrs. French gave her husband another gun-barrel glare. "Crawford, if it'll help, we'll go through it as many times as it takes."

Mr. French glowered back. "Fine," he said, a muscle twitching in his jaw. "It's just that I blame myself for what happened. And now I feel so damned helpless . . ."

"You blame yourself?" asked Kane. "Why?"

"Because I should have installed better security around the house. Hell, there are areas in the backyard where anybody could climb over the fence from the next street."

"Accusing yourself won't bring her back," Mrs. French pointed out. "Let's get on with this."

When her husband didn't reply, Mrs. French reached for a pack of Parliament cigarettes, lit one, and inhaled deeply. "We discovered Jordan missing early Saturday, so I'll start with Friday morning," she began, exhaling a cloud of bluish smoke. "That was June thirtieth, the day after her birthday. We'd all been out late the night before, and she had trouble waking up for her makeup-call at the studio."

"Christ, Beth, do you have to smoke in here?" grumbled Mr. French.

Mrs. French took another drag on her cigarette. "Yes, Crawford. I do."

"Let's get back to your daughter," suggested Kane. "Where were you on the previous evening, Thursday night?"

"We all went out to dinner to celebrate her birthday," Mr. French answered tersely.

"Where?"

"What's that got to do with—"

"I don't know right now," said Kane, cutting Mr. French off. Although sympathizing with the Frenches' loss, Kane was quickly losing patience with Jordan's stepfather. "Maybe somebody saw her and followed her home. Where did you eat?"

"The Ivy," Mr. French answered. "On Robertson."

"I know the place. Go ahead. You went to The Ivy for dinner on Thursday night, and Jordan had a hard time waking up Friday morning."

"That's right," Mrs. French continued, picking up the story. "Jordan is shooting a feature—" She paused, then started over. "Jordan was shooting a feature film at Paramount. The principal photography had to be completed during her *Brandy* hiatus, which was due to end mid-August. Things were hectic, to say the least. Her call-time was five in the morning, so we had to be up at a little after four."

"You went with her to the studio?"

"Always. Anyway, that morning she wouldn't get out of bed. She felt hot, so I took her temperature. It was a hundred and one. She had a cough, too."

"She had a sore throat?" said Kane, not recalling the coroner mentioning the presence of inflammation in Jordan's nasopharynx or throat. "So you called the studio and said she wouldn't be coming in," he continued, making a mental note to review the autopsy findings.

"Jordan made the call."

"Detective Peyron's report stated that Jordan had her own private cell phone. Was the call to the studio made on it?"

"I think so."

"Did she ever use your house telephones, or your cell phones?" asked Kane. He had already procured a warrant to check all calls made on Jordan's private house line and her cell phone; confirmation that she had occasionally used her parents' phones would enable him to do the same with those as well.

"Sometimes."

Kane pulled a notebook from his pocket and made an entry. "Fine. Go on. What did she do all day?"

"Mostly she stayed in bed, at least while I was home," Mrs. French continued. "I was gone for a few hours taking care of personal items. I'm on the LA Museum board and active in a number of charities, though I haven't had much time for them lately."

Kane turned to Mr. French. "What about you? When did you leave for work?"

"I got back from a bike ride a little before seven, showered, and left around seven-thirty," Mr. French answered, unconsciously scratching an angry rash on the back of his left hand. "Poison oak," he explained, noticing a quizzical glance from Kane. "I mountain bike two or three times a week. Took a spill into a patch of it last Wednesday."

"Looks nasty. Did you talk with Jordan before you left?"

"When Beth told me she was sick, I looked in on her. She was sleeping."

"And you didn't see or talk with her again till you got home that night?"

"No. When I got home, she was in her room watching TV."

"Any visitors that day?"

"Not that I know of."

"Did she eat anything that evening?" Kane asked casually, beginning to weave critical questions into the parents' recap of Jordan's last twenty-four hours.

"She didn't join us for dinner, but she may have fixed something for herself later," Mr. French answered.

"Like what?"

"I don't know. Jordan liked preparing her own meals."

"All right, go on. Tell me about that night."

Mr. French shook his head. "There's not much to tell. We went to bed around ten. I checked on Jordan before turning in. She was asleep. The next morning she was gone."

"And you didn't hear anything?"

"No. Our bedroom is on the second floor at the other end of the house."

"No sounds of a struggle?"

"No."

"Do you own a pet?" Kane persisted, remembering seeing a chain-link dog run beside the garage.

Mr. French sighed impatiently. "We had a German shepherd. Greta. She died last year."

"So you didn't hear anything?"

"No," snapped Mr. French. "How many times do we have to say it?"

"What about Jordan? The guy smashed her window to get in. *She* must've heard something."

Mr. French shrugged. "She was taking cold medicine. Maybe it made her too drowsy to wake up."

"All right. In any case, whoever broke into her room came over the fence or through the gate," reasoned Kane. "I saw a keypad out by the speaker. Who has the entry code?"

"Our maid, for one," answered Mrs. French, grinding out her cigarette in a crystal ashtray and reaching for her Parliament pack, defiantly ignoring a look of disapproval from her husband. "You don't think *she* might have had something to do with it?"

"I'm investigating all possibilities. Who else knows how to get in?"

Mrs. French lit a fresh cigarette. "Well, there's my tennis coach. The landscape company has the code, too. That's about it, except for close family friends."

"I want to speak with *everyone* who knows how to open that gate," said Kane, levering himself from the armchair. "Friends included. I'd appreciate it if you would write out a list for me right now, Mrs. French. While you're doing that, I need to confer with Detective Deluca. I'll be back in a minute."

Leaving the parents in the living room, Kane made his way back to the entry, arriving in time to see two SID officers carrying a plastic-wrapped mattress out the front door. At the far end of the driveway, he also noticed a CBS news van outside the gate. Standing with a group of people beside the van was a man whom Kane recognized as Brent Preston, one of the network reporters who had shown up at the reservoir on the day Jordan's body had been discovered. Kane stared a moment, his eyes narrowing. Then, grumbling under his breath, he strode down a hallway to the right, passing an enormous kitchen and a wood-paneled den on the way. When he arrived at Jordan's bedroom he found Deluca standing outside in a flower garden, leaning in through an open window.

Stopping in the doorway, Kane glanced around the brightly decorated bedroom. Posters of rock bands and classic movies covered the walls; bookcases crammed with stuffed animals and CDs bracketed the window; a desk and computer flanked the bed. Near an adjoining bathroom, the doors to a walk-in closet stood open, revealing neatly arranged shelves stacked with sweaters and blouses, poles laden with skirts and dresses, and racks displaying at least a hundred pairs of shoes.

Deluca sat on the sill and swung his legs into the room. "Appears the guy got in through here," he said, fingering a gouge in the window frame. "Used something to jimmy the window."

"Seems like that would have made a some noise," Kane noted, inspecting the damaged frame.

"Yeah. Seems that way," Deluca agreed. "You see the news van out front?"

Kane nodded.

"Damn, how do those dirtbags find out so fast?"

Kane shrugged. "Who knows? So what else do you have left to do?"

Deluca passed a palm across his chin, rubbing a coarse stubble that typically darkened his face before noon. "Not much. We've taken Jordan's clothes, mattress, bedding, address book, letters, and so forth. Everything but her computer. That's next."

"Find anything Peyron missed?"

Deluca nodded. "There were a couple of messages on Jordan's phone service, but they could have come in after Peyron was here. When I checked her house line, I got those beeps. You know, the ones you get when the phone company records calls for you."

"What were the messages?"

"I don't know. I don't have Jordan's access code. Want to ask the parents for it?"

Kane thought a moment. "No. They probably don't know. Anyway, Banowski's at GTE right now getting Jordan's phone records. Contact him and have him pick up her messages, too."

"Anything else?"

"Just wind this up. And make sure nobody talks with the media on the way out."

"No problem."

Upon returning to the living room, Kane found Mrs. French at an antique desk completing the list he had requested. Mr. French stood with his back to the room, staring out the window. "I see the news hounds have arrived," he noted with disgust, turning to face Kane. "Are your men finished?"

"Nearly." Kane crossed to the desk. "Are you done with that, Mrs. French?"

Jordan's mother made a final notation and handed her list to Kane. "I think that's everybody," she said. "I included their addresses and telephone numbers. Is there anything else you need?"

Kane folded the paper and shoved it into his pocket. "As a matter of fact, there is," he said. "I want you and your husband to do two things for me. But before we get into that, I have to explain something." He spread his hands apologetically. "You won't like what I'm about to say, but there's no getting around it. In any murder investigation involving a child, the parents *always* have to be ruled out as suspects. Now, I realize you have been cooperating and that you want the killer found as much as I do, but this has to be done."

"There's a murderer out there, and you're investigating us?" snarled Mr. French. "You think we had something to do with Jordan's death?"

"I didn't say that. I said ruling you out as suspects has to be done so the investigation can proceed."

"And how do you intend to rule us out?" Mr. French demanded.

"As I said, I want you to do two things," Kane replied. "First, in order to exclude any forensic evidence that didn't come from the killer, we need to get blood and hair samples from both of you. Second, I would like you to voluntarily submit to polygraph exams."

"You want us to take lie detector tests? Christ." Mr. French's nostrils flared. "All right, if that's what it takes to light a fire under your investigation, that's what we'll do."

"I'm glad you understand," said Kane. "When can you come down to the station?"

"The funeral is on Sunday, and we have family flying in from back East," answered Mrs. French. "Would sometime next week be acceptable?"

"That would be fine." Kane handed her his card. "Call when you're ready. And thank you for your cooperation. I'll be in touch."

With that, Kane turned and headed for the front door, thinking that although Mr. French had been less than cordial, he understood the man's frustration. And despite Mrs. French's veneer of Beverly Hills snobbery, toward the end he had found himself starting to like her.

"Detective Kane?" called Mrs. French.

Kane turned to see that Jordan's parents had followed him out. "Yes, Mrs. French?"

Jordan's mother swallowed, seeming close to tears. "I . . . I want you to know that we loved our daughter," she said, taking her husband's hand.

"I know you did," Kane said gently.

"No, you don't," said Mr. French. "You don't know us from Adam's cat. But we *did* love her, and we always will. I know you don't like me, Detective, and I don't blame you. I've been acting like an asshole. I admit it. But I can't help myself. I want whoever killed Jordan caught. And when he's caught, I want to see him punished. We didn't kill our daughter," he added quietly, putting an arm around his wife. "For Christ's sake, find the person who did."

\*     \*     \*

"C'mon, Mom. There has to be more to it than that."

"Hold on, Ali," my mom's voice came over the phone. "I have something on the stove."

122

Sitting in my dorm room, I gazed pensively out the window, waiting for my mother to come back on the line. Minutes earlier I had watched the latest Jordan French coverage on the *CBS Evening News*. The lead story had been the police search of the Frenches' estate, this time executed with a search warrant in hand. It was an exclusive CBS network story, and one that I knew was again attributable to me.

I still hadn't reconciled my feelings regarding the role I had played in Brent's recent on-air exclusives—first the ransom note disclosure, and now this. I believed that the public had a right to know what was going on in Jordan's murder case, as long as it didn't interfere with the police investigation—and I didn't see how anything I had revealed so far would make any difference in the long run. Plus I hadn't actually divulged anything I had been told in confidence; my revelations were just bits and pieces I had either picked up or concluded while hanging around my dad. True, I knew was in a unique position because of my father's connection to the case, and from an ethical standpoint that's where things got sticky. I also knew how my father would view things if he ever found out the role I'd played, which was probably unavoidable. After all, he *was* a detective. He would undoubtedly suspect my involvement in the leaks once he learned that I was working for CBS, and I couldn't put off telling my parents about my new job much longer.

"C'mon, Mom," I repeated when she came back on the line. "What exactly did the doctor say?"

"I told you, he said I'm fine."

I sighed, still staring out the window. "What about your nosebleed on the plane? And your fainting spell and being tired all the time?"

"There was a slight problem with one of my lab tests," Mom admitted. "Low platelets or something. I probably need to start taking Geritol. Dr. Porter said there's nothing to worry about, but he wants me to see a blood specialist for more tests."

"More tests? What kind of tests?" I asked, detecting what I thought was note of concern in my mother's voice.

"Ali, I'm fine. Dr. Porter just wants to be on the safe side. I'm going back tomorrow. Travis is dropping me off at the clinic in Santa Monica, and your dad's driving me home."

"Why does Dad have to drive you home?"

"Because Dr. Kratovil requested it, that's why."

"Dr. Kratovil?"

"She's a hematologist. Ali, you're getting all worked up over nothing. We'll talk about this tomorrow night at dinner. You're still coming, aren't you?"

"Sure," I said, recalling that I had promised to join the family for dinner on Wednesday.

"You'd forgotten, hadn't you?"

"Of course not," I said quickly, deciding that I needed to start writing things down. I have a great memory for facts and figures, but appointments are sometimes a different matter—especially if they involve something I don't want to do. "Actually, uh, I have some news to announce tomorrow night myself," I added, deciding that whatever the consequences, I couldn't put off telling her about my job at CBS any longer.

"Oh? What?"

"I'll tell you at dinner. Look, why don't I pick you up at the doctor's office on my way to Malibu?" I suggested, changing the subject. "Save Dad the trip."

"Your father wants to do it. But thanks."

"I'll see you tomorrow night, then."

"Okay, honey. Don't be late."

## 11

Catheryn glanced up as a door beside the reception counter opened into the waiting room.

"Mrs. Kane?"

Nervously, Catheryn closed a magazine that she had been futilely trying to read for the past half hour. She reached beside her for her husband's hand. "Yes?" she said, looking up at the nurse who'd spoken.

"Dr. Kratovil would like to see you and your husband now."

Attempting to hide her apprehension, Catheryn rose from her seat and followed the nurse down a long corridor, Kane at her side.

Catheryn had arrived at the hematologist's office earlier that afternoon, minutes before her two-thirty appointment. Kane, who had taken time off from work and arrived shortly after Travis dropped her off, had waited in the reception room while Catheryn underwent a procedure that had turned out to be far more involved than she'd expected. Following a review of her records and a check of the blood smears sent over by Dr. Porter, Dr. Kratovil, a slight woman in her late thirties with hazel eyes and a sympathetic smile, had asked Catheryn to undress and put on a hospital gown. The doctor left the room briefly while Catheryn changed. Upon returning, the doctor examined Catheryn carefully, paying special attention to the bruises on her arms and thighs. Afterward she instructed Catheryn to lie on her side, stating that it was going to be necessary to obtain a bone-marrow aspirate and biopsy from Catheryn's left hip.

Working with her nurse, Dr. Kratovil draped the area with surgical towels, cleaned the skin over Catheryn's left hip with Betadine, and administered a local anesthetic. Explaining the procedure as she worked, the doctor then made a tiny incision with a scalpel and inserted a large-bore needle with a cutting stylette on the end, using digital twisting to cut through cortical bone on a portion of Catheryn's pelvis called the posterior iliac crest. Until then everything had been relatively painless, but when Dr. Kratovil attached a syringe to the needle and used it to draw a sample of bone-marrow aspirate, Catheryn experienced a painful sensation of pressure. The nurse held her hand, telling her it would soon be over.

Giving Catheryn a break, Dr. Kratovil removed her gloves and spent several minutes away from the examining table. Some of the marrow aspirate she injected into a petri dish, stained, and pipetted onto microscopic slides; the remainder she saved in a test tube. Next, after using a microscope to examine the slides, she regloved and completed the biopsy by reinserting the needle and coring out a plug of marrow that was subsequently pushed through the extraction needle with a small wire and expelled onto a sterile gauze pad. As the doctor placed the biopsy plug into formalin fixative, she explained that it would be sent, along with the slides and the test tube aspirate, to the pathology department at St. John's Health Center, a nearby Santa Monica hospital.

"Pathology department?" said Catheryn uncertainly.

"Standard procedure," replied Dr. Kratovil. Then, covering the puncture site on Catheryn's hip with gauze and an elastic bandage, she added, "Keep this dry for twenty-four hours."

Though the hematologist had been reassuring throughout the biopsy, toward the end Catheryn had detected what seemed to be an overriding tension in the physician's manner, especially when she had been squinting through the microscope. Now, as Catheryn was about to hear the results of her tests, she began to suspect that Dr. Kratovil had requested Kane's presence for reasons that went far beyond providing transportation.

Catheryn glanced around Dr. Kratovil's private office as she entered. The small space was modest but well appointed. Perched on one corner of an oak desk were several framed photos of a smiling teenager. "Your son?" asked Catheryn, glancing at the pictures.

Dr. Kratovil nodded. "Jared turned eighteen this summer. He'll be enrolling at Stanford in the fall."

"I have a son and daughter in college myself," said Catheryn, struggling to keep her voice even. Then, turning to Kane, "This is my husband. Dan, Dr. Kratovil."

"Pleased to meet you," said Kane, reaching across the desk to swallow the doctor's outstretched hand in his. "What's this all about?"

"Why don't you both take a seat?" Dr. Kratovil suggested.

"Is something wrong?" asked Kane.

"Please," the physician said, motioning toward a couch facing the desk.

Kane followed Catheryn to the couch. As they sat, her hand once more found his.

"What's going on with Kate, Doc?" Kane asked again.

Dr. Kratovil looked at Kane, then at Catheryn. "I want you both to prepare yourselves for difficult news," she said, her face like stone. "I'm going to have to tell you things I would rather not say, things you may not completely understand at first, but I need to get this over so we can move on. You have a blood disease, Catheryn. It's a cancer of the white blood cells in your bone marrow called leukemia. This is a grave diagnosis, a life-threatening medical emergency comparable to a major heart attack. Left untreated, it will be fatal. Nonetheless, we have excellent nonsurgical treat—"

"Hold on," Kane broke in. "You're saying Kate has cancer? That's not possible."

"I'm afraid it is."

Stunned, Catheryn shook her head. "But I've been fine. Tired, perhaps, that's all. I recently went on a trip . . ."

"You're sure about this?" asked Kane. "Is there any chance you've made a mistake?"

"None," said the physician. "There's no doubt about the diagnosis. Catheryn has a malignancy known as acute meyloblastic leukemia, or AML, type M-2. Fortunately, it's one of the leukemic subtypes that is more amenable to therapy than others. Nevertheless, treatment will have to begin as soon as possible."

"I have rehearsals starting this week," Catheryn said numbly. "I can't—"

Dr. Kratovil cut her off. "You have no choice. Curing your cancer is paramount. All other details of your life—your job, social engagements, family duties—are now secondary. It would be best to initiate treatment within the next day or two, and it will require your complete time, cooperation, and commitment over the coming weeks and months. If you want to get a second opinion, it will have to be done immediately."

"No, I . . . I trust your judgment," Catheryn stammered. "I just can't believe this is happening."

"I know," Dr. Kratovil said sympathetically. "That's a common reaction, but you have to accept that you have a disease so we can do something about it."

"You're sure?" Kane asked again. "There's no chance you're wrong?"

"No."

"Then we want the best possible treatment. Pull out all the stops. Money is *not* a consideration."

Dr. Kratovil nodded. "Treatment will necessitate long stays at the hospital and will be costly. I mention this only because I want you to be prepared."

"Kate's got health insurance with the Philharmonic," said Kane. "She's covered under my policy at work, too. We'll come up with anything else we need, don't worry. No matter how much it is."

"Is leukemia hereditary?" asked Catheryn. "I mean, will my children . . ."

"The official answer is that leukemia isn't a familial disease," Dr. Kratovil replied. "We may learn more as time goes on, but in your case, given the circumstances, your family history, and the presentation of your illness, I can say with confidence that your children are not at increased risk."

"Good," said Catheryn.

"We'll beat this thing, Kate," said Kane, his voice hardening with rock-solid conviction. Then, to the doctor, "Tell us about the treatment."

Dr. Kratovil leaned forward in her chair. "As I indicated, we have excellent nonsurgical treatments for leukemia, and the five-year survival rate for Catheryn's type of AML is good."

"Nonsurgical. You're talking about chemotherapy," said Catheryn.

"Yes. Depending upon how your disease responds, chemotherapy will probably run several courses, each lasting around four weeks. During the first course, or remission-induction phase, you'll be given a combination of antileukemic drugs that will destroy most of the cancerous cells in your body. Unfortunately, the drugs will also destroy normal white blood cells, and there will be difficult side effects. You'll lose your hair starting around day fourteen, and you'll eventually suffer an almost complete lack of appetite, requiring that you be fed intravenously. With the new anti-emetic drugs available, nausea and vomiting probably won't be a major problem, but you'll lose weight and may become feverish. On the up side, your type of AML rarely affects the central nervous system, so drug administration into the spinal fluid probably won't be required."

Catheryn ran her fingers through her hair, glad to be concentrating on the mechanics of her treatment rather than the reality of her disease. "That's something, I suppose."

"I know all this sounds terrible, but I don't want to minimize the discomfort you'll have to undergo," Dr. Kratovil went on.

"You're doing a pretty fair job of not minimizing anything so far," Kane noted with a frown, placing an arm around Catheryn.

Ignoring the interruption, Dr. Kratovil looked at Catheryn and continued. "As the cancerous cells are killed, your natural immune system will also be incapacitated, and opportunistic infections will have to be fought with antibiotics. Because of clotting problems you'll be covered with bruises, and you'll regularly need blood and platelet transfusions. After the four-week induction phase, assuming everything goes well, you'll be in remission. You'll feel as though you're on the mend, and you can go home for a week or so to regain your strength. Unfortunately, if we stopped treatment at that point, the malignancy would recur.

"So what happens next?" asked Catheryn. "More chemo?"

"Correct. You'll return to the hospital for a second round of treatment. This continuation or consolidation phase will be similar to the first: five days of drug administration followed by three weeks of recovery while your bone marrow regenerates. That time will be a bit easier on you, with fewer blood and platelet transfusions, and afterward you can go home again. Following that, and depending on your postremission recovery, there are various treatment options open."

"Let me get this straight," said Kane. "Kate goes through two months of chemo, and then there's *more*?"

"Yes, although one course of action would be to do nothing unless she experiences a relapse," Dr. Kratovil explained. "Another plan would be to proceed with a further consolidation phase, continuing the chemotherapy until we're confident the cancer is completely gone."

"Are there other alternatives?"

Dr. Kratovil hesitated. "One last option would be to have a final session of combined chemotherapy and total-body irradiation, completely eradicating *all* white blood cells in Catheryn's body."

"Ensuring the cancer wouldn't recur?" asked Catheryn.

"That's the idea. On the downside, the latter course would irreversibly destroy your own natural immune system, requiring a bone-marrow graft. The graft tissue would have to come either from cells harvested from you during remission and subsequently purified, or from a closely matched donor. Which reminds me. Do you have any living siblings?"

"No."

"Are your parents alive?"

"Just my mother."

"You mentioned children."

"We have three. Travis, Allison, and Nate."

"We'll want to test them for compatibility." Dr. Kratovil jotted something on a pad of paper. "Your mother, too. But we're getting ahead of ourselves. At the moment, the main thing to understand is that after the induction and consolidation phases, we'll have to make a decision regarding future treatment. Now, I know I've thrown a lot at you, and I'll be more than happy to answer any questions you might have."

When Kane didn't respond, Catheryn spoke. "I only have one. I've heard that people with leukemia often undergo months of treatment, only to die soon afterward. I realize there are no guarantees, but if that's going to be the case, I want to know right now."

"Jesus, Kate," said Kane. "Don't talk like that."

"No, I want an answer."

"Kate, she said the five-year cure rate was—"

"I know what she said. Now I'm asking about *me*." Catheryn turned, her eyes finding the doctor's. "Despite all this treatment you've discussed, am I going to die anyway?"

Dr. Kratovil met Catheryn's gaze. "Not if I can help it," she said quietly. "I promise you that."

# 12

After dinner at the beach house on Wednesday, Mom called a family meeting. A leaden feeling in the pit of my stomach, I trailed my siblings into the living room, wondering what the topic of discussion would be. Because Travis and I were now away at school most of the time, family meetings had become an infrequent event in the Kane household, and when they did occur, they were typically held at my father's behest. Though in principle any family member could call a meeting, for my mother to have convened one was unusual, and I sensed it had not been called lightly. Does she already know that I've dropped out of summer session? I wondered. I shook my head, deciding that couldn't be it. There was no way Mom could have found out. Not yet, anyway.

What, then?

The evening meal had been unusually subdued, monolithic lulls in the conversation more the rule than the exception. Throughout dinner I had detected what seemed an undercurrent of strain between my parents, but not as if they were fighting—a rare occurrence these days. It was more like they were hiding something. As I slumped down on the living room couch between Travis and Nate, another thought occurred. Oh, no . . . I'll bet someone from UCLA telephoned after I withdrew from my lit class, checking on my housing arrangements.

Mom crossed the room and sat in an armchair facing the couch. Dad stood behind her, a hand resting on her shoulder.

"You two look about as cheery as a pair of funeral directors," I observed nervously. "What's up?"

When neither of my parents answered, I raised my chin defiantly, deciding to take the initiative. "Okay, Mom, let's lay our cards on the table," I said guiltily. I had intended to inform her of my decision to accept the CBS job offer; I just wished I could have been the one to break the news about withdrawing from school. Well, too late for that. "I know what this meeting's about. Look, I was going to tell you. Last night I said I had some news, remember?"

"What are you yammering about?" asked Dad.

"I remember, Ali," said Mom, silencing Dad with a glance. "What is it?"

"You mean you don't know?"

"Know what?"

"That I, uh, that I was offered a summer position at CBS. I thought somebody from UCLA student housing had called."

"Working part-time would be fine, but what does that have to do with student housing? You're not thinking of dropping out of summer session?"

"I can't do both, and this is a great opportunity. It'll give me a chance to see whether—"

Mom cut me off. "Out of the question. You need the credits from your literature course to transfer to USC. Your education is more important than any summer job. Besides, how would you get to work?"

"I'm only lacking four units, and I've already contacted the USC admissions office," I said. "They told me I could make up my missing credits during my first quarter at SC. As for getting to work, Trav lent me his Bronco for the rest of the summer."

Mom turned to Travis. "Oh? I wondered where you car was."

"I wouldn't have been driving it much, anyway," explained Travis, clearly regretting being caught in the middle. "I'll be gone most of July and August with my recitals."

Mom frowned, returning her gaze to me. "Why this sudden interest in working at a TV station? When you changed your major to journalism, I thought it was to find an outlet for your writing."

"TV news needs writers, too," I reasoned. "It may not be print journalism, but working at CBS would be a great start."

"You have this all figured out, don't you, young lady? Let me guess. If you drop out of summer session, I don't suppose you plan on living at home, do you?"

"No. I would like to keep my room at UCLA to be closer to work. Don't worry, I'll be getting paid, so I can handle the rent."

"We'll talk about this later," said Mom. "Unless it's too late to discuss. You haven't already dropped your literature course, have you?"

I shifted uncomfortably. "This was the last week I could withdraw. Plus I had to give them an answer at CBS."

"You can't simply—"

"It's done," I broke in, my voice filling with rebellion.

"If your mother says to, you'll *undo* it," my father warned.

"Dad, be reasonable. I'm old enough to make my own decision on this. I'm not a kid anymore. I'm about to turn twenty."

Dad scowled. "That depends on what comes out of your mouth next. Are you going to do what your mother says?"

"No."

"I beg your pardon? To the untrained ear, it sounded like you just said no."

"I can't reregister at UCLA. It's too late. Besides, you're not being fair. There's no reason I shouldn't do this."

"Damn it, Ali." Dad shook his head in exasperation. "How'd you get to be so hardheaded?"

"I'm the way *you* taught me to be," I shot back. "You've always said that if I thought I was right, to challenge authority."

"When I told you that, I didn't mean me."

"You also said to decide what I wanted, and then to do whatever it took to get it. Remember?"

"I remember. And you'd better remember who you're talking to. You're skating on thin ice here, cupcake. You and I need to have a little conference after this meeting is over."

I ducked my head, sensing from the set of my father's jaw that I had gone too far.

Nate, who had long ago learned to lie low when older family members clashed, finally spoke up. "What *is* this meeting about, anyway?"

Mom sat straighter in her chair. She glanced at Dad, then took a deep breath. "At the doctor's office today, I received some bad news," she said. "They did a biopsy of my bone marrow. It seems I have a disease in which my white blood cells are growing out of control."

"Leukemia?" whispered Travis, his eyes widening.

Mom nodded. "But the kind I have has a good cure rate, and I have a fine physician," she added. "Her name is Dr. Kratovil. She said she would be glad to talk with all of you kids and answer any questions you have concerning my treatment."

"Is leukemia malig—what's the word?—malignant?" asked Nate.

"Yes, honey. It is. But that doesn't mean I won't get better."

"And you said everything was all right," I said. "Just a slight case of cancer."

"Ali, shut the hell up!" snapped Travis. "This isn't the time for wisecracks."

"I'm sorry, Mom," I said quickly, feeling ashamed. "I didn't mean that. I say stupid things when I'm upset."

"I know, Ali. It's all right."

"How did you get sick?" Nate asked in a small voice.

"Nobody's sure what causes leukemia," Mom explained. "Exposure to chemicals and radiation can play a part, but there is a lot doctors still don't know. They *do* know it's not contagious, and it's not passed through the genes. You three aren't at a higher risk because I've developed this illness."

"But how do you get rid of it?" Nate persisted.

"That's the hard part," said Mom. "Over the next months I'll be receiving chemotherapy at St. John's Health Center in Santa Monica. During that time I'll miss things in all your lives, and I'm sorry for that, more than I can say. I wish I could protect you from the uncertainty we're facing, but I can't, so we'll just have to be strong and help each other get through this. Understand?"

"Sure, Mom," Travis replied. "I'll cancel my recitals—"

"No. I don't want you to do that. You're to continue with your piano engagements as planned."

"But—"

"Please, Trav. Canceling your recitals isn't necessary. I've talked with Grandma Dorothy. She's coming down from Santa

Barbara to stay here while I'm in the hospital. She'll look after Nate and keep things running."

"I don't need looking after," objected Nate.

Mom smiled. "I know you don't, but I'll feel better knowing she's here. And she wants to come. Now that Grandpa is gone, I think she's kind of lonely."

"Well . . . it *would* be nice having her visit," Nate conceded.

"She thinks so, too."

"When are you going to the hospital?" asked Travis.

"Your dad's driving me to St. John's first thing Friday morning".

Nate looked dismayed. "That soon?"

"I'm afraid so. I have to start treatment right away so I can get better," Mom replied. Then, forcing a lightness in her voice, "Who wants to ride in with me?"

"I do," Travis replied.

"We all do," I said.

My mother turned to her youngest. "Nate? Do you want to come?"

Nate looked away. "Will you be all right?" he asked, voicing the question on all our minds.

Mom glanced at my father, then back at Nate. "As I said, Dr. Kratovil is an excellent doctor, and my condition was discovered early. I'm going to receive the best treatment poss—"

"But will you be all right?"

Mom hesitated for a long moment. "You deserve an honest answer, Nate," she said at last. "You all do. The truth is, I don't know what's going to happen. We'll simply have to take things one day at a time. Okay?"

Instead of replying, Nate crossed the room and threw his arms around Mom's neck. Mom hugged him tightly, clearly wishing she had been able to answer his question differently. "Don't worry, honey, I'm going to be fine," she whispered, willing her words to be true. "You'll see. I'm going to be fine."

After the meeting, Dad and I descended to the redwood deck, out of earshot of the other family members. Our exchange did not begin well.

"Just what in God's name do you think you're doing?" Dad demanded, dispensing with the preliminaries.

"You're referring to my working at CBS?"

"No, I'm referring to your changing laundry detergents. Of course I'm referring to your job at CBS. I swear, kid, I keep thinking there must be some pharmaceutical explanation for your behavior. What are you on? Jesus, we have enough problems right now without your pulling a stunt like dropping out of school to work at some scumbag news station. Which reminds me. Is Lauren Van Owen still the bureau chief over there?"

"Uh . . ."

"I knew it. Damn, I can't believe she's doing this."

"Doing what?"

"I have to spell it out? It's simple. She figured I'd be investigating the Jordan French case, so she—"

"Does everything have to be about you?" I broke in, chafing at my father's assumption that I had been hired at CBS simply because of my connection to him. "Ms. Van Owen offered me the position on Tuesday, *before* you assumed the French case. Your involvement with the Jordan French investigation had nothing to do with it." Not exactly true, but in my anger I had no difficulty suppressing my doubts—at least for the moment.

"Is that right?"

"Yes, it is. Why is it so impossible for you to believe I could achieve something on my own?"

"It's not. Hell, you're a Kane. When you set your mind to something, it gets done. But this will cause trouble, and Van Owen knew it when she hired you."

"In all fairness, she made the position conditional on my telling you and Mom."

"So why didn't you?"

"I did."

"*After* you withdrew from school," Dad pointed out angrily. "Putting things as diplomatically as possible, Ali, your behavior on this sucks."

"If that's being diplomatic, what's your blunt version?" I asked, nervously attempting a smile. "Delivering it strapped to a cruise missile?"

"You have a real talent for sarcasm, you know that?"

"I'm sorry, Dad. But I want this job."

"Tough."

"Are you going to call Ms. Van Owen and get me fired?"

Dad hesitated. "You really want this?"

"Yes, sir."

"And you can make up your summer credits at USC and still graduate with no loss of time, like you said?"

"Yes, sir. Please let me do it."

Dad vacillated a moment longer. "Okay," he sighed. "It's against my better judgment, but as this is the first thing you've shown any interest in for a long time, I'm going to say yes. Your mother won't like it, and normally I wouldn't cross her when her mind's made up. But in this case, as it looks like it's a done deal anyway, I'll run interference for you. Just don't screw up."

"Thanks, Dad."

"By the way, I don't think it would be the best thing for your mom to know who you're working for."

"There's nothing still, uh . . ."

"Between Lauren and me? Hell, no. I just think your mom has enough on her mind right now without throwing Van Owen into the equation. Speaking of which, with all the lousy news stations in town, how'd you wind up at CBS?"

"Just lucky, I guess."

With a disgusted shake of his head, Dad stared out over the darkened beach, his eyes raking the horizon. A three-quarter moon had risen at the foot of the bay, illuminating the ocean with restless flickers of silver and gray. "One more thing, Ali," he added quietly. "I know that you and your mom have been locking horns recently about just about everything, which I suppose is normal for mothers and daughters, but these next few months are going to be hard. Really hard. Don't make them worse."

On the drive back to school, I thought about my father's words. At the time, his admonition not to make things worse for Mom had seemed unnecessary. Of course I wouldn't make things worse. Mom's illness constituted a family crisis, and during a family crisis, in the dogma Dad had drummed into Travis and Nate and me all our lives: *Kanes stand together, no matter what.*

When I was younger, those words had held little meaning. The heartbreaking loss of my older brother Tom had changed everything, the strain his death had placed on the fabric of our household eventually leading me to embrace the spirit of my father's simple precept. No, I swore to myself as I drove through the night, I would never do anything to make my mother's ordeal more difficult. Yet despite my conviction, doubts I had earlier pushed aside kept returning.

Am I being selfish by taking this intern position? I asked myself. Trav offered to cancel his recitals. Maybe I should do the same—quit my new job at CBS and move back to the beach to help out. But even if I did, what good would that do? Grandma Dorothy is coming to stay. And naturally, Mom insisted that Trav continue his recital tours. She wouldn't want genius boy's budding career to suffer simply because she's sick. But when it comes to something I want . . .

Jeez, what's wrong with me? I wondered in disgust, despising myself for my envy. Shaking my head, I again resolved to heed my father's warning. Things would be difficult enough for our family over the next few months. I couldn't make them worse. I just couldn't. If I were needed at home, or my working at CBS caused problems, or whatever, I vowed to take any and all steps that were necessary to make things right.

No matter what.

# 13

Sweeping back her long auburn hair with her fingers, Catheryn closed her eyes and raised her face to the shower's soothing jets, letting the water stream into her mouth and across her shoulders and over her breasts, its warmth flowing the length of her legs to the tiles below. Steam filled the bathroom, but she turned up the water temperature even higher, as if the near-scalding spray could somehow burn away her cancer. Though the time to leave for the hospital was fast approaching, she lingered a few minutes more in the shower's cleansing embrace. Finally, with a reluctant sigh, she turned off the water.

As she tipped her head and gathered her hair in a thick rope to twist it dry, an unsettling thought occurred. What did Dr. Kratovil say? Two weeks before she started losing it?

Oh, well. At least she would save on shampoo, she thought wryly as she stepped from the shower and grabbed a towel from a rack by the door. After wiping the steamy mirror above the sink, she inspected herself in the glass, examining her lean torso, firm breasts, and a stomach still as flat as the day she had married. She had always been proud of her body. Now, with insidious and unexpected cruelty, it had betrayed her.

"How's it coming in there, gorgeous?" Kane yelled from the adjoining bedroom. "Need any help?"

Catheryn began drying her legs. "I think I can handle things in here just fine, Dan."

"Too bad. I wouldn't mind handling 'em a bit more myself," Kane replied, lowering his voice suggestively.

"You've already taken care of activities in that department quite nicely, thank you," said Catheryn, smiling at Kane's salacious tone. In truth, their lovemaking the previous night had been glorious, their impromptu rendezvous beneath the covers that morning even better. Nevertheless, each time desire had carried them away, Catheryn had sensed a trace of desperation tingeing their passion, the specter of her impending medical treatment adding a darker color to what had always been a joyful sharing of their love. The children were acting differently around her as well, offering to help at odd times, doing chores that would normally have required reminding. Despite everyone's good intentions, their anxious solicitude had progressively made Catheryn feel like a guest in her own home.

"Whatever you say, sugar," Kane called. "Although in my opinion, when it comes to that particular activity, you can't get too much of a good thing. I'll go make sure the kids are getting dressed."

Catheryn heard the strain in his voice. "I'll be ready in twenty minutes," she called back, attempting to sound lighthearted and almost succeeding. "And before we leave, would you please clean up that mess you left on the dining room table? What were you doing with my back issues of *Architectural Digest*, anyway?"

"Something to do with work," Kane replied. He rarely discussed details of his investigations with Catheryn, and by tacit agreement, she seldom asked.

"Just because I won't be around for a while is no reason to let things go."

"Yes, ma'am."

Catheryn finished drying herself, wrapped a fresh towel around her damp hair, another around her torso, and stepped into the bedroom. The small bag she had packed the previous evening lay open on the bed, a collection of pictures on top. She picked one up, a shot of Nate when he was four. The family pet at the time, a black Labrador retriever named Sammy, sat nearby, the dog's eyes intent on a stick Nate was laughingly holding above his head. Catheryn paused, remembering how much Nate had loved that old dog. Putting off dressing, she flipped through several other photos she had chosen to take to the hospital. One showed a much-younger Travis performing in his first piano recital. Another, taken the summer before her oldest son, Tom, would have started college, depicted Tom and Kane grinning foolishly on a high-school football field, arms around each other's shoulders. The next was of Allison and Travis at Allison's fifteenth birthday party. The two were sitting on the old downstairs swing—Travis unaware his picture was being taken, Allison smiling innocently, her index and third fingers poking up behind her brother's head in the familiar "rabbit-ears" prank.

As Catheryn turned to the final photo, she heard Kane enter the room. "Everybody's ready when you are," he announced, coming up behind her and putting his arms around her waist. "I remember that one," he added, peering over Catheryn's shoulder. "Mexico. One of the busboys took it."

"I recall," Catheryn murmured, studying a shot of the entire family on a vacation they had taken two years back, a week after their house had been reduced to char and rubble. Homeless and with most of their possessions gone forever, they stood grouped before a palm-thatched palapa on a beach in Mazatlán. Kane, an arm around Catheryn, his leg in a cast, was sporting a tastelessly loud Hawaiian shirt and baggy shorts. Catheryn was wearing a tiny black bikini, a straw hat, and a carefree smile. Travis, Allison, and Nate, browned from a week of surfing and lounging on the beach, were clowning in the foreground.

"Those were good times," said Kane softly.

Her vision blurring, Catheryn placed the pictures into her bag. "Yes," she said, turning to her husband. "Despite all that had happened, they were. With the exception of when our children were born, I think those were some of the happiest moments of my life."

Gently, Kane took Catheryn's face in his hands. "I love you, Kate."

"Oh, Dan," Catheryn whispered. "I love you, too." Closing her eyes, she raised her lips to his.

Kane returned her kiss, circling her protectively in his arms. "We'll get through this."

Catheryn kissed him again, longer this time, a familiar passion beginning to stir as Kane tightened his embrace. Pulse quickening, she pressed against his strong body, her mouth warm on his. Finally, with a gasp, she placed her hands on his chest and pushed him away. "Let me get dressed or we'll never get out of here," she laughed.

"What's the rush? The hospital's not going anywhere."

"But . . ."

"One more kiss," said Kane, running his hands down the curve of her back and unfastening the towel.

"And then you'll let me get dressed?"

Sensing her resolve slipping, along with the towel, Kane drew her to him again. "Maybe. We'll talk about it later."

\*     \*     \*

On the ride to St. John's, I sat wedged between my brothers in the back of our family's green Expedition. The late-model Ford, a recent addition to the household that an auto-dealer friend of Dad's had picked up for him at auction, was a definite improvement over our former vehicle—a battered red Suburban that had been the family car for as long as I could remember. Still, the ancient Suburban had held fond memories for me: riding to my First Communion, driving lessons Dad had given me in a Pepperdine University parking lot, leisurely trips our family had taken every summer up the coast to Oregon. I missed it.

I had driven to the beach earlier that morning to accompany Mom to the hospital. I had barely seen my father before we left the house for Santa Monica, but I'd sensed that a strain still remained between us from our conversation on Wednesday night. Since then Dad's recent visit to the Frenches' estate had been televised both locally and nationally, with Brent's on-the-scene coverage culminating in an exclusive revelation that a search warrant had been obtained by police to reenter the house. But if my father had deduced that I was Brent's source of information regarding the search warrant—especially now that Dad knew I was an intern at CBS—he hadn't said anything. At least not yet. It was something for which I felt thankful. With all that was happening, I couldn't face another argument.

Nonetheless, as our family drove toward Santa Monica, a deeper tension than the one between Dad and me permeated the car—a tension eased only occasionally by forced conversation and falsely cheerful remarks about the weather, Nate's baseball team, and a recent proposal by the New York Philharmonic to schedule another presentation of Travis's piano concerto. As we neared the Health Center, I felt as if I were mired in a dark and endless nightmare. I glanced at my parents in the front seat. At that point Dad was mostly concentrating on his driving. Mom sat beside him going over a checklist to ensure that everything would function smoothly in her absence.

"Ali, don't forget that Grandma Dorothy is coming down from Santa Barbara this afternoon," said Mom, turning to me in the backseat.

"I know. My room's all ready for her," I replied. I had insisted that Grandma use my bedroom while staying at the beach—opting to use our house's small guestroom whenever I returned home.

"Believe it or not, I'm actually looking forward to seeing the old broad," Dad noted.

"She loves you, too," said Mom. "Although considering the way you two butt heads, I can't imagine why."

"She appreciates class, sugar."

Trying to lighten things, Mom winked at us in the back seat. "Of course she does. I, however, don't see the connection."

"Unless you're talking about low class," offered Nate, halfheartedly making an effort to join in.

"Or *no* class," Travis added, sensing the lines of battle being drawn in one of our family's good-natured patriarchal challenges—a diversion on car trips usually reserved for longer journeys when Dad had been mellowed by hours of driving.

Though normally I would have been the first to join in the mutiny, I remained silent.

Playing along, Dad scowled at us in the rearview mirror. "Last time I checked, my arm still reached to the backseat, rookies."

"Don't threaten the children, Dan," laughed Mom. "That's my job. Speaking of which, while I'm gone I want all three of you kids to help around the house and do whatever Grandma Dorothy says. That goes double for you, Nate."

"Yes, ma'am."

144

"And Allison, I want you to come home as often as possible, despite the demands of this . . . job you've taken."

"Okay, Mom," I said, stung by her tone but determined not to show it.

"I'll help, too," said Nate.

"I know you will," Mom said, again referring to her list. "In fact, as Travis and Allison will be gone a lot, you'll have to work especially hard. It'll be your job to see that Callie is fed and walked every day. And don't forget to keep her water bowl filled."

"I won't," Nate promised, reaching behind him to stroke Callie, who was curled comfortably in the rear luggage compartment. "Don't worry, I'll take good care of her."

"Good. Another thing, don't forget to—"

"Put away your list, Kate," Dad interrupted. "Please, sugar. Everything is going to be fine."

"But—"

"But nothing. You just get better. I'll tend to the troops."

After taking West Channel Road to San Vicente Boulevard, Dad jogged right on 20th Street, taking a back route to the hospital. Minutes later, as the walls of St. John's Health Center rose into view, a premonition of doom gripped me. As had all the Kane children, I'd been born at St. John's, but I had rarely visited since. I vaguely remembered accompanying Dad and my older brothers years back when we had picked up Mom and newborn Nate. Then, the multistoried building with its rows of windows and curving glass columns had been filled with promise. Now, following a recent round of reconstruction that had all but obliterated any vestige of the old health center, it seemed as if a pall had settled upon the impersonal-looking new structure, threatening heartache and sorrow for any who dared to enter its walls.

Dad pulled up at the curb, dropping us off near the entrance. Then, after snagging a rare parking spot on Santa Monica Boulevard and jamming a fistful of coins into the meter, he rejoined us. When we arrived in the lobby, we found Dr. Kratovil already there waiting by the information desk.

"Sorry we're late," Mom apologized as we hurried in.

"Don't give it a thought." Dr. Kratovil nodded warmly to Dad, then turned to us. "I'm Dr. Kratovil," she said, extending a hand to Nate.

Nate, who had insisted on carrying Mom's bag into the hospital, set the small suitcase on the floor and shook the physician's hand. "I'm Nate Kane," he replied gravely.

"And you must be Allison and Travis."

"Yes, ma'am," said Travis.

Not trusting myself to speak, I remained silent.

"Your mom is going to spend some time getting checked in," Dr. Kratovil continued. "In the meantime, there's a good cafeteria here, at least it's pretty good. If you want, we could go get a hot chocolate or a bite to eat, then see your mom in her room upstairs."

"Do we have to?" asked Nate, sidling closer to Mom.

"No, of course not," answered Dr. Kratovil. "But I thought it might give us time to talk."

"C'mon, Nate. I've never known you to turn down food," I said lightly. "We'll see Mom when she's done."

"You're not getting out of here without saying good-bye, if that's what you're worried about," Mom added. "Go on, Nate. I'll see you shortly."

With Nate reluctantly bringing up the rear, we followed Dr. Kratovil down a broad corridor and took an elevator to a brightly lit cafeteria on the second floor. Though no one was hungry, Travis and Dr. Kratovil got steaming mugs of strong black coffee. Nate opted for hot chocolate. My stomach tied in knots, I had nothing.

"So," said Dr. Kratovil after we had seated ourselves at a table near the door. "You must all have questions. Who wants to begin?"

No one spoke.

"It's all right. You can ask anything you want."

"Is Mom going be all right?" Nate finally ventured, cutting to the heart of the matter with childlike simplicity.

Dr. Kratovil paused before answering, three pairs of eyes upon her, awaiting her response. Finally she spoke. "When talking with family members about a disease such as your mother's, I don't believe in sugar-coating the risks," she said. "I don't know for certain whether your mother will recover, but she has a good chance. She's young and strong. We caught her leukemia early, and she has a type that's amenable to treatment."

"Mom said the chemotherapy will make her sick," said Travis. "How sick?"

"Very. We'll be giving her extremely toxic chemicals designed to kill cancerous cells, but their effect on the rest of her body will be devastating. She'll need all the support we can give her. A month from now when she's in remission, she'll be able to go home for a while. Then she'll come back for another course of treatment. After that, depending on how things go, further therapy may be required."

"Like what?"

"Possibly a third and even a fourth round of chemo, which may or may not be combined with radiation and a bone-marrow transplant," answered Dr. Kratovil. "But those are decisions we'll make later. Which reminds me—before we rejoin your mother, I want you all to swing by the hospital laboratory with me."

"For HLA testing to see whether any of us are a human leukocyte antigen match for Mom," I said, recalling some research I had done on the internet. "In case she needs an allogenic marrow graft."

Dr. Kratovil regarded me curiously. "How do you know those terms?"

I shrugged. "I did some checking last night. Am I right?"

Dr. Kratovil nodded. "You are. The chances are extremely slim that any of you will be an acceptable match, but as your mother has no siblings, testing you three children for HLA compatibility is worth doing. With any luck, however, if a transplant is needed Catheryn may be able serve as her own donor by using what is known as an autologous or 'rescue' graft—employing her own purified cells to reestablish her immune system. There's a national donor registry too, if we need allogenic, or nonrelated, marrow from someone else."

"Will she have tubes and needles stuck in her arms?" asked Nate.

"We have a better way now, Nate. We'll place something called a Hickman catheter into your mother's chest, and it'll stay there the whole time. It's easier than repeatedly starting new IVs, and the catheter has three separate channels for administering drugs, drawing blood, and giving IV nutrients."

"How about hospital visiting hours?" asked Travis. "Can we come whenever we want?"

"You can, within reason, but please don't visit if you have a cold or the flu or anything contagious," cautioned Dr. Kratovil. "Along those lines, many physicians require that visitors wear latex gloves. I think touching and hand contact are important, so we can dispense with the gloves as long as you wash your hands thoroughly with alcohol when you arrive. Another thing. No flowers."

"Bacteria in the water?" I guessed.

"Correct. Balloons are fine, as are pictures, drawings, books, and videos. And a cot can be set up in your mother's room, making it possible for a family member to occasionally stay overnight."

"I'll stay with Mom," offered Nate.

"I think Dad will have dibs on that," I said. "But maybe we can take turns," I added, noting Nate's crestfallen expression.

Dr. Kratovil finished her coffee and set down her cup. "Any other questions?"

All three of us shook our heads.

"In that case, it's time for me to get to work. I think your parents should be done registering by now, so let's stop at the lab and then see how they're doing."

After having blood drawn at the hospital laboratory, Travis, Nate, and I returned with Dr. Kratovil to the main lobby. The doctor stopped briefly at the registration desk, then accompanied us to the oncology unit on the fourth floor. There we rejoined

Mom and Dad in a hospital room overlooking the city of Santa Monica and the Pacific Ocean beyond. To the right of the door into Mom's room lay a large bathroom; straight ahead, facing a television mounted on the opposite wall, was a hospital bed attended by several chairs, a bedside stand, and a brace of complicated-looking monitoring machines.

When we arrived Mom was still unpacking, laying out toiletries and a few articles of clothing on the bed. Dad stood to one side, hands sunk deep in his pockets.

"Hi, Mom," I said. "Getting settled?"

"Hi, Ali," she replied. "Yes, I'm making myself at home. It's a wonderful room, don't you think? It has a much better view than the ones in the old maternity ward."

"It's great," I agreed, the room suddenly seeming too small. "What's next?" I asked, wishing our entire family, including mom, could simply get up and leave and never come back.

"Your mother has a number of preliminary tests scheduled," Dr. Kratovil answered, checking her watch. "As they'll take several hours, this might be as good a time as any for you all to say good-bye."

"Already?" asked Nate.

Mom smiled reassuringly. "You can visit tomorrow when I have more time, honey. Come here and give me a hug."

His chin trembling, Nate crossed the room and threw his arms around Mom's neck. "'Bye, Mom."

"We'll visit first thing tomorrow," said Travis, bending to kiss Mom on the cheek.

"You'd better," she warned with a mock frown. "Ali?"

"What, Mom?"

"Come here and say good-bye."

Slowly, I walked to the bed. Once more feeling as if I were trapped in some unspeakable nightmare, I placed my arms around my mother and gave her a hug. "See you tomorrow," I said softly.

# 14

Our entire family visited Mom at the hospital on Saturday and again on Sunday. Both times my father, preoccupied with my mother's worsening reaction to her chemotherapy, had little to say to any of us, including me. As he still hadn't mentioned my role in a CBS news crew being present at the Frenches' house on Tuesday, I was beginning to believe he hadn't made the connection.

Monday morning, following a mostly sleepless weekend, I left for CBS before 6 AM to avoid rush-hour traffic. When I arrived at the newsroom, Lauren Van Owen was already present. "Quite the early bird, aren't you?" the bureau chief remarked as I entered.

I shrugged. "Couldn't sleep. Figured I might as well get something done."

"A compulsive worker," Lauren noted approvingly. "I like that in an employee. Speaking of which, I want to compliment you again on that tip you gave Brent. Your hunch about the police search really paid off. Our share numbers were up dramatically on that story."

Despite conflicting feelings on the subject, I allowed myself a brief moment of pride at the bureau chief's praise.

"Speaking of which, I need a body to sit on the Frenches' house today," Lauren continued. "Think you can handle it?"

I stared in surprise. "You want *me* to go?"

Lauren smiled. "Unless you have something you would rather do."

"No. I mean . . . I'll be glad to go. What do you want me to do?"

"Like I said, you're just a body. Take a cameraman up there and watch the house. If anything develops—another police visit, for instance—have the cameraman start shooting and call for reinforcements. Brent is covering the President's California campaign trip, but he can be reached if something breaks. Stay in touch."

"I will. And thanks."

"You're welcome. You earned it."

Three quarters of an hour later I turned off Sunset Boulevard and headed up Mandeville Canyon. Sitting beside me in the Bronco, Max Riemann, one of the CBS staff cameramen, finished the dregs of his coffee and glanced out the window. "Ain't been up here in years," the older man noted idly. "Sure a lotta goddamned trees." Then, seeming embarrassed, "Sorry. Didn't mean to cuss."

"Forget it," I said. "I have older brothers. Plus my dad's a cop."

Riemann nodded. "I heard that. Lead investigator on the French case. Your covering this story causing any trouble at home?"

"A bit," I admitted, turning on Westridge Road. "Concerning my working for CBS, my dad's attitude can be summed up in one simple word: stupid."

But as I proceeded up the twisting canyon lane, I felt a renewed sense of unease, wondering whether Lauren's motives for sending me to the Frenches' house had more to do with my father than me. Stubbornly, I pushed away my doubts. What difference does it make? I asked myself. Lauren is giving me a chance, and I'm taking it. Period.

Just before 8 AM, I eased the Bronco to a stop in front of the Frenches' wrought-iron gate. Deciding a position across the street would provide the best vantage point, I parked in a vacant lot opposite the house. As I killed the engine, I noticed a late-model maroon Ford partially concealed behind a clump of oleander bushes near the rear of the property. Leaving Max to ready his video equipment, I climbed from behind the wheel, wondering about the Ford. It appeared too new to be abandoned, so why would someone leave it parked there?

Curious, I made my way across the vacant lot, approaching the vehicle from the side. When I was a dozen yards away from the car, I saw that two men were sitting in the front seat. I stopped, not having considered that the Ford might be occupied.

All at once I recognized one of the men in the car: Detective Paul Deluca.

Puzzled, I began walking again. As I neared the Ford, I saw that Deluca had been following my progress. The man beside Deluca said something. Deluca shook his head.

Upon arriving, I gave Detective Deluca a sunny smile, feeling a bit foolish for my stealthy approach. " Hi, Paul. What brings you out here?"

"Morning, Ali," Deluca replied, lowering his window. "If I didn't already know you were working for the media, I might ask you the same thing. Speaking of which, you should have mentioned your new job the other day when you called the squad room."

"Sorry," I said, realizing from his tone that Deluca must have figured out who tipped the CBS news crew on the day of the search, meaning my father knew as well. "At the time I was just trying to locate my dad," I explained lamely. "After that things sort of snowballed."

"Snowballed, huh?"

"It's the truth."

"Don't be so defensive," said Deluca. "I believe you. By the way, I'm really sorry about your mom. I hope she's gonna be okay."

My stomach dropped at the mention of Mom. "Thanks, Paul," I said numbly. Then, changing the subject, "So what *are* you doing here? Think the kidnapper might come back?"

Deluca hesitated. "Off the record?" he said evasively.

"Of course. I know better than to blow a police stakeout."

"Fine. *Off the record*, we think whoever did it might come back. Happens all the time. We're checking for cars cruising the area, people who don't belong, anything out of the ordinary."

Deluca's partner, a heavyset man with sagging jowls and a florid complexion, raised a pair of binoculars. "I'll be damned," he said. "Now he's comin' back from the other direction. How'd he manage that?"

I turned to see a large, muscular man wearing a brightly colored wind shirt, biking shorts, and helmet, pedaling a mountain bike toward the Frenches' gate. Without removing his feet from the pedal clips, the man steadied himself on the gate keypad and punched in several numbers. The metal barrier swung open. Moments later the biker coasted through the opening and down the long driveway, vanishing around the side of the garage.

"Mr. French?" I guessed, watching the gate swing closed.

Deluca nodded. "He took off around an hour ago, going *up* the hill when he left. Must've made a loop."

"Well, we'll never know, seeing as how we couldn't get past the dead-end at Queensferry," the other officer complained.

"You *followed* him?" I said, surprised.

"We trailed him," explained Deluca, shooting his partner a look of exasperation.

"Why?"

"To make sure no one else was following. Listen, Ali, we have work to do, so why don't you—" Stopping midsentence, Deluca stared over my shoulder. "Aw, hell. This thing's turning into a circus."

I glanced toward the street, noting a caravan of media vehicles pulling into the lot beside my car. One was an NBC news van, another had a CNN logo.

Deluca grabbed a cell phone from the dashboard. "Beat it, Ali."

"Right, Paul. See you later."

Mulling over my puzzling exchange with Deluca, I returned to my car. Something was wrong. Granted, it made sense for detectives to be watching the Frenches' estate. I had taken an active interest in many of my dad's cases over the years, and I knew that criminals—especially those who had engaged in a killing that involved rape or sexual rage—often returned to the scene to gloat, to relive their act, or even to taunt authorities. Although the coroner's report had yet to be released, because Jordan's body had been found nude, it was being widely speculated in the press that a sexual assault had taken place. But that didn't explain why Deluca and his partner had followed Mr. French. Watching to see whether someone else was following him didn't add up, either. What interest would the killer have in Mr. French? Before I could come up with an answer, I heard a car engine cough to life. An instant later Deluca's maroon Ford rumbled past, fishtailed onto the street, and headed down the hill.

Max regarded me curiously as I slipped back behind the wheel. "Anybody we know?"

"Cops," I said, rolling down my window. Though the morning was just beginning, the temperature had already risen into the seventies, promising another day of sun and smog for the Southland. "I think we just blew their stakeout."

"We weren't the only ones," Max remarked as another news van, this one from KCBS, slowed in front of the Frenches' gate.

The Channel 2 van stopped, backed, and turned into the lot, parking next to me. Seconds later the side door opened and three men piled out. One of them Mike Cortese. He started toward the rear of the van, smiling in surprise when he noticed me in the Bronco. "Hi, Ali," he said.

"Small world," I replied coolly, still a bit nettled about the way Mike and I had last parted. Of course I hadn't wanted him to kiss me . . . but he should have at least tried.

"That it is," Mike agreed pleasantly. Then, noticing Max, "Haven't seen you in a while, Riemann. How's it going?"

"Not bad, Mike. Yourself?"

"Can't complain." Mike surveyed the other news teams present. "The vultures are circling."

"Present company excluded, of course," I noted dryly.

"Not hardly," Mike snorted. "KCBS is here with the rest of the hounds to do an on-the-scene update, same as everybody else—the stricken family's house displayed in the background, our intrepid correspondent breathlessly listing all the things we don't know and haven't learned since yesterday. How about you?"

"Just watching the house."

Mike looked surprised. "They're already sending you out on location? Well, good for you, Ali. Beats getting coffee for the guys in the newsroom, eh?" he added with a grin.

Despite Mike's smile, I heard the acknowledgment in his voice. "That's for sure," I agreed.

"Did you notice Mr. French cranking up the hill just now?" asked Mike. "The man's got excellent taste in bikes. That titanium frame he was riding costs over four grand."

I whistled softly. "Four thousand dollars, just for the bike frame? How do you happen to know that?"

"I ride a bit myself." Mike glanced at the KCBS van, where one of the men who had arrived with him was assembling some sound recording equipment. "Well, time for me to get to work."

"Don't let me stop you."

"Hey, Ali?"

"What?"

Mike leaned closer, resting his forearms on the Bronco's open window. "How's about us getting together later this week? I know it's not much notice, but I have tickets to a screening at the Directors Guild on Wednesday. They're showing a film that a friend of mine worked on. Afterward, maybe we could grab a bite to eat. What do you say?"

"I . . ."

"Do you like Mexican? I know a place that's fantastic."

"I thought your favorite was Italian."

"I'm an equal opportunity eater. How's seven o'clock? I'll pick you up at the dorm."

I had enjoyed my time with Mike on the night we'd gone to Westwood. I also appreciated the role he had played in my being hired at CBS. But there was something about his challenging eyes and taunting grin and the disconcerting way he seemed to know what I was about say, even before I knew it myself, that made my pulse quicken with an emotion I couldn't quite define. Whatever it was, something about Mike got under my skin, and I resolved then and there to end things with him—deciding that Mike Cortese was definitely not for me.

But as I opened my mouth to reply, something peculiar happened. Although my brain had decided to cut Mike loose, evidently the rest of my body hadn't signed on to the plan, for instead of the curt words of refusal I'd intended . . . to my surprise I heard myself accepting.

\*     \*     \*

Kane sat at his desk in the squad room, hunched over a stack of forensic reports that had come in earlier. It had been a busy and, for the most part, sleepless weekend. Though it was only ten in the morning, he was already exhausted.

With the exception of visiting Catheryn at St. John's, Kane had worked through most of the weekend questioning people who knew the keypad combination to the Frenches' gate, following up on the canvass of neighborhoods bordering the reservoir, and interrogating Javier Peña, the sex offender that Carl Peyron had turned up as a suspect. The results of Kane's efforts had been fruitless, as had a surveillance of Jordan's funeral. Kane had even talked with an officer who had spent time in the Frenches' home during surveillance of the family's telephone line. The officer's assessment of the parents had confirmed Kane's earlier impression that although Mr. French was difficult and abrasive, both he and his wife seemed genuinely distraught over their daughter's loss.

Grimly, Kane began paging through a pile of lab reports, going through them anew to ensure he hadn't missed anything. The first, a test for free histamine and serotonin in the tissues surrounding Jordan's wounds, indicated that the welts on her back and buttocks had been antemortem, meaning she had been alive when she'd been beaten, whereas the ligature marks and sloughed skin on her wrists and ankles had occurred after death. The next item was a toxicology screening for drugs present in Jordan's body. Nothing of significance had turned up, not even the cold remedy that Mr. French had suggested could have made his daughter drowsy. The search of Jordan's room had proved disappointing as well. No blood, sperm, or seminal fluid had been found on her mattress or any of her bedding, underwear, or clothes. A hacker in the LAPD Automated Information Division who'd examined Jordan's computer had discovered nothing useful on her hard drive or backup material either, and although a survey of friends whose names had been gleaned from Jordan's address book was still ongoing, to date that approach had failed to produce any new leads. In fact, upon contacting individuals who had left messages on Jordan's service on the Friday before her disappearance, Kane had yet to find anyone who'd spoken to her that day.

With feelings of misgiving, Kane flipped to a microscopic analysis of tissues taken from Jordan's body at autopsy. Most of those results had been unremarkable, with the exception of a number of vaginal slides that showed a condition known as chronic interstitial inflammation—a localized reaction to abnormal physiologic stress. Taken with the focal area of vaginal erosion and the missing hymen noted earlier, it was a histological finding suggestive of sexual abuse having taken place over a period of time. Suggestive, but not definitive.

After initially reading the report, Kane had called Dr. Walter Chang, the coroner who'd performed the autopsy. Chang had cautioned that the vaginal inflammation could have resulted from any of a number of causes—chronic infection, for example. Recalling that Mrs. French had said Jordan's reason for missing work was because she had been coming down with the flu, Kane had also queried Chang about the presence of inflammation in Jordan's lungs, throat, or nasopharynx. Chang had assured them there had been none.

"Morning, Dan."

Kane looked up, finding Lt. Long standing by his desk. "Lieutenant. What's new?"

"Not much. How's Kate doing?"

"About as well as can be expected," Kane sighed. "I'll be spending nights at the hospital for a while. If you need to contact me and I'm not home, try my cell phone."

Long nodded. "Listen, I know the French case is heating up, but if you want to take some time off, feel free."

Kane shook his head. "I want to work. Keeps my mind off things."

"Okay. But if you need a few days or whatever, let me know." Changing gears, Long glanced at the forensic reports on Kane's desk. "What do you think?"

Kane knew that Long had already read copies of the reports. He also knew that they were both thinking the same thing. Wearily, he passed a hand across his face. "I have more ground to cover before forming any conclusions," he answered.

"So how are you proceeding?"

Kane paused to marshal his thoughts. Then, without referring to notes, he began enumerating elements of his investigation on the fingers of his right hand.

"One: Peyron wants to stay involved, so I've had him dragging in every known sex offender in the area. So far he's come up with two other possible candidates besides Javier Peña. Neither looks promising.

"Two: Deluca's been going through Jordan's address book and contacting friends who might be able to shed some light on what happened—did she have a secret boyfriend, was someone following her, did she use drugs, and so forth. By the way, I pulled the stakeout on the Frenches' residence. Things are pretty busy up there right now, and I don't want our surveillance unit getting spotted by the press.

"Three: Banowski is still working the reservoir-gate angle, checking with anybody who has a key to fire road locks—DWP, Southern California Edison, Fire Department personnel, and Van Nuys Division cops.

"Four: I'm currently interviewing all employees and friends of the Frenches' who had access to the house. I have yet to contact the maid and Mrs. French's tennis coach. So far I haven't been able to get in touch with Jordan's family doctor, either."

"I seem to recall that you asked the parents to come in for testing?"

"Uh-huh. I downplayed it as much as possible, but I told them we needed hair, blood, fingerprints, and polygraph exams."

"And they agreed?"

"Yeah."

"I thought you didn't hold much faith in polygraphs."

"I don't," Kane admitted. "I just wanted to see whether they'd come in and be tested." Like most seasoned police officers, Kane distrusted polygraph exams—typically labeled "lie detector" tests by the uninformed—aware that the exams didn't reveal lies but merely measured *stress* experienced by a subject during questioning. The results, which were subjectively based on recorded changes in pulse rate, blood pressure, and perspiration, could be inconclusive or even erroneous if over the course of the exam the suspect wasn't particularly stressed by guilt or fear of punishment.

"So when are the parents coming in?" Long asked.

"They said sometime this week," replied Kane. "By the way, I ran a CLETS check on them," he added, referring to a California police database whose acronym stood for California Law Enforcement Telecommunications System. In addition to accessing a diverse range of California criminal and civil records, the system was hooked into the federal network, including FBI and military-service archives. "Neither parent has a criminal record or warrants outstanding," Kane continued. "Mrs. French is a governing member of the Los Angeles County Museum of Art and sits on numerous charity boards; Jordan's stepfather graduated from Harvard Business School and is a senior vice president of CyberTech Development Corporation, an Orange County firm selling digital-compression software and high-speed modems."

"Anything come back on the DNA testing on the ransom note?' Long asked.

"The Touch DNA analysis is underway," answered Kane, brightening slightly. "No results yet, but I did hear that there were apparently cells present on the adhesive side of the self-stick stamp, and we stand a good chance of getting a profile."

"So if that pans out, when the parents come in we'll run their DNA against the sample on the stamp."

"Right. But first we have to get them in for testing, and at present that's strictly voluntary," Kane said. "Speaking of the ransom note, I'm looking into a hunch on where the cutout words came from."

"Anything you want to share?"

Kane shrugged. "It's a long shot. I'll let you know if it pans out."

Long let his breath hiss between his teeth. "I don't mind telling you, Dan, I don't like the way things are shaping up."

"Me, neither," said Kane. "I want to believe the parents, but a lot of things don't compute. No follow-up on the ransom note, for instance. And not even *one* stray hair being found in Jordan's bed. Did someone change the sheets? And if so, why? Then there's the autopsy report indicative of chronic sexual abuse, not to mention there being absolutely no sign of inflammation in Jordan's throat or lungs—supposedly the reason she didn't go to work that day. No cold medications were found in her system, either. And why didn't Mr. and Mrs. French hear anything that night?"

"There could be perfectly reasonable explanations for all of those things," Long pointed out, playing devil's advocate.

"I know. But unless we come up with another suspect, I'll have to look hard at the parents."

"You realize the can of worms you'll be opening?"

"Unfortunately, I do," replied Kane, recalling similar, well-publicized cases in which the bereaved parents of a missing child became the primary focus of a police investigation. In instances like the Susan Smith drowning murders in South Carolina, police had been vindicated; others, including the heartbreaking homicide of a young girl in Colorado, had blown up in investigators' faces.

"I conferred with the DA this morning after I read the forensic reports," said Long. "Mr. Gerrard made it abundantly clear that he won't proceed against anyone, *especially* the parents, without sufficient evidence. He's not taking this to court on probable cause. Plainly put, he's not going to stick his neck out on this."

"Not surprising. The prick's up for reelection soon," Kane noted sourly.

Long nodded. "If someone gets stung, he wants to make sure it's us and not him. On the other hand, I'm getting daily calls from the mayor's office, our own Chief Ingram, and every news agency in town. They all want to know when we're going to have a suspect in custody."

"What are you saying, Lieutenant?"

"I'm saying that the clock's running on this, and there's a shitload of pressure coming down for an arrest. I'll keep the heat off you as much as I can, but as I told you before, there are those at headquarters who hope you screw the pooch on this." Long seemed about to add something more, then stopped. "Damn," he sighed. "Remember when we started out in police work, thinking we were going to make a difference?"

"Nah. I was always in it for the money."

"Yeah, sure," Long chuckled. Then, more seriously, "Dan, you're one of the best investigators I've ever worked with. If anyone can close this case, it's you. Whatever happens, I'll give you all the support I can."

"Thanks, Lieutenant," said Kane. "Don't worry, I want whoever murdered that kid. No matter how this plays out in the press, I'll bring in *whoever* did it—even if it turns out to be the parents."

"Fine. Just do it fast."

Later that day Kane pulled to the curb on Robertson Boulevard, a half block down from The Ivy restaurant. By then a late-lunch crowd had begun drifting into the trendy West Hollywood power spot where the Hollywood elite came to see and be seen. Killing the engine, Kane stared at the two-story bricked structure, wondering why its street-side patio with white table umbrellas, trellises of flowering bougainvillea, and enclosing picket fence looked familiar. Giving up, he shoved a handful of coins into a parking meter and crossed the road to the restaurant where the Frenches said they had celebrated their daughter's fourteenth birthday.

Several couples stood out front, waiting for their cars at a sidewalk valet station. Kane slipped past them and climbed a short flight of steps to the restaurant patio, still plagued by a feeling that he had been there before. He still hadn't figured it out when he reached the hostess station, an antique oak lectern set beneath a vine-covered awning that led into the main restaurant.

"One for lunch, sir?" asked a pert young woman standing there, giving Kane a crisp smile.

Kane flipped out his ID. "Not today. I'd like to speak with the manager, please."

The young woman's smile wavered. "Is something wrong?"

"Relax," said Kane, repocketing his ID. "I'm running a background check on Jordan French's activities prior to her abduction. I was told she had dinner here with her family three weeks ago. Thursday, June twenty-ninth, to be exact. Were you working that evening?"

"Uh . . . yes. Thursday's one of my nights." The young woman pursed her lips in thought. "I recall they came in around eight. Jordan and her parents."

"Anything unusual happen?"

"Like what?"

"I don't know—anything out of the ordinary. An argument at their table, a fan pestering Jordan, whatever."

The hostess hesitated. "Not that I noticed, but I was busy here out front most of the night. Let me get the manager."

As she hurried off, Kane checked a menu posted nearby on a large easel, then let his eyes travel the patio, recognizing several movie stars having lunch. On the far side of the terrace he spotted an older actor who had won an Academy Award some years back. The man was sitting with a gorgeous, long-haired brunette who bore a pronounced resemblance to Rene Russo. Seeing her jolted Kane's memory. A film buff, he suddenly realized why the restaurant looked familiar, remembering that The Ivy's bricked patio had been used for a pivotal scene in the movie *Get Shorty*.

Moments later the hostess returned, followed by a tall man wearing a bow tie and a mint-green jacket. Kane extended his hand. "Detective Kane, West L.A. homicide."

"Bert Kline," the man replied, nervously pumping Kane's hand. "It's just awful what happened, simply awful. I'll be glad to assist in any way I can. What is it you want to know?"

"Anything you could tell me about the night Jordan and her parents came in for dinner might be useful."

Mr. Kline thought a moment. "I'm sorry, but I don't recollect anything out of the ordinary happening that evening," he said regretfully.

"Maybe Detective Kane should talk with Terry," suggested the hostess, who had remained close by. "I'm almost certain he waited on their table."

"Is Terry here today?" asked Kane.

"That's him over there," answered the manager, pointing across the patio to a young man with thinning brown hair and a close-trimmed mustache. Order pad in hand, Terry was conversing with a rowdy group of older women who, from the thicket of bar glasses on their table, appeared more interested in drinks than lunch.

"Fine," said Kane, turning back to the manager. "One question first. Are any records kept of what customers eat for dinner?"

Mr. Kline looked puzzled. "You mean like the order slips that go to the kitchen? I'm afraid not. Once a bill is totaled, the order slip is discarded."

"Thanks. You've been helpful," said Kane. Turning, he started across the patio. "I may need to talk with you again," he added over his shoulder.

"Anytime."

Kane intercepted Terry as the young waiter was making his way back to the bar. Though initially as flustered as the hostess had been, the young waiter quickly proved cooperative. It turned out that he had indeed been the Frenches' server, and he recalled that Jordan had been celebrating her birthday. When asked about unusual occurrences, he shrugged. "Anything unusual? Not really. Except . . ."

"Except what?" Kane pressed.

"Well, it may not be for me to say, but Mr. French *was* hitting the wine pretty hard that night. He was slurring his words toward the end."

"How about Mrs. French?"

"She was fine."

"And Jordan? How was she?"

"I don't know," Terry answered. "I've served her a number of times over the years, and she was usually fairly friendly and outgoing. That night she seemed . . . quiet. Like she had something on her mind."

"Remember what she had for dinner?" Although Kane asked casually, his eyes never left the waiter's face.

Terry smiled. "Same thing she always has. Seafood capellini."

Kane felt his pulse quicken, recalling the gastric contents discovered at Jordan's autopsy. According to the coroner, Jordan's last meal, a pasta with red seafood sauce, had undergone a period of digestion of three to four hours before she'd died. But how could that be, unless . . .

"Seafood capellini. I noticed that on the lunch menu," said Kane, his mind still picking at the ramifications. "You serve it for dinner, too?"

"Uh-huh. It's a house special," said Terry, his voice dropping into a waiter's practiced cadence. "Clams, shrimp, scallops, and mussels simmered in white wine, garlic, tomato sauce, and a touch of cream—served over fresh angel hair pasta with a sprinkling of parmesan cheese."

"And Mr. and Mrs. French?"

"I think Mr. French had a steak, but I'm not sure. I don't remember what Mrs. French ordered."

Unconsciously, Kane began cracking his knuckles. "One last thing, Terry. Did the Frenches take home leftovers?"

"I didn't box anything for them, but one of the busboys may have," answered Terry. "That's their job, along with clearing tables. Do you want me to find out who was working that night and ask?"

"I'd appreciate it."

"No sweat." Terry scribbled a telephone number on the back of a napkin and handed it to Kane. "This is my home phone. If I'm not here at work, try me there.

Kane shoved the napkin into his pocket. "I'll check with you later. And thanks."

"Glad to help. I liked Jordan. She was a good kid."

Returning to his car, Kane puzzled over the discrepancy between the estimated time of Jordan's abduction and the conflicting evidence given by her partially digested final meal—a meal that according to Terry she had eaten *two nights* before being abducted from her house. Of course, as with much of the other evidence that had been piling up, there could be another explanation. Jordan could have taken home leftovers from The Ivy and eaten seafood pasta as a snack the following evening.

Kane suspected it was doubtful that anyone at the restaurant would be able to say with certainty that the family *hadn't* taken home part of their meal—making the gastric contents questionable as a means of establishing Jordan's time of death. But despite the uncertainties involved, it was one more thing that wasn't adding up. More and more, Kane was beginning to examine a possibility that he had originally considered only out of necessity. Unthinkable as it was, either one or both of Jordan's parents might have been responsible for her death. It wouldn't be the first time a parent killed a child, nor would it be the last. Still, nothing definite existed, and the case could still take off in another direction.

Nevertheless, in the words of Lt. Long, Kane didn't like the way things were shaping up.

# 15

Later that week I returned to my dorm room, exhausted from the day. Lately it seemed as if work, visiting Mom, and sleep were becoming my daily routine, with no time to see friends—even McKenzie. McKenzie and I did manage to keep in touch, however, by texting and an occasional phone call, like the one that had just come in from her. Having stepped from a hurried shower, I stood dripping in my dorm bathroom, towel around my waist, cell phone in hand.

"Hi, Ali. I'm glad I caught you," McKenzie's voice came over the line. "Seems like I haven't talked with you in ages. How's your mom doing?"

"She's doing all right, considering," I replied, experiencing a sinking feeling at the mention of my mother. I had spent time with her at the hospital after leaving work that evening, and although Mom's spirits had been good, I'd been shocked to see the decline in her appearance. "The chemo's really knocking her for a loop, but she'll be fine," I added, not allowing myself to consider any other possibility.

"Of course she will. How's your family holding up?"

"Nate's taking things hard, but Grandma Dorothy is staying at the house now," I replied. "She's been spending a lot of time with him—driving him to baseball practice, reading with him, that kind of thing. As for Trav, he acts like he's in a fog, practicing all the time. I think he's throwing himself into his music and preparing for his next recitals to forget what's happening to Mom."

"Trav's leaving again?"

"Uh-huh. He wanted to cancel the last of his Van Cliburn summer performances, but Mom wouldn't let him."

"And your father?"

I recalled the strain I had seen growing in Dad's face over the past days. "They set up a cot for him in Mom's room. He's been sleeping at the hospital," I answered. "He's also been making friends with all the nurses and hospital staff, doing his best to ensure that Mom gets the best possible care. He's even been bringing in extra food that friends and neighbors have been dropping by our house. Everyone at St. John's loves him."

"Sounds like your dad. So how's your job going?" McKenzie asked, steering the conversation in another direction. "Seen any more of that cute cameraman?"

All at once I remembered my date with Mike. "Shoot, look at the time," I groaned, glancing at the clock on my desk. "I have to get ready to go out, Mac. How about if we meet for lunch later this week and catch up? Maybe tomorrow or Friday?"

"Sounds great. Where are you off to tonight?"

"I have a date."

"A date? With who? Sorry. With *whom*?"

"Mike Cortese."

"You're going out with Mike again?" squealed McKenzie. "That's great! I want all the details."

"Mac . . ."

"No excuses. And call me for lunch."

After hanging up, I hurried to get ready, oddly apprehensive about going out with Mike. Why hadn't I just said no? I wondered for the hundredth time since accepting.

Because you want to see him, a defiantly honest part of my mind replied.

Frowning, I decided that whatever my feelings, I had agreed to the date, so I was going out with Mike and that's all there was to it. Once I had finished drying my hair, I walked to the closet and selected a short, summery dress and a pair of low-heeled sandals that showed off my legs. After slipping into my clothes, I applied a touch of mascara to my eyes, a hint of gloss to my lips. Hair up or down? I wondered.

Down.

Using an antique silver clasp Mom had given me on my eighteenth birthday, I fastened my hair loosely in the back and inspected my reflection in the bathroom mirror. Not bad, I thought, resolving that if this were the last time I went out with Mike, it would be *my* decision, not his.

"Ali! Someone's here for you," Mrs. Random called up the stairs.

"Be right down." Grabbing my purse, I took one last look at myself in the mirror and headed for the door. As I made my way downstairs, I saw Mike waiting at the bottom of the staircase, talking with Mrs. Random. The housemother, normally a sobering influence on any male visitor entering the dorm, was smiling at something Mike was saying. They both glanced up as I reached the lower landing.

"Hi, Ali," said Mike. "You look fabulous."

"Thanks," I said, taken aback by Mike's appearance. He had been casually dressed the night I'd accompanied him to Westwood—his thick black hair tousled, the shadow of a beard darkening his face. Tonight he was cleanly shaved, his hair neatly brushed, and he had on a stylish pair of slacks and a tan sport coat that despite his rough features gave him an air of polish and poise. "You clean up amazingly well yourself," I added.

"I'll take that as a compliment," laughed Mike, putting an arm around me. "C'mon, I'm parked outside in the red. Good night, Mrs. Random," he added to the housemother. "Nice meeting you."

"You too, Mike. I hope to see you again."

"You certainly charmed her," I noted as we made our way to the street. "It took me months to get in her semigood graces, and even that status is still shaky. What's your secret?"

Mike opened the passenger door of his pickup for me. "Turns out she and my mother went to Santa Monica College together," he answered. "They haven't seen each other since, but she recognized my name."

I slid in, watching as Mike circled the front of the Toyota, noting the way he moved with the unmistakable grace of an athlete. "Small world," I said as he climbed in behind the wheel. "Your mom will be surprised."

Mike started the pickup and pulled away from the curb. "My mother died a few years ago."

"Oh. I'm sorry."

"It's all right."

"Is your father . . . ?"

"He's been gone a long time now." Mike fell silent. Then, turning east on Sunset Boulevard toward Hollywood, he asked, "How are things at the network? Gone a few rounds with Liz yet?"

"Not yet," I answered. "I'm keeping in shape for the match, though."

Mike smiled. "Yeah, you seem fit. What do you do for exercise besides rescuing people from heavy surf?"

"I jog almost every morning before work, play a little volleyball, and hit the UCLA gym once in a while. How about you?"

"I mountain bike whenever I can. Been riding with the same guys since high school."

"You mentioned mountain biking when I saw you at the Frenches' estate. By any chance are you familiar with the area Mr. French was riding that morning?"

Mike thought a moment. "Probably. Topanga State Park is close to his house, and I've ridden most of the trails and fire roads there. Why?"

"No reason. Just curious."

On the drive to Hollywood Mike and I talked comfortably, our topics ranging from Mike's job at KCBS to my recent trip to Washington, D.C. By the time we reached our destination, the Directors Guild of America building, I found to my surprise that I was actually enjoying myself, my earlier apprehension about my date with Mike forgotten. "I've never been here before," I said, admiring the DGA building's sweeping curves and towering angles. "It's an interesting-looking structure."

"You'll like the theater inside, too," said Mike, glancing at his watch. "Plush seats, giant screen, Dolby sound. But we'll have to hurry. This thing's due to start in a few minutes."

Leaving his pickup in an underground lot, Mike and I took an elevator up to a ground-level lobby thronged with people, many in suits and formal evening wear. By then most of those present were drifting toward a pair of double doors accessing a theater at the far end of the room. I gazed around, recognizing a number of television and motion-picture personalities. "When you said this was a private screening, you didn't mention that it was going to be a major studio event," I noted.

"I didn't know it would be this big myself," Mike confessed.

"Cortese!" someone yelled from across the crowd.

I turned, spotting a handsome man in his mid-thirties waving to us from the theater entrance. Mike waved back, then took my arm and began guiding me through the crush of people. Upon arriving at the theater doors, Mike introduced me to his friend, Don Sturgess, who had been the director of photography on the film we were about to see.

"Pleased to meet you, Allison," said Don, shaking my hand. "Are you an actress? Seems like I've seen you somewhere before."

"She was the star of that surf piece I shot at the Wedge several weeks ago," prompted Mike.

Don snapped his fingers. "You're the girl who rescued that kid and then wouldn't give your name, though you *did* give Cortese here a little grief regarding his deplorable chauvinistic tendencies, as I remember."

"Guilty as charged," I laughed, wondering whether there was anyone in town who hadn't seen that news clip.

"Where's the better half, Don?" asked Mike. "Bonnie couldn't make it tonight?"

"Our babysitter canceled at the last minute, so she's home with the kids. She said to say hi, and asked when you're coming for dinner."

"Say hi back, and tell her I'll call."

"I will. Hey, congratulations on your documentary being accepted at Telluride. I'm proud of you, pal."

"Thanks," said Mike. "I'm still working on final edits and laying down the last of the music, but it'll be ready by Labor Day weekend. I hope."

"It'll be ready and it's going to be great," said Don. Then, turning to me, "I don't know if you're aware of it, but Mike is one hell of a cameraman. Have you seen any of his work?"

"Just a shot of me covered with goose bumps on a dock in Newport Beach," I replied.

"And a fetching shot it was," laughed Don. "Seriously, Mike's got photos in galleries all over town, and in my opinion his film work is even better." He turned to Mike. "I swear, you're wasting your time shooting TV news clips. I have another feature coming up. Why don't I see if I can get you on?"

"Let's see how the festival goes first."

"I know it's a big step and you don't want to leave that comfortable little nest you've feathered for yourself over at Channel 2, but with your talent—"

Mike cut him off. "Thanks, Don. Let's talk after the festival."

"You can be one obstinate sonofabitch," Don sighed.

Mike smiled self-consciously. "So I've been told."

"Well, *I* liked it," I said, continuing an exchange Mike and I had begun following the movie—a high-budget science-fiction thriller about Earth's first contact with an alien race—and continued nonstop throughout the drive to a small Mexican restaurant near Santa Monica.

"I'm not saying I didn't like it," Mike countered, sliding a menu across the table. "The cinematography and special effects were excellent, the acting was first rate, and the twist at the end capped off things nicely. I'm simply saying that I didn't believe the two of them together," he added, referring to movie's star-crossed lovers. "There was no chemistry, no passion. They could have written him out and not lost a thing."

"I won't contest that," I conceded. "But every film doesn't need a love story."

"No, but it helps."

"I disagree. Personally, I think romance is highly overrated."

Mike looked at me closely. "You do, huh? Are we still talking about the movie?"

"That *was* the topic of discussion," I shot back. Irked at myself for my revealing slip, I glanced around the interior of the room, noting that nearly everyone there appeared to be Hispanic—a good sign in a Mexican restaurant. At the far end of the room, a decorative terra-cotta tiled roof set off the kitchen, beside which sat a small grocery-and-takeout stand. Strolling among the tables, an accomplished guitarist was strumming a rendition of a vaguely familiar Mexican song. Deciding to change the subject, I picked up the menu. "Guelaguetza," I said, reading the name at the top. "Come here much?"

"Fairly often," said Mike. "I enjoy finding little hole-in-the-wall places. Guelaguetza may not look like much, but the food here is fabulous and the prices are reasonable."

I frowned. "I love Mexican food, but I don't recognize one single thing on this menu."

"That's because this is Oaxacan cuisine—*auténtica comida Oaxaqueña*—not the typical guacamole, sour cream, and melted-cheese dishes you mostly find around L.A."

"That's for sure. What's *cecina?*"

"Leg of pork marinated in chili paste, then thinly sliced and fried."

"*Clayuda?*"

"A handmade corn tortilla."

"*Tasajo?*"

"Grilled rounds of beef. Absolutely delicious."

"Ah, here's something I recognize. *Mole* is a sauce, right?"

"Right," said Mike. "There are different kinds and colors: red, green, yellow, black. Most are made from chili, nuts, seeds, and Oaxacan chocolate. I'll tell you what. Why don't I order for both of us? Is there anything you don't particularly like?"

I replied without hesitation. "Brussels sprouts."

"Not a problem," laughed Mike, signaling the waitress.

Without referring to the menu, Mike ordered a variety of exotic-sounding dishes along with *horchatas*—sweet rice beverages garnished with chopped melon and purplish cactus-fruit purée.

When the food arrived, I found it as tantalizingly delicious as it had sounded. "Mmmm, you were right about this place," I murmured between bites, captivated by the layering of flavors in each piquant sauce, especially the tar-black *mole negro* with its lingering hint of bitter chocolate. "My taste buds think they've died and gone to heaven."

172

Our conversation continued unabated during the meal, Mike and I talking easily of our lives as we shared the wonderfully unusual fare spread before us. I learned that Mike had graduated from Lincoln High School in Santa Monica, then spent four semesters at Santa Monica College before transferring to UCLA for his last two years, graduating cum laude. Surprisingly, his undergraduate major had been mathematics, a course of study he admitted having followed simply because he was good at it. Instead of continuing the postgraduate highway to a career in academia, however, he had taken a left turn and applied to film school, deciding to pursue a lifelong love of movies. Accepted at both USC and UCLA, he had chosen UCLA, supporting himself by working as a part-time photographer at KCBS. After he graduated from film school, Mike's temporary job at the news station had turned permanent. It was something he seemed reluctant to discuss, although he spoke openly about everything else.

For my part, I found myself opening up as well. I talked freely of my family, my job on the school newspaper, my writing, and my recent decision to become a journalist. Mike raised an eyebrow at the latter but didn't comment, instead steering the discussion back to my writing.

"You write every day, huh?" he said, sliding a tray of different *moles* across the table. "With school and now your new job, how do you find time?"

"I get up early," I answered. "A perverted predilection I picked up from my dad."

"He gets up early and writes, too?"

"Not hardly," I laughed. "My dad's not exactly a lover of literature. His idea of a good book is one with lots of colored pictures."

"Somehow I find that hard to believe."

"Why?"

"Because you're his daughter. Plus I know a bit about cops."

"Perhaps I'm exaggerating a little," I conceded. "He does read the newspaper. The sports section, mostly. And the funnies."

"Yeah, sure. So you get up early . . ."

". . . go for a run, shower, and put in a couple of hours at the keyboard. Usually I'm out of bed by five-thirty or so. Lately with my job at CBS, I've been getting up even earlier."

"Sounds rough."

"Writing? Not really. I love it."

"Why?"

I hesitated, taken off guard by the question. "I suppose because it gives me a chance to do something creative," I replied, not certain myself. "I don't have any illusions about penning the Great American Novel or setting the literary world on its ear, but when I'm working on a story, when I'm completely *immersed* in it, I feel good. Like you do with your camera work, I imagine."

Mike remained silent.

"Even when I'm not at the keyboard, I'm constantly thinking about my plots and scenes and characters—especially when things are going well," I continued, warming to the subject. "You'd laugh if you saw my notepads. I have them stashed everywhere—beside my bed, on the dashboard of the car, in my purse. I'll be walking to class or watching TV or whatever and stumble across something I can use, so I jot it down. Sometimes I even wake up in the middle of the night with ideas that seem to percolate out of my dreams. It's as if my brain's chewing on things in the background without my conscious mind even knowing it.

"Have you had anything published?"

"Yep," I replied, unable to mask my pride. "Two of my short stories have made it to print—one in *Asimov's Science Fiction*, another in a mystery magazine you've probably never heard of. I've also been writing articles for the UCLA *Daily Bruin*."

"News and mystery and science fiction?" Mike mused. "Interesting mix. I would love to read some of your work."

"If you want, I'll give you a copy of the story that ran in *Asimov's Science Fiction*," I suggested. "It's not bad, if I do say so myself."

"What's it called?"

"*Daniel's Song*."

"I look forward to reading it. What are you working on now?"

"A novel."

"What's it about?"

"A family."

"Contemporary?"

"Yes."

"Where does it take place?"

"Los Angeles, mostly."

"Autobiographical?"

I glanced away. "Not exactly."

"At least give me a clue. How does it begin?"

"Two brothers are rock climbing in the High Sierra."

"And . . . ?"

"And they have an accident. Listen, I'd rather not talk about my novel."

"Why not?"

"Just because."

"Can I read it when you're done?"

Again, I looked away. "I don't think so, Mike. I'm not planning on showing it to anyone, assuming I ever get it finished."

"Then why are you writing it?" Mike asked.

"I don't know," I replied, failing to answer a question I had pondered more than once.

Twenty minutes later, as I finished the last of my *nicuatole*, a tasty gelatin dessert that had capped off the meal, I looked up to find Mike studying me pensively.

"What?" I asked.

"Nothing. Just thinking."

"About what?"

"About why someone who's obviously a budding writer would want to go into television journalism."

I frowned. "You're the one who got me the job."

Mike raised his hands. "I know, I know."

"Sorry. It's a sore subject," I backtracked, aware I had been on the verge of overreacting. "My mom's been riding me about it."

"And what do you say to her?"

"I try not to talk about it," I replied, recalling my argument with Mom on our flight to Washington. "She thinks that because my older brother Travis is a musical prodigy, I should be gifted, too. She won't accept something I learned a long time ago: No matter how hard I try, I'll never be in Trav's league in the creativity department. Not in a million years."

"How do you know if you don't give it a shot?"

"You sound like her."

"Sorry," Mike apologized. "So instead of writing fiction, you've decided to set your sights on a career in which hard work, guts, and determination can pay off. I understand that. But why TV news?"

"To tell you the truth, that wasn't my goal—at least not at first," I admitted. "Originally I pictured myself in print journalism. Now I'm not so sure. The problem is, nobody reads much anymore. The average American adult spends four hours a day in front of a TV. Can you guess how much time gets spent reading a book?"

"No idea."

"Four minutes," I said. "Which begs the question: Why bother writing? TV is what the public wants—short sound-bites combined with the raw power of pictures—and television gives it to them."

"Sounds like you've been talking with Brent."

"As a matter of fact, I have. He's been more than helpful, and he thinks I have a chance of making it in television news. Of course, right now I'm at the bottom of the heap, but I've already made some progress."

Mike nodded. "So I've heard. Brent told me that your tip about your dad's search warrant put CBS on top of the ratings again last week."

I detected a note of reservation in Mike's voice. "You don't approve?"

"I didn't say that."

"Then what? If I can use my father's position to get an inside track and nobody gets hurt in the process, why shouldn't I?"

Mike leaned forward. "Look, I'm not making value judgments here. What goes on between you and your father is your business. I'm just saying that I know how things are at CBS, or at any news station, and with your dad being the—"

I cut him off, again sensing his disapproval. "I'm a big girl," I snapped. "I can take care of myself."

"In other words, mind my own business?"

"Not in other words," I shot back, my anger getting the better of me. "Those words are fine."

The atmosphere abruptly frosting, Mike paid the bill and escorted me to the parking lot in silence. When we reached his pickup, he fumbled with his keys, inserted one in the passenger-side door, and unlocked the truck. But instead of opening the door, he turned to me. "Listen, I'm sorry about what happened inside," he said. "I didn't mean to insinuate that you can't handle yourself at CBS, or that the reason you were hired was because of your dad."

At the mention again of my father, I fought back another surge of resentment. "No, I'm the one who should be sorry," I said. "I didn't mean to blow up like that. I have somewhat of a temper, in case you haven't noticed."

"*Somewhat* of a temper?" Mike chuckled. "If we're going to keep going out, I'll have to remember that."

"Who says we're going to keep going out?"

"I do."

"In that case, I'll attempt to keep my temper under control."

Mike moved closer, still holding my eyes with his. "Good."

Awash in a rush of nervous anticipation, I tried to speak but couldn't. It was a moment I had expected, unsure whether I wanted it to come or not. But when Mike gently lifted my chin and brought his lips to mine, I closed my eyes and kissed him back, a shiver of excitement coursing up my spine.

Mike touched my hair, then let his hand drop to his side. "I've wanted to do that for a long time," he said. He held me in his gaze a moment longer, then opened the Toyota's passenger door. "I suppose I should get you back. Tomorrow's a work day."

"Mike?" I said, at last finding my voice. "I . . . I'm really sorry about what happened inside. It was my fault for being too sensitive. Aside from that, I had a good time tonight."

"Just good?"

I grinned. "Good's a start," I replied. "Let's leave room for improvement."

"It's a deal."

Again, I hesitated. "Mike, would you do me a favor?"

"Sure. What?"

"On our way back, could you drop me by Saint John's Health Center?"

Mike looked puzzled. "Is something wrong?"

"My mom's there. She . . . she's being treated for leukemia."

"Oh. I'm sorry, Ali, I didn't know. Of course I'll take you. I'll wait outside and drive you home afterward."

"That won't be necessary," I said. "I don't know how long I'll be. Anyway, my dad's staying with Mom till she's over the worst, so I can get a ride from him or take a cab."

"I'll be glad to wait."

"I appreciate your offer, but just drop me off. And Mike?"

"What?"

"I meant what I said about having a good time tonight. Thanks."

# 16

Still thinking of Mike's kiss, I pushed through the doors of the Santa Monica Boulevard entrance into St. John's, signing in at the visitors' desk inside. After riding an elevator to the fourth floor, I walked down a wide hallway leading to my mother's room. I hesitated when I arrived. When I had asked Mike to drop me at the Health Center, visiting my mother had made perfect sense, even at that late hour. Now, as I stood outside my mother's room, I began to have doubts. Maybe Mom was already asleep. My dad was staying over, too. Knock? I wondered.

I tapped gently.

No response.

I turned the doorknob and stepped inside. A glow from the lights of Santa Monica lit the small room, the dim illumination from the window augmented by a number of red and green LED readouts on the monitoring machines and IMED medication pumps stationed by Mom's bed. Accompanying the medical machines, several IV stands with fluid-filled bags stood guard beside her as well. Framed pictures of our family sat atop a mobile cabinet nearby; balloons and an assortment of Nate's drawings adorned the walls. Still fully dressed from work, Dad was slumped on a cot near the window. He glanced up as I entered. "Ali. What are you doing here?" he asked softly.

"I was in the area and thought I'd stop by," I replied, struck by the bone-weary exhaustion in his voice. "How's Mom?"

Dad sat up. "Today was a rough one. She's sleeping now. Don't wake her."

I moved closer to Mom's bed, my heart dropping at her appearance. Over the past days her features had steadily taken on a skeletal gauntness, as though her flesh were melting away.

"Dr. Kratovil said everything is going as planned," Dad went on numbly, his voice barely a whisper. "She also told me that the HLA blood tests came back today. Grandma, Travis, and Nate aren't even close, but it seems you would make an acceptable marrow donor."

"Me?" I said, surprised at the news—recalling from my computer research that typically only siblings stood a chance of being human-leukocyte-antigen compatible, with children of the marrow recipient rarely so.

Dad nodded. "The doc said something about your being a better match than the haploid-identical three-locus match they expected, whatever that means, along with also being ABO compatible. You're not perfect, but if we need a donor and the registry doesn't come up with somebody better, it looks like you'll do."

I also recalled from my internet inquiry that a six-locus match was considered ideal for an allogenic graft, but even that wasn't perfect unless the transfer took place between identical twins. Worse, allogenic bone-marrow transplants were dangerous, with grave side effects and a significant mortality rate. "It won't come to that," I said. "Mom will be fine."

"I know," Dad said.

"You're tired, Dad. Why don't you go home and get some sleep? I'll stay here tonight."

"Thanks, but no."

Not knowing what to say, I eased down beside my father on the cot. We sat in silence, staring at the bed. Minutes passed. Just as I had decided it was time to go, Dad's cell phone buzzed. He pulled it from his jacket pocket. "Kane," he said quietly. A pause, then, "Thanks, Lieutenant. She's doing okay. Hold on a sec." Covering the phone with his hand, he glanced at me. "Stick around. I want a word with you before you leave."

Dad stepped outside. After he closed the door behind him, I walked to the window, staring out at the lights of the city. Idly I listened to my father talking in the hallway, taking comfort from the gruff resonance of his voice. His words, at first fatigued, gradually rose in volume, turning angry. "Let me get this straight," I heard him say, his tones now rumbling through the door like distant thunder. "You're telling me that even with all the discrepancies in their stories, the DA *still* won't go for another warrant?"

A pause. "Dammit, Lieutenant, we're coming up cold on every other front. The parents are the only—"

Another pause, this time longer. "Yes, sir. I'll see you tomorrow."

I waited for my father to return. After several minutes when he didn't reenter the room, I glanced one last time at Mom and left. I found my father leaning against a wall outside, a scowl darkening his face. "Trouble at work?" I asked.

"You might say that."

"The French case?"

Dad looked at me sharply.

"Sorry. Couldn't help overhearing."

Dad took my arm. "C'mon, princess," he said, marching me down the hall. "You and I need to talk."

"About what?"

Instead of answering, Dad escorted me to a nearby stairwell. Once away from the hospital rooms lining the corridor, he said sternly, "What I want to discuss is this job of yours. I had an enlightening talk with Deluca today. You were the reason that a CBS news van showed up at the Frenches' house last Friday, weren't you?"

"I . . ."

"The truth, kid. It was you who tipped the news crew about my search warrant."

"What if it was?" I replied nervously. "I did the same thing anybody would have—put two and two together and came up with four."

"Great defense," Dad snapped. "You're no worse than all the other media scumbags."

"Don't you think scumbag is a bit harsh?" I shot back, unable to hold my tongue. "*Everyone* in the news is not the enemy. People have a right to know what's going on. Brent says—"

"That would be Brent Preston you're referring to?"

"Right. He says—"

"I don't give a damn *what* Mr. Preston says," Dad snapped. "I don't like it when someone gets in the way of my investigation. And that includes you."

"Dad, we don't have to be on opposite sides on this. We both want the same thing."

Dad sighed. "You want a handful of aspirin, too?"

"No, we both want to find Jordan's killer. Besides, nobody got in the way of your investigation."

"This time, maybe. What about the next? Ali, when I agreed to let you work at CBS, it was despite your mother's objections. She was mad enough to spit tacks about your dropping out of summer session, but I—"

"I already apologized for not talking with her first."

"Did it sound like I was finished?"

"No, sir."

"Then button your lip."

"Dad, I—"

"Allison, your role in this conversation is to listen," Dad warned. "As I said on the night you sprung this news intern job on us, I let you take it because it's the first thing you've shown any interest in for quite some time. Plus, I figured you're old enough to make a few of your own decisions."

"Even if they're wrong?"

Dad frowned. "Yes, even if they're wrong. *Especially* if they're wrong. It's one way to learn. It's no secret what I think of the press, but if that's what you want to do with your life, I'll support your decision—on two conditions. First, and most important, I don't want you doing anything else to upset your mother. I told you that before. Our family has enough problems right now without your making them worse. Understood?"

I nodded guiltily.

"Second, I want you to steer clear of the Jordan French investigation."

"But . . ."

"No buts. Every time there's a news leak on the case, I'm the one who catches hell. From now on, anything you hear me say that relates to work, *including* my discussion just now with Lieutenant Long, is off the record. Cross that line again and you'll wake up in the next zip code. I swear, I knew this job of yours was going to cause trouble." Dad shook his head.

"Granted, you're bright and capable and I've never know anyone who works harder than you to succeed, but do you really think those are the only reasons Van Owen hired you?"

I started to fire back a caustic retort but hesitated, for the second time that evening struck by a truth I didn't want to hear. "Actually, I thought it might have been because you and she . . ."

Once more Dad shook his head. "I told you, that was over a long time ago. Lauren and I are on good terms, and I consider her a friend. A good friend. But there's no way my past association with her would rate any special treatment for you. When it comes to the news, that woman is all business."

"So you're saying that the only reason she hired me is because of your connection to the Jordan French case?"

"It may not be the only reason, but it's sure as hell part of the equation. The thought must have occurred to you."

Again, despite my doubts, I pushed aside the possibility. "My working at CBS isn't about you, Dad," I replied stubbornly. "It's about me."

## 17

The next day Brent Preston appeared on the *CBS Evening News*, reporting that Mr. and Mrs. French were under police investigation for the murder of their daughter. He added that according to police sources, inconsistencies had turned up in the parents' account of Jordan's abduction, and that authorities had unsuccessfully attempted to procure a second and more comprehensive search warrant to reenter the Frenches' estate.

Brent's exclusive report, CBS's lead story of the evening, ignited a media firestorm that quickly turned into an international news frenzy—with every network, newspaper, and magazine rushing to cover these new developments. And though I tried to tell myself it wasn't my fault, I knew this latest break in the story was again because of me.

The following afternoon found McKenzie and me sitting in the CBS cafeteria having lunch. While I morosely toyed with a small green salad, McKenzie enthusiastically dug into an order of sushi, her eyes wide with excitement as she scanned the room for media personalities. Earlier that morning I had suggested meeting at Farmers Market for our luncheon date. McKenzie had insisted that we eat at CBS Television City instead.

"Jeez, Ali. Intern job or not, I can't believe that you talked with Brent about the case after your dad ordered you not to," said McKenzie, taking a bite of sushi. "Knowing your father, he has to be livid," she added, her star-struck eyes darting like dragonflies about the cafeteria.

"Dad and I haven't spoken since Brent's newscast," I said glumly. "And that wasn't exactly how it happened." In truth, I was embarrassed at the part I'd played in Brent's latest exclusive, and regretful about how things had worked out. I couldn't believe I had trusted Brent. It was a mistake I wouldn't make again.

"So how *did* it happen?"

"Not to make excuses, but you had to be there."

"So tell me."

I sighed. "There's not much to tell," I said, pushing away my salad. "The morning after I talked with Dad at the hospital, Brent asked me point-blank whether I knew anything new about the case. I admitted that I did, but I said that what I had learned was off the record. Brent kept after me, saying we were professionals and promising that whatever I revealed to him would be off the record, too. I didn't have anything definite, except I knew that detectives from my dad's unit had been watching the Frenches' house. I also knew they had followed Mr. French for some reason. Along with what I overheard at the hospital, it added up to Jordan's parents being under suspicion. When I eventually shared my conclusions with Brent, he said he had been thinking the same thing, and that he was going to do some checking. Guess what? 'Off the record' means you can't use something *unless it's confirmed by an independent source.*"

"And Brent got confirmation?"

I nodded. "It took a while, but a contact of his in the DA's office revealed that the LAPD had tried for a second search warrant to reenter the Frenches' house. Brent also learned that my dad had asked for authorization to look for a murder weapon, nylon cord similar to that found on the body, blood and hairs in the Frenches' cars, and material related to the ransom note. The rest is history."

"I'll say. It's all I've seen on the news since."

"Brent says it was bound to come out anyway. It was simply a matter of time, and at least this way CBS got to break the story."

"Thanks to you," McKenzie pointed out. "Not to sound crass, but Brent wound up looking really good on this. What did you get?"

"There wasn't any quid pro quo."

"Not directly, but you got something, didn't you?"

"I *am* being treated differently around the newsroom," I admitted. "No more running for coffee and typing other people's stuff. Instead, Lauren has me doing background research on the French case. She's given me added responsibility in other areas, too.   She's sending me out with Brent this afternoon, for instance."

"Back to the Frenches' house?"

I nodded.  "Brent is doing another update."

"With all that's been going on, I'll bet that place is a zoo."

"It is.  I've heard that the vacant lot across from their house looks like a swap meet.  News vans everywhere."

"Do you think they're guilty?" McKenzie asked, lowering her voice.

"Mr. and Mrs. French?"

"No, the Dallas Cowboys Cheerleaders.  Come on, do you think they did it?"

"I don't know," I answered.  "But if they did, there's a good chance some kind of sexual abuse was involved—at least according to the research Lauren's had me doing.  Most abused kids are mistreated by family members, neighbors, or persons they trust, and it's more widespread than you'd think.  Did you know that roughly a *third* of all American women admit to having experienced childhood sexual abuse at the hands of an adult male?  For some reason, kids often keep it secret."

"That has to be a hard thing for a kid to carry around."

"Really hard," I agreed, remembering the humiliation of my own rape, a shame I had kept hidden from my parents for more than a year afterward.  "I still have trouble believing someone could do that to his or her own child."

"Jordan struck me as being a normal kid, at least from what I saw of her on TV," noted McKenzie.  "It wasn't like she had any deep, dark secrets."

"She was an actress.  Maybe she was good at hiding them."

"Maybe."

"So," said McKenzie, popping a final piece of sushi into her mouth.  "Gimme the vitals on your date with Mike.  That was the purpose of this little get-together, as I recall."

"In your mind, maybe.  Not mine."

"You like him, don't you?"

"Yes, if it's any of your business," I replied.  "When he's not irritating me, I like him a lot."

McKenzie grinned. "Good. And of course it's my business. I'm your best friend. Where did he take you?"

"We went to a screening at the Directors' Guild, then to a Mexican restaurant."

"For a writer, you're sure stingy with details," McKenzie complained. "C'mon, it's me you're talking to. What's he like?"

"Well, he's not what I expected," I replied. "According to a friend of his, Mike is a talented cameraman and filmmaker. A documentary he wrote, shot, directed, and edited is being shown at the Telluride Film Festival this fall, but for some reason Mike is reluctant to take the next step up in his film career—even though his friend offered to help." I shrugged. "I haven't figured him out yet. I suppose changing jobs and putting yourself on the line can be scary, especially when it comes to doing something creative. Maybe he's afraid of failing."

"Did you share that trite little observation with him?"

I smiled. "Despite what you consider to be my lack of tact with men, my judgment's not *that* bad."

"Good to hear. Has he called you since?"

"I talked with him last night. He invited me out this weekend."

"And?"

"And I asked for a rain check. With things heating up at CBS, I'm pretty busy."

McKenzie shook her head disapprovingly, then changed the subject. "Anything new with your mom?"

"This is her last day of chemo," I answered. "After that she begins three weeks of recovery."

"And then she's cured?"

"Unfortunately, no."

"I'm sorry, Ali," said McKenzie. Reaching across the table, she took my hand. "If I can help in any way, please let me."

I abruptly felt myself on the verge of tears, something that recently seemed to be happening more and more. "Thanks, Mac," I said quietly. "I appreciate the offer."

\*       \*       \*

At that precise moment Kane was leaving the West L.A. station house, taking the stairs down from the second-floor squad room two at a time. He bumped into Deluca as he hit the bottom landing. Deluca appeared harried, a scowl darkening his features.

"That doesn't look like happiness I see on your face, partner," noted Kane.

"After you run the news gauntlet outside, you won't be oozing joy either."

"The camera crews are still out there?"

"That's an affirmative."

"Damn," said Kane, belatedly wishing he had parked behind the station rather than in the police lot across the street. "I figured they'd be gone by now."

"No such luck."

Since Brent Preston's latest on-air revelations, the West L.A. station had been besieged by the press. Worse, Jordan's parents had retained the services of a prestigious Beverly Hills law firm. Subsequently, on advice of their new attorneys, they had refused to undergo polygraph testing, submit hair and blood samples, or speak with police without legal representation, if at all. In a later press release, however, they had announced they were perfectly willing to assist authorities in any efforts directed at finding their daughter's *real* killer or killers. Sensing the mood of the media, the district attorney had expressed confidence in the investigation, while at the same time distancing himself from any accusation of the parents. Furthermore, despite Kane's renewed request for additional warrants to collect hair and blood samples from the parents, the DA had again played it safe—maintaining that there was insufficient evidence to justify a new search.

Not privy to details of Kane's investigation that were progressively pointing toward the parents, many newscasters had grown skeptical—some even suggesting that Mr. and Mrs. French were under suspicion simply because inept LAPD detectives had failed to turn up other viable suspects. Complicating matters, intense pressure was coming down from the top for an arrest. *Any* arrest. It was a course Kane knew would be a mistake. Accusing the sex-offender gardener wouldn't pan out, and thus far evidence against the parents was sketchy at best. A comparison test with the ransom note DNA, assuming an analysis was possible, could either rule out or confirm Mr. and Mrs. French as suspects, but it looked like that was not to be—at least not without a warrant. And for that, investigators needed something concrete. *But what?* Kane was furious at the DA's obstructive stance and the recent turn of events in the media, but there was nothing he could do about either.

"So who do you think leaked to the press this time?" asked Deluca.

"Probably some jackass in the DA's office, although it might have come from the coroner's office, too," Kane replied. "Both are full of holes."

Deluca hesitated. "I hate to bring this up, *paisano*, but now that Allison is working for the news—"

"Don't go there," Kane interrupted. "If I even *thought* Ali had anything to do with this . . ."

"You heard that the chief is talking about having everyone connected with the case take polygraph exams?" said Deluca.

"I heard," Kane sighed. Both men knew that their police-union contract forbid mandatory lie detector testing of LAPD personnel. They also knew that if requested, they had no choice but to comply. "First I'd like to see them start testing our local prosecutors, then work their way through the coroner's office," Kane added.

"That'll be the day," Deluca noted dryly. Then, brightening slightly, "If you don't have anything going right now, let's grab some chow."

"Can't. I'm on my way to Sherman Oaks to talk with Jordan's family physician," said Kane. "Which reminds me. Did you contact Mrs. French's tennis coach?"

"I'm just coming from there," said Deluca. "The guy has an airtight alibi for the time Jordan disappeared. Anyway, he doesn't seem like the kind who goes for the kiddy set, either. I did some checking and found he's been giving a few of his middle-aged female clients more than tips on their backhand, if you catch my drift."

"Any criminal record, money problems, that kind of thing?"

"Nothing."

"Could he and Mrs. French have had something going?"

"Possibly," Deluca conceded. "But even if they did, I don't see how it would fit." He thought a moment. "What about the fire-road angle? Anybody with keys to the gates look promising?"

"Nope."

"What about the phone records?"

"We *are* making some headway there," Kane conceded. "Banowski ran down all telephone calls made from the French residence for the week prior to Jordan's abduction. He has yet to locate anyone who spoke with Jordan on the day *before* she vanished. Incidentally, the call to Paramount that morning was made on her parents' line, although we still don't know who placed the call."

"What about the maid?" asked Deluca. "Turn up anything on her?"

Kane shook his head. "She's clean. No run-ins with the law, no record, nothing. And as far as she's concerned, the Frenches are a model family without a single enemy. She did confirm that they occasionally bring home food when they dine out. She said Mrs. French lets her eat their leftovers for lunch."

"What about Jordan's birthday dinner at The Ivy? Any leftovers from that?"

"The maid didn't know. Seems Mrs. French phoned her that Friday morning and canceled her regular cleaning day. Mrs. French told her that Jordan was sick and didn't want to be disturbed."

Deluca raised an eyebrow.

"I got a call yesterday from one of the waiters at the restaurant where the Frenches celebrated Jordan's birthday," Kane went on. "According to him, none of the busboys recalls boxing any leftovers for the family that night."

"What do you think?"

Kane paused. "To tell you the truth, Paul, I'm not sure of anything. When I talked with the parents, they both seemed genuinely distressed about losing their daughter."

"So if they weren't involved, why do they need a lawyer?"

Kane shrugged. "It's no secret how these things can go on a case like this. Remember the investigation in Colorado where that little girl disappeared and then turned up dead in the basement? Hell, in some ways I don't blame Jordan's parents. We've uncovered a lot of discrepancies, but as our sterling DA pointed out, all those things could have perfectly logical explanations."

"If you say so," said Deluca, raising an eyebrow.

"Look, I have to get rolling if I want to make it to Sherman Oaks and back before rush hour," said Kane, not missing Deluca's dubious tone. "I'll talk with you later."

"Give my best to our brothers and sisters in the media out there."

"Right," Kane grumbled, starting toward the reporter-choked entrance. "I'll do that."

# 18

Over the ensuing weeks, hungry for anything new, the news media subjected Jordan's parents to the most intense scrutiny imaginable. At Brent's request, CBS even hired an information broker, a private investigator who for a hefty fee amassed copies of everything from the family's medical records and possible criminal histories to their dates of birth and social-security numbers, details of Mr. French's employment, summations of Mrs. French's charitable activities, telephone bills, financial credit reports, and driving records—even descriptions of their automobiles and license plate numbers. Though besieged by the press, Mr. and Mrs. French steadfastly refused all interviews, communicating with the media only through their attorney and publicist. Eventually they abandoned their home and went into hiding. Which, of course, made interviewing them even more desirable.

It was while perusing Brent's list of Mrs. French's charitable activities that I hatched the idea of contacting the Los Angeles County Museum of Art, noting that for years Jordan's mother had held a seat on the LACMA board of directors. After calling the museum, I fibbed my way past several layers of telephone bureaucracy, finally reaching the director's office. Identifying myself as the representative of a private foundation interested in making a donation, I learned in the course of talking with a friendly administrative assistant that the museum board was convening that afternoon on museum premises for its monthly meeting. It was a gathering all available board members were required to attend. Recalling Brent's advice about looking out for number one, I decided that this was too good an opportunity to let pass. After making certain that Brent, who had departed earlier for Orange County, was still out of the newsroom, I hurried to Lauren's office.

After listening to my proposal, Lauren initially refused. "Out of the question," she said. "This is Brent's story. He'll handle it."

"Brent's in Irvine doing a spot on Mr. French's software company," I countered. "If we're going to have *any* chance of getting an interview with Jordan's mother, someone has to leave immediately."

"And that someone should be you?" Lauren said skeptically.

I nodded. "I totally agree. Thanks."

"Sorry, Ali. I need someone more experienced. One of the other correspond—"

"But you already sent me out with a cameraman to watch the Frenches' estate," I interrupted. "Why is this any different?"

"It just is," said Lauren, her tone cooling. "For one thing, the story has changed considerably since then. For another, you're not qualified to do an interview. Now, where do you think Mrs. French is going to be?"

I didn't respond. When laying out my plan to Lauren, I had purposely withheld the details of Mrs. French's engagement, saying nothing about the museum or its board of directors' meeting. Instead, I'd simply stated that I had a hunch where Jordan's mother would be later that afternoon.

Lauren stared. "You're not going to tell me?" she said, her voice hardening.

"Listen, she might not even be there," I reasoned, dodging the question. "It's a long shot. Why waste a staff correspondent? Let me check it out. I'll take one cameraman and be back in a couple of hours. If it doesn't pan out, nothing's lost. And if it looks like Mrs. French is going to show, I'll call for reinforcements," I added, lying.

"Absolutely not." Lauren scowled. "This has gone on long enough. Where is Mrs. French going to be?"

I still didn't reply, my temper beginning to flare. Lauren wasn't being fair. After all, I had been the one who figured things out. Why shouldn't I be the one to go?

"Damn it, Allison. Are you going to tell me or not?"

I shook my head, deciding I had gone too far to turn back.

"I could fire you for this," Lauren warned.

"What would that accomplish?" I retorted, part of me wishing I could start over, another part realizing it was too late. "C'mon, Lauren. Give me a chance. What have you got to lose?"

Lauren remained silent for several seconds, chewing it over. "All right," she finally conceded. "As you said, it's a long shot. But if you *do* get lucky, make sure you call immediately for help."

"Thanks," I said, heading for the door before the bureau chief could change her mind. "I won't let you down."

Accompanied by Max Riemann, the cameraman who had accompanied me to the Frenches' estate, I drove to the museum. After parking on a side street, I left Max in the car and walked back to museum grounds. Within minutes I located Mrs. French's silver Lexus in a private parking lot reserved for museum officials—matching the vehicle and license plate to the description given in Brent's information-broker report. I had been right. She *was* there.

Disregarding my promise to Lauren to call for backup, I hurried back to my car, then returned to the museum—this time with Max and his camera equipment. Careful not to attract attention, we positioned ourselves behind a concrete pillar at the rear of the parking lot, waiting for Mrs. French's meeting to end. It took several hours, but our patience eventually paid off. Initially, however, Jordan's mother made it clear that she had no intention of speaking with anyone—especially someone thrusting a microphone in her face.

"Mrs. French, do you have any comment on the LAPD targeting you and your husband as suspects in Jordan's murder?" I asked, walking briskly to keep up with Jordan's mother as she hurried toward her Lexus. Following close behind, Max kept his lens angle wide, bracketing both Mrs. French and me in a traveling two-shot.

Mrs. French increased her pace without responding.

"Many people think you're being treated unfairly by the police," I persisted. "Is there anything you want to say in your defense?"

Irritated, Mrs. French glanced at me. A look of recognition lit her eyes. "I know you," she said, stopping for a moment. "You're the girl who rescued that kid at the beach."

Though surprised, I ignored her question and tried to get back on topic, switching to another one of my prepared questions. "With all the confusion surrounding the investigation, do you—"

"My attorney has advised me not to talk about the case," Mrs. French stated, starting again for her car. Abruptly, she stopped. "Actually, there *is* one thing I would like to say," she added. "I want to thank all of Jordan's fans and friends who have been so supportive during this terrible time. Jordan was a wonderful, loving child, and I miss her terribly. I wish . . ." Mrs. French's words trailed off.

Though I felt a surge of compassion, I held the microphone steady. As Jordan's mother fought to regain her composure, I noticed Max slowly tightening his camera angle. "I want everyone to know how much I loved her," Mrs. French said at last, tears shimmering in her eyes. "How much my husband and I both loved her."

"And what would you tell those who think you were involved in your daughter's death?" I asked softly.

Mrs. French gazed into the camera. "I would tell them that it's a heartbreaking thing to lose a child, and being accused of her murder has made it all the more horrible," she answered, her eyes brimming. "We loved our child. We didn't kill her."

The spot was featured that night on the *CBS Evening News*. It was subsequently aired on every network affiliate across the country. Granted, nothing substantive came from my interview with Jordan's mother, but the emotional tenor of the piece was exactly what the viewing public wanted—an intimate moment with Mrs. French, a mother suspected of complicity in her daughter's death.

Ratings soared, with calls flooding in from people wanting to know whether Allison Kane was really the girl who had appeared in the beach-rescue segment a month earlier. Interest in me was spurred even more when the connection was made between me and Detective Daniel Kane, lead investigator on the case. Unlike the tabloids and other mainstream news stations, CBS chose not to comment on my family connection, but management privately indicated that further on-air appearances by me were under consideration—*particularly* in relation to the French case.

On the downside, Brent was incensed. It was his story, and I had scooped him. Eventually I managed to smooth things over, at least I thought I did, but in the process I saw a dangerous, vindictive side of Brent that I didn't like. I knew I had come close to burning a bridge, but at the time the chance to snag an interview with Jordan's mother had seemed worth the risk. Plus it was my idea, and Brent was the one who had told me to look out for number one.

But now, with reporters mobbing me in the Television City parking lot and the news-starved media suddenly concentrating on *me* and my connection to the case via my father, I began to regret my rashness. It was a regret that burgeoned as the story gained momentum, threatening to steamroll anyone in its path.

Two nights later, following a tiring day at work and an even more exhausting visit with my mother at the hospital, I lay on my dorm room bed. Glumly, I stared at the ceiling, thinking that my on-air debut as a network reporter hadn't proved as satisfying as I'd hoped. Covering the news was one thing; *being* the news was another.

My cell phone rang, jolting me from my thoughts. Rolling over, I grabbed my phone. "Hello?"

"Hi, Ali. Mike here. I thought I'd extend my congratulations on your breaking into the big time."

I hadn't talked with Mike since our date. His voice sounded reassuring, a familiar note in a world that seemed progressively spinning out of control. "Do you mean it?" I asked, recalling his low opinion of the news.

"Absolutely," said Mike. "You pulled off what no one else had been able to do—get one of the Frenches to talk on-camera. And to think I warned you to be careful around Brent. Knowing him, I'm sure he's fuming."

"There wasn't time for him to get there," I explained, sounding unconvincing even to myself.

"Don't worry, I'm on your side," Mike said lightly. "So how's about we get together tomorrow night for a little celebrating?"

"Friday?"

"Today's Thursday, so that sounds about right."

"Sorry, Mike. I can't. I'm visiting my mom tomorrow night."

"Oh."

"Our entire family is meeting at the hospital to mark the end of her third week. Seven more days and she's out, at least for a while."

"That's great, Ali. I'm really glad to hear that."

"Me, too. Listen, I've been swamped at work and visiting my mom, but after her release we're having a party at the beach. It'll be a combo birthday bash and a homecoming celebration for Mom. Sunday, the eleventh, beginning around noon. Would you like to come?"

"Sure," said Mike. "It's your mom's birthday?"

"No. Mine."

"Well, happy birthday in advance. How old will you be?"

"Twenty. And no presents."

"Whatever you say. Who's coming?"

"Oh, probably several hundred of our closest friends," I sighed, trying to sound matter-of-fact and almost succeeding. "My dad will invite all his pals at work, meaning at least half the department. Mom and my brother Travis will call their music associates, and there'll be at least thirty or forty neighbors—not to mention my kid brother Nate's baseball buddies. Plus, I invited friends from school. Even a few from CBS."

"Brent?"

"Actually, Brent sort of invited himself. Not that he isn't welcome, as far as I'm concerned, but with the French case and all, my dad . . ."

". . . may not be overly thrilled to see him."

"That's an understatement you would have to know my father to appreciate."

"I've met your father," said Mike.

"You have? When?"

"A long time ago. Listen, I have to go, but I appreciate the party invitation. I'll definitely be there. Text me the address. And again, congratulations."

"Thanks. See you, Mike."

After hanging up, I lay on my bed replaying our conversation, wondering how Mike knew my father and wishing I had asked. Finally giving up, I padded downstairs to fix myself something to eat, again thinking that Mike Cortese was full of surprises.

# 19

When I arrived at the hospital the next evening, Travis and Nate were already there, along with Grandma Dorothy. With all of us present, Mom's small room seemed almost festive. Adding to the party ambiance, Nate's collection of pencil-and-watercolor sketches had grown to blanket almost one entire wall. In addition, a tether of colored balloons rose from the foot of the bed, and a chocolate cake, its three candles still unlit, sat atop a nearby cabinet. The IV stands, monitors, and medication pumps were still present too, their forbidding presence a depressing reminder of why Mom was there.

As I entered, Mom turned toward me and smiled. By now having lost most of her hair, she wore a stylish white turban, and for the evening's gathering she had applied a touch of makeup to her face and lips. Despite all she had been through, she was still beautiful. "Hi, Ali," she said. "Just in time for cake."

"Hi, Mom," I replied, noting with relief that although she hadn't regained her appetite and was still being fed intravenously, her features had lost some of the skeletal gauntness that had accompanied the worst of her treatment. "Cake time, huh?" I said, crossing the room to wash my hands. "Want me to light the candles?"

"Let's wait for Dad," suggested Nate. "He's coming, isn't he?"

"He's coming," said Grandma Dorothy. "He called from work to say he might be a little late. I told him to get here on time, but of course he never listens to me," she added tartly, a look of fondness in her eyes belying her tone. "Irritating man. It would serve him right if we just went ahead without him."

I smiled at Grandma, not for the first time noticing her resemblance to my mother. Though in her early sixties, Grandma Dorothy was still a strikingly attractive woman.

"Let's give Dan a couple more minutes," suggested Mom. Then, turning to Travis, "Tell me about your Seattle recitals, Trav. How did they go?"

"Great," answered Travis. "Speaking of which, I talked with the Van Cliburn committee about canceling the last of my engagements. You'll be back at St. John's by then, and I—"

"No," Mom broke in firmly. "We've discussed this before. Grandma is taking care of things at home, so there's no reason why you shouldn't honor your commitments."

"But—"

"No buts, Travis."

Travis sighed. "Yes, ma'am."

Sliding into a chair beside Travis, I shot my brother a sympathetic grin. Then, to my mother, "You're looking better, Mom."

Mom reached out and gave my hand a squeeze. "Thanks."

"Hey, guess what?" said Nate from the other side of the bed. "I'm gonna get to play in the AAU finals."

"AAU?" Mom looked puzzled. "I swear, honey, I can't keep track of your baseball schedule these days. The last I heard, you were in a Pony League all-star tournament."

"Yep," Nate replied proudly. "We lost the last round of the sectionals, though. Anyway, the AAU finals are coming up. The team that won the regionals is missing a player. They want me to fill in."

"That's wonderful, Nate."

"Are you sure it's okay? I won't if you—"

"I want you to play," Mom insisted. "I'm just sorry that I'm missing so much of your season by being in here." Then, still holding my hand, she turned back to me. "At least one of my children isn't hesitant about getting on with her life."

"We all saw your news piece, Ali," said Travis. "Impressive, sis."

"Yeah," Nate chimed in. "That was really cool. Did you get paid a lot?"

"I wish," I said. "Although there is talk of letting me do other on-air spots. If that happens, I might get a raise. Maybe my press credentials, too."

"This *is* just a summer job, isn't it?" asked Grandma. "You still plan to transfer to USC in the fall?"

Faced with a question that had increasingly occupied my thoughts, I squirmed uncomfortably.

"Of course she'll be continuing her college education in the fall," Mom answered for me. "Dropping out of summer session was one thing; not completing her education isn't even up for discussion."

The mood in the room suddenly chilled. I withdrew my hand from my mother's grasp. "I haven't made up my mind one way or the other on that, Mom," I said slowly. "But what would be so wrong with my taking off a semester and getting some job experience? After all, if I want to be a journalist, why not—"

"Allison, hounding some poor woman in a parking lot is *not* journalism. You're a blossoming writer. It would be a terrible mistake for you to drop out of school."

"Dad thinks the poor woman you say I *hounded* may be involved in her daughter's death," I countered.

"Is that what *you* think?"

"What I think is not the point. Reporters aren't supposed to take sides."

"So what *is* the point?"

"The point is that Mrs. French is news. And people want to hear what she has to say."

"Even if she doesn't want to say it."

"Right," I retorted.

"How about if we cut the cake now?" interjected Nate.

"In a minute, honey," said Mom. "This is important." Paled from exertion, she started to add something but was overcome by fit a coughing. Scowling at me, Nate picked up a box of tissues and handed it to Mom.

Though regretting my quarrel with my mother, I pushed ahead anyway. "I appreciate your concern, Mom, but I'm old enough to make my own decision on this. And if I want to take time off from college, I don't see what's so wrong with that."

"What's wrong is that you should be focusing on your studies," Mom finally managed over her coughing. "Especially your writing. Journalism may prove to be a satisfactory outlet for your talents, Ali. But not like this."

"Nothing I do is ever good enough for you, is it?" I snapped, stung once more by her tone. "Mom, everyone can't be a concert cellist like you, or a prodigy like Travis. The rest of us have to make do with what we've got."

"You have a lot more going for you than you think, and I would hate to see you waste it," Mom said, struck by another fit of coughing. "Please trust me. I know I'm right about this."

"You're *always* right," I shot back, recalling that I had said the same thing to her on the plane.

"Ali, shut up!" Nate shouted. "Don't say another word to Mom. Just shut up."

I stared at my younger brother, startled by his outburst.

Nate glowered back. "Why do you always have to be so mean?" he demanded, close to tears.

"Nate . . ."

"Get out. We don't want you here."

I glanced at Travis, then at Grandma Dorothy. Neither met my gaze. With an angry shrug, I stood. "I'll call you tomorrow, Mom."

"Please don't go," Mom begged, her voice filled with hurt. "We . . . we haven't even cut the cake yet."

"I'm not hungry," I said. "I'm sorry I lost my temper," I added, regretting my earlier words but knowing I couldn't take them back. Feeling everyone's eyes upon me, I hurried out the door.

Seconds later, as I made my way down the hall, I noticed my father exiting one of the elevators on Mom's floor. Dad looked tired, the strain he was under clearly having taken its toll. "Party over?" he asked as I approached.

I avoided his gaze. "Not yet. They're holding off cutting the cake till you arrive."

"Why aren't you in there?"

"I have things to do at work."

"Is that right?" Dad looked at me sternly. "Well, speaking of that, I caught your interview with Mrs. French. Damn it, Allison, do you have any idea how much trouble you're causing me?"

I looked away, exasperated at walking out of one argument and into another. "What is this, pick on Allison night?"

"If the shoe fits, Allison. In case you don't know, everyone on the French investigation is taking heat about leaks to the media. Now that the word is out you're working for CBS, can you guess who the brass are looking at whenever the subject of leaks comes up? Me." Dad hesitated, then added, "And I'm not so sure they don't have good cause."

"What do you mean?" I asked guiltily.

"Well, for one thing, I told you that Mr. and Mrs. French being under investigation was off the record, and you agreed to keep your yap shut. Next thing I know, it's headline news. What'd you do, blab to someone at CBS? Lauren, maybe?"

I looked away. "I . . . I mentioned it to Brent," I admitted. "But I told him it was off the record. I didn't realize he could use it anyway if he got independent confirmation from someplace else. Which he did."

Dad's eyes narrowed. "Where?"

"The DA's office."

"That's what I thought." Glaring, Dad began cracking his knuckles. He glanced toward Mom's door down the hall, then back at me. "Do you understand the position you're putting me in?" he demanded, lowering his voice. "Have you seen the tabloids? 'Detective's Daughter Scoops Network Reporters!' You're making it look like I'm running some kind of Chinese fire drill."

"I can't help that," I said.

"Bull," Dad said, his temper now barely in check. "For one thing, you could quit that so-called job of yours."

"And what good would that do? The damage is already done. I'm not quitting my job. But in the future I'll do my best to stay out of your way on the French case."

"Like you have so far?" Fuming, Dad strode down the corridor without looking back.

I watched as my father entered Mom's room. Then, with a despondent sigh, I turned toward the elevators, again recalling my resolution never to do anything to make my family's problems worse.

Well, that promise is certainly shot to hell, I thought glumly.

Arriving at the elevators, I thumbed the call button, wondering whether I should simply quit my job at CBS, move home, and make everyone happy.

No, a stubborn part of my mind replied.

Why not?

Because it's not what *I* want.

And what is it that I want? I asked myself. What is it I want so bad that I'm willing to fight everyone to get it? Being a hotshot news correspondent like Brent? Seeing myself on television? Proving I can do something on my own? What?

No answer came.

With a chime, an elevator door opened. I stepped inside and placed a finger on the lobby button. Then, instead of pushing the button for the ground floor, I exited. On the day Mom had begun her treatment, my brothers and I had visited a small chapel on the fourth floor, not far from Mom's room. On impulse, I decided to visit it again.

With a final glance over my shoulder at Mom's room, I made my way down the hallway. After navigating several corridors and passing a nurses' station, I found the chapel. Glumly, I pushed through a heavy door into the deserted chamber beyond. Before me, several banks of wooden pews sat in front of a white-clothed altar. Smelling a cloying vestige of incense, I walked past a confessional in the rear, not quite sure why I was there.

Because it beats going back to an empty room at UCLA, my inner voice prompted.

Oh, shut up.

Exhausted, I eased into one of the rear pews, my mind filled with thoughts of my mother, and of my father, and of the burden my recent actions had placed on my family. In the solitude of the chapel, I reviewed my life over the past weeks, coming up with various rationales and justifications for the things I had done. Somehow, my reasoning always rang hollow. Worse, as the minutes ticked by, I found to my irritation that I was better able to argue my parents' position than my own.

Though in a chapel, I didn't feel like praying. Not surprising, as I hadn't prayed since losing my brother Tom. I still believed in God . . . mostly. I just couldn't understand how He could have let Tommy die. At first, after Tommy's death, I wasn't able to accept that it had really happened. Tommy's death had seemed so unnecessary, so *unfair*—like something that had happened in a dream. I kept hoping to wake up and find he was still alive, but of course that didn't happen. And as time went on, as days ground into weeks, and weeks into months, as Tommy's loss became real and the reality of his death replaced my denials with a flood of wishes and what-ifs and regrets, I accepted at last that the world can be heartbreaking and cruel, and as much as I wished it were otherwise, that terrible things can happen in life— things that will never, ever get better.

And now, with a hollow feeling of despair, I realized that God was threatening to take away my mother as well . . . and there was nothing I could do about it. Hot, bitter tears stung my eyes, blurring my vision. I fought them. Still they came. At last I lowered my head and let them flow, feeling more desolate and alone than I had since Tommy's death.

Time passed.

Behind me, I heard the chapel door creak open.

"Ali?" someone called into the room.

Travis.

"She's not here," I answered, furiously palming my eyes.

Moments later Travis joined me in the back pew, slumping down beside me on the hard wooden bench.

"Go away, Trav. I want to be alone."

He didn't reply.

"What are you doing here, anyway?" I asked.

Travis shrugged. "I might ask you the same thing. You haven't seen the inside a church for quite a while."

"Haven't seen any point. Actually, I'm not quite sure how I feel about God these days."

"Dad would consider that no excuse for not being a good Catholic."

I ignored my brother's attempt at humor. "Why are you here, Trav?" I asked again. "I thought everyone would be gone by now."

"I saw the Bronco still in the parking lot. I figured you were probably up here."

"Clever you. Are Grandma and Nate waiting downstairs?"

"No. Mom got tired toward the end. After we had cake, everyone left but Dad."

"You didn't ride in from Malibu with Grandma?"

"I borrowed a friend's car and drove here earlier." Travis glanced around the chapel, then changed the subject. "McKenzie says you've been dating somebody recently."

"I've gone out a few times with a cameraman who works at Channel 2," I answered, grateful to be thinking about something besides Mom.

"Any chance for new developments in the romance department?"

I shrugged. "Doubtful. Right now I'm trying to get something going with my life."

"Who says you can't do both?"

"I do. I'm not saying that having a relationship isn't right for some people, just not for me. It's going to take everything I have just to get ahead. In case you haven't noticed, I don't have the luxury of being a musical genius like you."

"Ali, you're gifted, too. Everyone who's read your stories thinks—"

"—I have potential," I finished, fighting a surge of anger rooted in a lifetime of living in my brother's shadow. "Or worse, that my work shows *promise*. We've had this discussion before, Trav, and it always boils down to the same thing. I could write from now till doomsday and never reach your rarefied level of talent, and we both know it. But if I work really hard, sometime in the distant future I might actually be good. But *great*? Never. Well, screw that. I have an opportunity right now to make something of myself at CBS, and I won't foul it up by getting sidetracked by anyone or anything."

"You're wrong about your writing, Ali."

"Who made you a literary critic?"

"Jeez, why do you act this way? And don't give me some line about wanting to have a career. You'll probably get angry at me for saying this, but ever since the night you were attacked—"

"Stop right there."

"I—"

"Please, Trav. Just . . . drop it."

Silence hung between us like a gathering storm. At last Travis asked, "What's going on, sis?"

"Nothing."

"C'mon, Ali. It's me you're talking to. What's up?"

I looked away. "Nothing."

"Dad mentioned running into you in the hall. I don't imagine that meeting was one for the family scrapbook."

"It wasn't."

Travis looked at me closely. "But your fight with Dad isn't what's really bothering you, is it?"

I remained silent.

"Please talk to me, Ali."

Finally I answered. "This may sound stupid, but for the longest time after Tommy died, I couldn't believe he was really gone," I began, my voice barely audible. "I just couldn't believe it. Then, when it finally did sink in that I would never see him or hear him or talk with him ever again, the realization was almost more than I could bear."

Travis gave my hand a squeeze. "Me, too," he said quietly. "And now Mom."

"And now Mom," I echoed. "I'm so worried. What if she—"

"Mom will come through this," Travis interrupted, his words a bit too forceful.

"I hope so. What I hate most is that even with all that's going on, she and I still can't be in the same room without getting into a fight."

"I know what you mean. Remember how Dad and I used to be?"

"Who can forget? How did you ever get things straightened out with him?"

Travis thought a moment. "Mostly, I think I just got older."

"Fine. I'll just wait to get older."

"Do that. And while you're at it, remember that no matter how pushy Mom can be, she only wants what's best for you."

"I know," I sighed. "That's what makes it so hard."

Travis shifted restlessly, seeming to have something else to say.

"What is it, Trav?"

Travis took a deep breath, then let it out. "Can I level with you, sis?"

"No. Just keep lying."

"At the risk of pissing you off again," Travis continued, "I'm going to give you some advice. It's this: Get your priorities straight."

"What's that supposed to mean?"

"Exactly the way it sounds. I know you have plenty on your mind right now—your new job at CBS and decisions about school and Dad getting on your case for screwing with his investigation. But maybe it's time for you to ask yourself what's *really* important. It's not school or work or any of those other things. It's family. It's the people you love and who love you."

"After you read that, did you eat the cookie?"

"I'm serious, sis."

Irritated at my brother's unsolicited advice—which I took to be tacit criticism of my position at CBS—I started to reply with another sarcastic retort but stopped, struck by a familiar chord in his words. "Mom told me something like that, too," I said instead, recalling my exchange with my mother on the plane.

Travis nodded. "I'm not surprised. Think about it, Ali. You may find it makes sense."

# 20

Wednesday, at a little before noon, Kane pulled up to the Paramount Pictures employee gate on North Gower Street, avoiding the tour entrance on Melrose Avenue. He lowered his window and identified himself, then waited impatiently as the gate guard placed a call to Ron Bannock, the studio chief of operations with whom Kane had spoken earlier that morning. A moment later the guard handed Kane a pass and waved him through. Following directions received previously over the phone, Kane eased his car down a long asphalt lane lined with sound stages, trailers, golf carts, sets, props, and film equipment. Everywhere he looked he saw extras in costume, grips pulling gear from the backs of trucks, electricians setting up lights, and men transporting equipment.

Wheeling through acres of Paramount real estate, Kane headed for a blue water tower he could occasionally glimpse between sound stages. He lost his way while navigating a snarl of streets deeper in, taking an unintentional detour past an enormous blue-sky backdrop and a clump of brownstone buildings that looked like they had been transported directly from New York's Upper East Side. Eventually he found the water tower he had spotted earlier. A number of cars were parked in an open square at its base. No sign of Ron Bannock. Deciding he would never find his way around the chaotic movie lot without assistance, Kane eased his Ford next to a white Mercedes, shut off the engine, and waited.

As Kane sat, his mind began chewing on details of the investigation. No matter how he tried to tell himself otherwise, he knew that unless something changed, the French case—mired in a media blitz and saddled with a self-serving district attorney—would soon stagnate. In Kane's experience, most homicide cases were closed quickly or not at all. Every day that passed, the murderer's trail cooled, witnesses' memories grew cloudy, evidence evaporated. And although Kane hated to admit it, he knew that progress on the case had nearly ground to a halt.

Upon questioning, Dr. Sidney Taylor, the Frenches' family physician, had staunchly maintained that Jordan could not have been the victim of chronic sexual abuse. Over the past six years he had seen her in his office on more than thirty occasions, and according to him, at no time had he detected any physical signs of sexual molestation, nor had he observed any of a wide range of psychological manifestations associated with abuse. Jordan had simply been a bright, normal kid. On the other hand, no vaginal exam had ever been done with a gynecological speculum, so physical symptoms might have been missed. Furthermore, given the circumstances of Jordan's death and that healthcare personnel were required by law to report suspected instances of child abuse, Kane surmised that Dr. Taylor was probably disinclined at that late date to admit he might have missed something.

In performing a background check on Jordan's parents, Kane and other members of the homicide unit had talked with neighbors, friends, and coworkers. Though Mr. and Mrs. French were generally well liked, they were also characterized as being extremely private. No one in their neighborhood had actually known them well, and the few casual friends of the Frenches that Kane had been able to find described Jordan's mother as being obsessed with her daughter's acting career—a typical "movie mom" who for years had fiercely shepherded Jordan's meteoric rise in the acting world. Working tirelessly, Mrs. French had procured an agent for Jordan by her third birthday, chauffeured her daughter to casting calls, and overseen her early work in TV commercials and daytime soaps. Eventually Mrs. French had been pivotal in Jordan's being cast in the prime-time family series, *Brandy*—and the rest was history. Though outwardly pleasant, Mrs. French was also described as a driven woman who, when challenged, could become as hard as tempered steel.

Mr. French's associates at CyberTech Development Corporation had depicted him as hardworking, intolerant of incompetence, and ruthless in business. Some at CDC had also added that he was an equitable boss whose door was always open. None of those interviewed admitted having knowledge of any spousal abuse, wife swapping, or any other unusual aspects of Mr. and Mrs. French's married life.

Of course, in the wake of Brent Preston's latest on-air revelations regarding the case, Kane's scrutiny of the Frenches had not gone unnoticed by the media, especially the tabloids. Sensational daily accounts of the Frenches' most intimate secrets, the bulk of which were attributed to psychics and other questionable sources, had become commonplace. Even distinguished correspondents, starving for something new, were indulging in an orgy of speculation.

Reacting to the situation as the case rocketed to international attention, the Frenches had hired a public relations firm through which they issued regular statements declaring their horror at having had a child murdered—a horror compounded by finding themselves under suspicion by the police. In their opinion, the investigating authorities were merely working to charge them with the crime, not to find the real killer or killers. As a result, their attorneys had notified Kane to either charge the Frenches with a crime or leave them alone, and that any attempt to contact them directly would be considered harassment. Things seemed to be going from bad to worse, and with pressure mounting for an arrest, Kane found himself praying for a break in the investigation. Given the way things were shaping up, he suspected one wouldn't be forthcoming.

"Detective Kane?"

Kane glanced up from his musing. Straddling a bike at the base of the Paramount water tower stood a young man wearing jeans and a golf shirt. Kane nodded. "Are you Ron Bannock?"

"Uh-huh. Sorry I'm late. Got hung up on something across the lot."

"Not a problem." Kane scrutinized the studio's chief of operations, having thought he would be older, fatter, and driving an expensive car—or at least one of the golf carts he had noticed on the way in.

"You were expecting someone in a suit?" Ron asked with a grin, noting Kane's questioning glance. "Sorry to disappoint you."

"I'm not."

"Good." Ron climbed off his bike, a wide-tired Schwinn. "Best way to get around," he added.

"Mr. Bannock, if you can get me where I want to go, I don't care if you're riding a camel."

"Fair enough," the young man chuckled. "And call me Ron. You mentioned wanting to visit the production office for Jordan's movie?"

"For openers."

"Okay, leave your car here and follow me."

Kane rolled up his window, exited the Ford, and locked the door. Ron, now walking his bike, started off toward a group of buildings on the east side of the square. "So what will happen to Jordan's movie now that she's gone?" Kane asked, quickly catching up to walk beside him.

Ron shrugged. "The director was under the gun to get Jordan's principal photography completed before the end of her *Brandy* hiatus. As a result, most of it's already in the can. They're having to rewrite the ending and shoot a couple of new scenes, but that's about it. This may sound callous, but Jordan's death won't affect things much, except maybe to sell more tickets."

"What about her TV show?"

"That's a different story," Ron answered. "The producers are replacing Jordan with another young actress and proceeding with a new season—in the hopes that the scandal will generate enough interest to get the series past a rough transition. Personally, I think it's gonna tank."

After walking past several trailers, Kane accompanied Ron into a nondescript, military-style building. The interior of the tan-and-brown structure appeared military issue as well, with utilitarian cubicles branching off a main hallway and a stained, acoustical-tile ceiling. As Kane stepped inside, a woman in her late twenties glanced up from a desk guarding the entry. "May I help you, sir?" she asked, removing a telephone receiver from her ear and covering the mouthpiece with her hand. Then, noticing Ron, "Oh, hi, Mr. Bannock."

"Good morning, Courtney. This is Detective Kane. He's investigating Jordan's death. He wants to ask you some questions."

"Of course." The woman spoke briefly into the phone, disconnected, and turned to Kane. "I'm Courtney Goodall, production coordinator on Jordan's film," she said, leaning across her desk to shake Kane's hand. "I recognize you now from TV. How can I help?"

"I'm getting a little background information," said Kane. "Who Jordan knew, did she have any enemies, stalkers, that kind of thing. In addition to talking with you, it would be helpful if I could question people she worked with."

Courtney thought a moment. "When Jordan started on the film, she brought over most of her support crew from *Brandy*. Wardrobe, makeup, even her teacher and social worker. Most of them are gone now and won't be back till *Brandy* begins shooting again."

"Social worker?"

"Union rules," Ron explained. "Every minor on the set has to have a parent present, along with a teacher and a social worker."

"Usually the teacher and social worker are the same person," Courtney added. "Come to think of it, Molly's still here with some of the other kids on the movie. She and Jordan were pretty close."

"Molly?"

"Molly Snazelle. She was Jordan's teacher-slash-social worker."

"Where can I find her?"

"Sound stage thirty-two. Take a left when you get outside—"

"I'll show him," Ron broke in.

"One thing first," said Kane, still addressing Courtney. "I understand that Jordan called in sick on the Friday before she vanished."

Courtney flipped through a calendar on her desk. "June thirtieth."

"Who took the call?"

"I did."

"Did she sound ill—coughing or whatever?"

"I didn't speak with Jordan. Her mother phoned."

"You're sure about that?"

"Positive," Courtney replied. "Mrs. French said that Jordan was coming down with the flu, and that she wouldn't be back till after the Fourth of July weekend."

"Thanks, Courtney," said Kane, turning for the door. "You've been helpful."

After trailing Ron past a block of sound stages, Kane entered a huge structure marked Stage 32. Recalling passing it on his way in, he glanced around the gigantic building's interior. High above, suspended from a grid of metal catwalks, a series of wooden platforms draped with wires, cables, and lights traversed the room, lending dimension to the colossally proportioned space. With the exception of the floor, gray soundproofing pads covered almost every other surface—walls, ducts, and ceiling.

Kane waited by the entrance as Ron conferred with several men on one of the sets—a gloomy façade that appeared to be the dungeon of a Medieval castle. When Ron returned, he informed Kane that most of the crew had already broken for lunch, but that Molly Snazelle was probably still in her trailer. Feeling like a kid being led around an amusement park, Kane exited the sound stage and followed Ron to a nearby trailer. Once there, Ron paused to answer a call on his cell phone. He spoke a few moments, then turned to Kane. "Sorry, Detective, I have to run," he said. "This is Molly's trailer. If she's not here, I'm sure she'll return shortly. I've also cleared it for you to talk with anyone you want to interview on the set, once they're back from lunch. Do you think you'll be able to find your way back to your car afterward?"

Kane glanced behind him, spotting the familiar blue shape of the water tower. "I'll find it. Thanks for your help."

"Anytime." Ron swung a leg over his bike. "And whoever killed Jordan, I hope you find him."

"We will," said Kane, wishing he were as sure of himself as he sounded.

As Ron pedaled off, Kane mounted a short flight of metal steps and knocked on the trailer's aluminum door. Seconds later a woman's voice sounded from inside. "Come in."

Kane ducked through the opening. Desks and worktables filled one end of the narrow interior; a blackboard and bookcase took up the rest. A woman with pale-blue eyes and a peppering of prematurely graying hair looked up from a salad she was eating at one of the tables. "Yes?"

"Ms. Snazelle?"

"That's right."

Kane flipped out his ID. "Dan Kane, LAPD. I'd like to talk with you about Jordan French."

The woman glanced at Kane's identification. "Certainly, Detective. What do you want to know?"

"To tell you the truth, Ms. Snazelle, I'm not exactly sure," Kane answered, bending to avoid a low-hanging light fixture as he moved into the room. "I'm trying to learn all I can about Jordan, get a sense of who she was. Mind if I sit?"

"Help yourself."

Kane dropped into a chair at one of the worktables, belatedly noticing that the seat was designed for a much smaller anatomy. Postponing her lunch, Molly slid into a chair opposite him. "The furniture's not exactly intended for someone your size," she said apologetically.

Kane smiled. "Don't worry about it. Courtney at the production office says you and Jordan were close."

"We were."

"So what was Jordan like? Who were her friends? Anything you can tell me might be helpful."

Molly considered a moment. "Well, because of her shooting schedule and not being in regular school, Jordan didn't have many friends her own age," she said. "She was a precocious child who kept to herself when she wasn't on camera. While performing she could be outgoing and vivacious, though in person she was often introspective and private. She threw an occasional tantrum, but for the most part she was a professional.

215

Everyone on the set liked her. She loved music, playing video games, and reading. Is any of this useful?"

"Precocious, huh?" Kane mused. "How precocious? Did she ever mention having a boyfriend, somebody special? Somebody she could have been having sex with?"

"No."

"She had plenty of fans, though. Any of them ever cause problems? Threatening letters, stalking, obscene calls?"

Molly shook her head. "Nothing out of the ordinary. I'm sure she would have told me if there were."

"You implied she was moody. Was she into drugs or alcohol?"

"Absolutely not. Aside from being a star, Jordan was just a normal fourteen-year-old girl."

Kane glanced at a publicity photo of Jordan pinned to a wall near the blackboard. The picture showed a girl with bright hazel eyes, long dark hair woven in braids, and a captivating smile. "You'd be amazed at how many fourteen-year-olds are using drugs and alcohol," he said, pushing away the mental image of Jordan as he had last seen her.

"That may be, but I don't think Jordan was one of them," Molly repeated firmly.

Kane decided to shift gears. "Ron mentioned that Mrs. French had to be present on the set while her daughter was working."

"Mrs. French had to be present on the studio *lot*," Molly corrected. "Mostly she stayed in Jordan's trailer. Jordan said her mother made her nervous when she was on the set."

"How did they get along otherwise?"

Molly hesitated. "Actually, for the most part, Jordan and her mother didn't," she said. "Don't get me wrong. Mrs. French is an extremely able woman, and Jordan owed a great deal of her success to her. But as a mother, let's just say that in my opinion, Mrs. French left a bit to be desired."

"Did Jordan ever mention her parents fighting?"

"Occasionally. I don't think Mr. and Mrs. French are very close either—at least from what I gathered from Jordan. She didn't say it in so many words, but I got the impression that Jordan felt guilty about her parents' problems, as if they were her fault. You know how kids are."

The trailer door banged open. A boy wearing Dracula makeup and a long black cloak burst inside. "Hi, Ms. Snazelle," he said, glancing curiously at Kane.

"Be with you in a sec, Leonardo," said Molly. "Could you wait outside till we're done?"

"That's okay," said Kane, rising. "I'm finished here. Thanks for your time, Ms. Snazelle."

Molly nodded somberly. "I'm not big on capital punishment, but I think whoever did that to Jordan deserves the death penalty."

"I couldn't agree more," said Kane, starting for the door. "I'll call if I think of anything else."

"Anytime."

An hour later, after conferring with several people on the set including the director, the assistant director, and Jordan's co-stars, Kane headed back to his car. Using the water tower as a guidepost, he retraced his path through the New York section of the lot, cutting past the brownstone buildings and circumnavigating a bricked enclave resembling Greenwich Village. As he walked, he reviewed what he'd learned. Dejectedly, he admitted it wasn't much.

True, at least he had verified that the call informing the studio that Jordan wouldn't be coming to work had been made by Mrs. French, not her daughter—leaving the time of Jordan's death still unresolved. His meeting with Molly Snazelle had established that friction existed between Jordan and her mother, and that Jordan might have felt guilty about her parents' marital problems. Both were common in cases of sexual child abuse. But where did he go from there?

Approaching the parking lot, Kane fished his keys from his pocket, absently noting that the white Mercedes was now gone, fresh oil stains in its place. After unlocking his car, he slid behind the wheel, cranked the engine, and started out the way he had come. Minutes later, as he drove through the studio gate and exited onto Gower, the thought occurred to Kane that in every detective movie he had ever watched, A led to B, which led to C, and so forth—ultimately resulting in a successful conclusion to the case. Neat, logical, satisfying.

It seemed to Kane that more often in real life, A led to B . . . which didn't lead to shit.

# 21

On the day before my twentieth birthday, Mom finally returned home. Enjoying a much needed respite from the nausea, vomiting, bruises, diarrhea, lab tests, blood and platelet transfusions, IV nutrients, and a host of other treatment-related indignities that had comprised much of her life for the past month, she looked stronger and healthier than she had in quite some time. Though I had been to Mass only sporadically since starting classes at UCLA, I attended Sunday services with the rest of our family the next morning, knowing my presence at Our Lady of Malibu Church was not optional. And surprisingly, as I sat next to my mother listening to a long, boring sermon, I found myself almost enjoying the ceremony.

Later I joined Mom in the kitchen as Dad cooked breakfast, a meal that despite offers of help from both Mom and me, he insisted on preparing for the family alone. Afterward, excited about the upcoming party that day, he marched out to the beach and began digging a pit in the sand above the high-tide line. Though I again offered to help, my father once more refused, saying that no one should have to work on her own birthday . . . dishwashing excepted, of course.

With nothing to do after the kitchen was cleaned, I retreated to the redwood deck outside and sat on the swing. Though it was barely nine, a brisk offshore breeze was already sweeping the beach, carrying down the green smells of the hills above our house. Wearing shorts and a tank top, I raised my face to the wind and wrapped my arms around my bare legs, my skin prickling in the cool morning air. Gazing out toward the water, I noticed that the tide had lowered considerably since I'd awakened, and a wide swath of sand now stretched to the ocean—isolated clumps of driftwood, seaweed, and rock piles littering the half-mile crescent that defined Las Flores Beach. Past a seaside berm, racing to elude uprushing tongues of foam, a platoon of stilt-legged terns pecked at the water's edge, their nimble dance with the waves casting flitting shadows in the slanting rays of the early morning sun.

I uncurled my legs and placed a sandaled foot on the deck, giving the swing a push. Then, lulled by the motion of the swing, I again hugged my knees and gazed out over the Pacific, listening to the sounds of Mom's cello drifting from the ground-floor music room behind me.

Deep and resonant, the tones of her cello had for me always been joined inseparably with the voice of my mother. As a child I'd heard her music and sensed it tugging at me, unleashing a flood of yearnings that I had been unable to fathom. As years passed and I had grown to realize the depth of my mother's gift, I eventually defined the emotions it wrenched from me. Respect, admiration, and pride in my mother's artistry had been there from the beginning, yet my feelings had also been tinged with resentment at the power it held over me. Worse, with the eventual knowledge that I would never measure up to my mother's perfection, came an abiding jealousy that Mom's genius had been passed not to me, but to my brother Travis.

A moment later I heard Travis on the keyboard, his playing joining Mom's in an intricate choreography of tone and rhythm. They were performing a piece for cello and piano that I recognized as Schubert's *Arpeggione*, a hauntingly moving sonata that Mom and Travis had played many times in the past. More a virtuoso showcase for cello than piano, the music progressed through a contrasting arrangement of winsome themes—Mom taking her fair share of the melodic burden but in the process making several uncharacteristic errors.

Feeling petty and small for the envy I routinely felt when hearing Mom and my brother play, I listened as the music proceeded to a sensual middle section as transparent and lovely as a waterfall. Next Mom and Travis set out on a spirited final movement, Mom again making mistakes only someone familiar with the sonata would detect.

As the sounds of the piano and cello died away, I found my eyes stinging with emotion, moved by the beauty of Schubert's composition and the artistry of Trav's and Mom's playing. Jeez, what's wrong with me? I wondered. I continued staring out over the horizon, deciding that if I were going to get through the day without making a fool of myself, I needed to do a better job of keeping my feelings in check.

In the distance offshore, I spotted a raft bobbing on the swells, the ten-by-ten-foot platform an illegal albeit inconsequential navigational hazard that Dad and other beach residents had placed some years back. McKenzie, Nate, and I had played an unexpectedly pivotal role in its launching as well. Seeing it reminded me of what had seemed a simpler time, hearkening back to an era uncomplicated by the uncertainties now facing me.

"How're you doing, honey?"

I turned to see my mother easing down beside me on the swing. "Good," I answered, quickly wiping my cheeks.

Mom gave the swing a push with her foot, then looked at me more closely. "Is something wrong?"

"No. It's . . . it's just great to have you home."

"It's great to be home," Mom replied, still regarding me with concern. "You sure you're okay?"

"I'm fine," I said, embarrassed that her music had affected me so deeply. "Your playing just now was fabulous. You haven't lost your touch."

"Liar. I was awful," Mom laughed, adjusting a floppy velvet hat she was wearing to cover her baldness. "Not practicing for a month takes its toll. According to Rachmaninoff, 'If you don't practice for a day, no one knows. If you don't practice for two days, *you* know. If you don't practice for three days, *everyone* knows.' I'll definitely have to spend some hours in the music room before returning to St. John's."

"It doesn't seem fair that you have to do the chemo all over again."

"No, it doesn't," Mom sighed. "Speaking of which, I'm going in on Wednesday for a checkup. Why don't you meet me afterward for lunch? We could eat at that Chinese place on the Santa Monica Mall you like so much."

"Sure, Mom." I hesitated, then changed the subject. "I can't believe Dad's attempting another luau," I remarked, gazing out to where my father had finished digging a large hole in the sand, several dozen yards from the volleyball court. He had been unnaturally secretive about his plans for my birthday party, but I had known what he had in mind from the minute I'd seen Dad and my brothers gathering kelp from the water's edge on Saturday. My father was currently lining the sand pit with stones. Nate was helping carry rocks, while Callie was trotting around proudly with a baseball-bat sized piece of driftwood in her mouth, futilely trying to get someone to play.

"The last time *was* kind of a disaster," Mom conceded, referring to a similar attempt Dad had made years back to roast an entire suckling pig. Refusing to fully cook, the pig had to be cut up and finished in the oven. As a result, everyone wound up eating long after dark. "He says he has it wired this time," she added hopefully.

"If he doesn't, today's crowd could turn ugly—which for most of Dad's cop buddies wouldn't be much of a stretch," I observed. "By the way, how many of our nearest and dearest did Dad invite?"

Mom smiled as she answered. "Well, most of his police associates are coming, of course, plus all of our neighbors. I invited musicians from the Philharmonic, Nate called his baseball teammates, Trav invited friends from SC, and you're having over people from school and work. There should be at least a hundred and fifty. Maybe more."

"Great," I grumbled, secretly pleased that my parents were turning my birthday party into such a production. Of course, it was also to celebrate Mom's homecoming, but I was still thrilled at the prospect. "It'll be wonderful to have the unwashed masses trooping through our house, just like the old days," I added.

"It'll be fun and you know it."

"Sure. About as much fun as watching Olympic curling."

"Oh, come on," Mom chuckled. "It's a beach party. Besides, no one will be 'trooping' through the house. Everyone will be outside."

Once more the sound of Travis's playing drifted from the music room. He was practicing passages from his recital repertoire—haphazardly stopping and starting, repeating different sections. Mom and I fell silent, listening to him play. "He's incredible, isn't he?" said Mom during a lull.

"Yes, Mom. Trav is getting better all the time."

My brother resumed his playing, this time attacking a particularly strenuous progression embedded in one of his recent compositions. "Did I tell you I got my press credentials last week?" I asked.

"I'm sorry, honey. What did you say?"

"I said I got my press credentials, along with my LAPD, Highway Patrol, and Sheriff's Department passes. A raise in pay, too."

"Congratulations, Ali," Mom said carefully. "I know how hard you've been working at your intern job. I just . . ." Her voice trailed off.

Afraid our old tensions were about to resurface, I resumed staring out at the beach without replying. I noticed that my father and Nate had finished lining the sand pit with rocks and were now constructing an enormous firewood teepee in the center, using driftwood from a pile stacked near the sea wall.

"What's bothering you, Ali?"

"Nothing," I replied. "Why do you keep asking me that?"

"Because I know you." Mom reached for my hand. "Something's on your mind, and it isn't just our disagreement about your news internship. What is it?"

I didn't answer.

"Ali, I love you. If something's wrong, I want to help. Please, Ali. Talk to me."

I finally responded, my words barely audible. "Mom, I know that your doctors are doing everything for you that's medically possible, but what if—"

Mom cut me off. "I'm going to get better. Now, I don't want to hear anymore about that. Not today. Especially not today. I'll be fine."

Wanting to believe, I searched my mother's eyes. And for a brief, chilling instant, I glimpsed the doubt behind her iron curtain of control. Shocked, I started to say something more.

Mom silenced me before I could speak, raising her fingers to my lips. "I'll be fine."

*     *     *

Hours later, having burned most of the driftwood that was stacked near the sea wall, Kane instructed Nate and Travis to shovel the remaining coals from the rock-lined pit into a shallow depression in the sand nearby, leaving only the fire-blackened stones in the pit as a source of heat. Then, after laying down a bed of bladder kelp taken from tangles of seaweed they had stored in several thirty-gallon trash containers, he layered in foil-wrapped food: a twenty-pound fresh Alaskan salmon, a dozen lobsters, buckets of clams and mussels, whole chickens and crabs, bushels of corn and potatoes, racks of marinated pork ribs, and pumpkins stuffed with seafood and vegetables—judiciously interspersing additional seaweed between layers and placing slower-cooking items on the bottom, faster-cooking ones higher up. The remainder of the kelp went on top, followed by a tarp and three inches of sand, leaving a small hole near one edge for steam to escape.

Satisfied with the status of the cooking pit but determined that nothing should go awry, Kane surveyed the growing party with an eye seasoned by many similar endeavors—though none in recent years, not since the old house had burned. Standing on the beach with his hands on his hips, he proceeded to go over a mental checklist, reviewing various other party preparations. Beer: kegs in ice tubs on the redwood deck. Soft drinks: cooling in chests beside the kegs. Porta Potties, a precaution to avoid overstressing the house's septic tank: two stationed on the street near the outside staircase. Trash cans: lined with plastic bags and strategically positioned around the deck. Serving tables: set with paper plates, plastic forks, and an assortment of appetizers, casseroles, and side dishes that early-arriving guests had already brought. Salads, both green and fruit: staying fresh in the upstairs refrigerator. Desserts: butter-pecan ice cream and a huge chocolate cake waiting upstairs, along with watermelon and baskets of fruit.

Everything was ready. As predicted by the tide tables consulted weeks earlier, the ocean was still receding, affording the luau pit a wide margin of safety. Overhead, the summer sun beat down from a cloudless California sky, sending the afternoon temperature into the mid-eighties. With a shrug, Kane decided that if he had forgotten anything, it was too late to rectify the omission. Although many of those invited had said they wouldn't be coming till later, by now over fifty guests had arrived, and like a runaway locomotive barreling down a mountain grade, the party was gaining momentum by the minute.

Deluca, Banowski, Kane's ex-partner Arnie Mercer, Lt. Long —the single member of the LAPD brass who had been invited— and various other police associates not camped out near the beer kegs were engaged in a clamorous competition on the volleyball court. Feet churning the sand, the generally overweight and out-of-shape police officers were offsetting their athletic shortcomings with boisterous enthusiasm and good-natured ribbing. Most of Catheryn's music associates, including Alexander Petrinski and a score of Philharmonic musicians, were gathered beneath the upper balcony, claiming a rare bit of shade. Escaping the hot sand, a number of younger partygoers had taken to the ocean, where several hundred yards offshore a dozen swimmers had crowded aboard the raft, with a dozen more in the water waiting to climb on. Along the hard sand at the water's edge, Travis, McKenzie, and Allison were sailing a Frisbee back and forth. Kane smiled as he saw Allison charge through the shallows to snag an errant pass from Travis, then tumble backward into an oncoming wave just as she snapped a perfect backhanded toss to McKenzie.

"Man, that grub's smellin' mighty good, Dan."

Kane turned to see Lou Barrello, an Orange County Sheriff's detective with whom he had worked several years before. "Hey, Lou. Glad you could make it."

"No way I'd miss one of your shindigs, amigo. From what I hear, your parties are the most fun someone can have while still wearing underwear."

Kane inspected his friend, noticing that Barrello's fire-plug body had grown even more padded over the past year, his balding pate even more devoid of hair. Following the death of his wife, Barrello had taken an early retirement and now skippered a scuba-dive boat berthed at Port Hueneme, a short drive up the coast from Malibu. "So how's the seafaring going?" Kane asked, shaking Barrello's outstretched hand. "Still puking over the rail every time the channel gets a little choppy?"

"Not me," Barrello retorted, his twinkling eyes belying a scowl as crusty as a tugboat keel. "We Italians are born with constitutions of steel. You must be thinking of someone else. One of your pansy Irish friends, maybe," he added with a grin. Then, his smile fading, "Seriously, Dan, why don't you and the family come up sometime? My treat. We still have space on a charter next weekend to the outer islands. Should be a great trip."

"I'll take a rain check on that," replied Kane. "We have a lot on our plate right now."

"I know," Barrello said sympathetically. "I was so sorry to hear about Kate. Believe me, Dan, I understand what you're going through. If there's anything I can do to help, anything at all . . ."

"I appreciate that, Lou. If there is, I'll let you know." Kane glanced at Barrello's empty beer cup. "Appears your drink needs a little freshening, pal," he said, changing the subject. "Can't have you getting parched out here in the hot sun."

"You don't have to ask me twice," said Barrello, sensing Kane's discomfort. "But I meant what I said. If there's anything I can do, anything at all, please let me know."

The two men negotiated a three-foot rise to the top of the sea wall, then fought through a throng of people crowding the deck, heading for the kegs of Heineken and Michelob chilling in tubs filled with ice. In an eddy formed in the flood of partygoers by the metal tubs, a knot of beer drinkers stood jostling for cup position beneath the flowing spigots. Using his low center of gravity, Barrello pushed forward and jammed his cup beneath the Heineken tap. "One for you, Dan?" he asked, grabbing another cup.

"I'm sticking to Coke," Kane answered. Ignoring Barrello's quizzical frown, Kane gazed across the deck, catching Catheryn's eye. He winked and smiled. Pausing in a conversation with Arthur West, the Los Angeles Philharmonic's principal cellist, Catheryn smiled back.

"Kane's still riding the Shirley Temple wagon," explained Arnie Mercer, who was waiting behind Barrello for a refill. "Didn't you know that, Lou? Dan swore off booze years ago. Gave up drinking right around the time he started squattin' to take a piss."

"Up yours, pard," Kane chuckled.

"Same to you," said Arnie, impatiently cramming his cup under the spigot and spilling half of Barrello's newly filled drink.

"As we're discussing personal matters, I heard Mercer's got his whole security crew switching to Maxi Pads," offered Deluca, who had followed Arnie up from the beach. "Says there's less chance of leakage on those troublesome heavy days."

"Screw you, Deluca," Arnie said.

"I'd rather pay a visit to your fiancée for that," Deluca replied with a grin. "Course, if Stacy ever sampled the Italian stallion here, she'd be dissatisfied with all other men, including you, for the rest of her poor unfortunate life."

"Funny, your wife mentioned that very same thing to me last night," Arnie shot back. "Which reminds me. I had to leave in a hurry, and I forgot my shoes under your bed. I'll swing by for 'em later."

"Check for my jock strap while you're there," chimed in Banowski, who had also drifted up for a refill. "It'll be the one that's all stretched out."

"In the butt area, maybe," said Deluca. "Besides, you wouldn't know what to do with a good-looking woman like Sarah. I've seen the dogs you go out with."

"When you're pokin' the fire, you don't look at the mantle," Banowski retorted.

"How are your wedding plans going, Arnie?" asked Kane, attempting to elevate the conversation.

"We're still on for this spring, but things are getting more and more complicated by the minute."

"Nothing against Stacy, but take my advice and forget the whole thing," advised Deluca. "You think things are bad now, wait till later. I'll tell you something about women. Once you marry 'em, they're never satisfied. It's like that old philosophical question: If a woman talks in the woods and there's no man around to hear her, is she still complaining?"

Arnie shook his head. "Damn, Deluca. I had no idea you were so deep."

"Plenty more deepness where that came from, *paisano*."

"So how's about keepin' it to yourself?" suggested Banowski, the thumb of his left hand unconsciously fumbling for a wedding band he hadn't worn in years. "None of us brought our hip boots." Then, to Arnie, "Not that I don't see eye-to-eye with our Italian friend here on marriage, though. In fact, here's *my* advice on the subject: Instead of tying the knot, just find some woman you really hate and buy her a house."

"Nice," remarked Kane, abandoning his attempt to raise the level of discussion. "Ever consider working for Hallmark?"

"I call 'em as I see 'em."

"Stacy's not that way," protested Arnie, beginning to bristle.

"They're *all* that way," Banowski replied.

"Not Stacy. She's perfect for me."

"Why? She own a liquor store?"

"Good one," laughed Arnie. Then, more seriously, "You may laugh, but after I retired from the force, I had time to think back over the years since Lilith and I split up, and I wound up asking myself what was the one thing in life I still needed."

"To go on a diet?" guessed Banowski.

"Plastic surgery?" quipped Deluca. "A shower? Listerine?"

"Aw, hell," said Kane before Arnie could respond. "Look who just waltzed in."

\*     \*     \*

Flushed from a dip in the ocean, I headed for the deck and rinsed off in our outside shower, then made my way back to a spot McKenzie and I had claimed on the far side of the volleyball court. As I grabbed a towel and began drying my hair, I glanced around, surprised at the number of people who had already arrived. Despite the crowd, I knew that the majority of those coming wouldn't show up until dinnertime. "I hope there's enough to eat," I observed, dropping into my beach chair beside McKenzie.

"There will be," assured McKenzie, stretching out her tanned legs and digging her toes into the sand. "Hordes of people brought food. Have you seen the serving tables? They're loaded with goodies. Especially desserts."

On the volleyball court before us, Travis and Christy White, my brother Tommy's former girlfriend, were playing a game of doubles against two young officers Dad had invited from the West L.A. Division. Travis and Christy had grown up playing beach volleyball and were an excellent team. In addition to disregarding any and all rules of acceptable ball-handling, their LAPD adversaries were compensating for their lack of skill by serving to Christy as often as possible. They were still losing. Having called "winners," Nate and a friend were stationed on the ocean side of the court, ready to retrieve wild shots before the ball reached the water. I watched the one-sided contest for a few minutes, then glanced toward the house, noting that Alexander Petrinski had abandoned Mom's music enclave to join Grandma Dorothy. The two were sitting side-by-side, perched on the edge of the sea wall. Petrinski touched Dorothy's hand, saying something that made her laugh.

I tipped my head. "Check it out, Mac. Trav's music teacher is making moves on my grandmother."

McKenzie turned toward the house, studying the older couple. "I think they look cute together," she observed. "By the way, what's new with you and Mike?"

"Nothing."

"He hasn't called?"

"He phoned twice. I've been too busy to see him."

"What's wrong with you, girl? You're going to screw things up, just like always. It's obvious he likes you, so why don't you—"

"I invited him to the party today."

"Oh. Well, I'm glad to see you're finally coming to your senses. When is he getting here?"

"I don't know. I thought he would be here by now." I again gazed toward the house, searching the crush of people milling on the deck. As I was about to turn back to McKenzie, I spotted Mike descending the outside stairway from the street. He was wearing shorts, sandals, and a brightly colored Hawaiian shirt. As he rounded the corner, I noticed Brent Preston following close behind, his crisply pressed slacks, loafers, and sport coat a sharp contrast to Mike's comfortable attire. A moment later my dad, who was conversing with friends near the beer kegs, also spotted the CBS network correspondent. Lips compressed in a hard, thin line, Dad started across the deck.

Without a word, I rose and headed toward the house.

McKenzie got up and hurried after me. "What's wrong?" she asked, running to catch up.

"Trouble," I said grimly. "I, uh, sort of invited Brent Preston. Dad's going over to talk with him. You'd better stay clear."

McKenzie laughed. "Are you kidding? I wouldn't miss this for the world."

By the time McKenzie and I reached the deck, Dad had already intercepted the sandy-haired newsman. Dad's mouth was smiling. His eyes were not.

"Hi, Brent. How's it going?" I blurted before my father could speak. "Dad, I want you to meet—"

"I know who he is. I take it *you* invited him."

"You take it right, Dad."

Dad's smile tightened. "It's your party, petunia, so I guess you can invite anybody you want. One thing, though," he added, addressing Brent. "This is a social event, pal. No interviews, no questions, and absolutely no discussion about police work. Is that understood?"

Brent nodded. "Of course. I can't stay long anyway. I just thought I would drop by and wish Allison happy birthday." He hesitated, and then went on. "Listen, Detective. I know you have a healthy distaste for the press. Nevertheless, you must know we're only doing our job."

Dad scowled. "I must, huh?"

"You may not like it," Brent continued evenly. "But it's the simple truth. The Jordan French murder has become a national obsession, and your news blackout has only made things worse. People want to know, and if authorities like you were more forthcoming, we in the press wouldn't have to pry."

"We have good cause for withholding details of the investigation, as I'm sure *you* must know," Dad shot back.

"Just as I'm sure you realize that it's our job to dig up as much as we can and report it."

"Even if it jeopardizes the investigation?"

Brent shook his head. "No one wants to compromise your investigation. But in all fairness, do you think you should be the sole arbiter of what the public gets to know?"

"As a matter of fact, I do."

"We have a difference of opinion on that."

"At least we agree on something, chum."

"Don't shoot the messenger, Detective," Brent went on, making one last attempt. "The news serves a purpose. For instance, how many other parents of murdered children would give anything for some public pressure to solve their cases?"

"Oh, I get it," Dad said slowly. "You're mobilizing public pressure to close the case. So you're actually helping? Gee, since you put it that way, let me be the first to apologize."

Recognizing the signs of anger stirring in my father, I stepped forward. "C'mon, Dad, this is a party. Brent will behave himself. Here, I want you to meet someone else," I said. "Mike Cortese, this is my father. Dad, Mike Cortese."

Suspiciously, Dad shook Mike's hand. "Are you a reporter?"

"No, sir," Mike replied. "A cameraman. I met Ali at Newport Beach on the day she rescued that swimmer."

"So *you're* the guy who plastered her mug all over the TV," said Dad. Then, looking at Mike more closely, "Cortese, huh? I know you. Your old man was a cop. Frank Cortese."

Mike nodded. "I met you at his funeral when I was twelve. I didn't think you would remember."

"Dad doesn't forget much," I said, staring at Mike in amazement. "How come you never told me your father was on the force?"

"The subject didn't come up," Mike answered. "I did tell you I knew something about cops, remember?"

I thought back, recalling Mike's words the night we'd eaten at the Oaxacan restaurant.

"Your father was a good man, Mike," Dad went on. "He and I went through the Academy together. How's your mom? Doris, right?"

"She passed away two years ago."

"I'm sorry. I didn't know."

At that moment Nate hollered up from the beach. "Dad, you'd better get down here! Some of your friends have decided it's time to eat."

"Damn," Dad said. He glowered once more at Brent. Then, shaking his head, he hurried down to the luau pit, barely arriving in time to prevent Deluca and Banowski from lifting the edge of the tarp.

"I feel like I just underwent the third degree," said Brent once my father was out of earshot.

"Don't let my dad throw you," I advised. "He's already had his daily ration of raw meat." Then, to McKenzie, who until then had been standing quietly behind me, "Mac, you know Mike and Brent?"

McKenzie smiled at Mike, then refocused her eyes on Brent, at whom she'd been staring for the past minutes. "I, uh, I met you in the newsroom, Mr. Preston," she stammered. "The other day when Ali and I . . . the day we went to lunch."

"I remember," said Brent, taking McKenzie's hand.

"I'm glad," McKenzie squeaked, her voice catching in her throat. She attempted to say something more but couldn't.

"Despite appearances, my friend McKenzie is remarkably intelligent, personable, and witty," I said somberly. "Unfortunately, at the moment she seems to have misplaced her brain. Want me to help you look for it, Mac? Blink once for yes."

McKenzie glared at me, blushing furiously.

"Nice seeing you again, McKenzie," laughed Brent. "And happy birthday, Ali. This looks like a great party, but unfortunately I have to take off. See you tomorrow at work."

"You're leaving?"

Brent nodded. "I promised Liz I would attend a wedding reception with her. Besides, I'm not really dressed for this. I just wanted to stop by and wish you the best." Moving closer, he kissed me lightly on the cheek, then turned and started for the stairs.

I smiled self-consciously, surprised by Brent's kiss. "My dad chased him off, didn't he?" I said to Mike as Brent headed up the stairs.

"If Brent had wanted to stay, he would have," Mike answered. "This isn't his kind of thing."

"Too bad," said McKenzie, at last finding her voice.

I grinned. "The silent one is back."

"Oh, shut up."

"C'mon, you two," Mike chuckled, linking arms with McKenzie and me. "The sun is shining, the waves are up, and if I'm not mistaken, that's a volleyball court out there. I suggest we head down to the beach."

By 5 PM, despite a rising tide, a wide expanse of sand still stretched to the water's edge. As shadows lengthened, more and more people continued to arrive—gradually swelling the party to several hundred guests. Earlier the celebrants had sequestered themselves in smaller segments, with Mom and her musician friends conversing on the deck, a rowdy LAPD contingent positioned near the beer kegs, volleyball enthusiasts gathered around the court, and kids splashing in the ocean. Now, ballooned by late arrivals, the party finally coalesced into a single organism with one thing on its mind: food.

With the dinner hour fast approaching, serving tables on the deck were now overflowing with casseroles, salads, and desserts people had brought. To provide additional space for food from the cooking pit, Dad overrode Mom's objections and ordered a squad of LAPD officers to carry down our dining table from the house. While Dad's men were busy with the table, Travis, Dad, and Nate began removing the luau tarp, releasing billows of steam laden with tantalizing, smoky scents. With the exception of a few charred potatoes on the bottom, the food proved to be perfectly cooked—chickens tender and juicy, garlic-seasoned salmon pink and delectable, buckets of clams and mussels steeping in their own juices, corn and other vegetables crisp and delicious, lobsters and crabs steaming in their shells, and racks of ribs tangy with a sauce Dad had spread on top before wrapping them in foil. After separating the food from its protective kelp and placing it on serving trays, Dad had Nate and Travis carry the feast-laden platters to the redwood deck.

Next Dad ordered my brothers to uncover the casseroles and side dishes on the serving tables, after which he had them bring down everything but the ice cream and birthday cake from the upstairs refrigerator. Clearly conscious of voracious guests watching his every move, Dad busied himself preparing the luau table—arranging plates and utensils at one end, shellfish and salmon at the other, vegetables, ribs, and chicken in between. A line had formed by the time he finished, with Banowski and Deluca predictably positioned toward the front.

"What's takin' so long with the chow?" Deluca clamored.

"Eating sometime this century *would* be nice," Banowski added.

"Hold your horses," Dad replied, grabbing a Coke from a nearby ice chest. "I have something to say before we dig in." Then, stepping atop the cooler, he let loose a long, earsplitting whistle.

At that moment Mike and I were sitting cross-legged in the sand near the sea wall, where we had been watching the predinner activity on the deck. I had momentarily glanced away to talk with Mike, but at the sound of Dad's piercing blast my head involuntarily snapped around. Like all the Kane children, I had grown up on the beach recognizing my father's distinctive whistle as a signal to come home—immediately and without argument. Returning my gaze to the deck, I saw Dad towering above the crowd. "Oh, no," I groaned as I saw him raise his arms for quiet. "He's going to give one of his toasts."

"Everybody pipe down," Dad bellowed, his drill-sergeant voice startling the entire assembly to silence. "We'll be serving the grub shortly," he went on. "But before that I have something to say. As you all know, my daughter Allison turns twenty today. It's a day for which the Kane family has a lot to be thankful."

Feeling heads turn toward me, I squirmed uncomfortably.

"First of all, my wife, Catheryn, has recently returned from the hospital and is now recovering her strength," Dad continued, turning toward the far side of the deck where Mom was seated with friends. "It's great to have you back home, Kate."

"Welcome back, Mom!" yelled Travis.

"Yeah, Mom!" Nate chimed in, followed by a round of applause from the crowd. Smiling, Mom raised her wineglass in response.

"Next," Dad added, "I want to point out that this isn't just *any* birthday for Allison. Starting today, she's no longer a teenager, and I know I speak for the entire Kane family—*especially* yours truly—when I say that we all breathe a sigh of relief now that the attitude-problems associated with having a teenager in the house are over."

"You forgot about me, Dad," Nate shouted.

"Damn. Well, we can at least hope you'll be easier," Dad chuckled after the laughter died down. "Seriously," he continued, fixing his gaze on me. "When Ali was born, I wasn't sure how having a daughter would work out. By then Kate and I already had Tom and Travis, and things had gone smoothly with them—at least for the most part. Boys I knew how to handle; a daughter was something else. But when I picked up Ali in the delivery room and looked down at that little red-faced bundle of joy, I knew things were going to be all right. And they have been. Having a daughter has turned out to be more rewarding than I ever dreamed, and I wouldn't trade her for anything in the world. Not to say there haven't been a few rough spots along the way. Truth is, I've probably butted heads with Allison more than all the other kids put together, and to this day we're still locking horns. Those of you acquainted with my daughter know that she's competitive, hardheaded, and stubborn. These are traits she *certainly* didn't get from me."

Once more Dad had to wait for the laughter to subside. "In addition, besides getting her mother's good looks and being smart to a fault, she's also a straight-A student and a talented writer to boot—several other things she didn't inherit from me, either."

"Hear, hear," yelled Lt. Long, who over the years had fought a losing battle with Dad over his sketchy departmental reports. More laughter followed. Then everyone again fell silent, waiting to hear the rest of Dad's speech.

"Bottom line, and most important," Dad went on, "those of you who know Allison also know that when the chips are down, she's someone you can count on. No matter what."

I looked up in surprise. I knew that Dad's poker metaphor was one of his highest compliments—one he used to indicate men on the force with whom he would trust his life.

Finding my eyes across the crowd, Dad raised his can of Coke. "I'm proud to be your father, Ali," he said. "And I'm proud of you, and of the young woman you've become."

Taken completely off guard by my father's words, I swallowed hard. Years back I had been present at another event when Dad had offered a similar toast honoring my oldest brother, Tom. At the time, convinced I was an outcast in the company of brothers, a weak little sister residing at the bottom of the Kane family food chain, I had expressed a bitter belief that my father would never voice comparable sentiments about *me*.

Sweeping his gaze across the assembly, Dad raised his soft drink can even higher. "Now before the food gets cold, I'd like you all to lift your glasses and join Catheryn and me and the rest of our family in wishing Allison a happy twentieth birthday, a long life, success in whatever career she chooses, and that she eventually provides her mother and me with a passel of grandchildren," he said, his voice ringing out strong and clear. "To Allison."

Cheering wildly, everyone joined in Dad's toast, raising cups and glasses in a tumultuous ovation. Unaccustomed to being the center of attention, I felt a flush spreading up my neck, warming my cheeks. Blinking back an unwanted rush of tears for the second time that day, I looked at my father and mouthed the words, "Thanks, Dad."

Dad grinned back. Then, readdressing the crowd, he uttered the words for which everyone had been waiting. "Let's eat!"

Despite my earlier concerns, there proved to be more than enough food for everyone. As the sun dropped over Point Dumé to the west, I went through the dinner line and then retired to my beach chair, having earlier positioned it closer to a fire that had been rekindled in the empty luau pit. Balancing a paper plate in my lap, I dug into my food, surprised at how ravenous I was. I hadn't eaten since breakfast, but it was more than that. The smoky flavors of the luau, seasoned with a hint of ocean from the sea kelp, begged another taste, and another.

Mike, who had scavenged a beach chair from the deck to sit beside me, started in on an enormous portion he had served himself. "Your dad's quite the chef," he noted happily, taking a bite of lobster.

"I'll say," I agreed. "This food is so good, I'd eat it even if I *weren't* hungry."

"And when would that be?" Travis quipped from across the fire pit.

Grinning, I unobtrusively shot him the finger and continued eating.

"With your father cooking the family meals like this, it's a wonder you're not as big as a house," Mike went on, smiling at the interplay between Travis and me.

237

"How sweet of you to say," I replied tartly, trying a forkful of a seafood and vegetable mix that I had scooped from one of the baked pumpkins. "We don't eat this way every night, you know."

"But we'd *like* to," Nate interjected from partway around the fire.

Across the flames, Travis and Christy nodded in agreement and kept eating. Also present in the group ringing the fire were McKenzie and a young LAPD officer she had met earlier that day, as well as Grandma Dorothy and Alexander Petrinski. At length, as the eating gradually slowed, people in the circle began striking up random conversations, discussing everything from sports and weather to the upcoming presidential election. "So how's the writing coming?" Mike asked me, gleaning a last morsel of crab from his plate. "You still working on that novel you mentioned? The one about two brothers who are rock climbing in the mountains?"

I shot a quick glance across the fire at Travis, relieved to see he was engaged in conversation with Christy. "You have a good memory," I said evasively.

"For some things. Can I read it when you finish?"

"Uh . . ."

"Yeah, yeah, I know," said Mike. "You're just writing it for yourself. Well, I would like to read *something* of yours. As I recollect, you did promise to give me one of your short stories."

I nodded. "*Daniel's Song*. I have a copy up in my room. I'll get it for you before you leave."

"I look forward to reading it. By the way, your dad was right."

"About what?"

"About you getting your mother's good looks. The resemblance is amazing."

"Not really," I said carelessly, pleased by Mike's compliment. "Mom's the real beauty in the family. You should have seen her before . . ."

"I can imagine," said Mike. "She's still gorgeous."

"She is, isn't she?"

"Yes, she is. You know, I had a really good time that night we went out," Mike continued. "We ought to do it again sometime."

"I'm pretty busy at the station right now, Mike."

"That's just during the week. Let's get together next weekend. How about if I pick you up first thing Saturday morning?" Mike persisted. "C'mon, Ali, you know the old saying. All work and no play—"

"—gets lots of work done," I finished. "What do you have in mind?"

"I don't know. We could take a hike, go for a bike ride, whatever you want."

"A bike ride? Like on the trails you ride with your friends?" I asked, recalling my conversation with Mike on our way to the movie screening.

"I had something less strenuous in mind. Say, taking the bike path down to Venice Beach and having lunch."

"Less strenuous, huh?" I said, my competitive streak surfacing. "Think I can't keep up?"

"That's not it. I only—"

"You know what I'd like?" I interrupted. "Can you locate the trail that Mr. French took on the day we saw him returning to his house?"

"Mr. French?"

"You said he was riding an expensive bike, remember? I talked with someone who followed him that morning. They said he rode up Westridge to a dead-end at Queensferry, then returned from the other direction. Think you can find the trail he took?"

Mike paused. "Well, there's an entrance to Topanga State Park at Queensferry," he said. "From there Mr. French must have ridden up Sullivan Canyon to the fire road, then taken the dirt section of Mulholland to a single-track that connects with Mandeville Canyon. I've ridden up Sullivan before, and it's tough. Really tough. I don't see why you want to go that way."

"I just do," I said, not completely certain myself, although part of my desire to take that route stemmed from a nagging curiosity I had felt upon seeing Mr. French, a man who had recently lost his daughter, returning from a bike ride as though nothing had happened. Another part I couldn't quite put my finger on, but it had bothered me since that morning.

"Have you done much mountain biking?" Mike asked.

"None."

"There are easier rides."

"Sullivan Canyon, Mike. Don't worry, I'll keep up."

Reluctantly, Mike nodded. "It's your funeral," he said with amused skepticism. "I have a friend's mountain bike you can use, if you don't have one of your own. I'll pick you up at six next Saturday morning. We'll want to hit the trail before it gets too hot."

"I'll be ready," I replied, bridling at Mike's funeral comment but trying not to show it.

"Good." Mike glanced at his empty plate, then toward the serving tables. "Time for seconds. Want me to get you anything? Salmon? Chicken? More clams?"

"I'm fine. Don't forget to save room for dessert."

"I'll worry about dessert when the time comes," said Mike with a grin, rising from his chair.

I watched as Mike topped the sea wall in an easy bound, disappearing into the crowd on the deck. Remembering his kiss outside the restaurant, I felt a sudden rush of heat. Uneasily, I wondered where our friendship was leading, realizing to my surprise that although Mike often provoked me as much as he attracted me, I was already looking forward to our bike ride next Saturday.

The last guest left at a little after midnight. Though a straggle of late-arriving partygoers stayed past eleven, most people departed following dessert, sated and spent from their day at the beach. Exhausted, Mom also retired early. Dad joined her, electing to leave the straightening up until the following day. Realizing that without at least a rudimentary cleanup, Callie and the other local beach dogs would have a field day going through the trash, Travis, Nate, and I policed the area, gathering up food scraps not already in trash bags and stowing leftovers in the upstairs refrigerator. Afterward, enjoying the solitude of the now deserted beach, I sat on the sea wall staring at the dying fire in the luau pit. To the east, a waning moon had risen over the foot of Santa Monica Bay, sending silvery shards of light shimmering across the ocean's surface.

"Quite a party."

Startled, I turned to see Grandma Dorothy standing behind me. "Hi, Grandma. What are you doing up so late?"

"Couldn't sleep." Dorothy kicked off her sandals and sat beside me, resting her feet on the cool sand at the base of the wall. "I don't think I'll eat again for a month."

"Me, neither," I agreed. "By the way, I was mortified at the way you threw yourself at poor Mr. Petrinski today. I had no idea you were such a hussy."

"I couldn't get rid of the man," Dorothy laughed. "He's nice, actually. We're going to a concert together next week at the Disney Center."

"Well, good for you. Be gentle with him, Grandma."

"Oh, hush."

I grinned at my grandmother, once more struck by Dorothy's physical similarity to Mom. Dorothy smiled back. "The party was good for your mother," she said. "I think it lifted her spirits."

"I do, too." I hesitated. "Grandma, can I ask you something?"

"What?"

I paused, trying to frame a question that I had wanted to ask my grandmother for a long time. Finally I said, "Did you and Mom fight much when she was growing up?"

"Of course," Dorothy replied. "That's the way things are between mothers and daughters."

"I'm serious, Grandma."

"I know you are, honey. And yes, your mother and I fought, sometimes a lot. Of course, I had her when I wasn't much older than you are now, so I still had plenty of growing up to do myself."

I hesitated, surprised by her answer. Dorothy and my mother seemed so close, I had trouble imagining them ever disagreeing, much less fighting. "Mom had me early, too," I noted. "She married Dad at nineteen."

Dorothy nodded. "That was one of the things your mother and I fought about. Bitterly, I regret to say. Not that I didn't approve of Dan. Quite the contrary. I simply thought they should have waited to marry until Catheryn had graduated from college. As things turned out, I was wrong."

"What was Mom like when she was growing up?"

Dorothy's eyes took on the faraway look of someone mentally revisiting things long past. "Your mother was precocious, inquisitive, and loving," she said. "She reminded me of you, Ali. She was also obstinate, opinionated, and rebellious," she added fondly. "In that respect she was like you, too. Perhaps worse."

"Really?"

"Really. Now, let me ask *you* something."

"Fire away."

"Are you happy?"

I hesitated, taken off guard by her question. "What do you mean?"

"Exactly what I said. Are you happy?"

"I . . . I'd like to think I'm working toward it," I replied. "Only sometimes I don't know what I want."

"As you get older, you may discover that getting what you *think* you want doesn't necessarily make you happy."

"What do you do, then?"

"That's something people have to discover for themselves," said Dorothy. "I *do* know that what makes for happiness isn't always a successful career, or money, or any of the other things that people expect to fulfill them."

"I suppose not," I agreed, wondering where our discussion was leading.

"There's a reason I asked you that question," said Dorothy, as if reading my mind. "You know that Catheryn and I have no secrets between us."

I remained silent, waiting for the other shoe to drop.

"I haven't mentioned this before now because I knew you didn't want to discuss it. And you probably still don't." Dorothy took a deep breath and continued. "Catheryn told me what happened to you on the night those men broke into your house. I know that you kept it hidden for a long time, and I can imagine what keeping that secret did to you. And to your mother."

"Grandma—"

Dorothy raised her hand. "Let me finish. Something like what you experienced is hard to get over, especially if you keep it bottled up inside. It's too much for someone your age to carry around by yourself. If you ever want to discuss it, I'm available."

I didn't respond, the memory of my rape coiling like a serpent in my mind.

"Now, I realize that on top of everything else, you have a lot of uncertainty in your life right now," Dorothy pushed on. "Your mother's illness, and this job at CBS that's driving your mom and dad crazy, and what to do about school and your career and the rest of your life. They're confusing things, things you may not know how to handle yet. Time takes care of many problems, but not all. So at the risk of sounding like a meddling old grandma, which I guess I am, I'm going to impart a few words of grandmotherly advice."

"Do I have a choice in this?" I asked.

"No."

"I didn't think so."

Dorothy smiled patiently. "I'm going to say this, whether you want to hear it or not. But I hope you hear me, Ali. It may not sound like much, but my mother told me this when I was about your age, and it's helped me through some rough spots." Dorothy took my hand. "Look inside yourself, Ali. Look inside and ask yourself what's truly important. When you know that, everything else will fall into place."

Long after Dorothy had returned to the house, I remained on the sea wall, watching as the fire subsided to a mound of glowing coals. With an unsettling sense of déjà vu, I pondered my

243

grandmother's words, recalling that Travis had told me essentially the same thing. Put another way, Mom had, too.

*The people I love are my life's real blessings.*

*Get your priorities straight.*

*Ask yourself what's truly important.*

I stared out over the moonlit bay, wishing things were really that easy.

# 22

I arose early the following Saturday, already thinking about my upcoming bike ride that morning with Mike. Forgoing my customary run, I donned my robe and worked at my computer until five-thirty, then slipped downstairs to the kitchen for a light breakfast of cereal and fruit. Afterward I crept back up the staircase, treading quietly. Upon returning to my dorm room, I shrugged off my robe and pulled on shorts, a tee shirt, and my running shoes, then tied a green nylon jacket around my waist.

The numerals on my desktop clock read: 5:51 AM. Time to go. After turning off my computer, I made my way back to the ground floor and stepped outside, waiting on the front landing. The sun was barely up. I donned my jacket, glad I had brought it. Minutes later Mike's Toyota pickup pulled to the curb, a pair of mountain bikes piled in the truck bed.

Leaning across the passenger seat, Mike peered up at the dorm, waving as he spotted me. I waved back, then descended the stairs and slid into the front seat beside him. Closing the door, I noticed the dark aroma of fresh-brewed coffee.

"Morning," said Mike, handing me a tall paper cup with a Starbuck's logo on the side. "I didn't know how you take it, so I left it black," he added, shooting an appreciative glance at my bare legs.

"Black's perfect," I replied, enjoying the warmth of the drink in my hands. Taking a sip, I inspected Mike over the rim of my cup, noting his colorful, long-sleeved racing shirt and tight-fitting biking shorts that accented the muscles of his thighs. His hair was brushed back from his forehead and looked damp, as if he had just stepped from the shower.

"I read your short story last night," he said as he dropped the Toyota into gear and pulled away from the curb. "Sorry it took me so long to get to it, but I've been jammed up at work and spending every other spare second making last-minute changes to my film."

"No problem," I said. Mike had called Thursday to confirm our ride, and I knew from our brief phone conversation that he was still struggling to ready his documentary for the Labor Day showing in Telluride. "At least you read it. What did you think?"

"First off," Mike said apologetically, "I don't usually like science fiction—"

"Everybody says that," I interrupted. "Though for the life of me I can't understand why. Half the successful movies made over the past twenty years have been based on science fiction, especially the blockbusters. Did you like the *Star Wars* series?"

"Of course. I—"

"*The Terminator? Close Encounters? Jurassic Park?*"

"Sure. What I'm trying—"

"*E.T., Back to the Future, The Matrix, Star Trek, Alien, 2001, Aliens, Blade Runner, Avatar*—"

"Ali, will you be quiet for a second? I'm trying to say your story blew me away."

"Oh."

"It wasn't what I expected. The setting was weird, but the people were real and your characters really got to me. Where'd you get the idea—a father who can't accept a deformity in his child, and as a result he winds up losing everything he loves?"

"I made it up."

"You named it *Daniel's Song*. Any connection to your father?"

"No," I said quickly.

"Well, wherever you got the idea, I liked your story. I liked it a lot. You're good, Ali. Really good."

"Thanks," I said, as usual more uncomfortable with praise than censure.

"I'd like to read something else of yours sometime."

When I didn't reply, Mike obligingly changed the subject. "I enjoyed meeting your parents last weekend. Especially your mom. How's she doing?"

"Getting stronger every day," I answered, recalling the disastrous luncheon date I'd had with Mom on Wednesday. After her follow-up visit at St. John's, we had met for lunch at the Santa Monica Mall. When I questioned Mom about her checkup, she had seemed distant, saying that everything had gone all right but adding that she'd made an appointment to see a bone-marrow transplant team on Friday. At Dr. Kratovil's suggestion, she was having this new consult done at the Ronald Reagan UCLA Medical Center, rather than at St. John's. Because I recalled from my discussion with Dr. Kratovil that a bone-marrow consult wasn't scheduled to take place, if at all, until after Mom's second round of chemo, I had queried her about it. Instead of answering, Mom instead had started in anew questioning my plans for the future. And as usual when that topic arose, our conversation had quickly degenerated.

Mike turned left at the light on Sunset. "I'm glad to hear she's improving," he said.

"Me, too. I'll give her your best when I see her. I'm having dinner at the beach with my family tonight."

"Well, say hi to your dad for me, too. And tell him thanks again for the party."

"Sure," I said, my mind still on my mother.

For the next few minutes we rode in silence. I sipped my coffee; Mike concentrated on the road. He turned right when we reached the light at Mandeville Canyon, then took a left on Westridge Road. Remembering my drive up the same route with Max Riemann several weeks back, I looked out the window, watching as a line of houses bordering the road slipped past. As we ascended higher on the ridge, the sun finally broke over the canyon's rim. Moments later I stared curiously as we passed the Frenches' estate. Outside their gate, a radio patrol car with a private security company logo on its door sat angled across the driveway. Otherwise, the grounds looked deserted.

Noticing my glance, Mike asked, "Anything new on the French story at CBS?"

"Well, for one, the tabloid reporters have finally stopped waylaying me outside the studio."

"That's good," said Mike. "Any other developments?"

"A few," I conceded. "On a hunch, I got the name of Jordan's family doctor from someone at her medical insurance company. Believe it or not, contacting Jordan's physician was an angle no one else at the news station had considered."

Mike smiled. "You're quite the detective, aren't you? Like father, like daughter."

I smiled back self-consciously. "Something like that. Anyway, Jordan's doctor admitted that the police had interviewed him, but otherwise he didn't want to talk. I kept him on the line and eventually got him to open up. He said that the questions he had been asked by investigators fell into two general categories: Had Jordan shown any physical signs of sexual abuse, and had he observed or had reported to him any psychological manifestations associated with childhood abuse—rebellious behavior, nightmares, depression—that sort of thing. According to him, the answer to everything was no. But in view of what happened, he could just be covering up any oversight he'd made."

"You mean because he didn't report it?"

"Correct. I thought it was a good lead," I went on. "Lauren gave it to Brent," I added.

Mike took a left onto a side street, then another on Queensferry Road. "Actually, I caught Brent's piece on Jordan's doctor last night," he said. "It was good."

"Yeah. It was terrific."

"The Jordan French case *is* his story, you know."

I didn't reply.

"Ali, for someone like you to have worked her way up the news ladder as far as you have in, what is it—*five weeks*?—is unheard of. Well, maybe not unheard of. I can remember a few instances when someone's rocketed up the ranks almost overnight, but it's rare, especially for someone as young as you. You've had a spot aired nationally, attracted management's attention in New York—at least from what I hear on the grapevine—and earned your press credentials. Incidentally, congratulations on that. You're on your way. Just be patient."

"Not something I'm noted for."

"You *are* ambitious, aren't you?"

Again, I didn't reply.

Riding the brakes, Mike coasted down a long incline, pulling to a stop at a dead end at the bottom of Queensferry. After parking a dozen yards from a wooden barrier blocking the road, Mike killed the engine, exited, and made his way to the rear of the pickup. Noticing that he hadn't brought a jacket, I left my windbreaker in the truck and helped him unload the bikes. Mike's bike had a brushed aluminum frame, knobby tires, suspension shocks on both front and rear wheels, and a water bottle mounted on one of the frame tubes. The bike he brought for me was slightly smaller, with a water bottle and similar tires but shocks on only the front fork.

After performing a quick equipment check on the bikes, Mike reached into the truck and grabbed bike helmets and two pairs of biking gloves from the rear seat. "Here, put these on," he said, handing me a helmet and a pair of gloves. Then, bending to loosen a clamp securing my bike seat, "You know how to work the gears?"

I pulled on the fingerless gloves Mike had given me, then donned my helmet and fastened the chin strap. Placing my hands on the handlebar grips, I inspected the shifters that controlled the bike's twenty-one gears. "Left hand shifts the front chain rings, right hand does the back sprocket?"

"Correct," said Mike. "You'll probably be in granny gear most of the time while we're climbing, so shifting shouldn't be a problem. Oh, and on the way down, be careful using the front brake," he advised, raising my seat. "Give it too much and you'll wind up doing a Polish wheelie—headfirst over the handlebars."

"Granny? As in grandmother?"

"That's the lowest gear."

"I figured," I said, pumping the brake levers to make sure which was which. It had been years since I'd ridden a bike, and even then my only experience had been on bikes designed for the pavement. Nonetheless, I felt confident I would be able to handle things. After all, riding a bike was, well—like riding a bike, right?

"Get on and see how it feels."

I placed a foot on the left pedal, pushed off, and swung over my other leg. At first the seat Mike had adjusted felt too high, but as I pedaled I soon found that the elevated seat position allowed my legs to extend almost completely on each downstroke, letting me use the full strength of my thighs.

"Looks fine," said Mike. He pulled on his own gloves and donned his helmet. "Let's do it."

I dismounted and followed Mike through a narrow gate designed to prevent the passage of motorized vehicles, rolling my bike vertically on the back wheel through the barrier. From hikes I had taken in the Santa Monica Mountains years back, I knew we were entering a portion of Topanga State Park where the use of trails and fire roads was limited to hikers, bike riders, and equestrians—an uneasy mix that shared the park in a spirit of begrudging tolerance. Nevertheless, as there had been no other cars parked at the bottom of Queensferry, I suspected it was unlikely that we would encounter anyone on our way up Sullivan Canyon at that early hour.

Once past the gate Mike threw a leg over his bike, clicking the metal inserts on the bottoms of his biking shoes into the pedals. As I remounted my own bike, Mike pulled over, bracing himself against the trunk of a eucalyptus tree. "We'll be heading up an old dirt service road that the gas company restored some years back," he said. "Thanks to the rains, it has mostly washed out again and is single-track most of the way up. There's water, rough ground, sand, shale, and plenty of climbing. There's also no rush, so we can stop to rest anytime you want. Just let me know."

"Don't worry about me," I replied. "We'll stop when *you* want."

Initially the ride proceeded down a short slope, following the last of the Queensferry pavement to a creek a hundred yards distant. At first, as I accelerated through the cool mountain air, I regretted not bringing my jacket. I regretted it doubly when we reached the creek bed and lost the sun. But as we turned right and started up the canyon, following what seemed to be little more than a footpath winding through the gravel and sand of the streambed, I quickly forgot about being cold. The ride was going to be a lot harder than I thought.

Unlike the chaparral-covered mountain slopes above, this lowermost stretch of Sullivan Canyon was dense with sycamore, oak, and cottonwood. Here and there, as the trail proceeded through banks of blackberry bramble and native grasses, I spotted sporadic flashes of color—the oranges, yellows, and blues of spring's resident wildflowers somehow persisting into the heat of summer. With the exception of several rain squalls that had pelted the Southland during July, Southern California had received little precipitation since spring. Despite the lack of rain, a spill of water still ran in the streambed, collecting in shallow pools behind logs and rocks. Though the creek now appeared tame, deep erosive cuts in the banks attested to the stream's power in flood. The flow of the creek gradually increased as Mike and I climbed higher, and on numerous occasions we were forced to cross. Following Mike's lead, I pedaled through each ford without falling, enjoying the cooling splash on my legs.

Despite the shade of the canyon and our occasional bracing charges through the water, I was soon perspiring heavily. Patches of perspiration stained my tee shirt under my arms and soaked a dark V on my chest. Worse, sweat kept trickling into my eyes, the salty sting an increasing irritation. My breathing growing labored, I repeatedly wiped my face on my shoulder, a risky maneuver while negotiating tricky terrain that more than once almost sent me careening into the streambed. Still, I refused to call a rest.

Mike continued smoothly up the steepening trail, the muscles of his arms and shoulders standing out under his shirt like strands of a hawser, his steel-corded legs pumping like pistons. Glancing back from time to time, he occasionally slowed to let me close the gap between us. Noticing this, I strained even harder, determined to keep him in sight. Running had toughened my body, but I quickly realized that my morning jogs had merely conditioned me for *running*, not biking, which seemed to require a whole different set of muscles. The low gear I was using had seemed ridiculously easy at first. Now, my legs turning to rubber, I wished I could drop the gear ratio down another notch. Maybe several.

Again and again I was forced to dismount and push my bike past washed-out sections of trail—interludes that provided little respite but at least gave me an opportunity to drink from my water bottle, something Mike managed to do while still riding. Twice he called back to ask whether I wanted to rest; each time I doggedly refused, insisting I was fine. My goal, however, had changed. No longer was I obsessed with keeping up. Now I simply wanted to make it to the top.

After forty minutes of steady climbing, Mike and I began ascending the right bank of the canyon, finally leaving the cooling shade of the streambed. Once more in the sun, we climbed a series of punishingly steep switchbacks to a rutted fire road topping the ridge, emerging from shoulder-high banks of yellow mustard weed on both sides of the trail. Mike stopped on a level section that offered a panorama of the canyon below. Heart thudding, lungs burning, shoulders aching, thighs cramping, I pulled up beside him.

Mike raised his water bottle and took a long pull. "Nice going," he said. "Not many could have made that climb their first time out."

I grabbed my own bottle, greedily guzzling the last of my water. "Not many girls, you mean," I gasped, wiping my mouth with the back of my hand.

"Not many, period."

"It wasn't so bad," I puffed. Heart still pounding, I looked down the way we had come. A swath of green marked the bottom of the narrow canyon, tracing the course of the streambed as it snaked toward the ocean. Ahead, the fire road we had joined climbed at a much gentler pace. "Where to now?" I asked when I had finally caught my breath.

"You still want to do the loop that Mr. French took back to Mandeville Canyon?"

I nodded.

"Then we go up."

Ten minutes of easier climbing brought us to the crest of an east-west ridge guarding the lower San Fernando Valley. Here the fire road exited through a gate onto an improved dirt road, its graded surface over twenty feet wide. After taking a single-track trail skirting the metal barrier, we again stopped to rest. "I didn't even know this road was here," I noted, surveying the sprawling cityscape below.

"Few people do," said Mike. "We're now on a portion of Mulholland Drive that's never been paved, thanks in part to lobbying by several equestrian groups that ride up here."

"Can you drive a car up here?"

"Sure. It connects with paved sections at both ends. But as I said, hardly anyone knows it's here. Great view, huh?"

"Gorgeous," I agreed, my eyes sweeping the distant valley. "What's that lake down there?" I asked, pointing to an irregularly shaped body of water nestled in the foothills a mile or so north.

"Encino Reservoir."

At Mike's words, my blood ran cold. "That's where . . ."

"Yeah," said Mike, picking up my train of thought. "Pretty inaccessible, huh? You can see why someone would consider it a good place to dump a body."

I stared down at the reservoir. As Mike had noted, it appeared unapproachable. Steep, brush-covered ridges formed its eastern and western flanks; an earthen dam comprised the northern terminus. Smatterings of housing developments dotted the hillside lower down—all clearly out of sight of the water. Because of its lofty location, Encino Reservoir was visible only from the air . . . and the section of dirt road on which we now stood. "It's a great place for someone to dump a body," I agreed. "But first that certain someone would have to know the reservoir was there."

"Ali, you don't think . . ."

"I don't know what I think," I said. And in truth, I didn't. After meeting Jordan's mother and hearing her emotional denials, I, like most in the media, had come to believe that Mr. and Mrs. French couldn't possibly have had anything to do with their daughter's death. Now I wasn't so sure.

Mike looked at me doubtfully. "Just because Mr. French rides up here doesn't mean anything."

"I know. On the other hand, as you pointed out, not many people even know that this road is here. I hate to say this, but now I can think of *one* person who does. And he's connected to the case."

Mike nodded thoughtfully. "Is that why you wanted to retrace Mr. French's bike route?"

"Maybe. Call it a hunch," I replied. Raking my eyes over the ridge, I spotted a cut in the hillside beneath a line of high-voltage power stanchions. I traced the trail as it snaked down the mountain, losing it behind a hill before it reached the water. "I think there's a way down to the reservoir over there," I added. "Let's check it out."

"It's an old access road. A locked gate is at the top. You can't get down that way."

I remounted my bike. "Let's check it out anyway."

After cranking past a small rise, I located the beginning of a narrow dirt road intersecting our unimproved section of Mulholland. An iron gate topped with outward-curving spikes blocked the road's entrance; a thick chain and a handful of interlinked padlocks secured the gate to a stout metal pole. Unlike the fire road gate we had encountered earlier, this barrier was accompanied on either side by an eight-foot-high fence topped with barbed wire.

I dismounted, leaning my bike against the fence. Disappointed that we couldn't continue to the water, I examined the locks on the gate. Two identical, circular-shaped padlocks at either end displayed Department of Water and Power markings—with one of the DWP locks hooked through a gate chain. Linked between the DWP locks were three smaller padlocks of various makes and shapes. A final padlock connected the second DWP lock to the opposite end of the chain, securing the gate. All the locks exhibited a reddish patina of rust and had probably been put there, I suspected, by different county agencies for their own use. None of the locks appeared to have been disturbed. The gate itself looked as if it hadn't been opened for years.

"Told you," said Mike, who had followed me to the locked entrance. "C'mon, let's hit the trail. We still have a lot of distance to cover."

"Hold on a sec." I peered through the gate, searching for signs of recent passage. Like the gate, the ground on the other side looked undisturbed, although I realized the rocky roadbed might not be soft enough to show tire tracks. Furthermore, any of the infrequent rainstorms that had blown across the Southland over the past weeks could have erased any tracks or footprints that had been left.

"I don't want to burst your bubble, Ali, but I'm sure the police investigated all this," Mike pointed out. "It's not something they would be likely to miss."

"No, it isn't," I conceded. "On the other hand, I'm not at all certain they know that Mr. French's morning bike ride takes him in plain view of the reservoir down there. For the time being, let's keep this between us."

"If you want."

"Promise?"

Mike smiled. "Cross my heart. Anyway, it's probably just coincidence."

"Maybe." With one last glance at the reservoir, I remounted my bike.

"You have something in mind, don't you?" Mike looked at me curiously. "What are you going to do?"

I shrugged. "I don't know. Yet."

# 23

After Mike dropped me off at UCLA, I lay on my dorm room bed, contemplating my discovery. True, Mr. French's knowledge of the reservoir's presence might be coincidental, as Mike had suggested. On the other hand, like my father, I accepted coincidence as an explanation only when all other avenues had been exhausted. Yet no matter how I racked my brain, I couldn't decide how to proceed. In the end I resolved that my best course lay in simply turning over the information to my dad and letting him take it from there. And if I were lucky, maybe there would be something in it for me. Having made that decision, I couldn't wait to talk with Dad.

Later that evening I drove to Malibu for dinner with my family, arriving at the beach at a little past six. Although the dining room table was set and a pot of a delicious-smelling stew sat simmering on the stove, the house appeared deserted. Wondering where everyone was, I made my way to my parents' bedroom. "Mom?" I called through the open door. "Dad?"

No answer.

Thinking they must be downstairs on the deck, or possibly taking a walk on the beach, I entered their bedroom and stuck my head out an open window near the bed. Not spotting them on the deck, I scanned the beach, failing to see them there, either. Disappointed, I decided to check the music room downstairs. As I left the bedroom, I passed my parents' desk—an oak secretary where Mom paid bills and Dad, though complaining the desk was too fancy for his taste, occasionally worked as well. A thick, three-ring binder on the desk caught my eye. A single word, inscribed in my father's bold cursive, was written on the binder's spine: French.

Over the years Dad had brought home similar books. Though I had never looked into one, I knew that LAPD homicide detectives referred to them as murder books. I also knew that they contained all pertinent documents and information relating to a case.

Curious, I returned to the bedroom and looked out the window again. Then, on impulse, I went to the desk and picked up the binder, not really intending to open it. It felt heavy, the files and reports crammed between its blue plastic covers as thick as a dictionary. I hesitated, my curiosity building.

Against my better judgment, I opened the book. Ignoring a surge of guilt, I quickly flipped through its contents, pausing on a grisly photo taken at the reservoir. Nauseated, I continued turning pages. I stopped when I came to the coroner's findings, a pivotal report that had been sealed at my father's request.

Most of the autopsy protocol—a multipage document containing anatomical drawings, photographs, swab results, histological summaries, and laboratory findings—proved too dry to hold my interest, and I skimmed through the pages rapidly. As reported in the sketchy details given to the press, the cause of Jordan's death had been a subdural hematoma. Details that had not been disclosed to the public included the absence of water in her lungs and stomach, as well as the presence of areas of vaginal erosion and tissue inflammation. Someone had underlined the latter, penning "chronic sexual abuse?" in the margin. As I was about to move on, another underlined section caught my eye—an autopsy analysis of the gastric contents. Jordan's last meal, pasta with a red seafood sauce, had undergone a period of digestion of three to four hours before she'd died. The digestion duration had been circled twice, with the addition of another question mark.

"What the hell are you doing?"

I turned, my heart dropping. "Uh, hi, Dad."

My father's eyes narrowed. Furious, he strode across the room and ripped the murder book from my hands. "Damn it, Allison!" he thundered.

"Dad . . ."

"What gives you the right to go through my files?"

"I . . . I didn't mean to pry," I stammered. "I came in here to find you and Mom. When I saw the book, I just thought I'd take a peek. I apologize, Dad. I have no excuse for going through your stuff. None at all. I'm sorry. I'm really, really sorry."

"Sorry doesn't cut it."

I looked down, unable to meet my father's glare.

"If details in these files are made public, it could ruin any chance I have of closing the investigation. Not to mention getting me fired."

"I won't say anything."

"How much did you see?"

"Not much."

"The truth, Ali! What did you see?"

"I looked at a few pictures, read a bit of the autopsy report."

"What part of the autopsy report?"

"The part about there being signs of chronic sexual abuse."

"What else?"

"That the stomach contents had been digested three to four hours before she died."

"Damn!" Dad exploded.

"Dad, I won't say anything about this to anyone. It's off the record."

"Like the last time?"

"No, not like the last time. I screwed up then. I won't do it again."

"You may not live to do it again," Dad warned. Then, as if struck by something in his own words, his thoughts seemed to turn inward. Slowly, the anger bled out of him.

I hesitated, puzzled by his abrupt change of mood. "Dad, I really am sorry," I repeated. "I was wrong to look through your files. But now that we're on the subject, can I ask you a question?"

"No."

I continued anyway. "I understand how releasing the sexual-abuse material could compromise your case, but what do the gastric contents have to do with anything?" When Dad didn't reply, I pondered a moment. "I suppose if you know when a final meal was eaten, the degree of digestion could be used to determine when someone died," I reasoned, answering my own question.

"Drop it," Dad ordered.

"So the stomach contents are important, and your circling the digestion duration could mean there's a discrepancy in the time of death," I went on.

"I said drop it."

"Yes, sir."

My father scowled at me, then turned toward the door. "C'mon. Time for dinner. We've been waiting to eat till you got here."

"Dad? You think they did it, don't you? Off the record?"

My father turned back. Wearily, he passed a hand across his face. "To tell you the God's honest truth, I don't know," he replied, still seeming oddly distracted. "My head's telling me one thing; my gut's saying something else. Now, let it go, Allison. Please."

"There's a reason I asked," I said. "I learned something today about Mr. French."

"And that is?"

"First of all, he's a mountain biker. He rides the trails and fire roads behind his estate. At least he did before he and his wife moved out of their house."

"Deluca mentioned that. So?"

"So I went up there this morning with a friend and retraced one of the routes Mr. French rides," I explained, having trouble containing my excitement. "Guess what? The dirt trail he takes runs in plain sight of Encino Reservoir."

Dad shook his head. "Just because he knows the reservoir is there doesn't prove a damn thing."

"But there's a road from Mulholland down to the water."

"A locked gate is at the top. Nothing was touched."

"It looked that way to me, too," I admitted, disappointed at my father's reaction. "There were no tracks on the other side, and none of the six or so padlocks on the chain appeared to have been tampered with, either. But I got to thinking. What if someone had a key to one of those locks?"

"We interviewed everybody who has or could possibly get a key," Dad replied impatiently. "Southern California Edison personnel, fire department workers—even LAPD cops. We came up empty."

"Oh."

Dad again started for the door, then turned back. "How many locks did you say?" he demanded, his eyes suddenly gleaming like a gun barrels.

Puzzled, I pictured the gate in my mind. "There were two big ones," I answered. "They had DWP stamped on them. Three smaller locks were linked between those two big DWP locks, and a final padlock at one end."

"So that makes six total? You're absolutely certain?"

I nodded. "I'm positive."

My father's expression hardened. "Damn. I should have checked that myself."

"What's wrong?"

Dad didn't answer.

All at once I understood. Two DWP locks plus three more for the other agencies that Dad had mentioned—SCE, the fire department, and the LAPD—made *five* locks, not six. "Someone cut the chain," I reasoned aloud, everything falling into place. "Then he repaired the cut chain by inserting an extra padlock. Whoever did it even used an old lock so it would match."

"This is off the record. All of it. You understand that," said Dad. It wasn't a question.

"Of course," I agreed. "But when the time comes, can I break the story about the locks? I'm the one who—"

"Allison, is your new job all you think about?"

"What's wrong with that? If I don't report this, someone else will. It might as well be me."

"And how is it supposed to look when it's *my* daughter breaking an exclusive story on *my* case?" Dad demanded angrily. "I'd have hell to pay explaining it to the department. What's more, every other news agency would scream foul."

"That's their problem," I countered stubbornly. "I came up with this. And if they don't like it—tough."

Dad scowled. "It will still look bad, no matter how it happened."

"So when have you ever cared about how things looked?" I pointed out. "Especially to the press."

"You have a point there," Dad conceded with a slight smile. He thought a moment. "You want to break the story when the time comes? Fine, as it's eventually going to come out anyway, you have a deal. Provided you keep your mouth shut till I say."

"Agreed," I said. "Now, what about tomorrow?"

"I beg your pardon?"

"You're going back to the reservoir, aren't you? I want to be there."

"Out of the question."

"I won't reveal the part about the locks. How about if—"

"No."

"Think about it, Dad. Some positive coverage right now could help your investigation. You know—police are working hard to uncover new leads, and so forth. And wouldn't having me there on the ground be preferable to having some news helicopter circling around overhead?"

Dad glared. "What do you mean, news helicopter?"

"Forget I said that," I backtracked. "C'mon, Dad. Please?"

"You're not going anywhere near that site." Dad hesitated, then continued. "But if you want to do something from a public road, I guess there's nothing I can do to stop you. But I still don't like it."

"Thanks, Dad."

Just then Mom called up from the music room below. "Dan, has Ali arrived yet? Nate and Travis are starving."

Dad crossed to the window. "She's here," he called down. "C'mon up. Let's eat."

Minutes later we all gathered at the dining room table. I sat next to Nate, Mom took her customary place beside Travis, and Dad sat at the head of the table. Dorothy, who had returned to Santa Barbara the day after the beach party, was conspicuously absent. Though she would be rejoining us when Mom began her second phase of chemotherapy, everyone already missed her, especially Nate.

Dinner that night, normally a high point for our family, seemed hollow and reserved. Like an unwanted guest, a shadow of uncertainty sat at our table, its presence sensed by everyone. The meal, a thick lentil stew, squares of cornbread, and a mixed green salad that Mom had prepared, was hearty and filling. Nevertheless, our family's customarily freewheeling conversation fell flat at every turn. Dad tried to be attentive, but his concentration drifted repeatedly during a discussion of Nate's AAU baseball finals later that month. Even Mom had trouble keeping her mind on Travis's rundown of the pieces he planned to perform for his remaining summer recitals.

Throughout this I kept my eyes down, guiltily suspecting that the family tension was because of me. Eating like a robot, I reviewed my confrontation with Dad, still puzzled by his reaction. Though I had no intention of disclosing anything I had learned from his murder book, I knew that in examining it I had been completely and unforgivably out of line. Dad's reaction had been justified, but his anger had been nowhere near as scathing as I'd expected . . . or deserved. He had even tacitly agreed to my presence at the reservoir the next day. It had seemed as if his mind were elsewhere.

Following dinner, Nate and I cleared the dishes. Dad brewed a pot of coffee while Travis helped Mom serve pecan pie and ice cream for dessert. Ten minutes later we all rejoined at the table. Nate finished his ice cream and pie in record time, and shortly afterward asked to be excused.

"Please wait till we're all done, honey," said Mom, taking a sip of coffee.

"Callie needs a walk," said Nate. "She hasn't been out much all day."

Hearing the word "walk," our yellow Labrador looked up from her wicker basket in the corner, quizzically raising her ears.

"You can take her out in a minute."

"Aw, Mom . . ."

My mother glanced at Dad. From my place across the table, I saw something pass between them. Dad nodded, covering Mom's hand with his.

Mom took a breath, then slowly let it out. "Nate, there's something I need to tell you, something I need to tell you all."

"What is it?" I asked nervously.

Mom glanced once more at Dad. "When I went in for my checkup on Wednesday, I got some bad news," she said quietly. "Dr. Kratovil says I'm undergoing a relapse."

Abruptly, I realized why my mother had seemed so preoccupied during our lunch at the mall.

"What does that mean?" asked Travis.

"It means my cancer has come back."

"I thought the chemotherapy was working."

"So did I," said Mom. "Most patients achieve remission following the first round of chemo. Apparently I'm one of the ones who don't."

"What about more chemo?" I asked.

"Dr. Kratovil thinks that would be a waste of time, even with a new combination of drugs," Mom answered. "She thinks we need to do something different."

I shook my head. "But—"

"Things aren't all bad," Mom interrupted, forcing a smile. "I had a conference with the UCLA transplant team. They think I'm a good candidate for a bone-marrow graft. Unfortunately, given the aggressiveness of my cancer, there's no hope of purifying my own stem cells for the procedure. I'll need a donor. They're hunting for someone with my exact marrow type. If one isn't found soon, I'll have to ask you, Ali."

Shocked by the news of my mother's relapse, I swallowed hard, feeling as if the floor had dropped out from under me. "You don't have to ask, Mom. Of course I'll do it. I'm just glad I'm a good enough match."

"You aren't perfect, as we all know," said Mom, making an attempt at humor. "They may want to do a few more tests on you, but Dr. Kratovil thinks you're close enough."

"Slow down," said Travis. "I don't understand how this transplant is supposed to work."

"It's fairly simple," said Mom, seeming relieved to be shifting to a technical discussion of her treatment. "Some of my white blood cells are reproducing out of control. Prior to my bone-marrow graft, I'll receive X-rays and a high dose of chemotherapy that will kill *all* of my white blood cells, good and bad alike. Permanently. The cancer will be gone, but then I'll no longer have a functioning immune system. That's where the bone-marrow graft comes in. I'll be given someone else's white blood cells, and they will reproduce and take over the job for my missing ones."

"If a transplant is that easy, why didn't they just do one to begin with?" asked Travis.

"Well, it's not *that* easy," Mom admitted. "There can be complications."

I recalled the transplant information I had read on the internet. As Mom said, there could be complications. Until the graft took, assuming it did, the recipient was subject to any number of life-threatening infections. Worse, a transplant had to match its host closely or the graft cells would try to reject their new body, resulting in a condition known as graft-versus-host disease. From what I had been able to glean from my research, a bone-marrow transplant was a risky, potentially fatal procedure.

"What kind of complications?" Travis persisted.

Mom's control momentarily slipped, and for a split second I saw in her eyes the same flicker of doubt I had detected on the morning of the luau. "I did some reading on that, Trav," I said quickly. "For one, a transplant recipient often gets the allergies of the donor. Imagine, my white cells might make Mom allergic to housework, Brussels sprouts, foreign movies, and cleaning her room. Worse, she could wind up with my biggest allergy of all— hating being told what to do."

Though no one laughed, Mom gave me a grateful smile. "Things can always go wrong, Trav," she said softly. "But I'm in good hands. I'm going to recover."

"I know, Mom," said Travis. "When will this be done?"

"My insurance authorization should come through soon, but the doctors want to give me a few weeks to regain my strength before proceeding," Mom answered. "I'll probably be admitted to UCLA before the end of the month. There was some talk of waiting until a better-matched donor than Ali turns up. Unfortunately, that could take months or even years, if it happens at all. Because Allison's marrow type is acceptably close to mine, the doctors think the benefits of waiting are outweighed by the dangers of allowing the disease to progress. They want to proceed as quickly as possible. They're going to keep looking for a better match, but if they don't find someone soon, Allison will be my donor. I'm telling you all this so you'll know what's happening. But I don't want you to worry," she added. "I'll be fine. I promise."

"You said that before," said Nate, who until now had remained silent. "You said your treatments were going to make you better."

"I know, honey."

"The chemo was all for nothing." Nate shook his head. "You'll never get better, will you?"

Mom started to tell Nate he was wrong. Seeing the look on his face, she stopped midsentence. And this second time that her guard was down, we all saw her uncertainty, reading it in the tightness of her lips and the slump of her shoulders as plainly as if she had confessed her fears aloud.

Head down, Nate rose and walked from the room. Callie climbed from her bed and trotted after him, close at his heels. A moment later we heard the bang of the downstairs door out to the beach. With a sigh, Dad pushed away from the table.

I stood quickly. "I'll get him."

"That's okay, Ali."

"No, I want to," I insisted, hurrying from the room before my father could object.

After descending the stairs and making my way outside, I crossed the deck to the sea wall. Stepping to the sand below, I gazed up and down the deserted beach. By now the sun had painted a final smear of orange on the western horizon; to the east, the evening star glittered over Santa Monica like a distant diamond.

Not spotting Nate, I headed to the water, where the ebbing tide had exposed a wide swath of sand. Past the shoreside berm I noted a fresh set of tracks bordering the ocean. Walking briskly, I followed the trail. Rounding a rocky outcrop, I spotted Nate sitting on the sand fifty yards up, Callie at his feet. To me, something about their lone figures looked as defeated and forlorn as an abandoned farmhouse. Nate glanced up as I approached, then rubbed his eyes and resumed staring at the ocean. Callie gave me a perfunctory tail-thump, then lay her muzzle on her paws.

I stopped beside my brother, not knowing what to say.

"Go away," Nate said.

Ignoring his order, I sat beside him.

"Go away."

"Listen, Nate," I said gently. "Normally I save being nice to you for special occasions. This is one of those times. I want to help."

Nate scooped up a handful of stones and began flicking them at the water.

I rested a hand on Callie's head, working my fingers into her soft yellow fur. "Nate, I know we haven't been piling up the Kodak memories in our family lately," I went on, "but you're not helping Mom by acting this way."

"You're one to talk," Nate spat, angrily winging a rock at the ocean.

"Just because Mom and I don't get along sometimes doesn't mean—"

"Shut up, Ali. You don't care about anybody but yourself."

"That's not true, Nate."

"Yeah, right."

Without thinking, I took my brother's shoulders and turned him to face me. "I *do* care about Mom," I said fiercely. "Don't ever say I don't."

Nate glared back, his eyes red-rimmed and swollen.

"I don't know why Mom and I go at each other like we do," I said. "I wish things were different. Trav gets along with Dad, now. Maybe later, Mom and I will too."

Nate shrugged free of my grip. "What if there isn't a later?"

"There will be. Mom will get better."

"How do *you* know?"

"Because she has to."

"That's not good enough." Nate turned away. "You know what, Ali?" he went on. "I just realized something. All these years Dad has been telling us that if we wanted something bad enough, *no matter what it was,* we'd get it."

I didn't respond.

"You wanna make the team, you gotta *want* it, bucko," Nate went on harshly, lowering his voice in a surprisingly passable imitation of our father's. "But you gotta want it *bad*, sport. Hard work, determination, and desire will get you anything you want. *Anything.*" Nate gazed out at the waves. "He was lying. You don't always get what you want. No matter how bad you want it."

Again I remained silent, taken aback by my brother's bitterness. Nate had always been the most optimistic member of our family, able to find silver in even the darkest cloud. I sighed, struck by the thought that even with those you loved, it was impossible to ever fully know another person.

A troop of terns skittered along the shoreline, their beaks probing the sand for a final morsel before nightfall. As they passed, an offshore breeze whistled up the beach. Hearing the wind before it reached us, Nate and I both lowered our heads against the pelting grains of sand that followed. The gust plucked at our clothes. When it was gone, we sat without speaking.

Slowly a sprinkling of stars crept into the darkening sky, leaving only a faint tinge of red on the western horizon. At last I rose to my feet. "C'mon, Nate," I said, brushing sand from my legs. "I'm cold. Let's go back."

"You go. I'll see you later."

"I'm not going home without you." When Nate didn't respond, I took his arm and tried to pull him to his feet. I quickly gave up, aware for the first time that my little brother was no longer little. Somehow, while I hadn't been looking, the skinny younger sibling I'd always been able to push around had grown into a stronger. A lot stronger.

"Please, Nate," I said. "Mom needs you right now. She needs us all."

Nate's face opened for an instant, then closed. Wordlessly, he stood and began walking slowly down the beach toward the house. Callie bounded to her feet and took her place out front, leading the way back. I dropped in beside Nate, walking with him along the water's edge. Halfway to the house Nate glanced over at me, then once more gazed straight ahead. "Ali?"

"What?"

"Thanks for coming to get me."

"Sure, Nate," I said quietly, slipping my hand into his. "That's what big sisters are for."

# 24

During the night a tropical storm that had been stalled for days over the Pacific finally moved onshore, and first light revealed banks of thunderheads squatting over the mountains, with more threatening on the horizon. His overcoat collar turned up against a raw wind gusting from the north, Kane stood on a narrow fire road that led down to Encino Reservoir, staring out over the wind-chopped water.

Allison had been right. There *were* six locks on the upper gate chain: the same five present on the lower gate . . . *and an unauthorized sixth.* Calls to the various agencies confirmed that none of them had placed an extra padlock. Kane had suspected all along that the distance to the reservoir from surrounding neighborhoods made it impractical for someone to have carried in a body, even the body of a child. No, whoever dumped Jordan French's body had cut the gate chain and then *driven* to the reservoir—or at least to a spot nearby. And upon leaving, he had repaired the break in the chain by inserting an extra padlock. Kane shook his head, berating himself for not having checked the upper gate himself.

Turning from the reservoir, Kane glanced up the dirt road behind him. At the top of the ridge he could make out several patrol cars from the Van Nuys Division. An SID unit was there too, its members carefully removing the chain and its extra lock from the upper gate. On the road in between, officers were combing the brush. Below him, Deluca, Banowski, and several other members of the West L.A. homicide unit were working their way up from the water. The odds were unlikely that any tire tracks, footprints, or other evidence would be discovered at this late date—especially considering that the area had been well tromped during earlier canvasses. Nevertheless, it had to be done.

Again Kane swept his eyes over the choppy water at the south end of the reservoir, glad to be working. Activity kept his mind from thoughts of Catheryn, kept him from obsessing about her treatment. Focusing on the investigation, he attempted to place himself in the killer's shoes. It was probably night when he dumped the body, Kane reasoned. Where would he have chosen?

Kane narrowed his eyes, scanning the surrounding area.

Someplace not too far from the road. Someplace hidden.

A quarter mile from where Kane stood, the access road dropped sharply, joining another road that twisted up from the valley. Near this junction lay the easiest approach to the water, and the very section of shoreline where they had found the body. From where Kane stood, it looked open and exposed.

Not there. The killer would have wanted more privacy for what he had to do.

Kane started walking. He had originally insisted that in addition to examining the outer fence and gates for signs of tampering, the inner fence also be scrutinized. Areas in both were in disrepair, but no suspicious breaches had been found. Miles of outer and inner fencing circled the reservoir, however— offering ample opportunity for something to have been overlooked. On a hunch, Kane began rechecking the interior chain-link fence. Along the way he detoured around several patches of poison oak, recalling the rash he had noticed on Mr. French's hand.

Ten minutes later he found a cut in the inner fence.

It was hidden behind a clump of poison oak, invisible unless viewed from precisely the right angle. After pushing aside some branches, Kane knelt and examined the cut. Someone had made a vertical three-foot incision in the fence, then repositioned the severed sections. Kane leaned closer, noticing something caught on a strand of wire at the bottom. Using a ballpoint pen, he teased free a tattered tag of black plastic. Trash bag? he wondered. He gazed at the reservoir. The slope leading down to the water was steep, but not too steep for someone determined to make it.

After withdrawing an evidence bag from his pocket, Kane inserted the torn piece of plastic he had found, stuffed the baggy into his coat, and returned to the fire road. He arrived in time to see Deluca and Banowski approaching from below. Deluca was telling a joke, as usual punctuating his story with animated arm sweeps, his expressive Italian hands shaping his words. "So the grizzled old RAF officer lecturing to the women's group says, "Yes, ma'am, that's correct. A Fokker is definitely a German aircraft. However, these particular Fokkers were flying Messerschmitts.'"

"Good one," snorted Banowski, nodding to Kane as they arrived. "Reminds me of the one about the—"

"Save it," said Kane, cutting him off. "Which one of you comedians brought the handset?"

"I did," said Deluca, reaching into his coat and pulling out a mobile radio. "What's up?"

"I found a break in the fence." Kane pointed to the clump of poison oak concealing the cut. "Somebody went to a lot of trouble to hide it."

"So our man didn't drive all the way to the water?" Banowski said doubtfully, glancing toward the spot Kane had indicated. "He cut the fence and hiked down? Why?"

Kane shrugged. "Who knows? Things might have looked too exposed by the dam for his taste. It's also possible he didn't realize that DWP workers had left the inner gate unlocked. Or maybe he thought there was a night watchman. Whatever the case, I think our guy dragged the body down to the water right there."

"And the corpse broke loose from whatever was anchoring it and floated to where we found it," Deluca added. "Could've happened."

Kane nodded. "Radio one of the cruisers and have them send the SID guys down when they're done with the gate. And contact the divers who searched the reservoir before. We need them out here for a second look."

"You want 'em out here now?"

Kane nodded again. "Right now."

\*　　\*　　\*

I hadn't slept much the night before, worrying about Mom. I heard my father rise early, but I remained in bed at the beach house until after he had left. Then, dressing quickly, I left as well, not talking with anyone on my way out. Pushing the speed limit, I drove to Westwood, attempting to contact Mike on his cell phone several times on the way. No answer. Upon returning to my dorm room, I located Mike's home number in the Palisades telephone directory. Feeling a growing sense of urgency, I called him there. The phone at the other end rang a half-dozen times before someone finally picked up.

"Hello?" a sleepy male voice answered.

"Mike?"

"I think so."

"It's Allison."

"Ali?" Mike yawned. "What time is it?"

"Early. Listen, I need a favor. I'm at UCLA. I know it's Sunday, but can you meet me here ASAP with your video camera? And bring your biggest telephoto lens—one that can pull in an image from a long way off."

"Hold on," Mike said, starting to wake up. "What's this all about?"

"I'll tell you when you get here."

"Tell me now."

I hesitated.

"What's the matter?" said Mike. "Don't trust me?"

"That's not it."

"Of course it is. C'mon, Ali. What's up?"

"I told my father about what we found on our bike ride," I replied. "He's searching the reservoir site again this morning."

"And if you call CBS, Lauren will probably send Brent."

"Not probably. Definitely. As you once pointed out, it *is* his story. All I'd get would be a pat on the back."

"And you want *all* the credit."

"I was the one who came up with this, not Brent," I said.

A long pause. "Somehow I find it difficult to believe that your dad's revisiting the reservoir simply because you discovered that Mr. French knew it was there."

"There's more to it."

"Such as?"

"Such as things I can't talk about. But believe me, my dad has good reason to suspect the Frenches."

"He does, huh? Then it has to be the autopsy."

"Why do you say that?"

"Because according to leaks, nothing useful was found in the way of evidence at Jordan's house," Mike reasoned. "Nothing much turned up at the reservoir when her body was discovered, either. The autopsy is the only thing left."

"Are you going to help me or not?" I demanded, amazed that Mike had caught on so quickly, and angry with myself for having said anything to him at all.

"Not."

"Please, Mike. I wouldn't ask if it weren't important."

Another pause. "Look, if anyone at Channel 2 ever finds out that I shot footage on the Jordan French story and then simply handed it over to network instead of giving it to them . . ."

"It'll be our secret. Please, Mike?"

Silence.

"Please?"

"I'll see you shortly." Mike hung up without saying good-bye.

The trip to the reservoir took less time than I had expected. After picking me up in front of the dorm, Mike backtracked through Westwood and took the 405 Freeway north, exiting near Sepulveda Pass and then driving west on Mulholland. As he had said on our bike ride, the dirt section of Mulholland was easily accessible, and within an hour from the time I called Mike, we spotted LAPD cruisers and a strip of yellow POLICE LINE DO NOT CROSS ribbon barring the graded dirt road ahead.

I had originally hoped to get a shot of the locked gate above the reservoir. As that was now out of the question, I asked Mike to shoot several seconds of the police blockade, then had him drive back down the road to another overlook with a good view of the reservoir.

Over the next hour I had Mike record various shots of police officers stomping through the brush, investigators conversing by the water's edge, and a trio of divers combing the south end of the reservoir. All three men in the water were working at least a half mile from where Jordan's body had first been discovered. It was good video, but nothing definitive, nothing earthshaking. Simply another futile police search.

As I was beginning to think the whole thing had been a waste of time, Mike looked up from his camera, which he had positioned on a tripod near the side of the road. "Ali. I think they found something."

I raised a small pair of binoculars I had brought from my room. It took me a moment to locate the divers. One was in an inflatable boat, leaning over the bow. Another bobbed in the water nearby. The diver in the water passed a line to the man in the boat. The rubber-suited man in the inflatable craft pulled, straining to raise something from the bottom. Seconds later a yellow dive basket broke the water's surface. As the basket was hauled onboard, I could make out some kind of dark material glistening through the basket's knit holes. More of the black substance trailed over the basket's edge, muddy streams of water running from its folds.

"Looks like a trash bag," Mike observed.

I squinted through my binoculars. "Uh-huh. And whatever's in it is heavy. Are you getting this?"

"Every second."

"Good."

Shortly afterward another diver surfaced, passing a second line to the man in the boat. Another dive basket was raised, this one seeming even heavier. It too contained what appeared to be a plastic trash bag. This one had a length of cord trailing from it. Once the second basket was aboard, both divers squirmed into the boat. As one crawled forward to raise the anchor, the boat operator fired up an outboard motor on the stern, belching out a cloud of bluish smoke.

Lowering my binoculars, I checked my watch. If I wanted to make the New York deadline, I would have to hurry. Stuffing the binoculars into my purse, I reviewed a page of hastily scribbled notes I had written earlier that morning. Then, leaving my purse on the seat of Mike's pickup, I made my way several yards down the brush-covered slope.

"What are you doing?" asked Mike.

"Winding this up," I answered. "Can you get a shot of the boat, then pull back and get me with the reservoir in the background?"

"You're going to do a standup out here?"

"You have a problem with that?"

"Nope." Mike made an adjustment to the hooded lens of his camera. "Step to the left. Now down. Perfect."

"Will the camera mike pick up my voice?" I asked, wishing I'd had the time to get sound-recording equipment from the newsroom.

"It'll be fine," Mike assured me. "I'll cue you after the pullback. Ready?"

Over the past weeks I had analyzed Brent Preston's on-camera technique, studying other reporters' styles and approaches as well. I knew I could do it. This was my chance. "Ready," I said.

It had started drizzling several minutes earlier. After adjusting a plastic sheet covering his camera, Mike began shooting, framing the rubber boat heading to shore across the windswept reservoir. Then, twisting his long lens, he pulled back to reveal me standing in the brush. He raised a finger and pointed.

I gazed into the camera. Imagining I was talking to someone on the other side of the lens, I began. "Early this morning, acting on newly uncovered information, police investigators revisited Encino Reservoir, returning to the site where the body of actress Jordan French was found last month. Minutes ago, while searching an area far from where the body was originally discovered, police divers raised what appeared to be two large trash bags. Although the bags each appear to contain something heavy, at present the contents are unknown, but these new developments raise questions that are certain to shed new light on the case. This is Allison Kane, CBS News, Los Angeles."

Twenty minutes later, after shooting several more takes in which I added supplementary information suggested by Mike, I called the CBS newsroom. Explaining that it was an emergency, I obtained Lauren Van Owen's home and cell numbers from the news desk. After punching Lauren's home number into my cell phone, I waited impatiently for someone to answer.

By then the police search was winding down. The divers had exited the water and were loading their rubber craft onto a trailer, and a number of police cruisers had already departed. "C'mon, c'mon," I said aloud, absently watching Mike stowing his camera and tripod in the back seat of the Toyota. When no one picked up, I decided to try Lauren's cell phone. But as I started to disconnect, someone finally answered. "Van Owen residence. Candice speaking," a young girl's voice announced.

"Candice, this is Allison Kane," I said, remembering that Lauren had mentioned having a daughter. "I work with your mother. May I speak with her, please?"

"She's outside. I'll get her."

A thirty-second pause, then, "Allison?"

"Hi, Lauren. Sorry to call you at home, but I have something on the French case. Something big." I had mentally rehearsed what I planned to say next, but suddenly it seemed too brazen a move, even for me.

"What is it?" asked Lauren.

Despite my doubts, I pushed ahead. "As I said, it's big. And I have exclusive footage on it. But there's a condition to my turning it over."

"And that is?"

"It's my piece."

"Of course you'll get credit," said Lauren, her tone frosting. "We still have time to get Brent down to the studio and edit whatever footage you have."

"Brent's not going to be part of this. It's *my* piece."

"Allison, you're way out of line," Lauren snapped. "Brent is covering the Jordan French story. Period."

"Why can't I share?"

276

"I sympathize, but New York isn't going to let you waltz in and take over. Not to mention what Brent would say. I made an exception for you once when he wasn't available—"

"And it paid off," I interrupted stubbornly. "Look, I'm not out to steal Brent's story, but I got this on my own."

"Damn it, Allison . . ."

"It's mine. I want it."

A long silence. "You say you have footage? Who was the cameraman? Max Riemann? Let me talk to him."

"Max isn't here. I told you, I did this on my own."

Another deadly silence. "And this exclusive footage you got—*on your own*—it's good?"

"Better than good. It's gold. Not to mention that it's the only real development in the story for weeks. C'mon, Lauren. I want this. Do we have a deal?"

"What if I say no?" Lauren demanded.

"I'll either bury the piece or take it someplace else."

"You're not kidding, are you?"

"No."

Lauren hesitated. "Brent won't like this," she said angrily, her voice turning as hard as iron. "But if the coverage you have is as good as you say—and it had better be—it's your spot. How soon can you meet me in the newsroom?"

"Thirty minutes. Maybe sooner."

"Fine. And Allison? One question. How did you get to be so stubborn?"

I gazed out over the reservoir, remembering that not long ago my father had asked me the same thing. "It runs in the family," I said.

# 25

The following Friday Kane sat at his desk in the West Los Angeles station house, having arrived well before the start of his shift. It had been an overcast and soggy week, doing nothing to improve his mood. With an exhausted sigh, he reviewed a list of articles he had hoped to have included on a new search warrant—a warrant that the district attorney had once again refused to authorize.

Based on the new discoveries at the reservoir, Kane's abortive request for another court order allowing him to reenter the Frenches' estate had enumerated a long list of items to be taken, including all plastic garbage bags, nylon cord, and duct tape present in the house—materials similar to those recovered at the reservoir on Sunday. He had also petitioned for the authority to seize any metal-shearing tools that could have been used to cut the reservoir fence, pry bars or other instruments that might have made the forced-entry marks on Jordan's bedroom window, and any blunt objects like a baseball bat or golf club that could have served as the murder weapon. In addition, he had wanted to recover bolt cutters, padlocks, and associated keys; phone books and magazines; typing paper, envelopes, fireplace ash, and stamps that might be linked to the ransom note; and any personal computers, gloves, or pornography—especially child pornography. He had also asked to be permitted to examine the parents' clothes, shoes, and cars for blood, hair, fibers, and dirt from the reservoir road. Last, and most important, he had again requested that DNA samples be collected from the Frenches to be compared with the ransom note Touch DNA profile that had just come in—one bit of positive news in an otherwise bleak situation.

As before, the district attorney had maintained that there was no legal justification to authorize another search, including the procurement of DNA samples from the Frenches.

And reluctantly, Kane had to admit that the DA was probably right. The rock-filled garbage bags used to weigh down the body could have been purchased anywhere. The duct tape, nylon cord, and unauthorized padlock on the gate could have been purchased at a thousand different places, too. No footprints or tire tracks had been found at the scene, and no fingerprints had turned up on the newly discovered evidence. There was nothing to link *any* of it to the Frenches.

Frustrated, Kane had subsequently asked the Frenches to submit voluntarily to another examination of their home and to submit hair and blood for analysis. Responding through their attorney, they had refused. They did, however, publicly offer to work directly with district attorney investigators, provided no LAPD personnel were involved. This impossible stipulation tainted a proposal that to Kane was simply another play for sympathy in the press.

At any rate, Kane told himself, whatever he had hoped to obtain at the Frenches' estate had probably long since ceased to exist—and that was assuming the parents were guilty in the first place, something he still hadn't resolved. As he had told Allison, his brain was telling him one thing; his gut was saying something else. Although he kept chewing on details of the case that didn't fit, no matter how he went at it, he was having difficulty accepting that Mr. and Mrs. French could have murdered their daughter, trussed her up like unwanted garbage, and dumped her into a reservoir.

Nonetheless, despite its best efforts, the homicide unit had thus far failed to produce any new leads to the contrary. An investigation of the sex-offender parolee who'd worked for the Frenches had dead-ended, and another suspect caught stealing a stuffed animal left as bait at Jordan's grave had a solid alibi for the entire weekend of Jordan's disappearance. Questioning those with keys to the locked reservoir gates, talking with friends and employees of the Frenches' who had access to their estate, canvasses of the Encino Reservoir neighborhoods, and a general roundup of all known sex offenders in the area had all turned up negative.

Lacking other avenues, investigators were progressively being forced to revisit old territory—ground long since grown stale. As Kane had feared, without sufficient cause for additional search warrants and stymied by Mr. and Mrs. Frenches' refusal to cooperate, the investigation had stagnated.

Making matters worse, the Frenches had recently gone on the offensive by hiring their own investigators, declaring their intention of finding their daughter's killer themselves. Acting through their attorney, they had subsequently proceeded to inundate the homicide unit with an endless flood of "leads"—tips that invariably proved a waste of time, but leads that Kane and his team had to examine nevertheless. Capping off the whole sorry mess, the Frenches were now threatening a lawsuit, naming the LAPD and Detective Daniel Kane as defendants.

On the positive side of current developments, Allison's report on the last reservoir search had produced a surprisingly favorable effect on the public's perception of the LAPD. Airing Sunday night, her report had stressed that police were still working tirelessly to find Jordan's killer. Kane, of course, took heat on the story from every other news network, as well as from LAPD brass—the former contending that his connection with Allison gave CBS unfair access; the latter accusing him of leaking to the press. To each, Kane's reply had been the same: That's not how it happened. And if they didn't like it—tough.

Kane drained the dregs of his coffee, crumpled the paper cup, and tossed it into a waste can. As he did, he noticed Lt. Long entering the nearly deserted squad room.

Instead of proceeding to his office, Long perched his bulky frame on the edge of a desk across from Kane's. "You're here early," he noted.

"Couldn't sleep," said Kane. "It still raining?"

"Pouring. Damn, have you checked the mirror lately?"

"No."

"Well, don't," advised Long.

Kane ran a hand across the stubble covering his chin. "Thanks, Lieutenant. It's good to know there's at least one person in the department less tactful than I am."

"Dan, why don't you take some time off? With Kate's illness—"

"I want to work," said Kane, cutting him off. "There's nothing I can do for her at the hospital. If I don't keep busy, I'll go nuts. Besides, if I left, where would you find anyone fool enough to take over the French investigation?"

"Good point," Long conceded.

"You know, I've worked my share of high-profile cases over the years," Kane continued, deliberately steering the conversation from thoughts of Catheryn, "but this one takes the cake. I can't even turn around without tripping over some dirtbag reporter taking pictures and second-guessing everything I do. And assuming we somehow make an arrest and convince our nervous-Nelly DA to take the case to trial, it's going to get worse."

The two men fell silent, each contemplating an investigation that had turned into a no-win situation for everyone . . . especially the LAPD. "So how are things going with Kate?" Long finally ventured.

Kane shook his head. "Not good. They're still trying to locate an unrelated marrow donor, but unless they find someone soon, it looks like it will have to be Allison."

"Please tell Kate that everyone down here is pulling for her."

"Thanks, Lieutenant. I will."

Long glanced at the stack of files on Kane's desk. "Anything new there?"

Kane shrugged. "The ransom note DNA analysis finally came in. If we can get a DNA sample from the Frenches, or if we can come up with another suspect or suspects, it could prove critical. Otherwise . . ."

Long nodded glumly. "Anything else?"

"One other thing. Remember I told you I was working a hunch that I had on the ransom note?" Shuffling through the files, he found an SID lab report that had come in the previous evening. "It paid off."

Long leaned forward. "Go on."

Kane opened the report. "The ransom text was composed of words snipped from a glossy-style publication, remember? While I was at the Frenches' house, I noticed a number of similar magazines on their coffee table. You know, the kind no one reads but just has lying around for show—*Coastal Living*, *Architectural Digest*, *Elle Décor*, and so forth. When we were rebuilding the beach house, one of Kate's music associates gave us a subscription to *Architectural Digest*. Playing a long shot, I went through some back issues, comparing words in the magazines to those on a full-size photo of the ransom note. Eventually I got back issues of the other publications I saw at the Frenches' house and checked them, too."

"Hoping for a match?" Long said dubiously.

"I told you it was a long shot," Kane replied, passing him the report. "Don't worry, I did it on my own time. Anyway, it took a while, but in the end I got what I thought were a few hits—at which point I sent everything over to SID. They treated the ransom note background paper with a chemical that temporarily rendered it transparent, then used a high-intensity light to illuminate the printing on the flip side of each individual word. Bingo. They got a match. In fact, several."

Long flipped through the SID report, stopping at a section that showed words from the ransom note, with the writing on the reverse side displayed below. In an adjacent column was an identical word with matching print on the back. The words in the second column had all been cut from a recent issue of *Elle Décor*.

Long closed the report. "This doesn't prove anything."

"I know," Kane agreed. "Lots of people subscribe to *Elle Décor*."

"At least now I understand why you included magazines on your recent warrant attempt," said Long, handing the report back to Kane. "Good try."

"Yeah, except that the Frenches have probably burned everything by now. Assuming they did it."

Long frowned. "Right. Assuming they did it. Did you hear they took private polygraph exams yesterday?"

Kane shook his head. "Given by their own technicians, I assume?"

"Naturally."

"And passed with flying colors, no doubt."

Long nodded. "It was on the news last night."

282

"Well, you know what I think of lie detector tests," Kane snorted. "Even under the best of circumstances, they're questionable. And when administered by your own investigators, they're about as effective as one of those mystic power crystals they sell on the psychic hotline."

"Passing those tests did *one* thing for the Frenches," Long pointed out. "It helped them with public opinion. You know, Dan, along those lines, it might not hurt for you to give something to the media."

"I considered that. Then the tequila wore off."

"It wouldn't have to be anything major," Long persisted. "Something like this magazine thing might help defuse the negative spin that the Frenches have been putting on the case."

"Lieutenant, I don't want compromise my investigation—what's left of it—just to make myself look better on the six o'clock news."

"You're not the only player on the field here, Dan. This has become a national story. Hell, it's international. There's more at stake now than how *you* come off in the press."

"Is this you talking, Lieutenant? Or is it coming from higher up?"

Long didn't reply.

"No way I'm playing that game," Kane said, reading Long's answer in his silence. "I admit that the magazine angle isn't much, but it could be one more nail in the coffin if we get the case to trial. If we release it or other details prematurely, the Frenches will have all the time in the world to get rid of evidence and come up with a defense."

"All right, Dan," Long sighed. "It's your call . . . for now." Then changing gears, he asked, "So if the Frenches did it, how do you think it went down?"

"*If* they did it, it probably happened in one of two ways," Kane answered, happy to let their previous conversation lie. "Scenario one: Mr. French had been secretly molesting Jordan for years, probably beginning in her early childhood. Something went wrong the night of her birthday, and he killed her.

Afterward Mrs. French decided to make the best of a bad situation, and she helped him get rid of the body."

"And scenario two?"

"Mrs. French knew all along about the chronic abuse. It was eating her up, and she eventually killed Jordan in a fit of jealousy and rage. Again, Mr. French got rid of the body."

"So if one's responsible, they're both involved."

"Yeah," said Kane. "But if that's the case, the question is: Which parent actually did it? Unless we can turn one of them, I don't think we'll ever know."

"Even assuming we do get one to talk, there's the husband-wife confidentiality issue."

"I'll cross that bridge when I come to it," replied Kane. "As it is, to either solidify our case against the parents or to rule them out as suspects, we need to interrogate them and pick apart their story."

"What's the status on that?"

"*Our* attorneys are negotiating with *their* attorneys," Kane grumbled, remembering the wasted hours he had recently spent in a room so infested with lawyers that one department wag had noted there were enough attorneys present to talk themselves to death. "The Frenches are demanding to be interrogated together," he went on. "They also want an assistant DA in the room at all times, a doctor in case Mrs. French stresses out, a time limit, an advance look at all evidence, their own lawyers present at all times, the right to end the interview whenever they want, and a transcript of the proceedings."

"Sounds like more posturing for the media."

"Correct. They're also playing for time. I contacted the DA regarding the possibility of a grand jury subpoena to force them to testify, if they try to drag things out too long. So far no response from the DA. Whatever the case, I think that sooner or later the Frenches will have to come in. And when they do, you can be damn sure of one thing."

"What's that?" asked Long.

"When they *do* come in," Kane said tersely, "I'll be ready."

# 26

The rain that started while I was at the reservoir with Mike continued throughout the week, and by the following Sunday I was beginning to wonder whether the skies would ever again be clear. Feeling blue, I sat in my dorm room staring out the window and talking on the phone with McKenzie.

"Jeez, Ali. You're really not going to tell your mom?" asked McKenzie.

Though it was already after eight in the morning, the street outside my window was still as dark as dusk. To the west, rising on the horizon like an advancing army, storm clouds were massing over the Pacific, promising further precipitation in what had already been an unseasonable week of rain. Cradling the cell phone against my ear, I gazed across the road. On the far side of the botanical garden, the towers of the UCLA Medical Center rose in the early-morning mist. I felt a chill, knowing that soon my mother would enter those walls to start the most dangerous phase of her treatment.

"Hello?" McKenzie's voice echoed from the phone. "Ali?"

"Sorry. I was thinking about something else."

"What?"

"My mom."

"We were talking about your mother. You're not going to tell her you've quit college?"

"No," I replied nervously, still uncomfortable with a decision I had made on Thursday to take time off from school and see where my CBS job led. "Not yet, anyway. She has enough on her mind."

"Does your father know?"

"No."

"Well, at least that explains why you're still breathing," McKenzie noted dryly. "But you'll have to break the news sometime. You're supposed to start classes at USC in mid-September. That's just weeks away."

"I know."

"You've already notified USC admissions office that you won't be attending?"

"I told them on Friday."

"Jeez, Ali. Dropping out of UCLA summer session was one thing, but quitting college altogether? Do you like what you're doing at CBS that much?"

"Some of it," I replied. "After my piece on the reservoir, management offered to make my position at the L.A. bureau permanent. I figure I can learn more on the job than in some stuffy journalism class, so I said yes."

"When do you plan to tell your parents?"

"I'll tell my dad tomorrow, I guess. Mom's being admitted to UCLA in the afternoon. The whole family will be there. I'll tell Dad afterward, as long as he promises to let me break the news to Mom. So far he's been pretty understanding about everything— provided it doesn't upset Mom."

"And this will."

"Unfortunately . . . yes."

"Your whole family will be there?" asked McKenzie, backtracking. "I thought Trav had left again on his recital tours."

"He canceled them. Mom ordered him not to, but he did it anyway. Nate dropped out of his baseball playoffs, too."

"I'm sorry to hear that, Ali. I know how much Trav's recitals mean to him. Nate's baseball games, too. I hope everything works out. Tell your mother my family's praying for her."

At that moment my call-waiting beep sounded. "Hang on a sec, Mac." I switched to the second line. "Hello?"

"Ali? It's Mike."

"Hi," I said, wondering why he would be phoning so early. "Give me a minute. I'll be right back."

I reconnected with McKenzie. "Mac, I have to sign off. Mike's on the other line."

"You blow me off the minute a male admirer calls?" McKenzie complained, trying to sound insulted. "Actually, I like that. Shows you're getting your head on straight."

I smiled ruefully. "I'm glad somebody thinks so. I'll phone you later."

"You'd better," warned McKenzie. "The only time I see you these days is on TV. Remember, I want details."

Again wondering why Mike was calling so early, I clicked back to my second line. "Mike?"

"Still here. No one at the beach answered, so I thought I'd try you on your cell."

"It's Sunday. My family's undoubtedly at church," I explained. "What's up?"

"Nothing much. I just thought I might take advantage of a slight break in the weather to show you something."

"Now?"

"Yep, before it starts raining again. Are you game?"

"I suppose so. But what—"

"It's a surprise," said Mike. "It'll only take a few hours, and you'll like it, I promise," he added mysteriously. "I'll pick you up in a few minutes. We'll need to get going before the next storm rolls in."

"Does this have something to do with Jordan French?" I asked hopefully.

"No," Mike laughed. "Everything doesn't have to be about work, Ali. Are you coming?"

"Okay," I agreed after a slight hesitation, my curiosity piqued.

"Good. Do you have sturdy shoes?"

I hesitated again, trying to recall where I had left my hiking boots. "I think I have a pair around here somewhere."

"Fine. Wear them."

Twenty minutes later Mike's Toyota pulled up out front. Wearing shorts, boots, and a waterproof windbreaker, I climbed into the truck beside him. Though I tried to pry our destination from Mike as we drove up Hilgard and headed west on Sunset, he refused to divulge anything—saying only that I should trust him and that I wouldn't regret the trip. I was intrigued as well as irritated. Although I hate secrets, I finally gave up and rode in silence.

Instead of following Sunset to the coast highway, Mike swung right on Palisades Drive, heading up Santa Ynez Canyon into the Santa Monica Mountains. Minutes later we turned left on Verenda de la Montura and parked in front of a stout metal barrier. "This is it," he said, slipping from behind the wheel.

I exited the other side of the truck. "We're in the middle of the worst rainstorms of the year, and you want to go for a *hike*?" I said, eyeing a Topanga State Park plaque fastened to the gate.

"You'll see," said Mike.

"Tell me where we're going. I can't stand secrets."

"Tough," Mike laughed. "Let's get moving."

Reluctantly, I followed Mike through the gate and descended a narrow walkway. As we approached a streambed below, I could hear the roar of flowing water. When we reached the creek, I saw that the waterway cutting down Santa Ynez Canyon had been swollen by the recent rains, and in places it was threatening to overflow its banks. As Mike and I started up a dirt path bordering the raging stream, I also noticed spray-painted gang graffiti festooning a concrete culvert running beneath the road.

"Seems some of our inner-city brethren have visited recently," Mike remarked dryly, noticing my gaze. Then without looking back, he took off briskly up the trail.

I lengthened my stride to keep up, still wondering what we were doing there. At first the canyon rose gently, limbs of sycamore and live oak forming a dripping canopy above us. Lining the path, lupine, morning glory, and mariposa lily wildflowers gleamed like jewels amid thickets of buckwheat and fern. As we walked, I smelled the moldy odor of rotting leaves, mixed with an occasional hint of anise and sage from the hillsides higher up.

Soon the trail steepened, and the canyon's sandstone walls and limestone outcroppings gradually closed in. On both sides, streams newly born from the rains cascaded down steep inclines to join the flow of the main drainage below. Continuing on, Mike and I came to a dilapidated wooden fence, above which the storm-choked streambed forked. When I joined Mike at the water's confluence, I found him inspecting a large sandstone boulder with a circular depression on its upper surface. "Check this out," he said, indicating the rounded concavity. "Chumash Indians used this rock to grind acorns thousands of years ago."

"I thought the Chumash lived farther up the coast," I remarked. "At least that's what we learned in school."

"The Chumash had permanent settlements at the mouths of all the main watercourses around here," said Mike. "Point Mugu, Malibu and Little Sycamore Canyons, and La Jolla Valley. This place is full of history. Did you know that the treaty for the Mexican-American War was signed at the foot of Cahuenga Pass, right here in the Santa Monica Mountains?"

"No, but thanks for the history lesson," I replied crankily, still annoyed that Mike had yet to disclose our reason for being there. "You can put that in your book of things nobody cares about."

"Maybe I will," Mike chuckled. Then, taking my hand, he stepped into the icy current. "C'mon. We have to cross."

Hanging on tightly to Mike's hand, I made my way to the opposite bank, at times wading up to my thighs in the frigid water. Thankful I had worn hiking boots, I followed Mike up the left fork of the rushing stream, reaching another branch in the waterway a hundred yards farther on. There we reforded, this time taking the right channel. At a spit of land beyond, two stone chimneys rose from the underbrush—apparently all that now survived of what had once been an old cabin. Past the ruin, Mike and I climbed progressively higher into the canyon. The path, which had initially paralleled the stream, gradually deteriorated—repeatedly forcing us to detour up the steep hillside to circumvent narrow sections of creek and impassable rock faces. After a strenuous section of boulder-hopping, Mike called a rest. "We're nearly there," he announced, sitting on a stone outcrop. "Let's take a breather."

"No argument from me," I said, sitting beside him. A constricted section of streambed had forced us to bushwhack a route higher on the ridge, and from our elevated position we had a clear view down the canyon. From where we sat I could see no trace of habitation, no indication that man's hand had ever touched the land below. Visible only were the sandstone cliffs, the rugged mountains higher up, and ominous banks of thunderheads rising on the horizon.

Enjoying the impromptu hike despite Mike's continuing refusal to tell me where we were going, I closed my eyes and listened. In the distance I could hear the liquid trill of a bird piping its staccato song; nearer, over the rush of the stream and the rustle of wind in the chaparral, I could make out the intermittent "kr-r-reck—ck" of a Pacific tree frog. From higher on the ridge came the ghostly hoot of an owl. Amazed that such an untouched setting still existed so close to civilization, I opened my eyes. When I did, I found Mike studying me.

"So how're things going at work?" he asked, not seeming the least bit embarrassed to have been caught staring.

"Great," I replied. And they were. The numbers on Sunday's exclusive reservoir report had been stellar, ratcheting me up the network ladder several rungs in one stroke. Unfortunately, my reservoir report had also fed a growing tension between Brent and me. Despite Brent's ill feelings, New York had requested that I do another network spot, and later in the week Lauren had dispatched me to cover a heat-transfer-tubing leak at the San Onofre nuclear power plant south of Los Angeles. With Max Riemann's help I turned in a short but professional clip that aired nationally, being used to fill a vacancy in the news schedule. Afterward Max had labeled me a natural, saying I possessed a "red-light reflex" that enabled me to connect with the camera. It seemed to me, however, that my on-camera composure was simply a matter of having a good memory, being able to ad-lib, and not being cowed by anyone or anything—traits I had developed growing up in the Kane household. But whatever it was—my seeming confidence, my cut-to-the-chase interviewing style, or even the spillover from my televised rescue effort at the Wedge—one thing was becoming increasingly clear to everyone at CBS, especially corporate management: According to the numbers, the viewing public liked Allison Kane.

Nevertheless, even when I reported on an unrelated story like the power-plant leak, I suspected that the Jordan French factor, as

I had come to think of it, was in play. Because of my family ties, I had become solidly linked in the public consciousness with the ongoing murder investigation. Though to date CBS had made no on-air mention of it, my Dad's being the lead investigator on the case was something about which every other network, newspaper, and tabloid had reported in depth. In a sense, I had progressively become *part* of the story, and as such I often found myself dodging aggressive, irritating questions from other correspondents. Since Sunday's reservoir report, in order to avoid a gaggle of waiting reporters outside work, I had started parking my car in the Farmers Market lot and using the back-alley door into the newsroom. It was a situation I didn't relish, but one that I hoped would ease with time.

Mike shifted on the rock outcrop, trying to get comfortable. "Congratulations on the reservoir piece," he continued. "That spot you did on the San Onofre power plant was excellent, too. I knew you were going places."

"You did, huh?" I said, feeling myself flush with pride. "Well, a lot of it is thanks to you—including my getting the job at CBS in the first place. I couldn't have done the reservoir piece last weekend without you, either. I really appreciate your help, Mike."

"My pleasure," said Mike. "Speaking of which, you didn't tell anyone I shot that footage, did you?"

"No. I think Brent suspects, but he hasn't said anything."

"What about Lauren?"

"She didn't push it. Don't worry. It's our secret."

"Good. Like I said, if that information were to get out, I would definitely be in hot water over at Channel 2. Speaking of which, how's everyone at network handling your success? Liz, for instance?"

I smiled. "Green with envy. As for Brent, he was furious about my scooping him again. Lauren, on the other hand, has been surprisingly supportive. Management called from New York on Friday to offer me a full-time position. I think she had something to do with it."

Mike raised an eyebrow. "Full-time? Are you going to accept?"

I nodded. "I can't pass up an opportunity like that."

"I'm happy for you, Ali," Mike said quietly. "As long as it's what you want."

I couldn't read what was in Mike's eyes. "They may have something big for me coming up soon," I went on. "CBS has been negotiating with the Frenches' publicist and lawyers, trying to set up an interview. Assuming it happens, guess who stands a good chance of being involved."

"You?" said Mike, his expression still betraying nothing.

"Uh-huh. Oddly enough, it was at the request of Mr. and Mrs. French. In fact, it was one of their stipulations. I'm not sure network will go for it, but if CBS gets the interview, Jordan's parents want me there."

"Why?"

I shrugged. "I suppose that aside from the obvious tie-in with my father, they think the interview will play better to the public if they're being questioned by a young woman not much older than their daughter. You know, like when a rapist hires a female attorney to handle his defense, or when someone accused of a hate crime gets an African-American lawyer to plead his case. Plus, after my interview with Mrs. French at the museum, Jordan's parents probably think I'm sympathetic."

"Are you?"

"I was at first. Now I'm not so sure."

"Mr. French's knowing about the reservoir location changed your mind?"

"There's more to it than that," I said, recalling the material I had seen in my father's murder book.

"We talked about that last Sunday," said Mike. "You indicated there was something in the autopsy report implicating the parents."

"I didn't say that. You did."

"And you didn't argue," Mike pointed out. "I can keep my mouth shut, Ali. I'm right, aren't I? There's something in that report. That's why your dad kept it sealed."

Once again I regretted having broached the subject. I trusted Mike, but I had made a promise to my father. When I didn't reply, Mike pushed on. "The body was submerged in water for weeks, so there couldn't have been much evidence left—fingerprints, fibers, and the like," he reasoned. "It had to have been something else, such as her being beaten, or maybe even sexually molested. But how could that tie in with the parents, unless . . ."

"Let it go, Mike. Please."

Mike snapped his fingers. "That's it, isn't it? There was some kind of sexual abuse going on, and it showed up in Jordan's autopsy. That's why the police are all over her parents, just like the tabloids have been saying."

"Mike, I can't talk about this."

Mike looked at me quizzically, then lifted his shoulders. "Whatever you say. I guess I don't blame you for wanting to protect your story."

"It's not that."

"Right." Mike stood, stretched, and checked the sky. "You know, I probably shouldn't say anything, but I overheard my news director talking about you the other day. Something about stealing you away from network and hiring you as a local announcer for KCBS."

"Really?" I said excitedly.

Mike smiled. "Really. See, you're not the only one with secrets. C'mon, let's hit the trail."

Mulling over Mike's surprising revelation, I followed him down an embankment, rejoining Mike by the stream a dozen yards farther on. From there the walls of the canyon closed in again, once more making for difficult going. Eyes lowered, I picked my way over the tricky terrain, concentrating on my footing. As we turned a bend, I was struck by a rush of mist and the roar of falling water. Startled, I raised my head.

We had come to a stone grotto. Rock walls towered over us on all sides. Fifty feet up, gigantic boulders were wedged in a narrow opening of the waterway. Over the top of the uppermost boulders, a curtain of water hissed through the morning air, falling in a broad, crystalline sheet to a shallow pool near where we stood.

"Oh," I whispered.

Mike grinned with pleasure at my reaction. "Most of the year this stream is just a trickle. As you can see, it's worth getting up here after a rain."

I stared, at a loss for words.

"I knew you'd like it," said Mike, taking my hand as he stepped into the water. "This is one of my favorite spots." Then, making for the far bank of the pool, "There's a way to the top. The view from up there is amazing."

A stinging spray bathing my legs, I allowed myself to be led past the base of the falls, awed by the power of the rushing water. To the left, dangling from an unseen anchor, a knotted rope trailed down the face of a nearly vertical rock wall. When we reached the bank, Mike grabbed the rope and tested it, letting it take his full weight. "It'll hold," he said. "You go first. I'll catch you if you slip."

"We're going up there?"

Mike nodded. "Unless you don't want to."

I squinted up the stone face. Thirty-five feet of strenuous climbing would bring me to a ledge, after which it appeared an easy scramble to the top of the falls. But first I had to get there. And if I slipped making it to the ledge, my landing would be crippling, even in the unlikely event that Mike managed to break my fall.

"Give it a try, Ali. If you can't make it, just slide down the rope."

Though I wanted to say no, I couldn't. "I'll make it," I said. I grabbed the rope. It felt rough in my hands, the knots thick and knobby. I gave the line a tug. It felt solid, but still I had misgivings. Though fearless regarding most physical endeavors, I hate heights. Nonetheless, despite my fear, I leaned back and placed my feet against the wall.

"That's it," said Mike. "Now just walk your way up."

Nervously, I started up the slippery rock, alternately moving my hands and feet. My forearms quickly felt the strain, but I resisted the temptation to stop partway. Forcing myself to continue, I inched my hands up the rope knot by knot, progressively scrabbling my feet higher on the wall. Though it was a struggle, I made the ledge in one continuous effort.

"Way to go," Mike hollered from below.

"Nothing to it," I yelled back, fighting to catch my breath.

Mike grabbed the rope and began climbing, making it look easy. Seconds later he joined me on the ledge. Then, worming our way through a flared chimney formed by the boulders above us, we continued to the top. Once there Mike led me to a flat sandstone ledge overlooking the surging falls and the pool below. I sat carefully, dangling my legs over the edge. Seeming oblivious of the drop, Mike nonchalantly eased down beside me.

I didn't say anything for several minutes, letting my eyes drink in the pristine landscape. Despite the effort required to get there, I conceded that Mike had been right. The view from the top *was* breathtaking. In addition to the expanded horizons provided by our airy vantage, the torrent sluicing past touched a powerful chord of excitement within me. Staring at the hypnotic arc as it fell to the pool far below, I felt as if I and the rocks and the whole world around us were vibrating with the thrum of some monstrous, well-oiled machine. Lifting my eyes, I gazed at the sky, drawn by a flash of movement. Wheeling above a distant ridge, a red-tailed hawk traced slow circles in the sky.

Noticing my glance, Mike leaned closer. "There's still plenty of wildlife around here," he said, raising his voice to be heard above the roar of the water. "Deer, coyotes, bobcats, even mountain lions. But you have to be lucky to spot them."

I tried to imagine the canyon as it must have been when the first Native Americans visited thousands of years ago. I could almost believe that nothing had changed since then. "Do you get up here often?" I asked.

"No. I usually save coming up here for special occasions."

"Like during a flood?"

"Sometimes," Mike laughed.

"I suppose you bring all your girlfriends up here," I remarked, immediately wishing I could retract my words.

"You're the only one I've ever invited," said Mike. "I come here to be alone and think. It's always been a good place for me to work things out."

"I have a place like this myself," I confessed, surprised by his reply. "My own spot where I go when I need to be alone."

"Where is it?"

"The botanical garden at UCLA, across from my dorm," I answered. "A stream runs down the middle and there's a waterfall there, too. Nothing like this, but it's beautiful too . . . and quiet. There's a bench just past a footbridge, right beneath the tallest tree in the exhibit. From there you can't see any of the campus buildings, or any of Westwood, either. Just flowing water and stands of bamboo and beds of exotic plants."

"Sounds nice. Maybe I could visit it with you sometime."

A gust whistled up the canyon, lifting my hair and raising a crop of goose bumps on my legs. My nylon jacket had kept my upper body mostly dry, but my shorts were soaked, as were my shoes and socks. Shivering, I lowered my head against the wind. Seeing this, Mike scooted closer and put an arm around me. I shifted uncomfortably, though I found I liked the feel of Mike's touch. And his arm around me *did* make me warmer, though not simply by shielding me from the wind.

For a time Mike and I sat enjoying the stormy morning. Gradually, to the accompaniment of distant rolls of thunder, the sky darkened as yet another squall began sweeping onshore. Soon clouds tangled the sun in shadow, sailing in like a menacing armada. Seconds later it began to drizzle, threads of rain stitching the waterlogged hillsides around us. Before we knew it, what had started as a gentle sprinkle turned into a pelting deluge. Behind us, a creek that had been trickling down the slope abruptly swelled, carrying down a clatter of rocks and gravel from higher up.

Mike glanced up the hillside, then at the roaring stream spilling over the falls. "We have to get out of here," he said.

"Do I detect a note of urgency?" I asked.

"If the water rises much more—and it will if it keeps pouring like this—we won't make it out," Mike answered tersely. "Sorry, Ali. I didn't think it would start raining again till later."

"Can't we climb up and find a trail higher on the ridge?" I asked nervously.

Mike stood, pulling me to my feet. "Maybe farther down. The canyon's too steep here. Let's go."

Mike and I retreated through the boulder caves, pausing when we came to the rope ledge overlooking the pool. My breath caught as I stared over the sheer drop.

"I'll go first," said Mike. Without awaiting a reply, he grabbed the rope and leaned backward. Feet against the sandstone wall, he rapidly worked his way down, quickly arriving at the edge of the pool. "You ready?" he shouted up the face, taking a position below me at the base of the cliff.

"Not really," I called back, my stomach churning as I placed my hands on the top knot. Belatedly remembering that Travis had once told me that down-climbing is often more difficult than going up, I backed to the edge of the precipice, sensing the void looming behind me. I hesitated when my heels reached the drop-off.

"You can do it," Mike yelled, cupping his hands to his mouth.

A streak of lightning sizzled across the sky, striking a ridge not a half-mile distant. An instant later the thunderclap startled me into action. Narrowing my eyes against the rain, I leaned back and began inching my feet down the wall.

Fear and adrenaline gave me an initial burst of strength. Nevertheless, my hands and forearms, exhausted from the climb up, soon cramped. Worse, rain had wet the rope, making it difficult to grasp. In an effort to descend more quickly, I accidentally let one of my feet slip off the rock. The other foot quickly followed. A heartbeat later I found myself dangling, suspended only by my hands. I glanced down, instantly wishing I hadn't. I attempted to get my feet back on the wall. Couldn't. Willing myself not to panic, I struggled to wrap my legs around the rope, trying to keep from falling. No good.

"Slide down the rope, Ali."

"I . . . I can't."

"Yes, you can. I'll catch you if you fall."

I knew I had to do something. Soon. My hands were failing. My legs were all but useless on the slick rope.

"Move, Ali. Now!"

I forced myself to slacken my grip. I began sliding downward. Slowly, I descended in jerky stops from knot to knot.

I eased down several feet.

And another foot.

And another.

Nearing the rocks below, my grip suddenly gave out. I was falling! I heard myself scream as the slippery knots began banging through my hands . . .

Mike's strong arms caught me before I hit the ground.

Unnerved by my fall, I lay in Mike's embrace, resisting the impulse to bury my face in his chest. Gently, Mike set me on my feet. "You okay?"

"I'm fine," I replied shakily, grateful for Mike's strength and filled with a new respect for Travis's sport of rock climbing. That, and the realization that it was definitely not for me.

"Good." Mike brushed a dripping strand of hair from my face. "Let's get out of here."

With Mike in the lead, we fought our way downstream, at times crossing waist-deep torrents, at times circumventing narrow sections by scrambling up slick, muddy slopes—all the while pelted by the wind-whipped downpour. After what seemed like hours, we finally arrived back at Mike's truck—wet, tired, chilled to the bone, and laughing at our folly.

"I swear, Mr. Cortese," I said, attempting to wipe a spatter of mud from my legs, "you sure know how to show a girl a good time."

"Glad you enjoyed it," Mike replied, scraping his boots on the curb beside his Toyota. "I'll be sure to call you when we get our next monsoon."

"You do that," I retorted, still shaken by my fall but giddy with relief that we had made it back. Then, gazing at my filthy hiking shoes and mud-smeared legs, "In the meantime, is there somewhere I can hose off before going home?"

"We can clean up at my place," said Mike. "It's on the way."

## 27

Mike's house, a modest, one-story bungalow that he had inherited from his parents, sat behind a hedge of holly trees on the corner of Galloway and one of the east-west streets dividing Pacific Palisades above Sunset Boulevard. Though small, the house was attractive and well maintained, with stained-glass windows, hardwood floors, and white plastered interior walls that curved at the top to spacious, nine-foot ceilings. The rain had stopped by the time we arrived, at least for the moment. Mike cleaned our boots with a hose near the garage, then offered to toss my mud-encrusted clothes into the washer while I warmed myself in a hot shower. Still shivering from our hike, I gratefully accepted.

Twenty minutes later, my skin pink and tingling from the shower, I dried myself with a thick towel, brushed my hair back from my forehead, and pulled on a pair of sweatpants and a soft cotton workshirt that Mike had given me to wear while my clothes were drying. Not finding him when I padded barefoot from the bathroom, I wandered into the living room, idly checking the contents of an oak bookcase against the far wall. Three upper shelves contained hardcover novels by popular authors: Clancy, Grisham, Conroy, King. Another held a collection of leather-bound classics by Stevenson, Melville, Dickens, and the like. But it was a small section of books on the bottom shelf that caught my eye.

Kneeling, I scanned the titles. All were texts on advanced mathematics. Recalling that Mike had mentioned being a math major in college before switching to film, I pulled out a volume on differential equations and flipped through several pages of indecipherable symbols, then replaced it on the shelf.

"Planning a career in science?"

I turned to find Mike standing in the doorway. He had showered and changed from his muddy clothes as well, and he was now wearing sandals, jeans, and a denim shirt. Though he had made an attempt to comb his thick black hair, it still looked disheveled. "Science? Not hardly," I answered with a smile. "Speaking of which, where's your slide rule?"

Mike grinned. "Gave it up years ago, along with my pocket protector," he answered good-naturedly. "Besides, nobody uses slide rules anymore. It's all hand-held calculators now. You want something to drink while we're waiting for your clothes? They still have a bit to go in the dryer."

"What do you have?"

"Coffee, Coke, juice, and milk. I can make sandwiches too, if you want."

"I'm not hungry, but something to drink would be nice," I replied. "Do you have anything stronger than Coke?" Though I had yet to reach legal drinking age, while at UCLA I'd attended parties where liquor flowed freely, and on occasion I had joined in—at times getting more than a bit tipsy. That notwithstanding, I didn't consider myself much of a drinker, and I wondered why I had asked. With an embarrassing flash of insight, I realized it probably had something to do with proving to Mike that I wasn't a kid.

Mike raised an eyebrow. "Something stronger? What do you have in mind?"

Wishing I hadn't asked, I struggled to think of an appropriate drink. "How about some brandy? That's supposed to warm you up, isn't it?"

"It'll do that, all right," Mike agreed. "Hang on. Two brandies coming up."

After Mike left, I continued my tour of the living room, perusing a gallery of black-and-white photographs on the walls. Some were landscape portraits of areas I recognized as Joshua Tree National Monument, Glen Canyon, and Death Valley; others detailed vaguely familiar sections of Los Angeles. But most of Mike's photographs were of people, all kinds of people—men and women, children and adults—each uniquely seeming to fit the scene in which he or she had been captured. One showed a grizzled old man fishing from the Malibu pier; another was of a young girl bending to examine a crab on the beach; a third portrayed a lovely woman sitting in a wicker chair, her eyes shining with what appeared to be a melancholy mix of love and regret.

Mike returned minutes later, a cut-glass snifter in each hand. "Here you go," he said, passing a glass to me. "Cheers."

I touched the rim of my snifter to Mike's, swirled the amber liquid, and took a sip. The fumes stung my nose. Determined not to betray my inexperience, I swallowed, the fiery liquor burning my throat and lodging like a white-hot coal in my stomach. "Good," I choked, my eyes watering.

"That it is," Mike agreed, politely pretending not to notice my distress. "I saw you checking my photos. What do you think?"

"I like them," I said when I had recovered enough to talk. "Especially the ones of people. There's something in them that makes me feel, I don't know—as if I'd like to get to know the subjects. Who's this, for instance?" I asked, pointing to the photograph of the woman in the wicker chair. "She's quite beautiful."

"That's my mom. I took it the year she died."

"I'm sorry. I didn't know. She looks so young."

"She was."

To fill the awkward moment, I took another sip of brandy. This time it went down more easily. Curious, I again examined the photo of Mike's mother, wondering about the look in her eyes. "How did she die?"

"Breast cancer."

I felt a chill, realizing that the parallels between my life and Mike's ran deeper than I thought. A father on the force, a mother with cancer . . . "My mother isn't much older than yours was when she died," I observed numbly.

"I know. Don't worry, Ali. Your mom is going to recover."

"I hope so."

"She will," Mike repeated firmly. Then, lightening his tone, "Listen, we still have some time before your clothes are dry. Let's go into the den. There's something I want to show you."

I raised an eyebrow. "Your etchings?"

Mike chuckled. "No, my documentary. I have it on DVD. I'm not done making last-minute revisions, but I would love to hear what you think."

Welcoming the diversion, I trailed Mike down a short hallway, passing a spacious bedroom on the way. I glanced through the open door, noting a rack of surfboards in one corner, a set of weights and an exercise bench in another, and a large bed against the far wall. Continuing on, we reached a cozy chamber just off the entry. To the left beneath leaded-glass windows, a couch and coffee table took up most of the small room. Opposite the couch was a floor-to-ceiling bookcase packed with DVDs, CDs, and various pieces of electronic equipment including a large-screen TV. After closing the drapes to darken the room, Mike turned on the TV.

"What's your film about?" I asked, settling myself on the couch and curling my legs beneath me.

Mike shoved a DVD into the player. "The Los Angeles River. Ever hear of it?"

"Not really, unless you mean that concrete flood channel running through the city."

"That's the one, although it wasn't always confined to a cement sluiceway," said Mike. "Actually, the river played a critical role in the history of Los Angeles. More than people know."

"And you wrote and directed this film yourself?"

Mike smiled proudly. "Shot it, too. Did the whole thing on a shoestring. Friends at Channel 2 crewed for me on weekends, and an announcer buddy of mine did the narration.

"So your film's a history of—"

"Why don't we just watch it?" Mike suggested. He hit the play button on the DVD console and crossed the room, sitting beside me as the opening frames of his film flashed up. Conscious of Mike's nearness, I took another sip of brandy and concentrated on the film.

Titled *Forgotten River*, Mike's documentary opened with a brief history of the Los Angeles River, tracing the waterway's course from its headwaters in the San Gabriel Mountains to its mouth at the Pacific fifty miles distant. Over historic photographs and ancient film clips, a familiar-sounding voice described the river as the first Spanish expedition had found it: a seasonal stream lush with oak and cottonwood, its waters alive with salmon and trout, its reaches inhabited by bears, antelope, deer, and wolves. Surprisingly, the river that Angelenos nowadays knew only as a polluted flood-control channel was the prime reason for the founding of the Pueblo of Los Angeles—in time to become the city of the same name. And until the completion of the Owens Valley Aqueduct in 1913, the waterway that the Spanish had named the Porciuncula—sometimes no more than a trickle, sometimes a raging torrent—had supported all of Los Angeles's water needs for drinking, irrigation, and bathing.

Describing the subsequent construction of dams and concrete channels to protect the watershed from flooding, Mike's film told a common tale of man's subversion of nature, but it was the way his images brought the story to life, not the subject itself, that held my attention. In much of his work Mike used a distinctive cinematic style to record details others might have missed, interspersing historical narrative and interviews with people who had played various roles in the river's history—survivors of early floods, construction workers who had built the dams and channels, and citizens from community organizations currently battling to rehabilitate the riparian habitat. Most interesting to me, however, was the way Mike captured people in his lens and showed something revealing about them, something others might have missed.

Mike's work ended with a montage that, given the subject, proved far more moving than I would have thought possible. As the credits rolled, I realized to my surprise that his documentary had somehow transcended the story of a ruined river, in the end becoming a larger chronicle of the hopes, passions, and dreams of those who had lived the history of Los Angeles's forgotten waterway.

Leaning forward, Mike picked up the remote control and turned off the TV. He looked at me nervously. "Well?"

I set down my empty snifter. I had finished my drink partway through the film, and the liquor had imparted a warm, comfortable glow. "I'm impressed," I said quietly. "You're more talented than you let on."

"Thanks," said Mike, setting his own empty snifter beside mine. "I think."

"I mean it. I liked your film, Mike. A lot."

"Anything you would change?"

"You want my opinion? Are you serious?"

"I'm dead serious. As I said, I'm still making revisions. Any suggestions you might have are welcome."

I thought a moment. "Well, the only thing I could possibly criticize is that it left me feeling a little depressed."

"It's a depressing subject," Mike pointed out.

"I know. It's just that people want to feel good after seeing a film. Any film, even a documentary."

Mike frowned. "The subject doesn't really lend itself to humor."

"I'm not suggesting you make it a comedy," I said sympathetically, accustomed to editing my own writing and knowing how brutally painful it could be to change, or worse to delete, something I had sweated blood to create. "But why not close on a ray of hope? For one thing, you could brighten things in your concluding montage by adding a few more positive images."

"That might work," Mike conceded. "I've known something was missing from the ending. I think you've put your finger on it."

"A bit of uplifting music at some point might help, too," I went on. "Mendelssohn or Vivaldi, perhaps."

Mike remained silent for several seconds, seeming lost in thought. "I don't know about classical, but you're right about the music, too," he said at last. "Do you have any idea how much work you've just cost me?"

"You're going to make the changes?"

Mike nodded. "I'm leaving for Telluride first thing Tuesday morning, so I'll have to work like crazy to get everything completed before then. But yeah, your changes will definitely improve the film. I only wish someone had pointed this out before," he added. "You have a good eye, Ali. Any other suggestions? No holds barred."

"Okay, let's see it again," I said, flattered that Mike valued my opinion. "I thought the narrative was perfect, so this time let's run your film with the sound off. That way I can concentrate on the images."

"Whatever you say." Mike turned on the TV again and restarted the DVD. Using the TV remote, he pressed the mute button. Seconds later his documentary began anew, this time without sound.

Once more captivated by Mike's photography, I watched as his images marched across the screen. Mike sat quietly beside me on the couch, as if awaiting my judgment. But partway through the documentary I realized that he wasn't watching the film. He was watching me. Curious, I turned, my heart beating more quickly as I met his gaze. Inside, I felt something stir—part attraction, part panic.

Seeing the question in my eyes, Mike raised a hand to touch my cheek. Then he leaned closer and brought his lips to mine, tentatively at first, barely touching. A surge of excitement shivered through me, a disturbing yet tantalizing sensation I remembered from the first time we'd kissed. Mike's lips were warm, his mouth tasting of brandy. Pulse racing, I placed my arms around him and kissed him back. Mike pulled me closer and kissed me again. My breasts pressing against his chest, I parted my lips to the touch of his tongue, a sensual warmth building inside me.

We kissed for what seemed like forever. Hours passed, or maybe it only seemed that way. At one point I became aware that Mike's film had ended, but I didn't care. I hadn't known being with someone could be so exciting, so perfect. I never wanted it to end. As if in a dream, I felt Mike kissing my neck and the naked hollow at the base of my throat. "God, you're beautiful," he murmured, his strong hands running up the curve of my back. A voice inside told me to stop. Ignoring it, I returned his embrace, my lips and body growing insistent with a passion I had never before experienced.

Slipping his hands beneath my shirt, Mike's fingers traveled the bare skin of my shoulders, gently massaging muscles that were already stiff and sore from the climb. Waves of desire shivering through me, I moaned with pleasure as his touch loosened knots I wasn't aware I had. Still massaging my shoulders and back, Mike pulled me to him and kissed my mouth once more, his touch on my skin leaving a fiery brand everywhere in its wake.

Without willing it, my mind suddenly returned to the night of my rape, to the memory of another man's hands on my body. All at once an overwhelming sense of panic gripped me, squeezing me like a fist. Heart pounding with irrational terror, I pushed Mike away. "I can't do this," I said.

"What's wrong?"

"Nothing. I . . . I want you to take me home."

"Is there someone else?"

"No."

"Then what is it?"

"I told you. Nothing."

"Ali, I know you like me," Mike said slowly. "But from the beginning, every time we've started to get close, you've backed away. Why?"

I didn't answer.

"C'mon, Ali. We're friends, aren't we? Don't shut me out."

"I'm not shutting you out. I just don't want to talk about it, okay?"

"No, it's not okay. Tell me what's going on. You at least owe me that."

"I don't owe you anything," I shot back, attempting to cover my embarrassment.

"Maybe not, but I wish you would tell me what's going on in that head of yours anyway," Mike said patiently. "Unless you think it's better to hide your emotions. What's the matter? Are you afraid?"

"No."

"Then talk."

"All right," I spat angrily, fighting tears of self-consciousness. "You want to know what's wrong? I was raped four years ago and I haven't been with anyone since, that's what's wrong."

Mike stared. "Jesus," he said softly, reaching to take my hand. "I'm sorry, Ali. I'm so sorry. I didn't know."

I tore my hand from his grasp. "I don't want your pity."

"No, I don't suppose you do." Mike paused. "Four years ago. That would have made you around sixteen. Do you want to talk about it?"

I palmed away my tears without answering.

"Have you told anyone else?" Mike asked. "Or did you keep it to yourself?"

"I told my parents, although not right away," I replied, surprised by his question, and wondering how he had known to ask. "Afterward I saw a woman at a rape-counseling center. Later my mother made me visit a shrink. I quit after two sessions. Aside from that, you're the only person I've ever told."

"And since then you've never . . ."

". . . been with anyone? No."

"And now you're not sure how you feel about things."

My eyes briefly touched Mike's, then looked away.

"Listen, Ali, I know a few things about rape."

"How would you know the first thing about rape?"

"You'd be surprised," Mike answered gently. "For instance, I know that rape isn't an act of passion; it's an act of malice motivated by a desire for dominance and control. I know that being raped in a supposedly safe place like your home or fearing for your life during the attack can make things worse," he added. "Afterward, women who have been raped often go through periods of shock and denial—followed by fear, depression, anger, and disgrace. Symptoms can range from nightmares to a complete withdrawal from social contact, with a survivor feeling as if she has the word 'raped' branded on her forehead. Many women suffer posttraumatic stress disorder for years, along with panic attacks and problems with sexual intimacy."

Puzzled, I shook my head. "How do you . . . ?"

"KCBS ran a week-long special on rape last year. I was a cameraman on the shoot."

"You have quite the memory, don't you?" I said. "What other little gems did you pick up?"

Mike thought carefully before answering. "I learned that for a survivor to recover, she has to take control of her life and make her own decisions," he said. "She needs to feel safe and strong, not helpless or weak. Sexually, the woman needs to feel in control and know that her partner will stop if asked, as well as abiding by any limits she sets."

"Sounds simple, the way you tell it," I said bitterly, feeling as if Mike had just laid me open on a dissecting table. "It must be wonderful to have all the answers."

"I don't have any answers, Ali. I just know that being raped didn't change who you are. That comes from inside, from a place no one can touch."

"You think so?" I said, unable to meet Mike's gaze.

"Yes, I do. What I'm trying to say is that I like you," Mike said softly. "I like you a lot, and I want to keep seeing you. I realize you have problems, which is understandable considering what you went through. I also know that you'll get yourself straightened out. Till then, I simply want to spend time with you. No pressure for anything else. What do you say?"

At last I looked into Mike's eyes. "I say you're too good to be true," I answered, realizing I had never before felt like this about anyone. "I don't want to be the way I am," I went on quietly. "Afraid of everything. Afraid of being close. I just don't know how to change."

Mike held my gaze. "Do you trust me?"

"What kind of a question is that?"

"The most important one anyone can ask. Do you trust me?"

"Yes."

"Then I'll make you a promise. I'll never hurt you, and I'll never do anything to you that you don't want."

I nodded that I understood. Though comforted by Mike's conviction that I would eventually overcome my fears, in my heart of hearts I wasn't so sure. *But if not now, when?* my inner voice whispered.

"Mike?" I said, determined to put my terrors behind me. "I know I'm asking a lot and that the moment has probably passed, but . . . do you think we could try again?"

"Ali, you don't have to."

"I know I don't have to. I *want* to. Can we?"

Instead of answering, Mike took my hand and led me down the hallway to the bedroom I had seen earlier. When we reached the doorway, he scooped me into his arms and carried me into the room. After kicking off his sandals, he gently lowered me to the bed and lay beside me on the comforter, propping himself up on one elbow.

"What happens next?" I asked nervously, feeling a wave of both apprehension and desire.

"Anything you want," Mike replied, combing his fingers through my hair. "But first you have to tell me."

"Tell you?"

"Yes. For instance, would you like me to kiss you?"

"I . . . I think so. Yes."

"Then tell me."

All at once I understood. Mike was giving me control. "I . . . I want you to kiss me," I said, my voice trembling.

Mike leaned closer and brought his lips to mine. I circled him with my arms, again detecting a sweet lingering of brandy as I opened my mouth to his. A rush of heat washed over me as Mike returned my embrace. Hesitantly, I slipped my fingers beneath his shirt and ran my hand over the hard, lean muscles of his chest.

"Do you want me to touch you, too?" Mike asked.

"Yes."

"Tell me."

"I want you to touch me." Shyly, I unbuttoned my shirt, letting it fall open. My nipples were already pointed and hard. I inhaled sharply as Mike brushed his palm across them, teasing them even more erect. Then he slid the shirt from my shoulders and removed it. Next he unfastened the buttons of his own shirt, shrugging it off.

Unsure of myself but unwilling to stop, I raised my lips to Mike's and kissed him again, my tongue now tentatively exploring, my body reveling in the warmth of his bare skin and the strength of his hands on my back and hips and legs. Never suspecting it could be like this, I shuddered with excitement at his touch. Running my fingers through his hair, I pulled his face to my breasts. "Kiss me," I whispered, shocked at my own boldness.

Passion mounting, I writhed with pleasure as Mike's lips moved lower, his hands cupping my hips, pulling me against him. Mike had said he would do nothing I didn't want, and I was certain he would stop if I asked. I also knew I wouldn't ask. I didn't want him to stop. This was different from the horror I had experienced in the past, a terror that had so changed my life. Now it was what *I* wanted. And I wanted more.

"Take off your clothes," I said huskily, emboldened by a power I felt unfolding within. I lowered a hand to Mike's belt and unfastened his buckle, then tucked my thumbs under the waistband of my sweatpants and rolled the soft cotton fabric over my hips. Drawing up my knees, I slipped off the sweatpants and dropped them to the floor. Mike stripped off his jeans and undershorts at the same time.

I came into Mike's arms once more, feeling the electric touch of our bodies and the burning hardness of Mike's need pressing against me. He kissed me, his lips warm and demanding, his hands finding my breasts and thighs and the fiery liquid core at my center. And then his mouth was everywhere upon me, bringing me to the brink of ecstasy. I arched my back, shuddering as wave upon wave of rapture swept over me.

"God, you're beautiful," Mike murmured again.

My breath coming in gasps, I pushed Mike onto his back and straddled him. Taking him in my hands, I brought my lips to his, my breasts pressing against his chest, my hair fanning over my shoulders. Mike returned my kiss, then looked into my eyes. "Tell me, Ali," he said hoarsely. "Tell me what you want."

"I want you, Mike," I replied, my fears dissolving, more sure of myself than I had ever been before. "I want you."

Fumbling at a nightstand beside the bed, Mike opened a drawer. Finding what he wanted, he slipped on a protective sheath as I kissed his cheek and neck, then lay still as I guided him inside. A moan escaped my lips as Mike entered me. Overcome with desire, I again brought my mouth to his. Then, moving with a rhythm as ancient as life, I slowly began rocking my hips, my need mounting with Mike's, our bodies joined in a hunger neither of us could deny. I cried out softly when I climaxed, my passion cresting and surging and flooding like a relentless tide. And again, moments later, I cried out anew as Mike joined me, everything simple and flowing and complete.

Afterward we lay together, our bodies entwined in comfortable silence. With my head cradled on Mike's shoulder, I watched as shafts of light filtered into his room, tracing a pattern of shifting shadows on the ceiling. Neither of us spoke, for no words seemed necessary. And as I lay in Mike's arms, I felt myself slowly filling with a certainty beyond understanding. Deep within, I knew that something inside me had changed . . . indelibly and for all time.

# 28

Monday. I sat at my desk in the CBS newsroom, staring at my computer screen. Though I tried to focus on work, my mind kept returning to thoughts of Mike. Several times I started to phone him but stopped, deciding it was too soon after the weekend to call and not wanting to give the impression of being clinging or needy. Besides, I wanted him to call *me*.

Picking up a pile of notes instead, I scanned a list of questions that I had been considering—questions Lauren had asked me to compile for the upcoming network interview with the Frenches. Assuming it happened. The Frenches, their retinue of attorneys, and their publicist were still negotiating with CBS over terms of the interview, and it seemed to me that things were progressing at the rate of continental drift.

For reasons of their own, the Frenches had continued to stipulate that I be their interviewer. As much as I wanted to participate, the Frenches' motive for wanting me notwithstanding, I knew it was a completely unrealistic demand, and it came as no surprise when CBS held firm on insisting that a more senior correspondent conduct the interview. After much discussion, however, to my delight a compromise was reached in which Brent and I would both participate. On another front, the Frenches had also demanded that a copy of all questions be submitted to them beforehand. CBS had refused. Although the parents had bowed to network policy on that particular point, many other contentious details still remained to be worked out. Nevertheless, despite ongoing problems, an interview date had been tentatively set for two weeks hence, with a national airing to follow.

As much as I tried to concentrate, I repeatedly found my thoughts returning to Mike. At last I reached for the telephone, realizing that if I wanted to get any work done at all, I needed to speak with Mike first. I dialed his home number from memory. Getting his answering machine, I listened to Mike's recorded voice but didn't leave a message. Next I phoned Channel 2.

After numerous delays, someone transferred me to one of the editing bays. Mike picked up on the third ring.

"I'm glad you phoned," Mike said, sounding tired. "I'm leaving for Telluride early tomorrow, but I was planning to give you a call and see whether we could get together tonight."

"Maybe," I said. "Mom is being admitted to UCLA this afternoon. I'm visiting her after work, and I don't know how long I'll be. Can I call afterward?"

"Sure. Give your mom my best, will you?"

"I will," I replied. Then, changing subjects, "How are the changes to your documentary coming?"

"Getting there," Mike sighed. "After you left, I worked on revisions straight through the night."

"You were up all night?"

"Yep," Mike answered wearily. "The only thing left to do now is to lay down a new music track over the ending montage, per your suggestion. By the way, you were right. Your changes are exactly what *Forgotten River* needed."

"I'm glad to hear it," I said, noticing Brent making his way across the newsroom. "Everyone at Telluride is going to love it."

"From your lips to God's ears."

"Don't worry, they will. How long will you be gone?"

"I'm not certain, but at least a week," Mike replied. "Screenings don't start until Friday, but I'm flying out early to get the lay of the land."

"Well, break a leg, or whatever you film people say."

"Thanks, Ali. Let's talk later. If it turns out we don't see each other tonight, I'll call from Colorado. In fact, I'll call every day. I miss you already."

"You'd better. See you, Mike."

After replacing the receiver, I glanced up to find Brent standing beside my desk.

"Mike?" he guessed.

I nodded.

A canny look flitted across Brent's face, quickly replaced by a smile. "So you two have been seeing a lot of each other?"

"Uh-huh," I said, not missing Brent's brief expression of what I construed to be disapproval. "Something wrong with that?"

"No, of course not," Brent said quickly. "Mike and I have been friends for years. He's a great guy. I just don't want to see you get hurt."

"What do you mean?"

Brent hesitated. "Look, I'm only saying this because I know Mike," he went on reluctantly. "The guy's a regular Don Juan— girlfriends lined up around the block. There's no way he'll ever get serious about anyone, including you. As long as you realize that, fine."

"Thanks for the tip," I said, staring down at my desk. "Did you want something else?"

"Not really, except I thought it was high time for you and me to bury the hatchet," Brent said with a shrug. "I admit I was angry at first about your reservoir piece, but I have to give you credit. You showed plenty of hustle on that, just like when you got your interview with Mrs. French."

"Thanks."

Brent extended a hand. "As it appears we'll be working together on the French interview, how's about we let bygones be bygones. Friends?"

I took his hand, relieved that our unspoken feud of the past weeks finally seemed over. "Friends."

"Good." Brent squeezed my hand, then released it. "I have work to do, but let's get together later and discuss how to structure our meeting with Jordan's parents." Without awaiting a reply, he started back across the newsroom.

\*　　\*　　\*

On the way to his cubicle, Brent pondered the wounded, doe-eyed expression he had seen on Allison's face when he'd spoken of Mike. She had been unable to hide her hurt, although she'd certainly tried. Things between her and Mike must have progressed further than he had thought. In fact, from the lost-little-girl look in her eyes, she was already in love with him, though she would probably never admit it.

Following the airing of Allison's reservoir piece, Brent had questioned every news cameraman at CBS. No one he had talked with had admitted shooting the footage she'd used, but *someone* had. At the time Brent had been fairly sure it was Mike. It was a bit of knowledge he had kept to himself, suspecting it might come in handy. Given present developments, Brent was now certain that Mike had accompanied Allison to the reservoir and shot her footage. The real question was: How had Allison known to be there in the first place?

Brent had contacted all his sources in the DA's office. He had also phoned an informant at the coroner's office. He had learned nothing. Whatever tip Allison had received about the reservoir must have come from another direction, and only one avenue came to mind: Detective Daniel Kane. But the lead detective on the Jordan French case wouldn't have simply handed over inside information to Allison, even if she were his daughter. She had to have procured it another way. Brent hadn't figured out that part yet, but it was the only thing that made sense. Which begged question number two: Did Allison know anything else? And if so, had she told Mike? On impulse, Brent lifted the phone and dialed KCBS. Moments later he had Mike on the line.

"How're you doing, buddy?" Brent asked casually. "I know you're probably swamped with getting ready for Telluride and all, but I wanted to call and wish you luck."

"Thanks," said Mike. "And swamped doesn't come close to describing it. I haven't even packed yet, and I'm still making last-minute changes to the film."

"One question and I'll let you go. Allison and I are hammering together another report on the Frenches. We're under time pressure, and Lauren asked me to double-check Allison's research and get corroborating statements."

"Ali's doing another spot on the Frenches? She didn't mention it to me."

"She's the secretive one, isn't she? Believe me, there are wheels within wheels in that girl."

A pause. "So what do you want to know?" Mike asked.

"Well, when Ali told me you were the one who shot that exclusive reservoir footage for her, I—"

"She told you? Damn."

Brent's pulse quickened. "Don't worry, your secret's safe with me," he said, trying to sound casual. "I realize if it got out, it would create problems for you over at Channel 2. Incidentally, that was clever the way you two came up with the reservoir angle in the first place."

"I just invited Ali on a bike ride," said Mike. "Whatever credit there is goes to her. She's the one who wanted to retrace Mr. French's mountain-bike route."

Brent thought quickly. "And she figured out Mr. French knew the location of the reservoir because he passed it on his bike rides," he said, part of the puzzle falling into place. But lots of people knew the reservoir was there. There had to be more.

Brent hesitated, reasoning that at some point Allison must have confided her discovery to her father, and whatever she had told him carried enough weight to spark his revisiting the area. That analysis was satisfactory as far as it went, but a piece of the puzzle was still missing. Not immediately coming up with an answer, Brent pushed on. "How much did she tell you about the autopsy?" he asked, taking a stab in the dark.

"The sexual-abuse angle? Just hints, like insinuating her father had solid cause to suspect the parents," said Mike. "At the time I thought she was being cagey to protect her story. Appears I was right."

Sexual abuse? Jesus! thought Brent, struggling to contain his excitement. The police must have evidence that old man French was molesting his daughter! But if that's the case, why hadn't Allison reported it? Maybe she hadn't been able to get confirmation. Well, maybe she can't, but I can, he thought. "On something this big you don't really blame her, do you?" Brent continued smoothly. "Anything you want to add?"

"Not really. Listen, Brent, I've gotta run, but please keep quiet about my shooting that footage for Allison."

"No problem," said Brent, his mind still racing. "Good luck at the festival."

"Thanks. See you when I get back."

After hanging up, Brent remained at his desk for several minutes, putting it all together. The part about Mr. French's bike rides resulting in a second police search of the reservoir still didn't make sense, but the fact Mr. French knew of the secluded reservoir site prior to the murder was newsworthy in itself. The real bombshell, however, was the child-abuse angle. Police investigators had to have cause for their dogged concentration on the parents, and the sexual abuse of a fourteen-year-old, especially chronic abuse, could have shown up at autopsy—even though the body had been submerged for weeks. Several of the tabloids had speculated on the child-abuse possibility from the very beginning, but this was different. This was real. And if there were evidence of sexual abuse in the autopsy report, Brent intended to reveal it.

He lifted the phone again. He needed independent corroboration, either from the DA's office or the coroner's office. Preferably both. It wouldn't be easy, but he had done this kind of thing before. When he told his contacts that CBS *knew for certain* that the autopsy results were consistent with chronic child abuse, someone would crack—especially if Brent said he was merely seeking confirmation from a second independent source.

It turned out to be more difficult than expected. Among other things, Brent had to call in markers and make promises he wasn't certain he could keep. But none of that mattered. Within an hour he had everything he needed: quotes, corroborating statements, even a pro forma "no comment" from the LAPD.

Time to talk to Lauren.

*       *       *

I stuck my head into the bureau chief's office. "You wanted to see me?"

"That's right," said Lauren. "Come in and close the door."

Glancing curiously at Brent, who was lounging cross-legged on the couch across from Lauren's desk, I stepped inside. "What's up?"

"Brent has put together a new piece on the French case. We're running it this evening," Lauren replied evenly. "Given the circumstances, I want to know whether you have anything to add."

Puzzled, I shrugged. "What story and what circumstances?"

"I'm sorry, Ali," Brent jumped in. "Mike called me this morning. He told me all about your bike ride and how you had discovered that Mr. French knew of the reservoir location—well before the murder."

I paled. "Mike told you that?"

Brent smiled sympathetically. "He also told me that you said there was evidence in the autopsy report proving that Jordan had been sexually abused. I just got confirmation from several independent sources. Ali, you know I had to follow up on this. I can't imagine why you didn't come forward with the story earlier, but this is too big to ignore."

Silently, I cursed myself for having confided in Mike. Although I hadn't told him that much, look what had come of it. Thank God I hadn't mentioned the time-of-death discrepancy.

"Why *didn't* you come forward with this?" demanded Lauren.

"I couldn't," I replied, still not wanting to accept that Mike had betrayed me, but seeing no way around it. "The sexual-abuse angle was something I got off the record."

"You could have gone to another source for corroboration," Lauren pointed out, raising an eyebrow.

"I know. But my father said that if it got out, it would jeopardize his case."

"That's *his* problem. *Ours* is to report the news."

"But if we disclose this, it will definitely screw up the investigation," I repeated, my stomach sinking. "Why not wait? If we hold off, my dad said we'll get an exclusive on everything when an arrest is made."

"Impossible. Now that it's out, we have to run with the story. If we don't, someone else will."

"But . . ."

"No buts, Ali. If you had come to me earlier, I might have been able to help. As it is, there's nothing I can do now other than give you an opportunity to get onboard. I'm asking you one more time. Is there anything you want to add?"

"No."

"In that case, Brent's piece will air tonight as it stands. And Allison?"

"What?"

"You have some thinking to do. We're in the news business. Your father is in the police business. Decide which side you're on."

# 29

Monday afternoon, Kane took time off from work to drive Catheryn to the UCLA Medical Center. Catheryn's first hours there were spent registering, filling out forms, and signing authorizations. Next, a white plastic hospital band encircling her wrist, she underwent yet another round of lab tests. Afterward she was taken to a private room in the Transplant Unit, located on the tenth floor of the west wing in an area known to doctors and staff as Ten-West.

Later Dr. Gary Miller, the transplant team's attending hematologist, stopped by Catheryn's room for a final review of her therapy. The radiation treatments, the first of which she would receive that evening, entailed three consecutive days of total-body irradiation, followed on the fourth day by a massive dose of chemotherapy. According to Dr. Miller, the goal of this combined approach was to achieve a condition know as pancytopenia in which all cells of Catheryn's immune system, normal and cancerous alike, were totally destroyed. After one day of rest, she would receive a bone-marrow graft taken from Allison. If everything went as planned, donor stem cells from Allison would reestablish Catheryn's immune system, leaving her cancer-free. Though Dr. Miller tried to sound reassuring without instilling false hope, his additional review of the risks involved left Catheryn with an encroaching sense of dread.

Dorothy, who had once more driven down from Santa Barbara to stay with the family, visited briefly, as did Travis and Nate. Catheryn also received numerous phone calls from friends and neighbors. Even Dr. Kratovil telephoned to wish her well and say that Catheryn would be in her prayers. Yet despite the calls and the presence of family, as the afternoon wore on Catheryn began to feel more and more alone, as if, like a shroud, her disease were descending between her and those she loved.

Lying in bed, she stared out the window, ruefully thinking that although the view from her room in the UCLA Medical Center was different from the one she had enjoyed at St. John's— she now had an aerial panorama of the palm-lined streets and high-rises of Westwood rather than those of Santa Monica—everything else about the room looked the same. Bland, colorless walls. Waist-high electrical receptacles and gas outlets. IV stands, monitoring machines, IMED pumps. A wall-mounted TV across the room. And everywhere, the hard, impersonal gleam of stainless steel. The family pictures and the collection of Nate's drawings that she had brought from home brightened things somewhat, but not enough.

Attempting to shake her feelings of foreboding, Catheryn tore her eyes from the window. Kane, who had stayed with her the entire afternoon, sat in a chair across from the bed. Lines of concern etched his face. "Penny for your thoughts," he said.

"They're not worth a penny."

"They are to me, sugar."

Catheryn shook her head. "I guess I'm a little scared," she said quietly. "Maybe more than a little." Rolling onto her side, she reached to a table beside the bed, retrieved a sealed white envelope, and handed it to Kane.

"What's this?"

"It's for the children," Catheryn answered. "Please give it to them if something happens . . ."

"Nothing is going to happen," Kane said firmly. "You're going to be fine."

"I know. But just in case, please take it."

"Okay, but nothing is going to happen," Kane repeated. He pocketed the envelope, then took her hand. "You're strong, we're in one of the finest hospitals in the country, and we have the best medical team available."

"You're right," Catheryn sighed. "I just hate being here. I hate being sick and weak and ugly like this. Most of all, I miss you and the children."

"Oh, you'll be seeing plenty of me," Kane said lightly, glancing at a cot that an orderly had set up for him by the window. "As for being ugly—hell, Kate, even with all you're going through, you're still the best-looking broad in this place."

Catheryn attempted a smile. "How would you know?" she asked, realizing Kane was attempting to lift her spirits and trying to play along. "Been doing a survey of all attractive females in the hospital?"

"Don't have to," said Kane. "Some things I just know."

*     *     *

Having come straight from work that evening, I knocked on Mom's UCLA hospital room door, then eased it open. Mom glanced up from her bed. She looked tired, shadows darkening the skin under her eyes, strain pulling at the corners of her mouth.

"Come in, Ali," she said.

Hesitantly, I stepped inside. "Hi, Mom. Dad. How's everything going?"

From across the room, Dad scowled at me without answering. "Everything's fine," Mom replied. Then, turning to my father, "Dan, could you give us a few minutes? I have something to discuss with Allison."

"Join the club," my father said. He strode to the door. "See you in a bit, Kate."

"Is something wrong?" I asked after he'd left.

"You could say that." Mom studied me for a long moment. "I had a disturbing conversation with Grandma Dorothy today. It seems she got a call from the accounting office at USC."

I lowered my head, knowing what was coming. "Could we talk about this later?"

"No. We're going to talk about it now," Mom said firmly. "The woman at the accounting office wanted to know where to return Dorothy's tuition money, as you wouldn't be attending classes at USC in the fall. Do you have an explanation?"

"I planned to tell you."

"You *planned* to tell me. When? Next Christmas? In any case, quitting school isn't something you just *announce*, young lady."

"I didn't discuss it with you because you'd have just said no."

"Correct. Dropping out of college is the worst thing you could do right now."

"Why?"

"I'm not going to give you a list of reasons," said Mom. "But you're just starting out in life, and—"

"—and it's *my* life," I interrupted. "In case you haven't noticed, I'm in the middle of something big at CBS. I want to see where it goes."

"Honey, you're capable of so much more. What you're doing on television is simply pandering to morbid public curiosity."

Stung by my mother's tone, I felt the barriers descending once more, years of alienation hanging between us like dirty linen. Angrily, I looked away. "Nothing I *ever* do is good enough for you."

"Ali, that's not true."

"Sure it is. From the beginning it's always been Travis, Travis, Travis. Well, I may not be a prodigy like Trav, but I'm doing what I can. And a lot of people think I'm doing a pretty fair job of it. Clearly, you're not one of them."

Suddenly seeming exhausted, Mom lay back and closed her eyes. "You and I can't even talk any more without getting into a fight," she said softly.

I struggled to find words that could pierce the walls between us. I could think of none. "I didn't come here to fight," I said.

"I know."

Silence.

"I should leave. Let you rest."

Mom opened her eyes. "I love you, Ali."

"I know you do, Mom." I rose and started for the door. "I love you, too," I added, knowing it wasn't enough. "I . . . I really should let you rest. I'll stop by tomorrow before work."

"All right." Mom stared out the window. "See you tomorrow."

Shaken, I stumbled into the hall. Ashamed of myself for arguing with Mom, now of all times, I turned to go back to her room. A strong hand on my shoulder stopped me.

It was my father.

"It's time we had another talk, petunia," he said, his voice ominously flat.

"What about?"

"Not here. Come with me."

With a sinking feeling, I trailed my father to the family waiting room at the far end of the corridor. I followed him inside. The room was deserted. Dad closed the door behind us, then turned to me. "What's this I hear about your quitting school?" he demanded.

"CBS offered me a full-time job. I took it," I replied nervously. "I can go to school later."

"And this is a decision that you figure you can make on your own?"

"It's my life."

"That it is, but others are affected by what you do," Dad said, his temper barely in check. "You should have discussed this with your mother and me."

I knew he was right, but I stubbornly replied, "If I had, what would you have said?"

"I'd have said that you're old enough to screw up your own life," Dad snapped. "Working for some dirtbag news station isn't my idea of how to improve the world, but if I couldn't talk you out of it, I'd have told you to do what you thought best."

"And Mom?"

"That's another story."

"And that's exactly why I didn't discuss it with her."

"You should have."

"Well, I just did, and she couldn't give me one good reason why I should stay in school," I said. Not exactly true, but I said it anyway.

"She couldn't, huh?" said Dad angrily. "Well, over the years I've learned to trust your mother's judgment on things, and simply because she couldn't give you her reasons doesn't mean she doesn't have good ones."

"Whatever they are, they aren't good enough."

Dad glared. "Your timing on this couldn't be worse, Allison. Your mother is on enough of an emotional roller coaster without your dropping this latest bombshell."

"I . . . I know," I said guiltily. "And I'm sorry. Lately I don't seem to be able to do anything right," I went on, suddenly remembering my recent meeting with Lauren. "Dad, there's something else I need to tell you. I screwed up at work. I made a mistake. I know I promised not to say anything about—"

Dad raised a hand, his eyes blazing. "I know all about it. Brent Preston called me at the station. He wanted my comments on a story he's airing tonight on the Jordan French autopsy. You promised to keep your yap shut about that, Ali. Instead, you went right out and told your pal Brent."

"That's not how it happened," I said. "I trusted someone else I shouldn't have, and he—"

"I don't want to hear your excuses," Dad interrupted. "Not right now. We have personal issues between us, princess. And by God when this is over, we're going to straighten them out. But what you're doing to your mom is another matter altogether," he continued, his voice as cutting as a whip. "I swear, I'm beginning to think I don't even know who you are anymore. One thing I do know. If you do one more thing to make life tougher on your mom, you *will* regret it. Is that clear?"

"Dad . . ."

"I only want to hear one thing from you right now," Dad said, his eyes as hard as granite. "Do you understand what I just said?"

"Yes, sir. I understand."

By the time I left the Medical Center, dusk had settled over the campus. Despondently, I shuffled past the darkened Biology and Plant Physiology Buildings, taking the pathway skirting the botanical garden to Hilgard. But instead of returning to my dorm room, I kept walking. It wasn't until I found myself in front of a parking garage three blocks away that I knew where I was going.

After retrieving Trav's Bronco from the parking space I had rented when he first lent me his car, I headed toward Pacific Palisades. I was fairly certain that Mike would be home packing for his trip. Instead of calling, I decided to confront him and have things out, face-to-face. I wasn't certain what I was going to say, but I knew it was something I had to do.

On the drive to Pacific Palisades, I kept searching my mind for some reason that would explain Mike's betrayal. In another part of my mind, the rational part, I knew there was none, nor could there be. Mike had been the only person besides my father who'd known I had retraced Mr. French's mountain bike ride. Mike had also deduced that evidence of child abuse had been discovered at autopsy, or at least he had strongly suspected it—a supposition that I had unwisely done little to dissuade. Now Brent knew these things, too. Brent said that Mike had told him, and Brent had no reason to lie. No, Mike had broken his promise of silence to me. Of that I was certain. There could be no excuse. With an angry flush, I remembered our time together in his bedroom, wondering what else he had revealed to friends like Brent.

Night had fallen by the time I reached Pacific Palisades. After turning right on Galloway, I proceeded up the narrow, tree-lined street. I slowed as I neared Mike's house, surprised to see him standing out front. Illuminated in the glow of a corner streetlight, he was talking to a tall, willowy blond girl wearing skintight shorts and a skimpy halter top.

I caught them momentarily in my headlights as I approached. The tawny-haired girl squinted briefly into the glare, then bent to finish tying shut the hatchback of her car—a late-model Honda with a bicycle hanging out of the rear. Then she turned to Mike and said something. Mike smiled. Smiling back, she put her arms around his neck and kissed him. Filled with a hollow pang of hurt and shame, I continued up Galloway without stopping.

I didn't look back.

On my return to Westwood, I stared numbly out the windshield, determined not to cry. It had been a bad day all around, but crying wouldn't help. Trying to look at the bright side, I told myself that things couldn't get any worse. I had definitely hit bottom. But as I made my way back to my empty dorm room at UCLA, a nagging doubt kept rising in my mind . . . telling me I was wrong.

Things could *always* get worse.

# 30

O n the following Saturday, after my customary cross-campus jog and several hours toiling on my manuscript, I saved my work and turned off my computer. Grateful for a break, I stood, stretched, grabbed my jacket, and started for the door. My appointment for the bone-marrow harvest was scheduled for 10 AM that morning, but the transplant team wanted me present an hour early for preoperative procedures. As I made my way down the hall, my stomach rumbled. Because my marrow would be taken under general anesthesia, I'd had nothing to eat or drink since the previous evening. Not that I had been hungry.

Following my preanesthesia assessment at the hospital earlier that week, I had worried constantly that something was going to happen to me—a fatal accident on the freeway while driving to work, for instance—leaving Mom without a marrow donor and no functioning immune system of her own. It was with relief that I realized the time for the marrow harvest had finally arrived.

The procedure I was about to undergo, as explained by Dr. Miller, hadn't sounded particularly complicated. I would be put to sleep and a series of needle punctures made into my posterior iliac crests—the fan-shaped bony structures forming the back of my pelvis. Approximately one quart of marrow would be taken from the hollow portion of my bones, after which I would be left with little more aftereffect than a very sore butt. The plastic pouch of harvested marrow, which Dr. Miller had described as looking much like blood, would be filtered to remove fat and particles of bone, then given intravenously to Mom. Simple.

But I knew it wouldn't be simple for Mom. My mother's ordeal at St. John's had been bad. This would be worse.

When I reached the landing at the bottom of the stairs, a telephone in the hallway began ringing. By convention, whoever in the dorm was closest at the time answered it. I hesitated, then ducked into a narrow alcove and lifted the receiver. "Hello?"

"Allison?"

It was Mike.

Without thinking, I started to hang up. He had been trying to call me daily since leaving for Colorado. I hadn't answered, nor had I listened to any of his messages. Suddenly I wanted to know what he had to say. "Hello, Mike."

"You're sure a hard one to get hold of," Mike said. "When I couldn't reach you at home or work, I finally decided to try the dorm and see whether anyone knew what had happened to you."

"I've been busy."

"I can imagine. Your big French interview is coming up, right?"

I didn't reply.

"How's you mother doing?"

"Not well."

"I'm sorry to hear that, Ali. Hang in there. She'll get better."

Again I didn't reply.

"I've missed you," Mike pushed on. "I've been really busy here at Telluride, but I did manage to watch Brent's autopsy piece on the news," he continued, struggling to carry the conversation. "I was surprised that you didn't do the spot yourself, as it was your information regarding the autopsy and the sexual abuse issue. Was that a network decision?"

My hand tightened on the receiver. I couldn't believe Mike was being so cavalier about his betrayal. Didn't he think I knew? "Are you trying to make some kind of joke?" I demanded.

"Joke? What are you talking about?"

"You tell me."

"If this is about your spilling the beans to Brent about my shooting your reservoir footage—"

I cut him off. "That's a laugh. I wasn't the one who spilled the beans—or whatever lame cliché you want to use to describe what you did."

"What *I* did? I don't understand."

"Sure you do," I snapped. "I'm hanging up now, Mike. I don't think we have anything more to say to each other."

"Ali . . ."

"On second thought, I do have one more thing to say. Don't call me anymore."

"Wait," Mike pleaded. "I thought we had something going between us."

"You mean between me and all your other women."

"*Now* what are you talking about?"

"You want me to spell it out? Fine," I said. "I thought we had something between us, too—at least until I saw you with your blond girlfriend the other night. I know I don't have any claims on you, Mike. We haven't made any commitment to each other. On the other hand, your being with me on Sunday like we were and then with someone else on Monday isn't the sort of relationship I want."

"That *was* you. I thought I recognized your car. Listen, Ali—"

"Whatever you have to say, I don't want to hear it."

"Sarah's an old girlfriend," Mike protested. "She came by to pick up her bike."

"Sure she did."

"It's true."

"The truth seems to be something you have trouble with," I said coldly, incredulous that after breaking his promise of silence regarding the French case, he actually expected me to believe him. "I judge people by what they *do*, not by what they say."

"You're not going to let me explain, are you?"

"No."

"All right," said Mike, his tone frosting as well. "In that case, I'll tell you something *you* have trouble with. Trust. You walk around in that protective shell of yours, so afraid of being hurt that you won't give anyone a chance—let alone the benefit of the doubt. Well, eventually you'll realize you have to trust someone."

"I do trust *some* people," I fired back. "But I choose them carefully, and you're no longer on the list. As for your amateur psychology, save it for someone who cares." With that, I slammed down the receiver and banged out the front door, ignoring curious glances from several girls coming up the steps.

## 31

Spurred by the growing media furor generated by Brent's autopsy story, the Frenches' publicist called CBS early the following week, requesting that the date for the interview with Jordan's parents be moved up. The network readily agreed, rescheduling the interview for the coming Thursday. It was widely rumored in the media that Mr. and Mrs. French, under threat of a grand jury subpoena, were likely to submit to a formal police interrogation as well. In light of that, I concluded that in addition to defusing the negative spin that Brent's autopsy piece had put on the case, the Frenches were attempting to garner national sympathy by preemptively going on-air with the viewing public first—another masterful example of playing the press.

The rest of the week dragged by, my early-morning hours spent toiling on my novel, my time at work devoted to last-minute preparation for the upcoming French interview, my evenings visiting my mother at the hospital.

Following the bone-marrow transplant, Mom had developed what Dr. Miller described as a neutropenic fever of unknown origin, a condition requiring IV treatment with broad-spectrum antibiotics and an antifungal medication. Along with intravenous feeding and daily doses of morphine, Mom was also receiving steroids and a drug called cyclosporin to combat graft-versus-host disease. Able to do nothing but watch as my mother grew weaker by the day, I kept as busy as possible, filling my waking hours with activity and dreading my dismal, sleepless nights. By Thursday morning, the day of the French interview, I was exhausted.

As scheduled, the Frenches arrived at the newsroom at precisely 10 AM. An hour later, after a review of procedural ground rules, the meeting with Jordan's parents got underway.

Despite showing the strain of past months, Mr. and Mrs. French held up well under initial questioning—painting themselves as wronged not only by police, but by an overly aggressive media as well. They described how, nerve-wracked by the journalistic attention they'd received, they had been forced to flee their home and live in hiding, shuttling from hotel to hotel, staying with friends, and shunning places they were known to frequent. But somehow, no matter where they'd hidden, they had always been found. In the end, according to Mr. French, they had simply accepted the impossibility of dodging the press and returned to their estate, becoming virtual prisoners in their own home.

Although I realized that I didn't deserve to be participating in the interview, I was determined to do my best. The trouble was, although I had written more than my share of hard-hitting questions, almost all had been given to Brent in what was clearly a news version of the "good-cop, bad-cop" interrogation strategy—my subservient role in the proceedings adding to the humiliation of knowing I wouldn't have even been there had it not been for my father's involvement in the case. That, and the Frenches' self-serving demands.

As the interview progressed, to my profound embarrassment, it became obvious to everyone that I had been cast as a sympathetic kid-sister, with Brent playing the more skeptical, seasoned correspondent, exerting a balancing influence. It was Brent, for instance, who broached the subject of why the Frenches had refused to cooperate with authorities by giving blood and hair samples, or by submitting to a formal police interrogation. Jordan's parents maintained that their refusal to cooperate with police investigators stemmed from the LAPD's clear intention of treating them as murder suspects, rather than seeking the real killer or killers of their daughter. In Mr. French's words, "The police came to our house convinced that we'd done it. They had a murdered child on their hands, and their knee-jerk reaction was to go after the parents. They didn't want to find out what actually happened. They just wanted to hang us."

Following up with a more friendly topic approved for me by network, I brought up similar examples of alleged misuse of power by authorities—instances including the McMartin childcare case and others in which lives had been ruined by what many considered a witch-hunt mentality on the part of investigators. Implied in my examples were the cautionary lessons to be learned. Naturally, Jordan's parents had wholeheartedly agreed.

Brent rebutted by asking Mr. French about his previous knowledge of the reservoir location, also bringing up the sexual-abuse aspects of Jordan's autopsy. On both issues Mr. French delivered a well-articulated response, pointing out that many people knew of the reservoir location, and that other explanations existed for the supposed child-abuse evidence discovered by the coroner. Mrs. French added that Jordan's doctor had unequivocally stated that during the numerous times he had seen Jordan over the years, *never* had he found any evidence whatsoever of sexual molestation.

Next I brought up the private polygraph exams that the parents had passed. Brent queried them regarding the LAPD contention that it was unlikely Jordan could have been abducted from her home without someone having heard a scuffle. I introduced a psychological profile of the killer that the Frenches had procured from an ex-member of the FBI's Investigative Support Unit in Virginia, stressing that the behavioral analysis had failed to match Jordan's parents in any respect. Brent questioned why no follow-up to the ransom note was ever received. And so on, back and forth. Although my father's being the lead investigator on the case was never mentioned, it hung in the air, shadowing the entire proceeding.

Toward the end, in a telling moment that summed up the overall tenor of the interview, I posed the only tough question I had been allowed. Point-blank, I asked Jordan's parents whether they had killed their daughter. It was a question that brought Mrs. French to tears.

"No, no, no," she replied, taking her husband's hand. "How could we do that? Think about it. The police would have everyone believe that we bludgeoned our daughter to death and then dumped her body in a reservoir. Next we wrote a phony ransom note, phoned the police to report her missing, and sat around waiting for the authorities to arrive. How could we do that? I mean, how could *any* parent do that? What sort of people do you think we are? We loved our daughter," she added quietly. "We would never have done anything to harm her. Never."

The interview aired the following evening as a CBS Special. To no one's surprise, it proved one of the most-viewed presentations of the year. Brent, Lauren, and I, as well as others from the newsroom, watched it in Lauren's office. In the edited version I came off as being even more sympathetic toward Jordan's parents, as if I considered them the injured parties. It was an effect that I knew had been carefully choreographed by network from the beginning. Conversely, Brent appeared even more the senior journalist, the one dealing with the nuts and bolts of the case. It was a part he executed with consummate skill. Afterward, disappointed and depressed, I returned to my room at UCLA.

When I arrived at the dorm, I found a stack of bills and letters that Mrs. Random had left for me on a narrow table inside the front entry. There was also a small package addressed to me, partially hidden beneath my pile of mail. Inside the package was a DVD labeled *Forgotten River*. No note.

After ascending the stairs to my room, I stripped off my clothes and took a long, hot shower, standing beneath the steaming spray as the water gradually eased the tension from my body. Twenty minutes later I stepped out, dried myself, and donned my robe. I briefly contemplated going to bed. I glanced at the DVD I had received in the mail. Though exhausted, I wasn't sleepy.

Deciding to watch the reedited version of *Forgotten River*, I flipped on my TV, shoved Mike's disc into my DVD player, and lay on my bed. Before long, despite my anger over Mike's betrayal, I was snared anew in the artistry of his work. He had taken my suggestions and improved upon them, laying down a classical music soundtrack over his ending montage and splicing in a number of more optimistic images throughout—including a shot of the waterfall we had visited in Santa Ynez Canyon. Though subtle, the changes he had made imbued the documentary with a note of hope that had formerly been missing, seeming to say that despite tragedy and hardship, life could be meaningful; and although bulldozed and trodden and cemented over in places, the beauty of nature still existed for those who looked for it.

But as the film ended, I felt anything but optimistic. More despondent than ever, I stared at the blank TV screen, wondering how things in my life could have gone so wrong. Raising the remote control, I turned off the set, at a loss about what to do next. I still wasn't sleepy. Crossing to my desk, I decided to put in a few more hours on my novel. I had nearly completed what I hoped would be my final revision, and work was going well. Thinking that my writing was the only thing in my life that *was* going well, I booted up my computer. As I was about to open my Word application, my cell phone rang.

"Allison?" Brent's voice came over the line. "Have you heard the news?"

"What news?"

"The preliminary numbers are in on tonight's broadcast. They're off the chart! Nobody's ever seen anything like it!"

"Great," I said, struggling to match Brent's enthusiasm.

"Great? It's better than great!" Brent raved. "It's like hitting a home run and winning the lottery all rolled into one. We really did it this time, Allison. C'mon, we're going out to celebrate."

"Now?"

"Right now. Victories like this don't come around every day."

"It's late, Brent."

"Late? It isn't even ten yet. Listen, I'm meeting Liz and a few friends at The Gardens for drinks. That's just down the street from you, right? I'm in my car heading to Westwood. I'll stop by for you on my way."

I wasn't dressed and my hair was still damp from the shower, but going out suddenly sounded better than staring at my computer screen. "All right," I agreed, starting to get caught up in Brent's infectious mood. "It'll take me a while to get ready. I'll meet you there."

Fifteen minutes later, after hurriedly drying my hair, dressing, and throwing on a touch of makeup, I left the dorm and headed down Hilgard on foot. As I turned the corner at the intersection of Glendon and Lindbrook, I spotted the tiled roof and rough brick exterior of The Gardens, the restaurant where Mike and I had eaten dinner earlier that summer. As I approached the entrance, a voice sounded from behind me. "Allison! Wait up."

I turned, spotting Brent exiting a nearby parking garage. "Got caught in traffic," he explained after crossing the street to join me. "My friends are probably already here," he added, seeming even more elated than he had on the phone. "Let's go join the party."

Brent escorted me through the front door. As we stopped at the hostess station, I glanced into the dining area. To my shock, I saw Mike sitting with Don Sturgess and several other people I didn't recognize. A thicket of champagne bottles and cocktail glasses littered their tabletop. As I was about to turn away, Mike looked up. Our eyes met. Then Mike saw Brent. Without a word, he pushed away from the table and started toward us.

I knew from talking with Brent that Mike had returned from the film festival earlier that week, but I still hadn't spoken with him. Irritated, I turned to Brent, finding him waving to a boisterous group in the bar. "There they are," he said, casually placing an arm around my shoulders. "Let's head in."

"Unfortunately, someone wants to talk with us first."

Brent turned. I felt him tense as he saw Mike coming toward us.

"Hello, Allison," said Mike when he arrived, his eyes flat and expressionless.

Despite my hurt at Mike's betrayal, the sight of him tugged at me. "Hello, Mike," I replied coolly.

Noting Brent's arm around me, Mike addressed his friend. "I take it you two are an item now. Congratulations."

Although Brent quickly removed his arm, I spoke before he could reply. "What I do is none of your business, Mike," I said.

Ignoring me, Mike shoved his hands into his pockets and stepped closer to Brent. "I guess congratulations are also in order for your big news special, Brent. Not to mention your piece on the Jordan French autopsy last week."

"Thanks," Brent said nervously.

Though Mike's mouth formed a smile, his dark eyes remained as hard as slate. "Speaking of which, I've done a little thinking about our last phone conversation," he continued. "You remember, when you called me before I left for Colorado." Mike stared at Brent as though he were examining something he had found in the gutter. "It took me a while to figure it out, but I finally did the addition. I've always said you would do anything for a story. I just didn't realize how far you would go."

Brent shifted uneasily. "I don't know what you're talking about."

"Sure you do." Mike moved closer.

"I . . ."

"We're going outside, hotshot," Mike said, his lips barely moving. "You and me. And as we're such *good* friends, I'll tell you what. I'm going to let you take the first swing. Maybe even the first couple."

Brent's eyes traveled the room, searching for a way out. Though he was as large as Mike and taller by inches, he was no match for his thick-muscled friend. "I don't want to fight."

By now several people were staring. "Too bad," Mike said, still not taking his hands from his pockets. "You should have thought of that earlier."

I stepped between them. "Stop it!" I ordered. I glowered at Mike, then addressed Brent. "Go join your friends. I'll be in shortly. I want a word with Mr. Cortese first."

Warily backing away, Brent retreated to the bar. Once he was gone, I turned to Mike. Though confused regarding what had just transpired, I intended to vent a rancor that had been simmering inside me all week. But as I started to speak, something in Mike's eyes reminded me of a look I had seen in one of his photographs . . . the one of his mother. And with that remembrance, my mind filled with thoughts of my own mother. And all at once, compared with my larger problems, Mike's betrayal didn't mean much anymore. Despite my anger, my bitter words died unspoken, my fury melting away. Abruptly, I just felt empty and alone.

As Mike saw the anger fade from my eyes, his own rancor deflated as well. "Sorry," he said. "Didn't mean to cause a scene."

Not knowing what to say, I glanced toward Mike's table in the dining room, again noting the champagne bottles. "I heard the festival went well," I said.

Mike nodded. "*Forgotten River* took first in the documentary category. PBS is airing it this fall."

"I'm not surprised. Congratulations seem to be in order for you, too."

"Thanks," Mike replied cautiously. "By the way, I'm leaving KCBS. Next month Don is starting that feature film he mentioned. He showed my documentary to the director, and the guy liked it. I was offered a job as the second-unit cameraman. I'm going to take it."

"Again, my compliments."

"Things appear to be looking up for you, too."

Mike's words rang hollow in my ears. "Couldn't be better," I said dully.

"I guess we both got what we wanted."

"I guess we did."

Suddenly needing to be alone, I stopped a passing waitress. "Excuse me, miss. Could you tell my friend Brent Preston that I'm going home? He's in the bar with—"

"I see him, Ms. Kane. I'll be glad to tell him."

Surprised at being recognized, I watched as the hostess made her way into the bar. Over the course of the summer I had somehow become a celebrity. It was a status I wasn't certain I liked, but at times it did have its advantages.

"Leaving?"

I looked at Mike for a long moment. Despite all that had happened, I still had things I wanted to say to him. Some were angry; some were not. I could find words for none of them. "Good-bye, Mike," I said instead. "Take care of yourself."

"Ali . . ." Mike hesitated. Then, with a sad smile, he looked away. "You take care of yourself, too."

Outside, the night air had grown chilly. I had worn only a light skirt and a sweater to the restaurant. Belatedly, I wished I had brought a jacket. Walking briskly to warm up, I headed back to the dorm. As I passed a line of Friday-night moviegoers on Glendon, I realized that I was retracing the same route Mike and I had taken earlier that summer. Though it had been only a few months ago, it seemed like an eternity.

Staying on well-lit streets, I turned on Le Conte at the edge of campus, starting toward the dorm. I paused when I reached the Medical Center complex. Without thinking I crossed the street, ducked into an ivy-covered parking structure, and ascended a flight of metal stairs to a broad plaza fronting the hospital. Seconds later I entered through a pair of sliding glass doors. After stopping in the lobby to sign the visitor's register, I hurried down a corridor to the West Wing elevators.

When I reached the tenth-floor Transplant Unit, all seemed quiet. I proceeded down the hallway, stopping at the nurses station to pick up a mask and gown—a hospital precaution required for all marrow-transplant visitors. Donning the mask and gown, I continued on, hesitating outside my mother's room. I didn't know why I was there, only that I had needed to come. I lifted my hand to knock. I hesitated, not wanting to wake Mom. Nervously, I cracked the door.

The interior of the room was dark. I slipped inside. In a faint light from the window I could make out the IV stands and IMED pumps beside my mother's bed, a spidery web of tubes trailing down to a catheter in Mom's chest. Not making a sound, I inched closer. As I did, I noticed my father sleeping on a cot near the window, hospital mask covering his nose and mouth, the rhythmic rasp of his breathing mixing with the hum of an air filter in the corner. Mom appeared to be asleep, too. After washing my hands with alcohol and drying them at the sink, I crept closer, stopping beside her bed.

Despite the dimness, I could see how heartbreakingly weak my mother had grown. Her face, puffy and swollen from the cortisone she was receiving, had taken on a deathly, ashen cast. The fever that had struck following her transplant, spiking as high as 104° at the worst, had retreated slightly, but Mom's condition still remained critical. Her white blood cell count was practically nonexistent, and the transplant team seemed increasingly unsure whether the bone-marrow graft would take. Against my will, I recalled a conversation I had overheard between Mom and Dr. Miller weeks before. Their discussion had involved the degree of resuscitation Mom wanted were she to develop life-threatening complications. At the time, the prospect of withholding heroic resuscitative measures had sounded ghastly. Now, the possibility that the situation might actually arise was becoming terribly real.

I stood beside Mom's bed, once more thinking that nothing in my life had turned out as I'd hoped. Nothing . . . especially my relationship with my mother. I had always believed that someday, even if it took years, we would be able to work things out between us. After all, Travis and my father had. Why couldn't my mother and I? Now, though I fought to banish the possibility from my mind, the thought kept returning that there might not be time.

And so I stood beside my mother in the darkness, more than anything wishing to mend the rift between us. Yet no matter how much I wanted it, I knew wishing wouldn't make it so. Finally, choking on a fear that I would never get the chance to make things right, I turned and walked out into the night.

# 32

Kane left the hospital at 6:15 AM, stopping briefly in Westwood to grab a sweet roll and a cup of coffee. Catheryn had been sleeping when he'd departed, and he hadn't awakened her. Her condition had stabilized over the weekend, but her fever still remained dangerously high, and the drugs and antibiotics didn't seem to be working. Though gripped by a sense of helplessness that had plagued him since she had first started treatment months earlier, Kane resolved for the moment to clear his mind of thoughts of Catheryn. Today was a day for which he would need all his powers of concentration. Today Mr. and Mrs. French were finally coming in for their formal interrogation.

Shortly after their CBS interview, the Frenches had notified authorities that with certain conditions and safeguards in place, they would agree to a police interrogation. It was an unexpected turn that still puzzled Kane. Given the circumstances, it was his opinion that no attorney in his right mind would allow Jordan's parents to voluntarily submit to a police interrogation, unless there were another factor at play. Of course, there was still the possibility of a grand jury subpoena to force them to testify, and in that case they would have to do so without their lawyers present. Granted, they could exercise their Fifth Amendment rights and refuse to cooperate with the grand jury, but that wouldn't play well in the media. A widely reported poll following their televised interview had reported that the public was generally unsympathetic regarding Mr. and Mrs. Frenches' refusal to be interviewed by authorities. Maybe finally agreeing was their idea of damage control. Or maybe they really were innocent, and they had experienced a change of heart regarding their cooperation. Whatever the case, Kane planned to make the most of the opportunity.

After running a yellow light on Santa Monica Boulevard and hanging a left on Butler Avenue, Kane approached the West Los Angeles station house. "Damn," he said aloud, noticing a phalanx of news vans again jamming the street out front.

Kane had hoped to avoid reporters by arriving early. "So much for that plan," he said aloud, deciding not to park in his normal spot across the street behind the courthouse. Turning a deaf ear to shouted questions as he passed the news crews, he continued on by the station, wondering whether Allison was among the mass of reporters blocking the entrance. Angrily dismissing the thought, he took a right on the south side of the station and parked in a private lot in back reserved for just such occasions.

As Kane entered the rear entrance of the building and made his way upstairs to the squad room, he mentally reviewed the French case, realizing much was riding on what happened that morning. Though there was no way to predict exactly what direction any given interrogation might take, Kane had always believed that preparation made the difference between success and failure. With that in mind, he had spent most of the preceding days going over the contents of the Jordan French murder book, reexamining every piece of evidence, and studying a recording and transcript of Brent and Allison's recently televised meeting with Jordan's parents—a record that upon request CBS had readily provided. Likewise, he had spent hours imagining how the questioning would go, assaying different ploys, tacks, and stratagems. He had done everything he could to prepare save one: He still hadn't resolved how to handle the sticky legal problem of his suspects' being man and wife.

As no other leads had panned out, Kane had progressively been unable to disregard a suspicion that at least *one* of the parents had been involved in Jordan's murder—a suspicion that had eventually become as pervasive as a dead rat in the walls. But if one of them did it, the other had to have at least known . . . and had probably cooperated in disposing of the body. *But which one?* Because of the husband-wife confidentiality rule, even if one were to confess, nothing said against the other was admissible in court.

Nevertheless, if one parent admitted committing the murder, it could implicate the other by extension. For example, if Mrs. French admitted killing Jordan, Mr. French must have known, as he had been in the house at the time of the murder. He probably had to have helped dispose of the body too, as his wife wasn't strong enough to do it alone. Furthermore, Kane could always maintain that evidence found as the result of one parent's testimony against the other fell into the "inevitable discovery" category—material that would eventually have been uncovered in another way—and should thus be admissible. Nonetheless, the confidentiality issue and the uncertainties it entailed would present a problem, and one Kane knew he would have to treat with care. At the very least, any mishandling could open the door to a plea bargain, an option he was unwilling to consider. If Mr. and Mrs. French killed their daughter, Kane wanted them charged with first-degree murder, nothing less.

At precisely 9:45 AM, the Frenches arrived. After battling their way through the brigade of waiting reporters, they entered the station house. Accompanying them were two attorneys wearing identical Armani suits—a lawyer present for each parent, as Mr. and Mrs. French were slated to be questioned separately. Included in the parents' negotiations, along with a demand that their lawyers be present and that they could end the interview at any time, had been a stipulation that they be questioned together. Kane had refused the latter request and on that point had held firm, wanting to preclude any communication between the parents during the interrogation so their individual stories could be compared for consistency. Kane had also declined to give Jordan's parents an accounting of evidence against them— another outrageous request made by their attorneys, and one Kane hadn't taken seriously. He had agreed, however, that a physician could be in attendance in the unlikely event that Mrs. French succumbed under the strain of interrogation. Jordan's parents had evidently decided a doctor wouldn't be necessary after all, as none was present. Neither were the representatives from the DA's office that they had fought so adamantly to have included—strengthening Kane's suspicion that it had all been more posturing for the press.

Mrs. French and her lawyer, a high-powered defense attorney named Jason Artz with whom Kane had tangled more than once in court, were led to a second-floor interview room. Mr. French and his counsel were taken to another room down the hall. Each interrogation chamber contained a gray metal table and chairs, and in Mrs. French's case, a clean glass ashtray. The rooms were also dressed with stacks of police files, detailed drawings of the Frenches' house, and items of physical evidence including the extra gate padlock, black plastic bags, and the knotted ropes recovered at the reservoir. Taped to the walls were forensic photos showing Jordan's body sprawled on the shore. Though lacking in subtlety, the presence of items associated with a case was a psychological ploy that Kane had often seen rattle a suspect into an admission of guilt. In addition, everything said in both rooms, even a whisper, was being recorded in a small alcove down the hall—something that wasn't revealed to the parents.

Figuring Mrs. French for the weak link, Kane elected to do the initial questioning on her, letting Deluca and Banowski tackle Mr. French. Although neither parent was under arrest, nor had they been charged with any crime, Kane began by reading Mrs. French her Miranda rights, having instructed Deluca to do the same for Mr. French. Next Kane reiterated his request that Mrs. French submit to a polygraph exam and give hair and blood samples. On the advice of Mr. Artz she again refused, saying that the results of those tests could do nothing to exonerate her and, depending on the extent of the police's mishandling of evidence, might even hurt her. Besides, she pointed out, she had already passed a privately administered polygraph exam.

Moving on, Kane eased into questions covering the days and weeks before Jordan's abduction, asking Mrs. French to describe her daughter's daily routine, things that happened at the studio, what Jordan did during her evenings at home—attempting to put Jordan's mother at ease and getting her talking at the same time. Throughout this opening phase Kane asked questions to which he already knew the answers, a technique he routinely used to get the measure of someone. Though initially nervous, Mrs. French settled down as things progressed, smoking constantly during the proceedings. At one point her attorney also started to light a cigarette. Kane politely informed him that there was a no-smoking rule in the building, and that the LAPD's making an exception for his client was a consideration not extended to him.

When Mrs. French's narrative reached the night of Jordan's birthday, Kane interrupted to query her about the presence of any strangers approaching their table at The Ivy, raising the possibility of a stalker. Next he asked her to elaborate on other items: what Jordan had been wearing that night, what she had eaten, what time the family had left the restaurant. He also casually slipped in a question about leftovers. By now having grown inured to answering Kane's battery of inquiries, Mrs. French responded to the latter by saying she couldn't recall having taken home any food that night from the restaurant.

Jumping ahead to the day of Jordan's disappearance, Kane asked Mrs. French to recount in detail everything she could remember, encouraging her to leave nothing out. He asked when her daughter had awakened that morning, how she had felt about not going to work, who telephoned the studio to say she wouldn't be in, what she ate, what calls she received, what she did during the day, what time she went to bed. Following that, Kane posed personal queries delving into the intimacies of the Frenches' marriage, most of which Mrs. French refused to answer. Lastly, his voice remaining neutral, Kane asked the most difficult questions of the morning: "Did you kill her?" "Do you know who did?" "Did you send the ransom note?" "Did you molest Jordan, or suspect that she had been sexually molested by your husband?"

To all, Mrs. French emphatically answered no.

After pretending to study his notes, Kane took Mrs. French through it once more, point by point, step by step. On issues about which she had been evasive or said she couldn't recollect, he tried other approaches, probing every inconsistency. And when they reached the end, he started anew. Mr. Artz sporadically asked Kane to keep his questions to the point, but for the most part—with the exception of conferring with his client before she answered some particularly difficult interrogative—he allowed Mrs. French to give what seemed to be a full and complete accounting of events relating to her daughter's murder.

Two hours into it Kane left the room, asking another homicide detective to stay with Mrs. French during his absence. Before departing, Kane privately told the detective that although Mrs. French could light up if she wanted, Mr. Artz was *not* permitted to smoke.

Keeping a prearranged meeting in the squad room, Kane and Deluca compared notes. It soon became apparent that Deluca and Banowski had experienced no more success with Mr. French than Kane had with Jordan's mother. The parents' accounts of their daughter's abduction correlated perfectly. A little *too* perfectly, in Kane's opinion. Nevertheless, both parents were steadfastly maintaining their innocence, and as yet nothing had come to light to prove otherwise. In an appraisal of Mr. French that Kane thought applied to Jordan's mother as well, Deluca summed up the interrogation thus far by saying, "If that guy's lying, he's one hell of an actor."

\*     \*     \*

"Excuse me, Brent. May I have a word with you?"

Brent Preston had just exited one of the newsroom editing bays, Liz Waterson at his side. Turning, he nodded curtly as he saw me in the hallway. "I'm busy right now, Ali."

"It won't take long. Could you give us a second, Liz?"

"Sure," the slim newswoman replied pleasantly. Though I knew Liz still referred to me as "mermaid girl" behind my back, over the past months the acerbic producer's antagonism toward me had been supplanted by something a little closer to respect. "See you later, Brent," Liz added with her trademark confectionery smile.

"I thought you were covering the Frenches' interrogation this morning," I noted after Liz had departed.

"I am," said Brent. "We got shots of the parents entering the police station. They'll be in there for hours, so I left the camera crew on location and came back to edit the initial footage we got." Brent checked his watch. "I'm heading back over right now. What did you want to talk about?"

I studied Brent for a long moment. "Well, for one thing, I've been thinking about your blowup with Mike," I said, broaching a subject that had been bothering me since last weekend. At the time, blinded by hurt and anger, I'd thought Mike's confrontation with Brent had been sparked by jealousy. Later, when I'd cooled down, I had begun to suspect there was more to it than that.

"Don't read too much into our little spat," Brent said smoothly. "Mike was drunk."

"He may have been drinking, but he wasn't drunk."

Brent folded his arms. "Okay, he wasn't drunk. What are you getting at?"

"Just this. In referring to your autopsy and sexual abuse story, he said *you called him*." I stared at Brent. "You told me that *he phoned you*. Which was it?"

"What's the difference?"

"It makes a difference to me." My tone hardened. "You also said that Mike divulged things to you about the French investigation—things I had told him in confidence. Is that how it happened?"

"Allison, I don't have time for this."

"What's more, Mike thinks that I told you he was the one who shot my reservoir footage," I continued. "Where did he get that idea?"

Guiltily, Brent looked away.

"You figured out Mike shot the reservoir footage for me, didn't you?" I persisted. "Then you started wondering what else he knew, so you convinced him I had confided in you—tricking him into telling you everything. No wonder he said you'd do anything for a story."

Brent's lip curled. "And I suppose you wouldn't?"

I shook my head, my suspicions confirmed. How could I have been so blind? "I wouldn't lie," I said. "And I wouldn't screw a friend."

"Oh, sure," Brent snorted. "And the check is in the mail. Like I said, I don't have time for this." He turned, heading toward the exit at the far end of the hall. "Let me know when you come back to planet Earth and we'll talk," he added over his shoulder.

Furious, I stomped across the newsroom and stormed into the bureau chief's office. "Lauren, there's something I have to know," I said, banging the door shut behind me.

Lauren glanced up from her desk. "Don't bother knocking, just barge right in," she said. Then, noticing the look on my face, "Listen, before you say anything, I know you're mad about not being at Frenches' interrogation this morning. It wasn't my call. But don't worry. You may have something even better coming up. New York is thinking about having you do a live update tomorrow for the evening news."

"Me?"

Lauren nodded. "It'll run live on the East Coast, so we'll shoot sometime after three-thirty. The idea is to have you go out to Jordan's grave for a recap of your interview with Mr. and Mrs. French, contrasting it with whatever we learn today about the parents' LAPD interrogation. Can you handle it?"

"I can handle it," I said. Part of me felt excited about the prospect; another part realized that the network executives intended once again to capitalize on my relationship with my father. "But that's not what I want to talk about."

"Oh? What, then?"

"Do you know where Brent got his information on the autopsy story?" I asked.

Lauren shrugged. "He got a tip from your friend Mike and followed up on it."

"Brent *lied* to Mike to get that tip. Then he followed up on information I had received off the record, information I had promised to keep quiet about."

"So if you promised to keep quiet, why did you tell Mike?" asked Lauren.

"I didn't mean to. Actually, he sort of figured things out himself."

"So what's the problem?"

I hesitated, more irritated with myself than anyone else for what had happened. "The problem goes deeper than Mike and

Brent," I said. "It goes back to the day you hired me. The only reason you gave me an intern position here was because of my dad, right? You figured I could provide an inside track on the Jordan French story, and I wanted the job so bad I didn't see the obvious. From the very beginning, you've been using me to get to my father. That's the sole justification for my being here at CBS. Tell me I'm wrong, Lauren."

Lauren shook her head. "No, you're not wrong," she said. "Of course I hired you because of your father. Anyone in my position would have done the same."

"I knew it," I said numbly. "I just didn't want to admit it, even to myself."

"But that's not the only reason I hired you," Lauren went on. "I meant it when I said you reminded me of myself at your age. You're smart, poised, determined, and you know what you want and are willing to do whatever it takes to get it. Don't let this thing with Brent throw you. I may have initially hired you because of your father, but you've more than proved yourself since. You're good, Ali. Actually, you're better than good— you're a natural. Plus you look great on-camera, and the public loves you. More important, they *trust* you. Hell, you're the hero who pulled a drowning kid from the ocean."

"Oh, I'm a real hero, all right," I said bitterly, thinking of the questionable things I had done over the past months. If Brent had been consumed with furthering his own career, *what about me?*

"Don't be so tough on yourself, Ali. Let me do that," Lauren continued lightly. "I probably shouldn't be telling you this, but after the French case winds down, Brent is getting bumped up to the Washington bureau. I've heard hints from New York that they're considering grooming you to take over his spot here."

"Let me guess what they'll have me doing: Tagging after my father and covering his next juicy murder investigation?"

"Ali, I understand your disappointment at the way things have turned out," Lauren sighed. "And unless I miss my guess, you're also in hot water with your dad," she added sympathetically. "Believe me, I know *that's* no picnic. But you'll have to get past this. There's too much at stake not to. Are you going to be all right?"

I thought carefully, deciding that Lauren deserved an honest reply. Despite all that had happened over the past months, I had grown to respect the bureau chief. Even more surprising, I had grown to like her. True, Lauren had used me, but never once had she lied.

At last I answered. "I don't know," I said. "As you told me earlier, I have some thinking to do."

*       *       *

Upon returning to the interview room, Kane found Mr. Artz rocked back in his chair—legs crossed, left foot twitching like a cat's tail. Mrs. French was impatiently tapping a cigarette into the ashtray. Kane waited until the detective he had left with Mrs. French and her attorney exited the room, then sat directly across from Mrs. French. Leaning forward, he folded his hands on the table.

"Listen, Mrs. French, I'm still trying to understand what happened," Kane said without preamble, easing into the next phase of his interrogation. "To do that, I want to talk more about your daughter. Not how she died, but what she was like when she was alive. Help me get to know her. How did she get along with other kids, what were her hobbies, did she listen to music, things like that. For instance, do you remember the day she was born?"

"Of course," Mrs. French answered.

"That was probably one of the happiest moments of your life, wasn't it?"

Mrs. French nodded, seeming surprised by the question. "Do you have children?" she asked suspiciously.

"Three," said Kane. "We had four. My oldest son died several years ago," he added. "I know what it means to lose a child, Beth. I know how it feels to have your hopes and dreams snuffed out in a single stroke. It's the worst pain I've ever experienced. No matter how it went down with Jordan, I sympathize with you. I truly do."

Mrs. French visibly relaxed, seeming to view Kane in a new light. And for the next thirty minutes, under his questioning, she spoke of Jordan's early years—telling of her second birthday party, her decision to be a movie star after seeing herself in a home video, her first television commercial when she was three, the German shepherd puppy they had bought for her when she turned five.

"Did you see any of yourself in her?" Kane asked.

"A bit," Mrs. French admitted. "I suppose all parents see a little of themselves in their children."

"Sometimes more than they want," Kane replied, thinking of his ornery, self-reliant daughter. "Did you consider yourself a good mother?"

"I did the best I could."

Deciding to change tactics once more, Kane remained silent for a long moment, letting the tension build. Finally he sat back in his chair and sighed. "I'll tell you something, Beth," he said, deliberately using her first name. "I have a gift. At least sometimes it's a gift. At other times it can be a curse, but there's nothing I can do about it. My gift, or whatever you want to call it, is this: I can spend a few minutes with anyone, and I mean *anyone*, and tell what sort of person he or she is. I can also tell when someone is lying, or at least holding something back. After spending the morning with you, I know you're not a bad person. The problem is, I'm having trouble believing the story you're telling me."

Mrs. French's eyes lost their warmth. "Oh?"

"It's little things—things that don't add up," Kane said, deciding the time had come to lay his cards on the table. At that point he had nothing to lose. If he were *ever* going to get Mrs. French to talk, that time was now. "For instance, if Jordan were forcibly abducted from her bedroom, why didn't you or your husband hear anything?" he asked. "I know your husband said she had taken cold medicine that made her drowsy, explaining why she didn't struggle and make a lot of noise. At autopsy, no indication of any such medication showed up in the toxicology screening. Plus, according to the detectives who were first on the scene, Jordan's room didn't look right. Everything was neat as a pin—no mud on the windowsill from where the intruder supposedly entered, no signs of a struggle. And when we examined the sheets on Jordan's bed, do you know what we found? *Nothing.* Not even one hair. The only way that could have happened is if the sheets were washed *after* your daughter vanished. According to your maid, you canceled her regular cleaning day on Friday, and she didn't return until the following Wednesday. So who washed the sheets? Can you help me with that, Beth?"

Mrs. French said nothing.

"Another thing," Kane pushed on. "We still haven't come up with anyone who spoke with Jordan on the day *before* you reported her missing. We examined her telephone record. Zip. Oh, she had messages from friends . . . all of them unanswered. We went through her address book and asked everyone whether they'd talked to her on Friday. Again, nothing. So here's a kid who normally yaks on the phone for hours, and suddenly she's not even returning calls. We also checked to see who contacted the studio on the morning she didn't go to work. You made that call, Beth."

"I told you, she was sick."

"Yes, that's what you told me," said Kane. "Unfortunately, the coroner doesn't concur with that either. He found no evidence that Jordan was suffering from the flu or anything else. Which brings me to my next question. It seems Jordan wasn't too sick to eat, because an analysis of her gastric contents showed that she had consumed a meal no more than four hours before she died. Here's the puzzling part: Her last meal was the same one she ordered at her birthday party on Thursday night. Seafood capellini. That was *thirty-six hours* before you reported her missing. Do you have an explanation for that?"

Mrs. French paled. "She . . . she must have eaten leftovers," she answered, lighting another cigarette.

"I thought of that, so I talked with the waiter who served you at The Ivy," said Kane. "He'll swear in court that no one in your family took home leftovers that night," he added, lying.

"He's wrong."

"I don't think so. Another thing. We know that the words on the ransom note were cut from a back issue of *Elle Décor*, a magazine that you subscribe to, Beth."

"So do a lot of people."

"But the rest of them haven't had a daughter who was murdered," Kane pointed out. "And I'll tell you something else. I'll bet if I were to visit your house right now, I wouldn't find that back issue of *Elle Décor*, the one used to compose the note. The rest would be there, but not that one."

A frown darkened Mr. Artz's face. "As you don't have a search warrant, Detective," he said, "that's mere speculation."

"Speculation?" Kane reached behind him. After pulling down one of the forensic photos taped to the wall, he slid the grisly photograph across the table. Mrs. French's face froze as she looked at the picture, a shot of her daughter's nude, water-bloated body. "Well, while I'm *speculating*, Mr. Artz, I'll tell your client what *I* think happened to Jordan," Kane went on, speaking to the attorney but keeping his eyes on Mrs. French. "The daughter she loved. It's not a pretty tale, but feel free to tell me if I'm right."

"You're the one doing the talking," Mr. Artz observed dryly.

Kane tapped the picture. "This is the child you gave birth to, Beth. This is the baby girl you loved. I know you loved her because I can see it in your eyes. But as she grew up, things changed, didn't they?"

Mrs. French looked away. "I don't know what you mean."

"Sure you do. I'm talking about your husband and your daughter. The autopsy showed what had been going on."

"Jordan's doctor said there could have been any number of reasons for that. He said—"

"I admit there could be other explanations for what the coroner found," Kane interrupted. "There *could* be other explanations besides chronic sexual abuse. But we both know the real reason, don't we, Beth? It must have been difficult for you. You had to have known, or at least to have suspected. Or maybe you just didn't want to face it. Is that it? Was it that you didn't want to know?"

Mrs. French didn't respond.

"How did it feel to have your husband go to her room at night, instead of being with you?" Kane asked softly. "It must have hurt you deeply. Every time he went to her, it reminded you of your own failure, didn't it? He loved her more than you. It must have broken your heart to be jealous of your own daughter."

Still Mrs. French said nothing.

"Did you listen?" Kane asked. "I know you did. You couldn't help it, could you? You crept down the stairs and stood outside her door, listening to what they were doing on the other side. Did you let it go on until it felt like something had to give, something had to blow?"

Mrs. French stared at the picture, tears now starting in her eyes.

"That night something went wrong," Kane continued. "Your husband was drunk. There was an argument. Jordan wouldn't do what he wanted, so he lost his temper and beat her with a belt. Or perhaps it was you. You'd had enough. You confronted them and attacked your daughter in a fit of jealous rage. Jordan fought back. Maybe she threatened to go to the police, causing a scandal and ruining her career, a career you had worked so hard to build. In the scuffle you hit her—"

"No! I never . . ."

Kane shook his head. "I don't think that's how it happened, either. It was your husband, wasn't it? It was Crawford."

Silence.

Kane pressed ahead. "While your husband was beating Jordan, she accidentally hit her head on the stairs, a dresser, whatever. After things cooled down, she went to bed. The next morning you found her dead."

Hand quavering, Mrs. French raised her cigarette and inhaled deeply.

"Her injury was worse than you'd thought," Kane went on. "She'd suffered a concussion. Sometime during the night while she was sleeping, she must have fallen unconscious. Hours later she died. It was an accident, but you couldn't call the police because of the bruises and strap marks. Worse, she had been sexually abused for years, something you knew the authorities would discover if there were an autopsy. After you got over the shock, you and your husband took the only way out. Jordan was dead and there was nothing you could do to bring her back. You had to make the best of things and go on, so you staged an abduction and got rid of the body. Am I close, Beth?"

Again, Mrs. French didn't answer.

"You had to wait till dark to dispose of the corpse," Kane reasoned. "You contacted the studio and said she was sick, canceled the maid's day, and helped your husband wash Jordan's body and wrap it in plastic garbage bags. Then, when Crawford went to work as if nothing had happened, you spent the rest of the day cleaning Jordan's room. That night you and your husband staged a break-in, concocted a phony ransom note, and one or both of you drove her to the reservoir. We even know how you were able to get the car down to the water." Reaching behind him once more, Kane grabbed the extra padlock he had discovered. "All that was left then was to wait till morning and report her missing," he added, placing the lock on the table. "That must have been the longest night of your life, Beth."

A sheen of sweat glistened on Mrs. French's face. She lifted her head to look at Kane. And in that fleeting instant when their eyes met and Kane saw the depth of her anguish, he knew he had hit upon the truth. Until then he hadn't been certain. Now he was.

"It had to have been an accident," Kane continued, offering her the "out"—the point during any well-planned interrogation at which a suspect could confess while rationalizing his or her actions. "And it wasn't you who caused it. You gave birth to Jordan. What mother would hurt her own child? It was your husband, Jordan's stepfather, and even then it must have been an accident. It's the only explanation that fits."

Mrs. French's hand rose to her mouth, stifling a sob.

"Come on, Beth. Say it. Get it over with."

Mrs. French lowered her head, tears now running her mascara. "My baby's the only one I ever really loved," she whispered, her words barely audible. "She's the only one who ever really mattered. She'll forgive me when I see her again. I believe that with all my heart. She'll forgive me."

"Forgive you for what, Beth? Tell me."

"I think this flight of fancy has gone on long enough, Detective," Mr. Artz interrupted. "Unless you have any further direct questions, this interview is over."

Kane ignored him. "Killing a child is a terrible burden, Beth," he said gently. "You can't carry it alone. It has to come out. You can't go through the rest of your life with this secret. It will destroy you. It will destroy you, and your husband, and anything you ever hope to make of the rest of your days. Jordan is gone and things will never be right unless you tell what happened. This is a chance for you to do the right thing. It'll just take a second, and then it'll be over and you can start making amends. Tell me what happened."

Mrs. French raised her head, indecision written on her face. But as she began to speak, Mr. Artz pushed away from the table. "My client has nothing more to say," he snapped. "This meeting is over."

Mrs. French hesitated . . . and the moment passed. Struggling to compose herself, she opened her purse and withdrew a mirror, making an attempt to repair her ruined makeup. Then, still clearly shaken, she stood, stubbing out her final cigarette in the ashtray.

Kane reached into his pocket and withdrew a plastic evidence bag and a pair of latex gloves. "I'm sorry that's the way you want it, Mrs. French," he said, pulling on the gloves. "For the record, though, what brand of cigarette have you been smoking?"

"Parliament," Mrs. French answered wearily.

Kane lifted the ashtray and dumped its contents into the evidence bag. "I intend to submit this for DNA analysis," he explained, sealing the bag. "I'm establishing that you were the only one in the room smoking, and that all butts in this ashtray are yours."

"DNA evidence? To be compared with what?" scoffed Mr. Artz. "As I recall, no trace evidence of any kind was found on Jordan's body *or* at the crime scene. This is simply another feeble attempt to intimidate my client. You're fishing here, Detective. As I said, this interview is over. Good day."

"Good day to you, Jason," Kane replied. "Oh, one thing I neglected to tell your client. You're right about no trace evidence being found on the body, as it was submerged in water for so long. None showed up in Jordan's bedroom, either. Nor did we find saliva on the ransom-note envelope or the stamp. We *did*, however, find cells on the adhesive side of the self-stick stamp, something we didn't tell the media. Whoever sent the note was careful not to leave fingerprints or saliva, but they touched the sticky side of the stamp and left some cells there. We've done DNA testing. Now we're simply waiting to come up with a match. Unless I miss my guess, we just did."

Mrs. French stared. "You can get DNA from someone just touching a stamp . . . ?"

Kane nodded. "Just like we can from a cigarette butt."

"In the unlikely event that you *do* come up with a match, we'll contest it in court," said Mr. Artz calmly. "My client handled the envelope when she received it in the mail. Her DNA got on it at that time. In any case, juries are notorious for dismissing this type of evidence, what with cross-contamination, false positives, and sloppy handling techniques. As you know, the latter is something for which the LAPD has become famous. Or should I say infamous."

Kane scowled, aware that the issues raised by Mr. Artz were a weak link in the chain of evidence, assuming the case ever got to trial. Kane also knew what Mr. Artz was referring to with his snide remark about the department—recalling a high-profile celebrity murder trial years back that had been lost, at least in part, by LAPD investigators' questionable procurement and handling of DNA samples. It was a debacle that had given the department a lasting black eye, and a situation no one wanted repeated.

"That won't happen this time," Kane promised quietly. "Everything is being done by the book. If nothing else, you can bank on that."

## 33

Early the next morning, a radio call from a patrol car in the Palisades came in to the West L.A. station. The call was transferred to the homicide unit. Ten minutes later Kane was driving west, thinking that an already troublesome case had taken yet another turn for the worse. As he proceeded up Mandeville Canyon, he berated himself for not having seen it earlier. The clues had all been there . . . not that he could have done anything to change things.

*She'll forgive me when I see her again.*

Following the interrogations on the preceding afternoon, Kane had received word that the Frenches were opening negotiations with the DA's office to explore the possibility of a plea bargain. So far, as with their formal police interrogations, Jordan's parents had admitted nothing. Nevertheless, it appeared that rather than risk going to trial on first- or second-degree murder charges, they were considering pleading to a lesser charge of involuntary manslaughter. And despite the DNA comparison that could link Mrs. French to the ransom note, Kane realized there was a strong possibility that the district attorney would take the deal.

As the DA had repeatedly pointed out, the bulk of the case against Mr. and Mrs. French was circumstantial, and nothing had changed. The one potentially solid piece of evidence, a comparison of Mrs. French's DNA to the DNA traces on the ransom-note stamp, might not even pan out. If it didn't, there was still the possibility that Mr. French wrote the note, but Kane didn't think so. After his interview with Mrs. French, he was certain that she wrote the note. But even if a positive DNA match did come back on her, as Kane was sure it would, convincing a jury that the loving parents of Jordan French had murdered their daughter would still be problematic, as was so aptly pointed out by Mr. Artz.

On the positive side, a DNA match would give Kane probable cause for an expanded search, and the next time he entered the Frenches' estate with a warrant in hand, he would have the right to go over everything with a fine-toothed comb. As he had surmised earlier, it was likely that all evidence tying the parents to the murder had already been destroyed, but you never knew what might turn up.

Approaching the Frenches' estate, Kane noticed a fair-sized media contingent already assembled across the street. More were undoubtedly on the way. The entry's iron gate stood open at the head of the driveway. A private security guard was stationed there, barring the way. Kane flashed his shield, and the guard waved him through.

The house and grounds appeared to have changed little since Kane's last visit—landscaping well tended, hedges precisely pruned, flower beds immaculate. Water from a morning hosing was puddled near the tennis courts. Beyond the courts, two black-and-white patrol cars sat in the driveway.

Kane parked behind one of the cruisers. After identifying himself and conferring with a uniformed officer outside, Kane started up the steps to the house. The front door stood ajar. Halfway up the stairs he saw the body.

Mrs. French's lifeless form hung from a banister pole on the second floor, her bare feet suspended above the staircase's lower landing. Upended on the entry tiles below lay a chair that she had apparently used to position herself—kicking it away as her final act.

Nodding briefly to a pair of officers inside, Kane stepped inside. He peered up at the body, noting that Mrs. French had chosen a black, knee-length dress in which to die. Moving closer, he also noted that she had removed her wedding ring before using what appeared to be a dog leash and an attached metal choke collar to end her life. Crude, but effective. Near the top of the leash's thick nylon webbing, a childish hand had written the name "Greta."

"The husband says he found her like that when he woke up," offered one of the officers.

Tearing his eyes from the corpse, Kane turned. The patrol officer who had spoken, a young Asian whose nameplate read "Lowe," tipped his head to the left. "He's in there."

Kane glanced into the living room. Sitting straight and unmoving on the couch where Kane had first interviewed Jordan's parents, was Mr. French.

"He gave us this," said the other officer, a florid, thick-necked man whose plate read "Flinn." He handed Kane an irregularly shaped piece of paper that looked as if it had been scissored from a larger sheet.

Kane took the paper. In elaborate, flowing script, someone had written the words "May God forgive me for what I did," followed by the signature "Elizabeth French." Kane looked at the officer who had handed him the note. "Where's the rest?"

Flinn shrugged. "The husband didn't say."

"We already called the coroner," said Lowe. "Want us to help get her down?"

"Let the coroner's assistants handle it," Kane replied. Then, studying the body a moment longer, he noticed that several of Mrs. French's long, painted fingernails were broken off at the quick. In her final moments, it appeared that Mrs. French had changed her mind about dying.

Kane walked into the living room. Mr. French gazed at him briefly, then resumed staring out the window. "You won," he said. "Satisfied?"

"Nobody won," Kane replied. "Where's the rest of the note?"

"Gone. That part was meant for me. Nobody else."

Upon receiving the scissored paper from the officers in the hall, Kane had suspected that in unburdening her soul, Mrs. French had implicated her husband in Jordan's death as well. Now he was sure of it.

"Tell me something, Mr. French," said Kane, his hands unconsciously balling into fists. "It's just you and me here. I haven't read you your Miranda rights, so anything you say will stay just between us. I have most of it figured anyway. I only need your help on one point. I know you had been abusing Jordan for years. I also know that her death was probably an accident, and I know that you and your wife concocted a phony abduction story to cover it up."

Kane paused, unwillingly revisiting the crippling horror of losing his own son, momentarily gripped by the sense of bottomless, crushing loss that had accompanied Tommy's death. Shaking his head in disbelief, Kane finally continued. "What I can't understand is how you could truss up your child, a daughter you say you loved, and then stuff her into trash bags and dump her in a reservoir . . . as if she were garbage you needed to get rid of. How could you do that?"

"I didn't intend for any of this to happen," Mr. French said quietly. "I loved Jordan."

"What you did wasn't an act of love," said Kane, his voice as hard as granite. "Not even close."

"Regardless of what you think, Detective, I'm not evil," Mr. French replied, regarding Kane levelly. "I made mistakes, I admit it. But I'm not evil. And neither was Beth."

"You think you're going to cut a deal with the DA, don't you?" Kane demanded, fighting hard to control his anger. "Isn't that right, Crawford? You have it all figured out. You'll blame the killing on your wife, saying you just helped dispose of the body. As for the sexual abuse, you'll deny it. You're the only one still alive, so no one can prove otherwise. Well, I've got news for you, pal. That's not the way it's going to go down."

Mr. French looked away. "And why is that?"

"Because I'm going to do everything in my power to make sure it doesn't," said Kane, recalling the vow he had made at the reservoir. "You can count on it."

Thirty minutes later Kane stood on the Frenches' front landing, watching as the coroner's van pulled up behind the squad cars in the driveway. With a despondent sigh, he shoved his hands into his pockets, again remembering the promise he had made to a dead child months earlier. Somehow, fulfilling that pledge had brought him little satisfaction. Now that it was over, he just felt tired and soiled and sad.

\*     \*     \*

"Good Evening. This is Peter Samson for the CBS News Evening News. In Pacific Palisades this morning, the Jordan French murder case took another tragic turn with the grisly discovery of . . ."

Heart racing, I watched the monitor to the left of the camera, seeing the CBS anchor's face but not really hearing his words. In the wake of Mrs. French's suicide, the location for my live shot—a segment that I knew, once again, was being done to cash in on my relationship with my father—had been switched to the newsroom, with a camera feed linked directly to New York. I was positioned in front of the lighted CBS "eye" outside Lauren's office. The illuminated "CBS News Los Angeles" logo on the wall behind me was similarly lit. A "key" light glared at me from behind the camera, with several other spotlights shining down from above. To my right, I sensed Brent and Lauren and Liz and other members of the news team standing in the shadows. An expectant tension sizzled in the air.

A clock on the wall read 3:31 PM, making it 6:31 PM in New York. Mrs. French's suicide was the lead story that night. I would be on in seconds, my words going out live and uncensored to millions on the East Coast. Rebroadcasts to other parts of the country could be edited later, but not this one. For those few moments, I would *be* CBS News.

". . . shocking developments. Here with the latest from Los Angeles is CBS's Allison Kane."

A man beside the TelePrompTer who had been doing a silent countdown on his fingers pointed at me. A red light on the camera flicked on. Taking a breath, I gazed directly into the lens. "According to LAPD sources, Mrs. Elizabeth French, mother of murdered actress Jordan French, was found dead this morning in her Pacific Palisades home," I began, my apprehension abruptly forgotten. "Apparently she had taken her own life. Mrs. French left a note asking God to forgive her—a request authorities reportedly consider an admission of guilt in her daughter's death. In a related development, sources close to the Los Angeles district attorney's office revealed today that a plea bargain proposed earlier by the Frenches' attorney has been rejected."

The scrolling words on the TelePrompTer ended. At this point I was supposed to sign off and turn things back over to the anchor. Suddenly I knew I needed to say more. "On a personal note, I would like to add a few brief words."

I felt a current of panic sweep through the newsroom. Ignoring it, I continued. "We in the media called Jordan French's death a *story*, and that's the way we treated it—as if covering a young girl's murder were simply something to boost ratings. In our rush to report every lurid detail, we forgot that Jordan's death was a heartrending loss for those who loved her. We as journalists should be better than that, me included. This is Allison Kane, CBS News, Los Angeles."

The New York anchor came back on, moving smoothly to the next story as though nothing were amiss. My broadcast finished, I turned to a roomful of disbelieving stares.

Brent was first to recover. He strode forward, thrusting his chin within inches of my face. "You conniving little bitch!" he snarled, spittle spraying my face. "You're not fooling anyone with your holier-than-thou bullshit."

Though I flinched, I stood my ground. "Mike was right about you, Brent," I said. "For you, this job is about money and celebrity and getting to the top. Anything for a story. And if people get hurt and lives are destroyed in the process—tough."

"And you're different, I suppose."

"I plan to change."

"I'll believe that when I see it," Brent spat. "As for the Jordan French case, I won't apologize to you or anyone else for how I cover a crime piece. That girl's death was a national story, and people wanted to know what happened. We're a hard-news station and we told them. That's our job."

"Maybe it's *your* job. I want something more."

"And what would that be?"

"I want to do something I can be proud of," I replied. "Not like what we just did."

Brent's eyes turned cold. "Screw you, Allison."

"Same to you, Brent."

Lauren, who after the broadcast had rushed to her office to answer a flood of phone calls, signaled to me through her office door. "Allison, please come in here."

I turned, leaving Brent fuming. Upon entering the bureau chief's office, I stood in front of her desk, not bothering to close the door. "If you want to chew me out, go ahead," I said. "I know that I—"

"I don't intend to chew you out," Lauren replied, hanging up the phone. "Not right now, anyway. But don't get me wrong. I don't condone what you just did. I know you were probably following your conscience, but everyone here at the bureau is going to pay for it—especially me. Given the circumstance, however, I think I understand. You really are your father's daughter."

"Am I fired?"

"Not as far as I'm concerned," Lauren sighed. "Management may feel differently. We'll see. Even if they do want you out, I suspect that there will be a position waiting for you at another network. Maybe several."

I remained silent.

"But your unauthorized speech isn't why I called you in," Lauren added quietly, her expression turning to one of concern. "I'm sorry, Ali. I just got a call from your dad. He's at the hospital. He wants you over there right away."

# 34

Upon arriving at UCLA Medical Center, I found my father in the Transplant Unit waiting room. Travis, Nate, and Grandma Dorothy were there, too—Travis standing by the window, Dorothy sitting erect in an armchair nearby, Nate slumped beside Dad on a couch by the door. Overcome with foreboding, I stepped inside. Travis looked at me somberly. The others turned toward me as well. No one smiled. "What . . . what's wrong?" I stammered, afraid to hear the answer.

"Your mom's fever is back," my father replied, his words dropping like stones. "It's higher than ever. I got a call from Dr. Miller. He doesn't think . . ." Dad's voice broke. He looked away. "He said it was time to gather the family."

I clapped a hand to my mouth, feeling as if I'd been struck.

"I phoned Father Donovan," Dad went on quietly. "He's on his way."

Speechless, I felt my knees begin to buckle. The room started to spin. I couldn't breathe.

Dad rose and crossed the room, placing his hands on my shoulders to steady me. "Are you okay?"

I shook my head, trying to clear my vision. "I . . . I can't believe . . ."

Dad's strong arms encircled me. I buried my face in his chest, wanting to cry. I found I could not.

Wordlessly, my father led me to the couch and sat beside me, his arm still around my shoulders. Nate shifted closer on the other side, his cheeks streaked with tears.

"Can I see her?" I finally managed.

"In a while," Dad answered numbly. "The doctors are in there now. She's been delirious. They have her heavily sedated," he went on quietly, as if he were speaking to himself. "I talked with her earlier. She said she hated feeling weak. She said she hated the thought of not being around to see you kids grow up, of not being there to help you over the rough spots and share in your lives and see you get married and have kids of your own. Can you believe that? Even with all that's happening to her, she's thinking of us." Dad stared at his hands. "Weak? She's the strongest person I've ever known."

"Dad, I'm so sorry about everything that . . . that's been going on," I said miserably, knowing my words were coming too late. "Between Mom and me, and between you and me, and . . . everything. I'm so sorry about the way I've been acting—"

"Now's not the time, Ali."

I glanced at the others in the room, then back at Dad. "I just want you to know it won't happen again."

"I know it won't," said Dad, tightening his arm around me. "The subject's closed."

The room drifted into silence, each family member taking consolation from the other's presence, yet each lost in his or her own thoughts. Solitary, interminable minutes passed, turning into hours. At 6:30 PM Father Donovan, our parish priest, visited Mom and administered Last Rites. After he left, we all took turns sitting with Mom, whose condition swung from transitory moments of awareness to progressively longer spells of delirium and unconsciousness. Around 8 PM Dad insisted that Dorothy and the rest of us get something to eat in the hospital cafeteria. He kept watch on the tenth floor, saying he wasn't hungry.

Despite the antibiotics and other drugs being administered, Mom's condition steadily deteriorated. Later that evening, when I questioned an intern leaving Mom's room, the doctor answered evasively—saying that everything possible was being done and now it was in God's hands. In desperation, I attempted to pray. No matter how hard I tried, the words wouldn't come.

At a little before midnight, after taking my turn sitting with Mom, I returned to the waiting room, feeling like I was going to explode. I suddenly realized that I had to get away, if only for a few minutes. Plus there was something I wanted to bring back for Mom. I had cleared it with Mom's doctor earlier that week, and now I wished I had given it to her sooner. Fearing I was too late, I told Dad that I was going to get some air and that I wouldn't be gone long. He nodded without seeming to hear me.

Feeling guilty for leaving, I rushed to my UCLA dorm room across the street, changed clothes, and hurried back to the hospital, having been gone no more than fifteen minutes. Nothing had changed. Everyone was still gathered in the waiting room except Dorothy, who was taking her turn keeping vigil at Mom's side. Dad was pacing the floor like a caged animal, his long strides measuring the confines of the claustrophobic chamber. Travis sat slumped in a chair, staring at the wall. Nate had fallen asleep on the couch.

Numbly, I joined my younger brother on the couch. Though I tried to stay awake, I gradually found myself dozing, floating between the hateful reality of consciousness and the forgetful oblivion of slumber. Nod by nod, I drifted off. And as I slept, I dreamed.

*I'm younger, having just turned thirteen. Summer vacation is nearly over. Mom and I are driving down the coast highway, heading to the Santa Monica Mall to shop for new clothes and school supplies for the coming year. Mom is sitting behind the wheel of her old Volvo; I'm beside her in the front seat. It's a gorgeous afternoon, the sun strong and bright, a faint hint of approaching autumn in the air.*

*Mom is in a buoyant mood. Our entire family recently attended one of Travis's piano recitals, and she's humming a passage from a Chopin polonaise that Trav performed for his opening piece. Then, in a musical non sequitur, my mother switches to a different melody. It's a song she used to sing to me when she tucked me in bed. It's one of my earliest memories:* Summertime, *from the Gershwin musical* Porgy *and* Bess. *Listening, I think that even my mother's singing is perfect, hearing in her voice the beauty and grace and everything I'm not and never will be.*

*After the first verse, Mom glances over. "Remember this, Ali? Singing it used to be the only way I could get you to go to sleep."*

*"I remember."*

*"You should. God knows, you heard it enough." Mom embarks on the second verse, her voice heartbreakingly clear and true.*

One of these mornings, you're going to rise up singing,
Then you'll spread your wings, and you'll take to the sky.
But until that morning, there's nothing can harm you,
With your daddy and mammy standing by.
*A pause. Mom starts again.*
Summertime, and the living is easy,
Fish are jumping—
*She glances over. "C'mon, Ali. Sing with me."*
*I shake my head. "I don't feel like it, Mom."*
*Mom continues, still encouraging me to sing.*
—and the cotton is high.
Oh, your daddy's rich, and your mamma's good lookin',
So hush, little Ali, don't you cry.
*"C'mon, honey. You know the words. Sing with me."*
*Perversely, I refuse to join in—wanting to, but knowing I can't . . . and not knowing why. Unable to meet my mother's gaze, I stare out the window all the way to the mall.*

Travis nudged me awake. I sat up and rubbed my eyes. Shafts of sunlight streamed into the room through venetian blinds, splashing against the opposite wall. Dad was standing in the doorway, conferring with Dr. Miller. From my father's bleary eyes, I knew he had been awake all night. I straightened my shoulders, feeling guilty for having slept.

Dad and the doctor entered the room. Dorothy was the first to speak. "Has there been a change?"

Dr. Miller hesitated.

"What is it? What's happened?" Dorothy demanded.

"Catheryn's temperature has stabilized," the doctor replied. "Her white blood cell count is up, too."

"What does that mean?" asked Nate.

"It means that your mother is a strong woman. She's a fighter."

"Will she be all right?"

Again, Dr. Miller hesitated. "She has a long way to go, but she's turned a corner," he said cautiously. "Graft-versus-host disease may still be a problem, but the marrow transplant appears to be taking. I think the worst may be over."

"Is she awake?" asked Travis. "Can we see her?"

"Yes, you can. I don't want her overstrained, so go in separately and please keep your visits short." Dr. Miller turned to Dad. "She asked to see you first."

When Dad returned, he seemed changed. Though he still looked exhausted, a deeper strain that had been present in his face was gone. For the first time in weeks, he seemed at peace. "You're up, kid," he said with a tired smile, glancing at me.

"Me?" I looked at Travis and Dorothy and Nate, then back at my father. "But I thought she . . ."

"She wants to see you next. Keep it short."

"I will," I promised, grabbing a package I had brought with me from the dorm. Filled with apprehension, I stopped at the nurses station, donned a hospital mask and gown, and hurried down the hallway. Upon reaching Mom's room, I entered and closed the door behind me.

My mother gazed up at me from her bed. "Hello, Allison," she said weakly.

"Hi, Mom." I crossed to a cabinet near the bathroom, carefully set my package on top, and washed my hands with alcohol. Then, self-consciously, I moved to Mom's side.

Mom reached out, taking my hand. "Thank you again for being my marrow donor."

"You don't have to thank me," I said, feeling more guilty than ever.

"Yes, I do," said Mom. "You know, I've always thought of you as being a part of me. Now you really are."

I recalled our last conversation on the subject. "You may regret that. Dr. Miller said you're likely to get my allergies, remember?"

"Like your aversion to being told what to do?" Mom asked, playing along.

I smiled. "According to Dad, you've always had your own aversion to that." Then, my smile fading, "Mom, I'm so sorry for . . . for everything."

"I know, Ali. You don't have to say anything."

"I want to," I insisted. "I've been afraid that I wouldn't get to tell you this, and I need to get it off my chest. I only wish I had done it sooner." I paused, then continued softly. "I'm sorry about what I said to you on the plane. And I'm sorry about all the blowups we've had lately. Most of all, I'm sorry for shutting you out all these years. I didn't mean to. I just couldn't stop."

"But why? Is it something I did?" Mom asked. "Was it what you said on our trip to Washington? You accused me of putting our family second—implying that I regretted having a family because it interfered with my career. Was that it?"

"Maybe a little."

"Ali, I've done things in my life that I regret, but having you and Travis and Nate and Tom is definitely not one of them. When you have kids of your own, you'll understand."

I shook my head. "As I told you before, I don't think that particular scenario is in the cards for me."

Mom smiled. "And as I told *you* before, we'll see. But my career isn't the real issue between us, is it?"

"No." I lowered my eyes. Taking a deep breath, I pushed on. "Mom, all my life I've been doing what other people wanted. That, and vying with Travis for your attention, yours and Dad's—scrambling to find a place for myself in our family." I hesitated, then rushed ahead, my words flooding out now that I had begun. "When the job at CBS came up, I think I took it to prove something to you and Dad, and maybe to myself as well. I wanted to succeed so bad I didn't stop to think about how I got there, or even whether it was what I really wanted. That's what I need to find out, Mom. What *I* want. I know I can't compete with Travis and his music, but that doesn't matter to me anymore. I need to find my own music, so to speak. It may not be great, but at least it will be mine."

"Ali, your writing—"

"At this point I'm not ruling out anything," I broke in. "I'm going to return to college next week. It took some explaining, but I've reregistered for classes at USC. Maybe I'll keep working at CBS too, at least part-time—assuming they still want me. And I plan to keep writing. But the truth is, I don't know what I'm going to do with my life. Not yet, anyway. But when I find it, *whatever* it is, I'm hoping you'll support my decision."

Mom thought a moment. "I will," she said. "As long as you let me be a part."

I squeezed her hand. "Deal."

Mom regarded me pensively. "There's more, isn't there?"

"Yes."

"Tell me."

My throat tightened.

"Ali, if we're going to make a clean breast of things, we have to go all the way. What is it?"

Again I lowered my gaze. "Mom, I . . . I'm more sorry than I can say for not telling you what happened the night I was attacked," I said. "I wanted to. I just couldn't. I know it's been a barrier between us ever since, but I didn't know how to change things. I didn't know what I wanted from you . . . or from anybody, for that matter. All I knew was that I felt helpless and ashamed and that I couldn't stand anyone's pity. I told myself I didn't need anybody. I realize now how wrong I was."

"Ali, you should have let me help."

"I know," I said, my eyes stinging.

"Of all my children, I've always considered you the strongest," Mom said sadly. "From the beginning, you've been the strong one. Even with all that has happened over the years—Tommy's death and your rape and the night that man attacked us and our house burned and we lost everything—I've known you would be all right. But Ali . . . you don't always have to be so strong."

"I know," I whispered, tears that had eluded me earlier now flowing unbidden. I tried to stop them but couldn't, for with my mother's words came the realization that in my determination not to be a victim, I had turned my back on the very people I most needed and loved. "Jeez, look at me," I said, wiping my eyes. "I'm sorry. I didn't mean to . . ."

"It's okay, sweetheart," Mom said gently. "If we can't show our feelings, we might as well be men."

"You've been watching too much Oprah," I sniffed, laughing through my tears.

"Amen to that," Mom agreed.

Neither of us said anything for a moment, content to be together with the walls down. At last I drew in a deep, shuddering breath. "I'd better be going," I said. "Dr. Miller said to keep our visits short, and I think I've overstayed my time."

"You'll come tomorrow?"

"First thing in the morning. I promise."

"Good. I'll look forward to it."

I walked to the cabinet and retrieved the package I had brought from my dorm. Shyly, I returned to the bed and handed it to my mother. "Dr. Miller said it would be okay for you to have this."

Mom took the carton, a brand-new typing-paper box, a red ribbon securing the top. "The manuscript for your novel?" she guessed.

I nodded. "You'll be the first to read it. I've been working on it almost every day this summer. It still needs polishing, but it's close to being done. I haven't come up with a title yet," I added, "but I'll think of something. Maybe something with a music connection. *Beach Song,* or *A Song of Summer*— something like that. Anyway, I . . . I hope you like it."

Without speaking, Mom cradled the box to her chest.

"It's not completely autobiographical, but it is about a family like ours," I continued nervously. "We're all in it. You, and Dad, and Travis and Tom and Nate. Even me. Especially me," I said, finding my mother's eyes. "It's about the summer Tommy died and our family came apart and everything changed. I told the good parts and the bad, including the part about my attack, relating everything as honestly as I could. For the longest time I didn't know why I was writing it. I just knew it was something I had to do. Last night I finally figured out why. I wrote it for you."

Mom held me in her gaze for a long, silent moment. "Thank you, Ali."

"I love you, Mom."

"I know that, honey," Mom replied, her eyes shining. "I've always known that."

Later I rode the elevator down to the ground floor, exhausted and emotionally drained. Grandma Dorothy and my brothers accompanied me. Dad stayed with Mom, saying he would call us later. As we stepped from the elevator, Dorothy asked, "Which way?"

I headed left. "Follow me."

"I always feel like a rat in a maze when I'm in this place," said Travis, trailing me down a wide hallway.

"This is supposedly one of the biggest building complexes in existence," I remarked, having learned to navigate the interconnected structures of the Medical Center by taking shortcuts through its labyrinthine passageways to other areas of the campus. "I've heard it has more continuous miles of corridors than the Pentagon," I added absently, still preoccupied with thoughts of Mom.

Arriving at the lobby, I stopped in my tracks. At the far end of the room, a sea of familiar faces filled the reception area. Arnie, Lt. Long, Deluca, Banowski, and a huge contingent of other LAPD officers were present, along with McKenzie, Christy, and a host of neighbors from the beach. Also present were Petrinski and a dozen or more musicians I recognized from the Philharmonic. "What's everyone doing here? I asked.

"They're here for Mom," Travis answered. "They're here for us, too."

"But how . . . ?"

"I asked McKenzie to make some calls last night," Travis explained. "Guess things sort of snowballed."

Inexplicably, I again found myself on the brink of tears. "That's an understatement," I mumbled.

Within seconds, several people at the far end of the lobby saw us. Someone said something. Then everyone in the waiting area turned. I could see the same question in all their eyes.

Nate bolted forward. "Mom's going to be all right!" he yelled, heading across the room at a run. "She's going to be all right!"

Smiling, Travis and Dorothy set out after him. Travis turned back when he noticed I wasn't following. "Coming?"

"I don't think so," I replied, still trying hard not to cry. "I can't talk to anyone right now. Make some excuse for me, will you?"

"You sure?"

"I'm sure. I . . . I just need to be alone."

"Okay, Ali. See you later at the beach?"

"Maybe. I'll call." With a tired wave, I started back down the hall.

"Hey, sis?"

I turned. "What, Trav?"

"Welcome back."

After exiting the Medical Center via the Dental School lobby, I paused on the sidewalk outside, wondering what to do next. I didn't feel like seeing anyone, but I didn't feel like returning to my dorm room, either. More than anything, I needed to be alone. All at once I remembered the perfect place: my secret spot in the botanical garden. Caught in the whirlwind of activity that had recently been my life, I hadn't visited it all summer. Now seemed the right time.

Strains of the song from my dream still running through my mind, I crossed the street and took a narrow path leading into the exhibit. At that early hour the lush garden was deserted, and most of it still lay in shade. I descended the garden's western bank, passing empty picnic tables and cement benches along the way. Minutes later I reached a small stream that wound through the center of the exhibit.

Moving through dappled patches of sunlight, I approached a small waterfall cascading over a jumble of sandstone boulders. I stopped briefly to admire a chaos of red-flowering turk's cap running riot up the opposite bank. In the distance, the campus bell tower struck once, signaling the half hour. Otherwise, the only sounds I heard were the gurgle of the stream and an occasional scolding from one of the garden's resident squirrels.

Working my way deeper into the exhibit, I took a path branching to the right, proceeding a dozen yards downstream. I crossed the creek using a random arrangement of stepping stones. Then, picking another trail, I climbed partway up the far bank, making for a bench overlooking the stream—an intimate vantage from which only plants and trees were visible, a spot from which one could imagine that the rest of the world were a thousand miles away.

As I rounded an immense stand of bamboo, I froze. Someone was sitting on the bench in my secluded refuge. "Mike?" I said, an ache rising within me, a longing I had tried hard to forget. "What . . . what are you doing here?"

Mike looked up. "Waiting for you."

"How did you know I would be here?"

Mike brushed off my question with a shrug. "Lucky guess." Then, his expression turning serious, "I heard your mother took a turn for the worse. How is she?"

I took a deep breath, then let it out. "Not completely out of the woods. But . . . we think she's going to make it."

Mike's face filled with relief. "That's wonderful news, Ali. I'm happy for you and your family."

"Thanks, Mike," I said. "How . . . how did you hear about my mom?"

"I called CBS, trying to find you. Liz told me that your mom's condition had turned critical, so I rushed over. When I saw the crowd in the lobby, I decided to wait for you someplace else."

"Like here."

"Uh-huh." Using his palm, Mike swept clean a section of bench beside him. "Join me?"

I sat on the bench, still puzzled by his presence.

"I caught your speech on the news last night," Mike went on.

"They ran it on the West Coast?" I said, surprised. "I was sure they would edit me out for rebroadcast."

Mike grinned. "No, they left you in—including the last part. Some suit in New York probably decided that having one of their correspondents publicly examine her conscience gave the network credibility. They got to air a juicy scandal, grab ratings, and appear concerned with professional ethics at the same time. Besides, by then everyone had already heard what you said. Speaking of which, did you know that Brent is getting bumped up to the Washington Bureau?"

I nodded. "He deserves it. And Washington deserves him."

"Nice way to put it," Mike agreed.

Across the stream, rays of sunlight skittered across the hillside, moving with the swaying branches above. Reminded of the shifting patterns I had seen on Mike's bedroom wall, I watched this interplay of light and shadow for a moment, struck by the realization that no matter how one attempted to keep things simple, life somehow always got complicated. "You mentioned trying to contact me at the newsroom," I said. "What did you want?"

Mike took a long time replying. Then, instead of answering my question, he posed one of his own. "Ali, do you think it's possible for two people to start over?"

I didn't respond.

"I don't know either, but I want to try," Mike pushed on. "I've missed you."

Caught in a conflicting surge of emotion, I continued to remain silent.

"I have the day off," Mike continued. "I know a great open-air seafood mart near County Line. Neptune's Net. We could drive up for lunch, then maybe do a hike in the mountains above Point Mugu. Or hit the beach at Zuma. Or we could just talk. What do you say?"

"You're suggesting that we simply pick up where we left off?"

"No. I want to start over. From the beginning."

"That's not possible."

"Why not?"

"Mike, we both made some mistakes—mostly me, I guess—and for that I'm truly sorry," I replied. "But after all that's happened . . ."

"Please, Ali. We can't let things end like this." Mike took my shoulders and turned me to face him. "I wasn't being completely honest when I said that I've missed you. It's more than that. I know we haven't known each other long, but I liked you from the first moment we met. It's hard to describe, but I feel . . . *alive* when I'm with you. I love having you in my life, Ali. And I don't want to lose you."

My thoughts flashed back to a conversation I'd had with McKenzie earlier that summer. We had been driving to the beach, and McKenzie had been probing my opinions on romance.

*"Remember that story you wrote about a blind girl falling in love for the first time? It was so romantic, I cried when I read it. What was the title?"*

*"I don't recall."*

*"Sure you do. Your main character went through all these changes, only to finally discover what she truly wanted in life was to have someone who really* knew *her—what food she liked, her taste in music, what side of the bed she slept on, how to make her laugh."*

I glanced down at the bench where I had found Mike waiting. "You never answered my question. How did you know I'd be here?"

"Your secret spot? Actually, I wasn't sure I would recognize it." Mike craned his neck, staring up at a giant eucalyptus towering above us. "But when I found a bench beneath the tallest tree in the garden, I knew this had to be it."

"But how did you know I would come?"

"Does it matter?"

"It does to me," I replied.

Mike shrugged. "I just knew. I also know that we deserve another chance. Will you give us one?"

Again my thoughts traveled back, this time transporting me to a Thanksgiving Day years earlier, a day on which Nate and I had accompanied Dad to the cemetery where Tom was buried. Though our father had picked that particular time and place to make an announcement of his own, it was there, beside Tom's grave, that I had finally confessed the secret of my rape. Dad, in his rough way, had tried to reassure me. Sounding the depths of my memory, I could still hear his words.

*"When things go bad, really bad, just remember who you are . . . and hold to it."*

At the time I had considered my father's advice simplistic and facile. But before the year was out, on the night fire had destroyed our home, his words had returned to me with unexpected force, giving me the courage to face my fears.

*Remember who you are . . . and hold to it.*

But who was I?

For the first time since the summer of my rape, I looked deep inside myself, searching a place no one else could go. Some of what I found there I liked: resolve, and humor, and a bold, adventurous spirit—traits I had inherited from my father. Intelligence, nerve, and an uncompromising strength of character, things Mom had given me, were there as well. But there were other things, dark things—things I didn't want to face. Jealousy. Insecurity. Envy. Spite. And worst of all, a fear of failure that had made it almost impossible for me to open myself to others, a fear that for years had caused me to hide behind a mantle of sarcasm and cynicism and wit. And worse, to my shame, I realized now that following my rape, my resolve never to be weak again had driven a wedge between me and the people I loved.

*Remember who you are . . .*

At last I turned to Mike. I found him watching, awaiting my reply. "Lunch at County Line and a hike," I said. "And then what?"

"I don't know," Mike answered. "If you don't have plans, we could shoot over to my place, throw a couple of steaks on the barbecue, watch a video . . ."

"A video? Hmmm . . . I hear there's an award-winning documentary out that chronicles the history of the Los Angeles River."

"And it just so happens I have a copy," Mike said with a tentative smile.

I raised an eyebrow. "And I suppose you'll want to watch it with the sound off?" I asked, remembering our time together when we first viewed his film.

"Actually, I thought we would just take things one step at a time."

"A fresh start? Really?"

Mike nodded. "Really. What do you say?"

I stared at the flowing stream below us, hesitating a moment more. Finally I came to a decision. I didn't know what the future would bring, only that I wanted to be a part of it. There was a big, unpredictable, dangerous, beautiful, cruel, heartbreakingly wonderful world out there to explore . . . and I intended to, my eyes and mind and heart open for whatever might come, no matter what.

With a growing sense of confidence and an abiding trust in life, I lifted my eyes and met Mike's gaze. "A new beginning," I said softy. Still holding his eyes with mine, I answered his question at last. "I would like that, Mike," I said, meaning it with all my heart. "I would like that a lot."

# Acknowledgments

I would like to express my appreciation to a number of people who provided their assistance and expertise while I was writing *Allison*. Any errors, exaggerations, or just plain bending of facts to suit the story are attributable to me alone.

To Detective Lee Kingsford (LAPD, retired), I again owe a debt of gratitude. His gift of knowledge and friendship once more proved invaluable during the preparation of the manuscript. To Susan Gannon, my wife and muse with a sharp eye for detail, to friends and family for their encouragement and support, to my eBook editor Karen Oswalt, to Karen Waters for her help on the cover, to Mike Dunning for his back-cover photo, and especially to my core group of readers—many of whom made critical suggestions for improvements—my sincere thanks.

If you enjoyed *Allison*, please leave a review on *Amazon* or your favorite retail site. A word-of-mouth recommendation is the best endorsement possible, and your review would be truly appreciated and will help friends and others like you look for books. Thanks for reading!

~ Steve Gannon

# About the Author

**STEVE GANNON** is the author of numerous bestselling novels including *A Song for the Asking*, first published by Bantam Books. Gannon divides his time between Idaho and Italy, living in two of the most beautiful places on earth. In Idaho he spends his days skiing, whitewater kayaking, and writing. In Italy Gannon also continues to write, while enjoying the Italian people, food, history, and culture, and learning the Italian language. He is married to concert pianist Susan Spelius Gannon.

To contact Steve Gannon, check out his blog, purchase books, or to receive updates on new releases, please visit Steve's website at: stevegannonauthor.com

Made in the USA
Las Vegas, NV
24 November 2020